T0265902

THE HOUSE ON
COLD CREEK LANE

THE HOUSE ON COLD CREEK LANE

Liz Alterman

**SEVERN
HOUSE**

First world edition published in Great Britain and the USA in 2024
by Severn House, an imprint of Canongate Books Ltd,
14 High Street, Edinburgh EH1 1TE.

severnhouse.com

British Library Cataloguing-in-Publication Data
A CIP catalogue record for this title is available from the British Library.

ISBN-13: 978-1-4483-1400-3 (cased)
ISBN-13: 978-1-4483-1401-0 (e-book)

All Severn House titles are printed on acid-free paper.

MIX
Paper from
responsible sources
FSC
www.fsc.org   FSC® C013056

Typeset by Palimpsest Book Production Ltd., Falkirk,
Stirlingshire, Scotland.
Printed and bound in Great Britain by TJ Books,
Padstow, Cornwall.

Praise for Liz Alterman

"Liz Alterman is a masterful storyteller"
May Cobb, award-winning author of *The Hunting Wives*

"Fresh twists . . . Alterman is off to a promising start"
Publishers Weekly on *The Perfect Neighborhood*

"Well written from start to finish . . . perfect for fans
of domestic suspense!"
Manhattan Book Review on *The Perfect Neighborhood*

"Alterman deftly uses alternating perspectives to show
us the building tensions, leading to one surprising
twist after another. I couldn't put this down"
Catherine McKenzie, *USA Today* bestselling author,
on *The Perfect Neighborhood*

"In theory, *The Perfect Neighborhood* is the ideal place to raise a
family. In reality, it's disturbing and completely riveting . . .
Reading this book made me feel like I lived in Oak Hill, and I
refused to leave until every secret was uncovered"
Samantha Downing, internationally bestselling author of
My Lovely Wife and *For Your Own Good*

"The combination of super-relatable characters and nearly
unbearable suspense made it impossible to stop reading"
Sarah Warburton, author of *You Can Never Tell*,
on *The Perfect Neighborhood*

"Liz Alterman has crafted a riveting mystery that epitomizes
every parent's greatest fear. A page-turning whodunnit that also
packs an emotional wallop, if you love Lisa Jewell's dark
domestic suspense, don't miss Alterman's captivating new book"
Rebecca Taylor, award-winning author of *The Secret Next Door,*
on *The Perfect Neighborhood*

About the author

Liz Alterman is the author of *The Perfect Neighborhood*, *He'll Be Waiting*, and *Sad Sacked*. Her work appeared in *The New York Times*, *The Washington Post*, *McSweeney's*, and other outlets. She lives in New Jersey with her husband and three sons where she spends most days microwaving the same cup of coffee and looking up synonyms. When Liz isn't writing, she's reading. To learn more or say hello, visit LizAlterman.com

For my mom and mothers everywhere who carry it all.

"Few of us could bear to have ourselves for neighbors."
— Mignon McLaughlin

ONE

April
Laurel

Rob's words spilled into my ear, so urgent I could almost feel the giddy rush of his breath through the phone. 'They accepted the offer. We got the house!'

'You're joking!' I sat up. Mid-morning sun warmed my face. I'd been resting on the couch, pillows behind my back and beneath my knees – the same way I'd spent the past two weeks. Like a nocturnal ballerina, the baby pirouetted inside me most nights, leaving me exhausted for much of the day. But the excitement in my husband's voice – this news – jolted me awake. 'We got it?'

My mother-in-law, Susan, looked at me, eyebrows arched. I gave her a thumbs-up. She mimed clapping and wiped her forehead in mock relief. It would've been impossible for her not to eavesdrop in our tiny apartment as she and three-year-old Jasper worked on a floor puzzle a few feet from me. Their heads bent toward one another as the scene – a rabbit farmer in overalls surrounded by chicks – clicked into place.

Rob had spotted the white Cape Cod-style house on Cold Creek Lane less than twenty-four hours earlier during his routine scrolling. He sent me the link and arranged an early-morning showing with the listing agent.

After a quick tour, he'd FaceTimed me from the empty bedroom that would be Jasper's.

'It's perfect, Laur!' His voice echoed off the ivory walls. 'Let's make an offer. What do you say?'

I'd said fine, go for it. I never thought we'd hear within hours. I expected to wait days and then lose out to a couple with more money. And, honestly, I was fine with that. The closer it got to my due date, the less appealing moving seemed.

Rob and I began house-hunting in the fall after the first-trimester morning sickness subsided enough that I could ride in the car without turning nauseous. We'd ventured to sweet suburban towns west of Manhattan and found four homes we'd loved, only to get outbid every time. It was so discouraging, we'd stopped looking to avoid ruining the holidays. When we started again in February, inventory had been low with only a handful in our price range, so we'd had to expand our search.

'If everything goes smoothly, we could be in by June,' Rob said.

After getting our hopes up only to be disappointed so many times, this seemed too easy, too good to be true.

I heard the *tick-tock* of the blinker and pictured him in the car on his way to work. I was quiet a beat too long. My husband, well attuned to my shifting moods, asked, 'Laur? Laur, are you there?'

'I'm here.'

'I thought you'd be more excited. What's wrong? You and my mom getting along?'

Susan had been staying with us on and off for the past ten days, making sure I followed my doctor's bed rest orders – not easy with a toddler. She kept Jasper entertained, bundling him up every afternoon and whisking him off to the park, spoiling him with cocoa and mini cupcakes before making dinner each night. She returned to my father-in-law, Dennis, on the weekends and boomeranged back to us on Monday mornings. Some people would say I hit the mother-in-law jackpot, but with another person in it, our apartment took on the cramped feel of a crowded elevator.

'No, no. I mean, yes, I'm fine. We're all fine.' I nodded, as if Rob could see me through the phone. 'I *am* excited. It's just, well . . .' I pulled at a loose thread in the blanket covering my legs and burrowed my feet between sofa cushions. I turned my head away from Susan. I could already hear how childish I'd sound before the words passed my lips. 'It's our first house. I wish I'd been there with you.' I tried to keep my tone warm, not whiny. 'I'd like to walk through the rooms at least once before we buy it. You know, actually see the place we're going to be paying off for the next thirty years.'

'I know, but—'

'Can we go this weekend?' I interrupted. 'I won't get out of the car. We can drive by. I want to check out the street, the neighborhood. Is there a playground nearby?'

'You know what the doctor said: full bed rest until thirty-seven weeks. The next time you leave the apartment, it's to have the baby.'

I groaned, knowing he was right.

'C'mon, Laurel. We're almost there.'

Easy for him to say. It had been fifteen days and already I was stir-crazy. How would I manage another three weeks? I blocked the thought before my anxiety spiked and my blood pressure soared.

'Trust me, you'll love this place,' Rob continued. 'I promise.'

'What about the mortgage?' I'd quit my job as a part-time pastry chef a few months earlier when I started cramping and spotting and my doctor told me to stay off my feet as much as possible. We'd mainly used my bite-sized salary to justify dinners out, concerts, and the small luxuries we couldn't give up: Netflix, Spotify, our gym membership. Still, I wondered how we could afford this property.

'We're pre-approved!' Rob scoffed, all confidence. 'Unless you bought a Porsche and didn't tell me, we're good. I didn't even have to dip into Jasper's imaginary college fund. And the best part? I decided to drop the offer twenty grand and they still accepted it!'

When was the last time I'd heard my husband that happy? Why couldn't I let him have it? Doubts and questions looped through my mind, vultures circling, as I fiddled with the fringes on the throw blanket.

'They didn't insist on the asking price? In this market? That's crazy.' I shifted. The baby hadn't moved since our call began. Or maybe she had and I hadn't noticed with all the excitement. I took a sip of orange juice from the glass Susan had placed on our scuffed-up coffee table and waited to feel the baby's fluttery movements.

'Nope. No other offers.' Rob blew out a long exhale as if to say, 'Lucky us!'

No other offers. Was something wrong with the house and my husband wasn't telling me? Why did my mind always go to the darkest place? I knew *why*, of course. My mother had been murdered days before Christmas when I was twelve years old.

How much of my present unease was my past refusing to let me believe good things could happen? And how much was that ugly side of human nature that made us desire something more once someone else wanted it too? It reminded me of the way Jasper was only interested in the swings at the playground after all of them were occupied. Maybe we never outgrew it.

'Does it have a weird smell?' I hinted at my concerns. 'Mold? Be honest!' Pregnancy made me keenly aware of the slightest foul scent. I'd potty-trained Jasper early so we could stop using that diaper pail that didn't trap odors, despite the promising reviews.

Silence. Did we have a bad connection or was he hesitating?

'Rob?' The baby jabbed at my ribcage. I patted my stomach, relieved.

'It's perfect,' Rob insisted. 'Even nicer in person. Lots of windows. The floors were just refinished. The street's wide, trees on both sides.' He paused. 'There's a creek behind the house. We should probably put up a fence.'

'You saw it for the first time an hour ago! We don't even own it yet and already you're making improvements!' I teased.

'Didn't I tell you it would all work out?' Rob laughed as a horn blared in the background. 'I'm heading into the tunnel, I might lose you. We'll celebrate tonight when I get . . .'

It was nice to hear him sound like himself again. Since the pregnancy had turned high-risk, he'd been on edge, anxious. While those were my default settings, my husband typically sailed through his days carefree. He'd led a charmed life, so different from mine. I'd been anticipating tragedy since the night two police officers had stood in my childhood kitchen towering over my father.

Rob expected every moment to shine. Why shouldn't his good fortune continue, he reasoned. And, like a self-fulfilling prophecy, for a while, it did.

Sometimes now I wonder if Rob hadn't found the house on Cold Creek Lane – if we'd never bought it – would his luck have held out forever?

And if it had, would it have been enough to protect us all?

TWO

Early June
Laurel

The rows of headless tulips were what I noticed first when we pulled up to the house. Their green stems poked toward the cloudless spring sky. Not a single petal rested atop the mulched beds that flanked the slate walkway.

The second thing that struck me was how close the houses were to one another. It hadn't looked that way online. I chalked it up to trick photography and wondered what other disappointments awaited.

It was my first time seeing the white clapboard Cape Cod in person. I still hadn't been inside. After adding my signature to dozens of documents electronically, Rob handled the closing while I recovered from my C-section and engaged in an endless cycle of breastfeeding and diaper changing. Though we'd spent weeks worrying that the baby would come early, Poppy arrived within hours of her due date, a healthy eight pounds and seven ounces. Susan offered to watch the children so I could finally see our new home, but I was too exhausted to take her up on it. Besides, we owned the place. There was no going back.

'This is it!' Rob whispered as he pulled into the narrow driveway. 'Home sweet home!'

We followed the moving van the whole way. Jasper and Poppy had fallen asleep before we'd exited the tunnel. The darkness and the motion of the car delivered a one-two-punch that acted like baby NyQuil. I was so tired from sorting and packing in between caring for a newborn and a busy little boy, I wished we were relocating across the country and could just drive forever. But forty minutes after we locked the door to our apartment for the final time, we turned the corner onto Cold Creek Lane and were greeted by a glorious green canopy courtesy of soaring elms. Our two-story home, dwarfed by the size of the surrounding trees, looked like a dollhouse. Its curtain-less dormer windows stared like a pair of vacant eyes waiting to make up their mind about us.

I peeked into the back seat. Jasper's cheeks were rosy with sleep while Poppy's tiny head pitched slightly forward at an angle that would've given an adult a stiff neck for days. The only thing worse than no nap was one that got cut short. Poppy would awaken ravenous, Jasper sweaty and disoriented. I'd tried to prepare him by scrolling through the listing photos on our iPad. 'This is our new house!' I'd repeated as we practiced the address.

To the left of the driveway, just beyond a hedge of low shrubs, something caught my eye. A young woman swept her chestnut hair into a high ponytail, her long legs encased in black tights as she lunged on the front steps either heading out or returning from a run. AirPods plugged her ears.

'Our new neighbor.' I jutted my chin in her direction.

'Yeah, I met her the day of the home inspection. Really sweet. She can't wait to meet you and the kids.' Rob's head was turned in the opposite direction, his hand raised in a wave. I realized we were talking about different people. I twisted in my seat and spotted an older woman, her hair white and roundish as dandelion fluff. She held a bright yellow watering can above a flower box of geraniums and grinned at us. I forced a smile, but moaned. I wasn't in the mood to meet anyone. The thought of making small talk when we still had so much to do, such a long day ahead, wore me out.

The back doors of the cavernous moving van rattled open, snapping my attention to the street. The men we'd hired had two more jobs that afternoon so they wasted no time unloading our belongings, planting them on the grass like strange saplings.

I wished we'd arrived at dusk. Beneath the brilliant sunshine, the shabbiness of our old furnishings was on full display. I cringed at the tufted ottoman resting on its side, buttons missing, and the pale-pink sofa dappled with red wine and juice stains. As the contents of our apartment piled up, the lawn took on the appearance of a desperate yard sale.

'Here we go!' Rob's warm, hazel eyes were bright in the almost-summer light. He kissed me on the cheek before jumping out to let the movers in.

I watched as he slid the key into the lock and opened the turquoise front door. A wreath of browning forsythia hung crookedly below the panel of windows at the top. I'd meant to ask him to change the locks. How had I forgotten? I chalked it up to 'baby brain' and told myself I'd mention it later.

'Mommy!' Jasper whimpered, kicking the back of the driver's seat. 'Where are we?'

I turned around and patted his leg. His soft skin was still cool, but with the engine off, the car grew stuffier by the second.

'We're here! This is our new house!' I wished I felt as cheerful as I forced my voice to sound.

My son rubbed his eyes with the back of his fists and blinked. He strained against the straps of his car seat, fingers fumbling with the buckles. 'I wanna get out! I wanna get out!'

As I reached into the back seat, careful not to wake Poppy, a sharp tug where my incision was slowly healing pulled at my side. I winced as I stretched to free Jasper. He shot from the car. I hurried to catch him before he darted into the path of the movers carrying our hulking dresser with its nicks and missing knobs.

We watched it disappear into the house. When I turned back, she was there – the neighbor who'd been gardening, standing on the other side of the walkway, watery blue eyes fixed on my face.

'I'm Marian.' She extended her damp hand and remained unsmiling. 'Marian Murdoch.' She wore a white linen shift dress and small pearl earrings. Her expression softened when she looked at Jasper. As she bent down to meet him at eye level, her knees popped.

Some kids were shy. Not my son. Like a hothouse flower, Jasper blossomed beneath the warm glow of attention. The way he'd eagerly approach older kids, dogs, even men playing guitar in the park near our apartment made me nervous.

'Shouldn't he be scared of strangers?' I'd fret to Rob. 'Where's that innate sense of fear?'

'He sees the world as a safe place, Laur,' my husband had said. 'That's a good thing.'

'This is my new house!' Jasper beamed at Marian, who smelled like a mix of dusting powder, perspiration, and raw earth. 'Wanna see it?'

'Oh, I've been in your house many, many times.' She pursed

her lips like a small child sucking on a secret. 'Once you're settled, I'd love to . . .' She stopped mid-sentence and straightened to her full height, her gaze shifting. 'You're not going to leave that baby in a hot car, are you?' Her mouth hung open as she pointed toward the back seat of the Accord where Poppy's tiny feet flailed in the window.

How had I not heard her? At the sudden recognition of my daughter's cries, my breasts began leaking. I dropped Jasper's hand and flung my arms across my chest.

Just then Rob came striding down the steps. 'Morning, Marian! Nice to see you again,' he chirped, ever the salesman. 'You've met my wife, Laurel.'

'Well, she didn't introduce herself, no. But, Rob, I'm more concerned about your baby.' Her bony finger directed his gaze to the car.

'Geez, Laurel! What the—?'

'She just started . . . I . . .' As I lurched backward toward the car, that familiar flicker of doubt filled his eyes. I'd been so busy feeding everyone else that morning, I'd had only coffee. Jittery and lightheaded, I pulled Poppy from her seat and cradled her small, sweaty body with my shaky hands.

When I looked up, Rob and Marian were scowling while Jasper sing-songed, 'That's my sister! That's my Poppy!' He raced toward me, tugging on the long cotton maternity skirt that had become part of my daily uniform.

'Don't you have one of those whatchamacallems?' Marian snapped her fingers as if summoning the word. 'Carriers? Then you could keep the baby close and have your hands free.' She tilted her head toward our belongings spread across the lawn like litter. 'You've got your work cut out for you here.'

My chest tightened.

'Great idea.' Rob turned to me. 'Laur, where'd you put that thing?'

A high chair and a lamp were whisked inside as I tried to picture where I'd packed the blue baby sling. 'I . . . I . . . I don't know,' I stammered.

Jasper wriggled beside me. 'Potty, Mommy! Potty now!'

And so rather than take a moment to savor my first look inside our new home, to appreciate the built-in corner cabinets in the dining room or admire the fireplace, I rushed through the rooms in search of the toilet before I had another mess to clean up.

The day continued in a blur of putting away dishes and setting up small appliances, making Jasper's toddler bed, locating Larry, the ring-tailed lemur he refused to sleep without. His room had a sweet little window seat. I imagined filling it with throw pillows and reading to him in that cozy nook.

The house was clean and well kept. Though it was small, it seemed like a mansion compared to our apartment. The kitchen's ample counter space meant I had plenty of room to roll out dough for pies and pastries. I smiled, envisioning Jasper, cheeks dusted with flour, helping me. A washer and dryer waited in the mudroom on the first floor. The upstairs bathroom had double sinks. Rob had been right. It was perfect.

Briefly, I wondered about the former owners. Why hadn't they insisted on the asking price? Did they have children? If so, how many? Where were they now?

Those thoughts scattered as I looked around the rooms, mentally arranging our family photos, pondering which window treatments would work best: blinds, shutters, curtains?

Around two o'clock, as Jasper and Poppy napped, the doorbell rang. My stomach clenched – first out of fear that it would wake the children and then because I was sweating, makeup-less, and unprepared to meet another neighbor. I stayed in the kitchen while Rob opened the door. He carried in a large box. It held a woven seagrass basket filled with fluffy white towels rolled to spa-like perfection. A red bow and a note were looped through one of the handles.

Sorry we're not there to help on your big day. Wishing you good health and happiness in your new home and always! Love, Mom and Dad.

Susan had stopped trying to get me to call her 'Mom' years ago, but she still signed cards that way. I never got used to it. She and Dennis were with Rob's sister, Emily, and her fiancé, Colin, sampling the tasting menu for their August wedding.

When Rob had told his mother our move-in date, she'd said, 'Oh dear, I could ask Em to reschedule, but you know how brides get when you try to change their plans.'

'Don't give it another thought,' we'd told her. It would've been nice to have them there to help with the children at least, but we managed.

The dining room glowed a gauzy pink in the early-evening light as we sat down to dinner. Rob had picked up pizza in town and brought home a bouquet of peonies for me and a foam football for Jasper. I was struck by how much my husband and son looked alike with their brown hair and hazel eyes. Each had a sprinkling of freckles from the sun they'd gotten earlier while playing tag in the backyard, the sound of the creek burbling behind them mixing with Jasper's deep belly giggle.

Opening a bottle of sauvignon blanc, Rob turned to me. 'I know you've been under a lot of stress lately with . . .'

I waited. Would he bring it up? The man who murdered my mother had been released from prison the day before. We hadn't talked about it.

'With a new baby and a new house,' he went on. 'You've been really strong. I'm proud of you.'

'Thanks,' I said, disappointed he didn't address how hard the past few days had been for me. Maybe he didn't want to spoil the moment.

We clinked glasses and I took a small sip, knowing I'd have to feed Poppy in a few hours.

'All our dreams will come true here, Laur.' Rob smiled, dimples flashing. 'Just watch.'

Through the window, I watched Marian puttering in her garden, stealing side-glances at our home, and willed myself to believe him.

By the time we tumbled into bed, the heat of the day had relented, giving way to a cool evening. We were grateful. The house didn't have central air conditioning. We'd need to buy and install window units. Rob added it to his never-ending to-do list.

The landline, Wi-Fi, and cable TV hadn't been hooked up yet. I was glad for a break from the outside world. I couldn't bear the footage of Lyle Hartsell, my mother's killer, walking out of prison and into his new life. But I also couldn't look away. I'd seen recent photos of him online. His dark hair and scruffy beard were threaded with gray. Deep lines creased his cheeks and forehead, making him appear much older than his early fifties. He'd only been locked up for twenty years, but it had aged him twice that. Still, it was nothing compared to the crime he'd committed, the lives he'd cut short, the others he'd destroyed.

All week journalists had called our apartment asking for a statement. 'You were just twelve when your mother was viciously murdered, Laurel. What's it like to know Lyle Hartsell is going to be a free man?'

My hands had trembled as I deleted their voicemails. The move had kept me busy, offering me a brief distraction. But Lyle was on the move too, doing whatever he pleased, going wherever he wanted.

The thought gave me chills. I pulled the flat sheet up to my chin.

'We should change the locks,' I said to Rob, goosebumps creeping across my arms. He'd opened the windows, letting the light breeze filter through our bedroom, something we never could've done in the city with its horns, sirens, and three a.m. fights that spilled into the street after the corner bar closed.

'I don't think we have to.' He switched off the lamp without jotting it down on the small notepad he'd placed on his nightstand. 'The house was vacant when I saw it in April. It's not like the former owners are going to come back and let themselves in.'

'No, it's not that.' I turned toward him. 'People give out keys, maybe to a dog walker or a neighbor in case they lock themselves out. I think it's safer if we . . .'

'Stop, Laur. This is a fresh start, OK?' My husband punched an indent in his pillow and rolled away from me. 'Moving forward, right?' The edge in his voice told me the conversation was over.

I knew Rob believed setting up a lovely home in the perfect neighborhood would transform me into the woman and mother he hoped I could be.

If only it were that simple.

I inched closer and draped my arm across his chest, not wanting our first night in our new house to end on an unpleasant note. I was sore from unpacking, but happy, grateful, desperate for life to be good here.

'That's nice, isn't it?' Rob whispered, rolling over, his fingers brushing my cheek. Pale moonlight spilled through the curtain-less windows, brightening his face.

'Hmmm?' I moaned, already slipping toward sleep.

'The sounds – the crickets.' He went quiet. 'Is that a bullfrog by the creek?'

'I think it is.' I laughed and gave a half-hearted croak before nuzzling his neck.

Teen voices floated in, followed by the slap of a skateboard. It was early, not even ten p.m.

'Want me to close the windows?' I offered.

'Nah,' Rob said. 'We've got a whole new soundtrack here. Let's give it a try.'

I yawned and closed my eyes. 'Whatever you say.'

If I'd gotten out of bed that night, crossed the room, and walked to the windows, would I have seen the pair of eyes watching our home?

Would I have called to Rob in an uneasy whisper, urging, 'Come here. Look.'

Would I have kept my hand just below the sill, pointed, and said, 'We need to leave. Now!'

And if I had, would he have listened?

THREE

Corey

Ma shifted in her armchair as I zipped the keys into my pocket.

'Oh no, honey, don't go out there,' she said. 'The weatherman was just saying thunderstorms are expected through midnight.'

She pointed at the TV as if instructing the bald man in the brown suit to repeat his forecast for my benefit. They'd already moved on to a segment about the growing iguana problem.

If I stayed home, I'd fidget and pace. We'd end up fighting over something stupid like how to load the dishwasher. Or I'd wait until her head dipped toward her chest then dump my tea and replace it with whatever was left in the bottles I stashed in the back of my closet. Anything to make the ache stop. The hours were all endless, but the ones in the middle of the night when I couldn't imagine the sun ever coming up again? Those were the hardest. My loss was an open wound that grew and spread in the darkness until it became the only thing I could feel. I was desperate to numb it any way I could.

'I'll be fine.' I twisted the rubber band a third time, tightening my ponytail 'til my face tugged a little at the sides. Running was one of the few things that cleared my head. I was better after – if only for a bit.

'We could get a treadmill, you know, put it in the sun room.' Ma waved her fingers toward the French doors that opened to a tiny space she'd filled with white wicker furniture. 'Then you wouldn't have to go out, and I wouldn't have to worry.'

I bit my bottom lip not to shout, 'I'm thirty-six years old. You don't have to worry!' But I was an adult who behaved like an asshole teenager while squatting in her mother's retirement village condo. Her concern wasn't misguided.

'See ya later,' I grumbled and felt the unsatisfying click of her flimsy front door as I yanked it shut.

Outside, steam rose off the asphalt in vapory little clouds like ghosts who stuck around after the storm. It had rained earlier, not that it was a single degree cooler. Fucking Florida. A downpour every day. Not that I minded. I respected it. The routine. The violence of it.

I wasn't halfway down the block before my lungs started burning and that splintery pain in my shins reminded me how many miles I'd tried to put between me and my old life. I added more each night, not that it did any good. Mostly I ran in a circle, a dog chasing its tail.

Eyes down, I promised myself I wouldn't go to that neighborhood again. Not that street. Not so soon. But I couldn't help it. They made it too easy.

It started with sidewalk chalk, a hunk the size of a baby carrot. I'd knelt, pretending to tie my sneaker, and reached for it as natural as if it were mine and I'd simply left it in someone else's driveway by mistake. I squeezed it the whole way home, palm sweating like it was a hot coal, my raw need turning it into a diamond in my mind.

What made me take it? It was the color. Orange. Frankie's favorite. Earlier that day, I'd seen the girl who held it. She was maybe three or four years old, squatting in pink Crocs where the driveway met the sidewalk. Her dark curls, damp from running through a sprinkler, shielded her face as she scribbled. So much like Frankie I bolted upright in the passenger's seat. What was she drawing? I couldn't make it out. We'd passed too quickly. Ma and me barreling toward Publix, her yammering about coupons and the spoiled milk she insisted on returning. Of course, the quart leaked and her Corolla had smelled like a dumpster for days.

Once I'd gotten a glimpse of the girl, I couldn't get her out of my mind. I went back to the neighborhood that night and plenty of times since. I'd tried to stop, but the hunger for something that belonged to her always won. It felt like Frankie was leaving things there for me to find, calling to me from some distant place where she was still perfect, still mine, whispering, 'Don't forget me.'

I wound through the streets, passing strip malls and stray cats, until I found myself in front of the girl's house. I wasn't surprised to see the butterfly barrette, but my heart jackhammered just the same when I spotted it laying on the ground beside the back door of their Pathfinder. Like an owl, I spun my head around in all directions before I lunged for it – the cheap yellow plastic warm in my hand. Drunk with the thrill of touching it, I stood there for who knows how long.

'Cor?'

I barely heard my name over the hum of the streetlights buzzing in my ears.

'Corey! That you?'

Shit. I'd been in this swamp-ass town for eight months and barely knew a soul, not that I minded. Could somebody have followed me? One of those assholes from the bar where I drank some Saturday nights – a reward for making it through another pointless week. Blood shot to my face, hot and tingly as a slap. I stuck the barrette in my bra and turned around.

'Dave?' My boss from the garden center wrestled a lid onto one of his garbage cans. 'Girl, what are you doin' on this side of town at this time of night?'

My breath came in short, fast bursts. 'Running,' I panted.

'From what? Or should I say from who?' He winked and wobbled, swaying a little in faded swim trunks.

I couldn't tell him I was running from myself, from the memories of Frankie bending to sniff a daffodil, or the gentle weight of her on my lap in the window seat as I read *Charlotte's Web*, the smell of her strawberry shampoo burying itself deep inside me.

'Just getting some exercise.' My fingers itched to touch the barrette. 'I didn't know you lived here.'

'Why would you?' He laughed and rocked on his heels, wiggling the toes of his bare feet. 'Kinda far from where you said you live. Must be, what? Four, five miles? I'd offer to drive you home, but I've had a few.' He slapped the lid of his recycling can, bottles rattling like applause.

'I'm good, but thanks.' I took a few steps back. 'See ya tomorrow.'

'Be careful now,' he called as I turned and sprinted away.

After I rounded the corner, I squatted, back pressed against a palm tree, to catch my breath but mostly to make sure the barrette was still there.

When I got back to the condo, the lights were off but the TV was still on in the living room, sending shadows creeping across the walls. I hoped Ma'd be asleep, lulled by a stupid laugh track or bored by a big-haired lady selling fake sapphires on a home-shopping channel. But she was awake, face bluish-white in the alien glow of the screen. She stood slowly, cordless phone in hand.

'Corey!' She let out a long sigh. In relief? Disgust? 'I've been worried sick.'

I looked at the clock. Nearly one a.m. 'Sorry, I thought you'd have gone to bed.'

'I was just about to call the police.'

I flinched. She came closer, little puffs of air escaping her lips with each step, until she was inches away.

'You and I, Corey.' She shook her head. 'We're all each other has left.'

Her shoulders slumped and I braced for what would come next: tears, a lecture, same sad guilt trip. Instead, she folded her arms around me. The barrette inside my bra stabbed me in the chest.

I thought about resting my head on her shoulder, sinking into the silky softness of her quilted housecoat, inhaling the fabric softener she'd used as far back as I could remember, but I didn't want to dirty her.

'You have to be careful,' she whispered. 'There are dangerous people out there this time of night.'

I stood, arms limp at my sides, letting myself be hugged by this woman who was shrinking a little more each day, fighting the urge to tell her that the most dangerous person of all is someone with nothing left to lose.

FOUR

July
Laurel

We'd been in the house nearly two weeks. Everything was in its place. Technically, we were settled, but I knew in my husband's eyes we hadn't conquered the most important part of suburban life: fitting in.

Over the weekend, he discovered a local website filled with parent–child music classes, library programs, and swim lessons categorized by age and named for fish. He texted me the link and wrote: *Time to make some friends!*

For Jasper or me? I responded.

Both! He fired back with a smiley face to take the sting out of the implication.

Had he come up with that idea on his own or did he overhear his mother when she and Dennis had visited? The Wests were rarely subtle. After a week of dropping hints about wanting to see the children and the house, Susan invited herself and Dennis for Sunday dinner.

'Such an exciting time!' she'd gushed as she helped me cover the leftover London broil and blueberry cobbler. 'When the kids are little – preschool, play groups – that's when you find your tribe.'

'Absolutely! I can't wait,' I'd lied.

I wasn't sure I'd ever had a 'tribe.' When Rob traveled for work and I felt lonely, I tortured myself by replaying a conversation I'd overheard the day of my bridal shower. I'd been in the ladies' room when my future mother-in-law and one of Rob's aunts walked in.

They had no idea I was inside a stall, thanks to thick oak doors that spanned floor to ceiling.

'Seems like a sweet girl,' Rob's aunt had said.

'Oh, she is. Just lovely,' Susan crowed.

My heartbeat sped up. I'd wanted her to like me – to love me.

'Awfully quiet,' the aunt continued. 'Not many friends.'

I'd guzzled three peach Bellinis within thirty minutes of arriving to calm my nerves. The cocktails left me lightheaded. For a moment, I considered popping out of the stall and pretending not to have heard Susan and Dennis's sister. Instead, I froze.

'Whatever happened to the gal from grad school? The one he brought to Clay's wedding? Tall? She was so friendly, outgoing.'

I waited, mouth dry. Susan said nothing. I imagined her stopping mid-lipstick application to give her signature open-palmed shrug.

'Robbie's happy. That's all Dennis and I can ask for.' She had the decency to lower her voice before she added, 'Laurel hasn't had an easy life.'

'Yes, you'd mentioned,' Rob's aunt said.

My stomach pitched. How often had I heard that or something similar? How many times had I known people were talking about me and wondered what they'd said? It never got easier.

The stall grew hot as a sauna. I sank to the toilet in a cream dress I couldn't afford to dry clean and put my head between my knees the way the therapist had taught me the summer I was thirteen.

I wanted a tribe, but I had trouble trusting people, letting them in.

'Be open to new things!' Rob always insisted, dispensing his fortune-cookie wisdom.

I'd tried when Jasper was a baby, but the effort exhausted me. I wanted to meet moms who said, 'This is hard' and 'I'm struggling,' but I kept running into ones who elevated parenting to a competitive sport with humble brags about the challenges of having an 'advanced' child.

But this was our fresh start. Since we'd begun talking about moving last fall, Rob would randomly blurt, 'We could get a grill!' When we watched *Maine Cabin Masters*, he'd reminisced about the day he and his dad built a birdhouse. 'Jasper would love that!' he'd exclaim and begin searching online for kits.

In our new community, he expected me to reinvent myself, too.

He wanted me to get out there and make friends. Mothers met through their children and once everyone got along, they introduced the dads. I was the gateway to Rob's suburban fantasy life. He longed to attend block parties, coach Little League, get invited to poker nights with men who brewed beer in their basements and converted their garages into makeshift bars. His mother still kept in touch with most of their former neighbors. Even the ones who'd retired to the Carolinas or Florida planned to fly in for my sister-in-law Emily's August wedding.

It was Monday, not even ten a.m. The week yawned ahead of us. I owed it to Rob to try to be the perfect mom. I could do it by making one right choice at a time, by putting my children first.

'Hey, Jasper!' I peeked into the playroom where my son was sprawled like a starfish across a beanbag chair, watching cartoon dogs fight crime. 'Let's have a catch with the football Daddy got you!'

As Jasper bolted for the backyard, I slipped my phone into my pocket so I could listen for Poppy through the baby monitor app. After lunch, I'd check out the links Rob sent and register for classes so I'd have something to share over dinner.

I heard Jasper's scream before I slid on my sandals. Racing barefoot out the mudroom door, I noticed his hands first. Red and black chunks spilled out of them as he hurried toward me blubbering. 'Mommy! Mommy!'

'Honey!' I knelt beside him. 'What happened?'

'My football! It broked!' He handed me crumbly foam cubes wet with dew.

'Foxes.' The voice, husky and warm, floated over the low row of hydrangeas. I turned to find our other next-door neighbor. We hadn't met yet. I'd only caught flashes of her from a distance, leaving or returning from a run. Up close, her eyes were robin's-egg blue. Tall and toned, she had the natural, effortless beauty of a J.Crew model.

'It's all these condo developments.' As she tilted her head, her shiny dark hair fell in full waves over her shoulders.

I stood and touched my blond bob. I'd been shedding like an Akita since Poppy was born.

'They're displacing the wildlife.' She leaned down and looked at

Jasper as he sat in the grass attempting to piece the chewed-up ball back together. 'Don't worry, bud. I can get you a new one.'

Jasper's pout switched to a gap-toothed grin.

'You don't have—' I started.

'I work for a toy company. Got tons of samples inside.' She aimed her thumb over her shoulder toward her house.

'Your kids must love that!'

The words were out of my mouth before I realized my miscalculation. Her face, bright and open a moment earlier, darkened.

'I don't have any. Yet. Maybe someday.' She smiled, and a wave of relief washed over me, glad I hadn't offended her. 'This must be Jasper,' she said and he grinned at her. 'I heard your grandpa calling you last night, showing you all the fireflies.' She smiled at me again. 'These houses are so close together, it's almost like we're roommates.' She extended her hand. I admired her polished red nails, gleaming at the tips of her ringless fingers. 'I'm Addison Conroy, by the way. People call me Addie.'

'Laurel,' I said, wishing my sweaty palms weren't covered in the ruined football's foam particles.

'I wanted to stop by and welcome you to the 'burbs, but thought I'd give you some time to get settled. I figured you probably had enough random visitors. Speaking of . . .' She jutted her perfect chin toward Marian's house.

'Did I hear crying over here?' Like a ghost, Marian, in an ivory tunic, floated across the grass, scowling.

'My football, Mimi! Look!'

When Jasper had struggled to say 'Mrs Murdoch,' Marian suggested this nickname. I'd bristled, finding it overly familiar and grandmotherly, while Rob had nodded and proclaimed, 'Mimi it is!'

'Oh dear!' Marian's hands, ropey with blue veins, flew to her face. 'That's why it's so important to bring your things in at night.' Her gaze shifted from me to Addie and back to Jasper. 'It's going to be another scorcher.' She sniffed at the air. 'Are you wearing sunscreen, young man?'

'Nope!' Jasper giggled and tore off toward the creek.

'We weren't planning to spend too long—'

'Doesn't matter.' Marian shook her head and aimed a crooked finger at the sky. 'You're aware of what's happening to the ozone layer?'

Addie's full lips twisted in a smirk. I wondered if she was thinking what I was: *A climate-change lecture from a woman who spends much of the day watering her garden? That's rich.*

Just then Poppy let out a cry. For once I was thrilled she was cutting her nap short.

'I should go.' I pulled the phone from my pocket to check the baby monitor app. 'Jasper, come inside. Poppy needs us.'

'I can watch him out here for you,' Marian offered, 'after you put sunscreen on him.'

Addie shaded her eyes, but not before rolling them ever so slightly.

'Thanks, Marian, but we have plans,' I lied. 'Jasper! Let's go!'

Before walking back to her house, Addie touched my arm, her fingertips cool and soft. 'Stop by anytime. I have a feeling we've got a few things in common.'

FIVE

Laurel

Was it possible to be energized by an eye roll? To imagine an entire friendship based on a mutual dislike for an overbearing older woman? Or was it just that, after so many days alone with an infant and toddler in a place where I didn't know a soul, I was starved for any kind of connection?

Whatever the reason, I spent the rest of that day fueled by an adrenaline rush, the kind of adolescent-like thrill that comes from being in on the cool girl's joke.

Maybe it was curiosity. Addie wasn't like the others and that made her intriguing. One by one, a few women on our block had dropped by during our first week. They'd stood on our stoop, peering past my shoulder, questions dancing in their eyes: Who were we? What brought us to town?

They came bearing gifts: a bottle of wine, a basket of zucchini muffins, variations of *I'd love to see what you've done with the place!* hoping I'd invite them in.

'We're still unpacking.' I kept the door pulled tight behind me, not up for exchanging pleasantries and family histories.

One in particular made a strange first impression. I'd barely opened the front door when she blurted, 'You stole my house!'

'Sorry?' was all I'd managed, distracted by her piercing blue eyes, chin-length black hair and cropped bangs.

'You stole my house,' she repeated, unblinking. Then she nudged my shoulder and laughed, red lips parting to reveal small white teeth. 'I'm joking. Sort of. I'm Zoey.' She thrust out her hand. A tangle of leather bracelets circled her wrist. 'I rent the place behind the Barretts' house.' She pointed down and across the street. 'They call it a cottage; I call it a shed. Anyway.' She crossed her arms. 'I'd been saving up to make an offer and *whoosh*, you swept in.'

'Sorry?' I'd meant it as in *Sorry, what?* or *Sorry, start again.* She interpreted it as an apology for purchasing the house.

'Whatever. I'm over it.' She was tall. Unlike the others, she didn't need to crane her neck to get a glimpse into my home. 'I heard you've got a kid. My son Wyatt's four. He's with his dad this week, but I thought maybe the boys could hang. I work from home so summers are rough trying to keep the little dude busy.'

Was she looking for a playmate for her son or a babysitter? Intimidated by her height and dark eye makeup, I found myself mumbling, 'Sure, sounds good.'

'Cool.' She pulled out her cell phone. 'What's your number?'

I gave it to her. How could I not?

My phone buzzed in the pocket of my maternity skirt and I startled.

'Geez, you're jumpy.' The corner of her mouth hitched upward in a lopsided smirk. 'It's just me making sure you gave me the right number. Chill.'

'Right.' My face flushed.

Afternoon clouds rolled in as she drifted down our front steps. I closed the door, wishing I hadn't opened it.

Meeting Addie had felt like a relief, a refreshing breeze on a sweltering day. Could I stop by like she'd suggested? Would it look like I'd come to collect the football she promised Jasper? I pictured her nails, red as fresh strawberries, when she'd touched my arm and extended that invitation. I could make a pie and bring her a piece. That wasn't odd; that was neighborly.

After I fixed Jasper's lunch and nursed Poppy, I started a grocery list. I'd prepare a nice dinner: chicken marsala with garlic smashed potatoes and a strawberry cream pie.

Rob took the train to his office, leaving me the car. I was still new to running errands with an infant and a three-year-old, but if I wanted to make that dessert I needed the ingredients.

Whisking the children into their seats, I rolled down the windows and turned up the radio, the fresh air and the voice of Marvin Gaye making me feel free, weightless. As we passed Marian's house, I saw her standing in her front window, staring. For a moment, I felt sorry for her. Maybe she was lonely? I waved – a reflex. She didn't wave back.

Suburban supermarkets seemed like warehouses compared to the cramped bodega near our old apartment. As we entered near a maze of breads and bagel bins, the bright light hurt my eyes, already burning from lack of sleep. Jasper walked alongside me, refusing to get in the basket of the cart. How would I manage this on a regular basis?

In the canned fruit aisle, Jasper discovered a toy display and begged for everything at his eye level.

'Fine,' I said, worn down by his pleading. 'You can pick one.'

He cheered and chose a Lego race car. In the produce section, he touched and identified vegetables he recognized while I inspected the strawberries. Most were pink with green bottoms; they wouldn't do. But it was summer in the Garden State, there was bound to be a farmers' market nearby.

I paid for our items and told Jasper 'no' each time he tried to sneak a candy bar onto the conveyor belt.

Back in the car, I drove for miles, savoring the scenery and time out of the house. Was it something in the walls that zapped me of all my energy? Could Marian's judgey glare leach through the siding, penetrate the insulation? Was I worried Zoey would show up any moment expecting me to watch her son?

I focused on the road ahead, my hands on the wheel, not getting or making something, not carrying a small person.

'Where are we?' Jasper's voice floated up from the back seat. 'I'm hungry!'

'You just had lunch!' I fished a banana from the grocery bag and tossed it over my shoulder. 'We're almost there!' I had no clue where we were. Poppy began fussing. 'We're on an adventure,' I added. 'We're hunting for strawberries. Just a little longer, OK?'

'I can't open this!' Jasper whined, waving the banana in the air. 'I need the potty!'

'Of course you do,' I groaned under my breath, ruing the downside of toilet training.

After I'd given up and turned the car toward home, I spotted the pointed peaks of white and green tents. A farmers' market. I parked away from the heart of it and told Jasper to pee behind a tree while I eased Poppy into the baby sling.

We strolled past gourmet pickles and candied cashews until I spotted strawberries shining ruby red in the afternoon light. Poppy, hot but content, snuggled against me. I pressed my lips to her fine hair and inhaled the apricot oil I rubbed into her scalp to prevent cradle cap.

I glanced at the other mothers and children and reached for Jasper's hand. We looked like everyone else. I took a deep breath and heard Rob's voice in my head, the words he'd whispered when I was in labor, 'You can do this, Laur. You are doing it, and you're doing great.'

At a stand selling frozen banana ice cream, we stopped and I bought a cup topped with blueberries for Jasper.

'Yum!' he squealed after the first taste.

The vendor asked if she could take our picture and post it on their social media platforms. I crouched low, wrapped my arm around my son, and smiled. I'd show Rob later. He'd love it.

It wasn't until we were halfway to the car that I saw him – the man leaning against a tree near the parking lot. Sunglasses hid his eyes. He faced our direction and stood unsmiling, stroking a scraggly, brown-gray beard. My first thought was *Lyle*. I spun around, reached for Jasper, and dropped the containers of strawberries.

'Oh no, Mommy!' my son cried. 'Why'd you do that?'

'It's OK. We'll buy more.' With shaky hands, I gathered the bruised berries.

By the time I stood, the man was gone.

When we got home, my nerves were raw. I wanted to call Rob but then I thought of him saying, 'You've been really strong, Laur. I'm proud of you.'

I had no proof it was Lyle. Stress and lack of sleep caused me to imagine the worst. I fed Poppy and put her down for her afternoon nap. I let Jasper skip his to help with the pie, preferring to keep him close. He licked the whisk, giggling as we sat together at the table arranging the berries.

'Mommy, don't be sad!' He smiled, his cheeks dotted with whipped cream clouds.

In our old apartment, on cold gray afternoons, I'd let him nap in our bed instead of his crib. I'd rest beside him and read a book. When he awoke, sometimes he'd scoot up on his knees to study my face. With tiny fingers, he'd try to force my mouth into a grin. 'No be sad, Mommy,' he'd say.

I didn't want my son to turn out like my father. The closest my dad came to displaying real emotion was to sigh and say, 'What can I tell ya?'

I tried to explain to Jasper that sometimes I did feel sad, but I always loved him. I wanted to be honest, to let him know that you didn't have to pretend to be something you weren't. He wasn't old enough to ask why I wasn't perennially happy like his father was, he just accepted it and loved me anyway. It felt like a gift.

'Mommy's not sad when she's with you.' I dabbed his cheeks with a napkin. 'Now let's find you a music class!'

With the pie in the fridge, I left Jasper watching a show about a frog trying out for Little League while I took a shower. As I grabbed a towel, I heard a thud downstairs. My heart stuttered, my thoughts spinning back to the man at the farmers' market.

'Daddy!' Jasper squealed. I exhaled, relieved Rob was home.

At the back of the closet, I found a loose maxi dress the color of celery. I'd gotten a touch of sun that afternoon and my spirits lifted with the promise of summer.

'It smells amazing in here,' Rob said when I walked into the kitchen. 'I'm starving.' He kissed me lightly on the lips and studied my face. 'Is that mascara?'

'Daddy, my football broked, but we made a pie!' Jasper raced between Rob and the fridge, tugging at the door to show off our work.

'A pie!' Rob rubbed his palms together then grabbed a bottle of beer. He glanced around. 'The house looks great.'

Unlike many husbands, Rob appreciated the invisible labor required to keep up a home. In our apartment, he noticed when I'd scrubbed Jasper's highchair, dusted, or changed the sheets. He hadn't made the connection that I cleaned frantically when I was at my most anxious. Instead, he considered a tidy home a sign that I was in a good place emotionally, mentally.

I let him believe it.

As I stood at the stove plating the chicken and potatoes, he wrapped his arm around my waist, moved my hair to the side, and kissed my neck. He was always more affectionate when I made an effort.

'See?' he whispered. 'I told you.'

'Told me what?'

'You'd be happy here.'

Something inside me hardened. I hated when he acted like he could predict the future. I freed myself and turned around. 'I met someone today.'

'Uh-oh.' He laughed and stepped back. 'Is this where you tell me you're leaving me for the milkman?' He leaned against the sink and reached for the beer bottle, taking a long pull.

'The woman next door. Addie.'

'That's great.' He smiled. 'How many kids?'

'None.' My cheeks flushed, remembering my awkward assumption: 'Your kids must love that!'

'Huh.' He took another swig. 'Young? Married?'

'About our age. Maybe a bit older? Thirty-three, thirty-five? I don't know. We'd started talking in the backyard then Poppy woke up. I thought I'd bring her a slice of the pie Jasper and I made.'

'Getting to know the neighbors. I like it!'

All through dinner, as Rob said, 'Really delicious!' and Jasper chatted happily about peeing behind a tree at the farmers' market, butterflies filled my stomach. Was it a dumb idea to go to Addie's? What would we have in common?

Some mornings I watched her leave for a run as I nursed Poppy in the glider, slices of pale-lemon light slipping through the curtainless window. I envied her graceful gait. From weeks of bed rest and lack of exercise, my legs were weak, leaden.

On Thursdays – garbage day – she rolled up her single can on wheels. Had she always been on her own? I wanted to know more about her, but what if her *Stop by anytime!* was a throwaway line?

If I hadn't told Rob about my plans to visit her, I'd have bailed. But I *had* told him and he'd hold me to it, part of his ongoing mission to force me out of my comfort zone.

Before I left, I gave Jasper the Lego box I'd bought at the supermarket.

'Help me build it, Daddy!' he begged.

Rob turned the box around in his hands. 'Where'd he get this?'

'I picked it up at the grocery store today.' I used our silver kettle as a mirror to check my lip gloss.

'It says this is for ages eight and up.' Rob frowned.

'Well, I thought you'd do it with him.'

'It's not that, Laur. These pieces are small. He or Poppy could choke on them.'

My mind was already next door.

'OK, sorry.' I pecked him lightly on the lips. 'I'll be more careful next time.'

'Oh, speaking of careful,' Rob continued as I covered the perfect wedge of pie, 'I called an attorney today about setting up the will and guardianship for the kids. He's sending over paperwork.'

'OK, thanks.' My stomach flipped. I hated the topic yet I'd been the one to bring it up. Losing my mom made me all too aware that tragedy could strike at any moment. Fear that something could happen to Rob and me hovered like a storm cloud.

I pictured the man at the farmers' market. The odds that it was Lyle were minuscule. I needed to stop expecting the worst and focus on all the good surrounding me.

I stepped onto Addie's tiny welcome mat and rang her bell. Beneath plastic wrap, the pie suddenly looked sloppy as juice from the berries bled through the whipped cream.

Sweat trickled down my back. What was I doing there? What would we talk about? I considered heading home when the door opened.

'Hey!' Addie looked flawless in brown linen shorts and a white sleeveless sweater. 'I was hoping you might come by!' She stepped onto her porch.

'Ladies!' We turned. Zoey stood in the street wearing a short red mini-dress, holding a leash, a squat basset hound shuffling ahead of her. 'Hanging without me?'

'Never!' Addie called. 'She walks the Barretts' dog and they shave money off her rent,' she murmured like a ventriloquist. 'Have a good night, Zo!' Addie waved. 'Keep an eye on that one,' she whispered without moving her lips again, 'especially around your husband.' She glanced down, grinned, and in her regular voice asked, 'What do we have here?'

'It's a strawberry pie.' I offered her the plate, but she held up her hand.

'Before I accept this, I need to ask,' she sniffed, 'are you wearing sunscreen?' Her Marian imitation, complete with a crooked finger, was pure perfection, her warm laugh a portal to a more interesting world.

My unease melted away.

If a tribe could consist of a single person, I'd found mine.

SIX

Corey

I threw the Corolla into reverse, desperate to put the garden center in my rearview for the day. Maybe for good. The wad of cash in my back pocket was practically burning through the denim of my cutoffs, making me hotter and more uncomfortable than the cracked vinyl upholstery.

I was trapped, blocked by a landscaper's truck. Dave, my boss, was shooting the shit with the driver even as Ma's car coughed blue-gray exhaust clouds in their faces.

'C'mon!' I whisper-whined. 'Go!' I couldn't get out and ask them to move, not after what I'd done.

A knock on the car window made me jump. It was Desiree, balancing on her brother's ten-speed, the late-day sun lighting up her hazel eyes. Her lips moved but I couldn't make out what she was saying over the asthmatic gasps of air conditioning I'd cranked to full blast. I rolled down the window and tried to act normal.

'Wanna get fro-yo or—?'

'Can't today. Mary Lou needs the car.'

Her squint twisted into a scowl. 'You should really get your own wheels.'

'Right back at ya!' I nodded toward her bike's seat, which was being held together by duct tape and determination.

'Touché.' She pronounced it 'touche' so it rhymed with douche.

I'd started at the garden center in December when I figured if I didn't get out of the house and away from Ma, I'd destroy the only semi-decent relationship I had left. In April, Desiree got hired to help out on weekends. Our Saturday fro-yo routine began in May after she took a bad check from a customer without asking for ID.

I'd heard her babbling at the register. 'We accept checks, but I've never done this before. Gimme one sec.'

I could've helped her, but I was stocking those soy candles with the stupid names like 'Cabin in the Woods' or 'Jamaican Sunset.' Josh, the assistant manager, could've talked her through it. Instead, he leaned over my shoulder pointing at the candles and making crude jokes like, 'Can't wait 'til they come out with one called "Festival Toilet" that smells like my bathroom after I eat at Five Guys.'

When the check bounced a week later, Dave, who was usually pretty chill, flipped out. It wasn't like the customer bought a bag of potting soil or a bunch of daisies. They got away with more than five hundred dollars' worth of rare orchids.

After Dave lit into Desiree, I found her wiping her eyes in the gazebo out back by mounds of mulch and ugly statues tattooed with bird shit. The maternal side I'd tried to bury bubbled up, and before I could stuff it down, I heard myself asking if she wanted to get ice cream after work.

As we'd sat in a raspberry-colored booth under super-bright lights, Desiree told me she couldn't afford to lose the garden center gig. Her mom cleaned houses for rich people in Palm Beach and was constantly on Desiree to study and get good grades so someday she'd be the rich person, not the cleaning lady. Our age gap shrunk as we complained about our mothers. Getting fro-yo became a thing after our Saturday shifts.

'Maybe next week?' Desiree asked, fiddling with the broken gear shift.

'Definitely.' I nodded, stuffing down the anger rising in my chest.
I didn't like disappointing her, but even more, I didn't like that I
cared.

The landscaping truck lurched forward and Dave slapped the
tailgate. 'See ya Monday!' He offered a sweeping wave meant for
all of us before heading inside.

Desiree hopped on the bike and I gunned it out of the lot so I
wouldn't have to watch her pedal away.

Ma didn't need the car. I just couldn't sit there with Desiree. Not
with the money I'd taken from the register making my whole body
buzz like I had a beehive between my ears and a hornet's nest in
my chest.

It was a short drive back to the condo, so I got on the expressway.
Changing lanes, I kept checking for lights, listening for sirens.
Then I laughed. I was a petty thief, not O. J. fucking Simpson.
There'd be no slow-speed chase. Not for two hundred and forty-
three dollars.

Why did I take it? Because it filled the usual hole inside me with
something different, something dangerous. It wasn't exactly a life-
changing amount, and I didn't need the money. I had enough from
the sale of the house, though that should've been a shit-ton more.
Kenny and I had busted our asses to renovate that little white Cape
Cod. My eyes burned every time I remembered Frankie and me
gardening together, how she'd drag the hose and drink from it when
she thought I wasn't looking.

Something Desiree had asked that morning as we watered herbs
in the greenhouse, the unbearable humidity already blurring the
edges of reason, came back to me.

'If you could be any flower, which would you be? I'll go first.
Gardenia – perfect combo of darkness and light. Plus, they smell
good. Now you.'

'Probably oleander.' I plucked a withered basil leaf. 'Simple.
Pretty.' I didn't add 'mostly toxic, sometimes deadly.'

Desiree wanted to become a landscape architect. She geeked out
over plants and flowers. She'd even worried about the fate of those
stupid orchids that got her put on probation. She had her future all
mapped out. If she couldn't get a scholarship to UMiami, she'd go
to community college, then transfer.

Most of the time Desiree's questions were like that. Fun. Harmless. But last week, as we sat inside the yogurt shop, she said something that messed me up.

'What's your deal?' she'd asked in between taking a lick of dulce de leche and picking a gummy bear off a molar with a chipped blue fingernail.

I shrugged. 'No deal.'

'You seem, like, I don't know, smart, but you work part-time. You're above-average looking, but you live with your mom, and no offense—' She put down her purple spoon and held up her hands. 'You have no social life. Eating fro-yo with some random though incredibly interesting teen on a Saturday isn't exactly "lifegoals."'

'Gee, thanks.' I pretended to be offended. 'Maybe if the whole landscape architect thing doesn't pan out, you could get into life coaching or motivational speaking?'

She laughed and a sprinkle shot out of her mouth.

'Sorry.' She coughed and shook her head. Sometimes her pixie hair was aqua; others it was hot pink. Her mom only let her color it in the summer, so every couple of weeks it was a different shade. Even with her face polka-dotted with pimples and her sarcasm, I saw it—her beauty, her potential. So much good was still ahead of her. So much bad was behind me.

'I'm just, I don't know, curious, like, what'd you do before this? Like why, why are you here? Doing this?'

How could I tell her that I took this job because there was no background check, and none of the usual crap the government makes you fill out so they can stick their dirty hands deep inside your pockets?

'You know my whole deal; seems only fair I should know yours.' She bit her spoon and smirked. 'You know I can just google you.'

My stomach cratered. If she did, which headline would she click first?

'Just blocking out a bad marriage, taking a grown-up time-out, plotting my next move.' I'd tried to sound cool, casual, and that had done the trick. At least temporarily.

By the time I got back to the condo, the sun was sinking, making everything glow orange and pink. I could barely stand it. The high had worn off. All that was left was shame. That's how it had become; the window of excitement closed a little faster each time.

Wheel of Fortune was blaring when I walked in.

'This lady's a school teacher and this man in the middle? He collects stamps. He almost won an RV!' Ma clapped.

It never stopped amazing me. I barely cared about my own life, why would I give a crap about Bob from Denver and his almost mobile home?

'Hungry?' she asked during a commercial.

'I grabbed a burger with some people from work.' The lies came fast, easy as breathing.

'At eight o'clock, there's a birthday celebration for Irene Moffatt in the clubhouse. Tomorrow's her eightieth. Her son, Mike, the one who's a police officer, the one who lost his—'

'Yeah, you told me this morning,' I cut her off. I couldn't listen to Mike's sob story again.

'You're welcome to join me. There'll be cake.'

'I'm going for a run.'

'Working all day then exercising. I don't know where you get the energy.' She sighed.

'You know the running helps,' I said.

'I don't know, dear. Because you don't tell me.'

'I'm telling you now.'

I went to the guest room and took the money out of my pocket. It was damp. The electric charge I'd felt when I first held it was long gone. I opened the closet and knelt in front of the orange chalk and yellow barrette, things I'd taken from that little girl's driveway. The purple thermos I'd swiped from their Pathfinder a week earlier rested on its side. Frankie had one just like it, only peach-colored. I screwed off the lid and stuck the cash inside.

Ma was putting on lipstick at the mirror beside the front door when I came out in my running shorts and tank. 'Sure you don't want to join me?'

'Nah, but thanks.' A hangover-like headache was building. I needed to fix it.

We left the condo at the same time, each of us slowly gathering speed like trains moving in opposite directions.

* * *

I tried to force myself into a different route, but my legs refused to cooperate. I'd been back to that neighborhood once since I'd taken the purple thermos, but some asshole was washing his truck across the street so I kept running.

When I turned the corner onto the girl's block, my heart was already flip-flopping. I crossed the street, slowed my pace, jogged past Dave's house with my eyes shut tight. I opened them and saw it up ahead. Something in the grass. A sandal maybe? Just beyond their driveway. I moved closer. A small pink Croc.

'Cor!' Dave's voice stopped me cold. 'Corey Sutton!'

Shit! I pictured the camera in the corner of the ceiling behind the register at the garden center. It hadn't been working when everything happened with that bad check Desiree took. I'd heard Dave on the phone, apologizing to Doug Hall, the garden center's owner, promising to be more on top of things.

I turned, bracing for the worst. 'Hey, Dave,' I panted.

'Checked the register at closing today.' He took off his baseball cap and wiped the sweat from his forehead with his meaty palm.

'Yeah, and?' I bent forward, hands on my knees, struggling to catch my breath, praying I wouldn't hurl.

'Came up short.' He put his cap back on and raised a beer bottle to his lips, its label shiny as a silver dollar in the moonlight. 'By a lot.'

'Who counted?' My temples started to pound. 'Josh? He was probably baked out of his mind. I'll double-check it Monday.'

'Pretty sure Desiree took it. Can't prove it. Just a gut feeling.'

'I don't think she—'

'I know you tried to take her under your wing after that whole bad-check deal went down, but this reminds me why I stopped hiring kids.'

'Desiree's not like—'

'Left her a voicemail, told her I was cutting back on staff and she shouldn't bother showing up anymore. I'm not gonna call the cops. They'll just tell me to fix that stupid camera.'

I sank to the sidewalk.

'Hey, you OK?' Dave leaned toward me.

The beer on his breath made my stomach churn. 'I haven't eaten much today.'

'Lemme grab you some water. Got a couple hot dogs left over from supper, you're welcome to 'em.'

I waved him off and he disappeared inside his garage.

Laying on the warm concrete, everything started to blur. The glow of the streetlights mixing with flashes of the cash I'd stuffed in the purple thermos, Desiree laughing as she added a second scoop of gummy bears to her fro-yo, the little pink sandal waiting just steps away.

That open wound inside me was spreading, infecting others. I either had to get better or find the source of my sickness and kill it at the root.

SEVEN

Corey

The night before came back in splinters and flashes. Dave's face, pink as a whoopee cushion, hovering inches above mine, his thick hand pulling me to my feet, his words ('Might need you to take Desiree's shifts, if you're up to it . . .') echoed inside my skull.

I groaned and reached for my phone to see if he'd emailed the weekly schedule. It usually took him a few tries to get it right, depending on how many beers he'd downed while putting it together. Not that I was in any position to judge.

After I staggered home, I'd gone right for the bourbon in the back of the closet. Sipped straight from the bottle. No wonder my tongue felt thick and prickly as a cactus leaf.

I tapped the email icon and jabbed at the pillows beneath my pounding head. Waiting for new messages to load, I scanned ones I hadn't opened. Most were ads for housewares, clothes, kids' stuff. Things I didn't need anymore.

The weekly farmers' market newsletter from my old town popped up. I clicked on it, determined to unsubscribe. I'd tried a dozen times; the damn thing kept coming.

An aerial shot of the green and white tents made my stomach twist like someone was turning a corkscrew inside me. Frankie loved the farmers' market. The sunflowers, the cider donuts, the guy on stilts who made balloon animals on opening day.

I scrolled down and that's when I saw it: a photo of a woman with a baby strapped to her. She was squatting beside a boy eating ice cream, dimples denting his freckled cheeks. Something caught my eye. The name. I reread the caption. *Laurel, Jasper, and Poppy West enjoy their first farmers' market visit since moving to town.*

Laurel West. The woman who bought my house. I never met her. Kenny and the real estate agent handled everything, but I'd seen her name on the closing documents.

I pinched the screen, zooming in to get a better look at the person who was living the life that once was mine. Purple half-moons hung beneath her eyes. Her fingers were curled around her son's arm. I spotted something just behind them. A woman. Her straw hat, the color of hay, with a wide black ribbon, made me look closer. My old neighbor had one just like it. How many times had I seen her wearing it, prancing around like she was the queen of Cold Creek Lane?

It couldn't be, I told myself. *But what if it was?*

My face tingled as if I'd been stung by a dozen bees. I poked at the screen again, stretching the image. It didn't help. The woman was blurry, like she'd known the photo was being taken and had spun around to avoid it.

Was it really her? Was it a coincidence she was there? Or was she following this mother, plotting to ruin her life the way I suspected she'd destroyed mine?

Shit! I hurled the phone across the room. It hit the wall with a thud and landed on my half-empty duffle bag. I didn't want to get involved. I couldn't. The charges against me had been dropped on the condition that I quit 'playing detective.'

What if grief had messed with my mind and I was wrong about all of it?

What if I wasn't?

I pictured Laurel West's tired eyes. If I didn't warn her, who would?

EIGHT

Laurel

With summer in full swing, we fell into a lazy rhythm. While Poppy took her morning nap, Jasper and I played in the backyard. If Addie didn't have a work deadline, she joined us. We sipped iced tea in the shade of the soaring elms while Jasper pushed his bubble mower or ran through the sprinkler Rob had set up so the grass wouldn't die.

Before meeting her, my main topics of conversation revolved around my children – how much they'd eaten, if they'd pooped. Addie recommended novels and gushed about shows she'd binge-watched.

Could you become more interesting simply by knowing someone? That's how I felt after spending time with Addie.

'What about having Zoey and Wyatt join you?' Rob asked one night at dinner. He'd met Zoey that morning when he was heading to the train and she was walking the Barretts' dog. 'I'd think you'd have more in common with her.'

'*You* probably have more in common with her,' I'd joked. Rob, who'd spent his whole career in insurance sales, had learned Zoey worked as a claims adjuster.

He took a sip of beer. 'Seems nice. Her son's close to Jasper's age.'

'I don't know, Rob, she's . . .' I couldn't put my finger on it. 'Blunt? Tough?'

'She's a single parent.' Rob licked his lips. 'Probably has to be.'

'For a quick conversation, you sure covered a lot.' I pushed away my half-eaten pasta.

'All I'm saying, Laur, is be open to new things, new friends.'

I'd made a new friend. Addie. We may not have had as much in common, but maybe that's what made her more intriguing. It was pathetic, I supposed, but I hoped some of her coolness would rub off on me. Even her simple gestures, like the way she swept her hair into a bun and then let it tumble down, were graceful, elegant. When she crossed her legs, I picked up her peach scent. Was it perfume or moisturizer? I was lucky if I remembered deodorant.

She talked about her job and gave me the inside scoop on which toys would be 'must-haves' for the upcoming holiday season, whispering so Jasper wouldn't overhear. I shared a bit about my days as a pastry chef. I told her how baking a birthday cake or being entrusted to hide an engagement ring inside a profiterole made me feel as if I were part of something special, if only peripherally.

'Aw, I love that.' She smiled.

I didn't say that those occasions, however brief, stemmed the rising tide of loneliness that often consumed me.

'There's a little bakery about ten minutes away,' she added. 'They make this buttery brioche and the best paninis. We should go sometime.'

A fluttery feeling filled my stomach. 'That sounds amazing!' I blurted before I fully envisioned the trip. Would I bring Jasper and Poppy? I'd have to. We'd only been in town a few weeks. I hadn't looked for a sitter yet. I'd need to drive because of their car seats. I saw the interior of the Accord through a stranger's eyes – the worn upholstery, faded floor mats, rotting banana peels in a cupholder attracting fruit flies.

'Maybe we could go on a weekend so the kids can stay with Rob?' Other than the grocery store, I hadn't really taken them anywhere on my own. 'That way you won't have to hear me read an entire kids' menu aloud or listen to songs about trains or donkeys in the car.'

'Stop!' She touched my arm. 'Rob and the children should come too. I love kids.' She lowered her sunglasses as the morning haze intensified. 'I'd hoped to have my own by now.'

What could I say? *You're still young. You've got time!* I knew how even the loveliest words offered in comfort often rang hollow.

'Sorry,' she added quickly. 'I didn't mean to get all sad and self-pitying. I was engaged once. It ended badly.' She shuddered and raised her chin toward Jasper. 'Look at him! To be that young and happy again, right?'

I glanced at my son, who was waving to a bunny. He'd taken to suburban life instantly. Beyond him, Marian, in green rubber gloves that skimmed her elbows, hosed down her birdbath.

'Hi Mimi! Hi Mimi! Watch this!' Jasper called, trying his best to cartwheel across the lawn.

'Careful now. That grass is full of ticks!' Marian hollered before shifting her sharp gaze toward Addie and me.

If Marian was a pest, Addie was the repellant. When Marian saw us together, she didn't venture over. Instead, she remained penned in her yard like a dog aware of the limits of an invisible fence.

I tried to respect the boundaries of my emerging friendship with Addie as well. Of course, I'd wondered what had gone wrong with her engagement. Why would an attractive, single woman choose to live in a small town with zero nightlife – unless you counted the library's ongoing series: 'Smart Saving for Retirement.' What had brought her to Cold Creek Lane? Curious as I was, I told myself to be patient. In time, I'd get my answers.

Musical Munchkins began the final week of June. It was held in a church basement in the heart of town less than a mile away. I hadn't thought about the logistics until my in-laws brought us a double stroller during one of their Sunday visits.

'Rob mentioned Jasper's class is just up the street and I said, "Laurel needs a good sturdy stroller!"' Susan explained as Dennis wheeled it fully assembled into our living room. 'Rob agreed it would make him feel so much better to picture the little ones buckled in rather than think of you trying to get them in and out of the car in a crowded parking lot. Or, worse, if you had to park on that busy main street.'

I'd looked at my husband and wondered when he'd stop doubting my ability to keep our family safe. His eyes had'nt met mine.

The class met on Tuesday and Thursday mornings. From the first one, Jasper was enthralled with the bongos, the dancing, the prospect of making new friends. He walked up to the teacher, Miss Cheryl, and kids twice his height with a swagger I envied.

'I'm Jasper! That's Mommy and that's Poppy!' He pointed at me and then toward the corner where I'd parked the hulking stroller.

For my son's sake, I forced myself to remain rooted to the group circle instead of skulking away, pretending to nurse Poppy, who slept through crashing cymbals, tinkling tambourines, and toddler meltdowns. Following Jasper's lead, I introduced myself to the mothers and nannies. Most already knew one another from the winter and spring sessions.

At the end of the second class, a mom came over to apologize. One of her twins had snatched a triangle out of Jasper's hand. I hadn't noticed.

'Last fall, Miss Cheryl had to hide the triangle,' the mom confided. 'It was causing full-on wrestling matches.' She rolled her brown eyes. 'I'm Jill, by the way. Laurel, right?'

I nodded, impressed she'd remembered my name from the first class. She invited us to join her and another mom at the nearby park after class.

'We pack a picnic lunch and complain about our husbands while the kids throw wood chips at each other. You really don't want to miss it.' She laughed as one of her boys raced over and pummeled her thighs.

'Can we go, Mommy?' Jasper was by my side, his eyes huge and pleading. 'Can we?' Had he been that bored with me that he'd leap at the chance to play with the boy who'd just pried a triangle away from him?

'How about next week?' I suggested.

'Yay!' Jasper jumped up and down.

'Great!' Jill pulled her phone from her shorts pocket. 'Give me your number. I send reminders on Monday nights. Oh, and if you don't mind, no nuts. My Flynn is allergic.'

'Sure, of course, no problem,' I babbled, wishing I shared my son's enthusiasm.

All weekend Jasper asked me to count down the days until he saw his new friends at the park. I hoped Jill would text me. Who else was included? Would I like them? Would they like me?

Monday night my phone pinged. *Weather looks good for tomorrow. Let's plan on lunch in the park. Bringing grapes! See you then!*

And so we went. Jill re-introduced me to another mom from class, Trisha, who lowered herself onto the picnic bench and winced. 'Hemorrhoids.'

'TMI, my friend,' said Jill as she reconsidered popping a grape into her mouth.

United by Musical Munchkins and the usual motherhood topics, we chatted about bedtime battles and picky eaters. It was nice to commiserate, yet at the same time, I didn't want to dwell on subjects that already claimed so much of my headspace. Still, I was grateful. In corners of the park, other mothers and nannies stood or sat alone, scrolling through their phones, waiting for nap time. Without Jill's invitation, I'd have been among them.

When they found out we were new to the area, they told me about playgrounds Jasper might like and registration deadlines for fall and winter sports.

'Where'd you guys move from?' Jill asked.

'Manhattan.' Afraid it sounded snooty, I added, 'Not *Gossip Girl*'s Manhattan. Hell's Kitchen.'

'And where are you now? Which street, I mean?' Trisha asked.

'Cold Creek Lane.'

As silence fell over the table, the children's giggles and shrieks seemed louder, more shrill. Trisha's hands stopped unzipping her son Milo's lunchbox. Even the barely swaying branches of nearby trees stilled as I waited for them to say something.

'The Cape Cod, just a few in from the corner,' I added.

Jill's dark eyes darted toward her twins.

'Oh, that's such a nice part of town,' Trisha finally said.

'So far, so good!' I smiled.

They grinned without revealing any teeth and the conversation shifted back to dinner recipes and debating if taking a beach vacation with kids was harder than staying home. I listened, nodded at the right intervals, and tried to shake my simmering unease.

For Rob and me, the house on Cold Creek Lane was at the very top of our budget. Other streets had larger, fancier homes set farther apart from one another. During his childhood, Rob's family had moved three times within their town. Susan wouldn't rest until they were settled in the most exclusive section of the community. I couldn't imagine it. This one move had worn me out.

'Me and mommy have new friends!' Jasper told Rob at dinner.

When I explained that we'd met his Musical Munchkins classmates in the park, my husband beamed at me in a way I'd nearly forgotten. I wanted to bask in the glow of it, do whatever it took to make it last.

* * *

On Tuesday morning, I rushed around the kitchen packing sandwiches and snacks, slicing grapes into quarters so no one would choke.

'Why don't you invite everyone here for lunch after class one day? Then you wouldn't have to lug all this stuff to the park.'

The idea sounded as far-fetched as if he'd suggested I invite the royal family to pop by for tea. Rob's mom lived for entertaining. Each year, she hosted Thanksgiving and a New Year's Day open-house brunch, complete with signature cocktails. She made it seem effortless, but after years in the hospitality industry, I was keenly aware of all it entailed.

'No way,' I told him. Just picturing it – the shopping, cooking, straightening and post-lunch clean-up all while caring for two young children – exhausted me.

Rob rinsed his coffee mug and placed it in the dishwasher. 'Well, we have the room.'

When we lived in the city, I used our limited square footage as an excuse to avoid hosting gatherings.

'What if the kids trash the house?' I knew how much he appreciated a tidy home.

Rob glanced at the kitchen table cluttered with Jasper's toy trains and Poppy's pacifiers. 'Ah, yes, you're right.' He smirked. 'I forgot about all our heirlooms.' He raised his eyebrows hopefully and lowered his voice. 'You said a few of these kids are going to the same preschool. It would be nice for Jasper to start off with a couple of friends in September, wouldn't it?'

He had a point. Jasper was crunching his way through a bowl of cereal, his eyes fixed expectantly on my face.

'Fine,' I conceded. 'I'll ask them after today's class.'

'Yay!' Jasper waved his spoon in the air. Milk dribbled on the table. Rob wiped it up before kissing Jasper and me on the tops of our heads and walking out the door.

Through the dining-room window, I watched him round the corner toward the train station and attempted to ignore the obvious: he was trying to turn me into his mother.

I waited until all the wrappers had been tossed and the water bottles recycled before extending the invitation. If they said 'no' it would have been too awkward to continue sittting there. Such a small, dumb thing – asking a few women to lunch – yet my leg bounced beneath the picnic table, anxious as a teenager inviting a crush to prom. A heatwave had rolled in. Sweat slid down my sides, settling in the folds of my stomach, making me more uncomfortable.

As we corralled the children, rosy-cheeked and ready for naps, I asked if they'd like to come to our house Thursday for lunch.

'What a fun idea! I'll bring mini-bagels since that's the only effing thing Milo's eating this week.' Trisha laughed.

Jill pointed at her twins, Flynn and Donovan, who'd spent most of their time attempting to catch a squirrel while their uneaten ham and cheese sandwiches congealed in the early-afternoon sun. 'You sure you want these tiny savages in your house?' she asked.

'I'm sure!' I remembered the way they'd gone quiet when I said we lived on Cold Creek Lane and thought I should prepare them. 'Our home's still a work in progress. Nothing fancy.' I tried to capture Rob's breezy tone when he'd joked about our 'heirlooms,' but in my nervousness, my voice fell flat.

'Same,' Jill said. 'Last night, I found Cheez-Its and a watermelon slice under the couch. Oh and ants! Lots and lots of ants.'

'Gross!' Trisha fake-gagged. 'Though gotta admit I'm jealous your kids will even touch fruit.'

As we went our separate ways, my body pulsed with relief. The only thing harder than prepping for the playdate would've been telling Rob no one wanted to come.

On the walk home, I thought about what I'd make for lunch. Would I buy wine? Our furnishings were shabby, but each time Susan stopped by she brought something – new throw pillows, artificial plants that could've fooled a botanist, and a silver-edged mirror to hang above the fireplace. It was starting to look and feel like a home.

Jasper would be thrilled to spend more time with his new friends and Rob would be ecstatic, imagining invitations to backyard barbecues and dinner dates would soon come our way. Getting everything ready would be exhausting, but it was nothing compared to how happy it would make them. And really, including Jasper, Poppy and me, it was just three women and a handful of children. How badly could it go?

NINE

Laurel

The morning of the lunch, I lurched around the kitchen and dining room, powered by adrenaline, dizzy from lack of sleep. Poppy had been up three times and only settled as Rob's alarm sounded.

The night before, I dusted and organized the playroom, then stayed up until midnight preparing spinach and tomato quiches along with cheddar and dill scones. All that was left to do was assemble the individual strawberry shortcakes. As I leaned against the counter hulling berries, Rob returned from taking out the garbage.

'You didn't invite Marian or Zoey?' He scowled.

I shook my head. 'Just the moms from music class.'

'And Addie, right?' It sounded more like an accusation than a question as he rinsed his hands at the sink.

In a panicky moment Wednesday night, I'd texted Addie and asked her to join us. Jill and Trisha were nice but with Addie there the conversation wouldn't solely focus on Milo's limited diet or Jill listing the pros and cons of Tae Kwon Do. When Addie had written back: *Thx! I'll be there!* I started to think it might be fun. And if not fun, then at least not awful.

'Right, yes, Addie, too. Why?'

'Well, I just saw Marian at the curb and she asked if you and the kids were all right. She said she didn't see you out in the back-yard yesterday.'

'I was getting ready for this afternoon.' I waved my knife over the mini cakes cooling on racks beside the open window. The early-morning breeze had slowed, turning the air inside the kitchen from cool and dewy to warm and close.

'Well, I thought you'd included her, so I said something like, "They're great. You'll see them today at lunch." I could tell she was confused, so I invited her and Zoey, too. She and Wyatt were walking Harriet, the dog, and overheard.'

'Rob, stop!' I swatted him with a dishtowel. 'That would be a nightmare.' His expression didn't change. I stiffened. 'Tell me you're joking.'

'I'm not.' He didn't smile. 'I told them to come around noon.'

'You what?' I dropped the knife. Its thick handle clattered against the cutting board. 'Why? Why would you do that?'

'They're our neighbors, Laur.' Rob inched toward me, plucked a strawberry from the colander, and popped it into his mouth. 'You didn't think it was rude to exclude them? They're both pretty much on their own.'

'I told you I was already anxious about this.' Hot tears stung my eyes. 'I barely know these women, Rob, the last thing I need . . .' I lowered my voice, paranoid that they'd hear us through the open window '. . . is Marian here judging me!' I mimicked her gravelly voice and scolding tone the way I did with Addie. '"Is that apple organic? If not, you might as well feed him pesticide! Shouldn't that baby be wearing a bonnet?" And Zoey? Will she accuse me of stealing her house again? And why do you know the name of that dog?'

'Stop. You're just nervous. The house looks great. Food's prepped. You know what my mother would say: "In for a penny, in for a pound." What's a few more guests? It's all going to be fine.' He kissed me on the forehead and grabbed his travel mug of coffee. 'Gotta go. Text me later.'

A wave of guilt washed over me. We had so much: a good marriage, beautiful children, a new home. Had I been uncharitable? Unneighborly? After all, before I met Rob, I knew what it was like to receive few invitations, to be on my own.

Still, I needed to tell Addie before she walked in and found 'Meddling Marian,' as she called her, parked at my dining-room table. I texted: *Looks like we'll be having a few surprise guests today. Rob invited Marian and Zoey!* followed by three exploding head emojis.

Addie typed right back. *No way! Don't worry, I'll protect you!* with a winking emoji.

I smiled at the message, stuck the phone in my pocket, and added two place settings.

*   *   *

We were getting ready to leave for Musical Munchkins when the mail came.

'I got it!' Jasper raced past me. He'd developed a Pavlovian response to the squeak and slap of the mail slot. He scooped up the pile and handed it to me.

In between a take-out menu and a landscaper's flyer, I spotted an envelope the size of an invitation addressed to me.

'Mommy! Let's go!' Jasper tugged at my elbow as I slid my finger under the flap and gave myself a paper cut.

'Ouch!' I whimpered as Poppy began crying in her swing.

'Mommy!' Jasper whined.

'One sec.' I'd have assumed it was my mother-in-law sending me a recipe she found in a magazine, except the small, cramped handwriting on the envelope wasn't Susan's.

We were running late but my curiosity was piqued. It was so rare to get anything personal. I unfolded the sheet of loose leaf, my heart beating faster as I processed the words scrawled across the page: *I lost my family. Now yours is in danger.*

I read it again, the hairs on the back of my neck bristling, breath caught in my throat. I turned the note over. What was I expecting? A signature? I spun around, overcome with the sensation of being watched, then darted to the door as if I could catch the mail carrier, as if he could tell me who sent it.

I flung the door open and found Addie standing on our top step, one hand poised to press the doorbell, a glass bowl in the other.

'What's wrong?' she asked. 'You're shaking.'

'I . . . I just got this.' I held out the note; sweat beading on my forehead.

A 'V' formed between her sculpted eyebrows as she read the words.

'Where's it from?' She pointed to the envelope.

I hadn't thought to check the postmark. 'Florida?' My brain cycled through everyone I knew. Not a single friend or relative lived there. *Lyle Hartsell.* Is that where he ended up?

Addie sighed. 'I'm sure it's a scam. Something like this happened a few towns over. Turned out developers were trying to scare people into selling cheaply and quickly by sending creepy letters.'

'Really?' I asked.

'You didn't see it? I think there was a "Dateline" about it. You said it took you months to find a house, right? People resort to crazy things when real estate and money are involved.'

I thought of Zoey saying, 'You stole my house.'

Before I could mention it, Addie held up the bowl. 'I'm so sorry to do this, but I can't make it to lunch. Things are going sideways with this new client, and I have to be on a noon call with my boss.' She looked uncharacteristically flustered. 'If it wraps up early, I'll be back.' She extended her offering, squinting as blinding sunlight reflected off the foil that covered a tricolor pasta salad.

A throbbing began behind my eye. Marian and Zoey were coming; Addie was cancelling. I stood there numb, unmoving.

'I'll just stick this in your fridge.' She stepped into the living room, the loose skirt of her brick-red sundress dancing around her ankles as she twirled toward the kitchen. 'The place looks fantastic, by the way. I love what you've done – the pictures, the plants. So cozy!'

I followed her and set the note face down on the counter. 'I cleaned for today; it's usually a disaster.'

She moved a carton of eggs to make room in the crowded refrigerator, perfectly at home. She hadn't been inside until then. I wondered briefly if she'd been close with the previous owners.

'I have to get back.' Her mouth, shiny with a pinkish-brown gloss that made her blue eyes brighter, turned down at the corners. 'Again, I'm so sorry!' She dashed toward the door, light as a cat, as I lumbered after her.

'No, I understand. Thanks for bringing the salad. You didn't have to,' I called as she crossed the lawn.

'I hope you like it.' She smiled and gave a small wave before disappearing inside her house.

Any energy I had left leaked out of me as I loaded Poppy into the stroller. Jasper insisted on buckling himself, which took twice as long. As I pushed the children uphill beneath the broiling sun, I considered cancelling. I could've pretended Jasper had a stomach bug and sent an apologetic text. Jasper would be disappointed, but I could offer him an extra strawberry shortcake and he'd forget all about it. That was the beauty of children. They were so distractible, so forgiving. When Marian and Zoey appeared at the door, I'd tell them lunch was off and send them back home. But there was no point, I'd only have to reschedule, and prepare for it all over again. It was simpler to see it through.

As we sang the 'Hello' song and Jasper and I took turns playing the xylophone, I tried to stay present, but the note kept circling through my mind. It had to be Lyle or Zoey. Or maybe it was a scam like Addie said? How could I host this lunch when I was so distracted?

Poppy fussed in my lap as Jasper danced around more excited than usual. I recalled Rob's words: 'It's all going to be fine!' This was his idea, and where was he? Thirty miles away in an office, deciding where to grab lunch. In that moment, I was furious with him and with myself for listening to him.

Jill must've sensed something was off. She leaned over and smiled. 'There's still time to cancel!' She nodded toward Flynn, who was licking the mirror while his brother bopped him on the head with foam drumsticks.

I let out a rueful laugh. 'No, you have to come! If you don't, we'll be eating quiche for weeks.'

I had two bottles of Sancerre chilling. How nice it would be to pour a glass and feel it swim in my system, untying the knot that had settled between my shoulder blades after I'd read the note. But I couldn't serve it, not with Marian's cold, eagle eyes watching. She'd label me a 'day drinker.' I could already hear her chastising me for the lack of nutrients in the chicken fingers I planned to feed the kids.

'Good!' Jill said as Miss Cheryl strummed the opening notes of The White Stripes' 'We're Going to Be Friends.' 'We don't get a lot of invitations!'

I looked at Flynn who tripped his brother as they ran back to the circle. I should've canceled then.

I walked home while Trisha and Jill drove. Parked in front of the house beneath the midday sun, their white SUVs gleamed like dry-docked yachts.

Jasper hurled himself out of the stroller and raced to our front door. 'C'mon, guys! C'mon!' He beckoned with a wave of one plump hand, his other turning the knob. The door yielded, groaning open. With Addie stopping by and us rushing to get to class on time, had I forgotten to lock it?

Jasper marched the children toward the playroom. Flynn and

Donovan pushed past him to get the first look at the toys as Milo struggled to keep up.

'Your home is lovely!' Jill said, weaving her sunglasses through her mess of auburn curls and setting her handbag down.

'I cannot believe you just moved in!' Trisha did a three-sixty spin. 'We've been in our house for two years and our walls are still bare. It's pathetic!'

My spirits lifted. Each compliment was like a hit of dopamine. Maybe this was why Susan hosted so many parties. All the labor was worth it for the chance to bask in the glow of a little admiration.

I slipped Poppy into her swing and fixed everyone a glass of iced tea. The house felt stuffy, and I hoped the air conditioners, already chugging away, could keep up with the heat radiating off the kids and the oven as I turned it on to warm the quiches. *You should've made cold salads and sandwiches*, I berated myself.

Jill peeked into the playroom. 'The twins were so excited about this. Thanks again for hosting.' She rubbed my arm like we were old friends. Another hit of dopamine. It was a sweet scene. Jasper gave Donovan a tour of his play kitchen while Flynn knelt at the train table and Milo tossed the football in the air.

'They're welcome to go outside if they'd like,' I suggested. 'More room to run.'

Trisha winced. 'The creek makes me – you know . . .'

I didn't know, but nodded. 'No, right, of course.'

'It's so nice and cool inside,' Jill added though I'd noticed her fanning herself as the oven hummed, toasting up the room. 'Look how happy they are. Now, what can I do to help?'

The doorbell rang and my stomach dropped. I wanted it to be Addie; I knew it was Marian.

In a cornflower-blue dress nearly the same shade as her eyes, Marian stood grimacing at the crooked forsythia wreath I hadn't replaced. She thrust a bouquet of pink and white hydrangeas, blooms as big as softballs, at me.

'These are gorgeous. Thank you,' I managed as I watched a spider creep across the emerald leaves.

'Yours could look like this too if you watered them.' She peered past me into the living room. 'The former owner had quite a green thumb. It's a shame to let everything perish.'

Hearing her voice, Jasper raced through the kitchen. 'Mimi!' He launched himself at her, wrapping his arms around her legs. Flynn and Donovan piled on. Marian stood there encircled, patting their heads like Mother Goose.

'Marian!' Jill gushed.

'Marian!' Trisha echoed. 'What a fun surprise!'

Marian was beloved. I was bewildered.

'So good to see you all!' she exclaimed. 'I had no idea who'd be here. Last-minute invitation and all.'

I was about to shut the door when a small blond boy raced up the walkway.

'You must be Wyatt,' I said as he breezed past me, a ragged stuffed penguin in one hand, a toy flip phone in the other.

Zoey, looking cool and eclectic in blue linen overalls and a bowler hat, sauntered slowly behind him. 'So this is where the party's at?' she deadpanned. 'Here.' She handed me a bowl. 'Carrot slaw. Secret family recipe.' She winked and walked in.

I started to introduce her to Jill and Trisha but Zoey interrupted. 'We're acquainted.'

'That's right!' Trisha said. 'Was it Terrific Tadpoles or Galloping Guppies?'

'Does it matter?' Zoey laughed.

I placed the carrot slaw on the table and returned to the kitchen to put Marian's flowers in water as the conversation turned into a volley of 'How have you been?' and 'Look how big!'

As I removed chicken fingers from the oven, Jill appeared. 'Let me do that!' She sliced the tenders into skinny rectangles. 'Thank you for being mindful of Flynn's nut allergy.'

'No problem at all,' I said as I tossed the salad. 'You know Marian?'

'We met her about a year ago.' Jill looked up from making ketchup smiley faces on the kids' paper plates. 'She volunteers at the library. Sometimes she leads story hour.'

I imagined Marian taking delight in *shushing* adults and children alike.

'She babysat a few times,' Jill lowered her voice, 'but Flynn fell down the deck stairs, landed on a rock, and needed three stitches under his chin. Honestly, I think that little scar is the only way my mother-in-law can tell the twins apart.' She laughed as she arranged mini-bagels into a pyramid. 'Anyway, we haven't seen her in ages because Pete thought we should hire someone . . .' She mouthed the word 'younger.' 'Not that we really go anywhere – maybe out to dinner once a month. I still feel bad about it. Marian felt even worse. She brought Flynn a panda the size of a fire hydrant. You've seen my kids, they're maniacs. It could've happened on anyone's watch.' She arched her eyebrows in a look I couldn't read and walked toward the playroom, calling, 'Who's hungry?'

With the children parked around Jasper's train table, the adults moved into the dining room.

'This looks amazing, Laurel!' Jill said.

'Seriously!' Trisha broke a scone in half. 'I can't remember when I had a hot meal that I didn't have to cook, pay for, or pick up.'

Marian took a seat at the head of the table closest to the living room, while I sat opposite, nearest to the kitchen. Jill and Trisha sat on one side with Zoey across from them. I looked at the empty chair and hoped Addie would make it in time for dessert.

While they passed salads, I served the quiche. Crashing sounds spilled from the playroom – a tower of blocks toppling, a bucket of cars dumped. I stood to check on the kids, but Jill stopped me.

'Unless there's blood, let's ignore them and dig into this feast.'

The house was warm, but it smelled fantastic. Conversation and children's laughter floated through the rooms, replacing the usual cartoons and music videos.

Relief washed over me. Rob was right; it was going fine. I watched each woman take a bite, hungry for more praise. Since I'd stopped working, I'd forgotten how good it felt to receive a compliment.

Marian set down her fork. 'Do you have any water?' Her voice sounded different, coarser, wheezy.

'Of course. Let me grab some.'

I was standing at the fridge, the ice-maker churning and spitting cubes into the pitcher, when I heard the scream. My first thought was the children. Jasper. He was smaller than Jill's twins, who, by her admission, behaved like savages. It came again. An adult scream. Then another, followed by the sound of chairs scraping against wood.

'Call 911!'

'Get my bag!'

'Marian! Marian!'

'Oh my God!'

'Her airway's closing! Where's my bag? I need Flynn's EpiPen!'

I darted to the dining room. Marian's watery blue eyes were as swollen as a boxer's at the end of the final round. She gasped, her breath a faint whistle. Plates and silverware clattered to the floor as her thick-knuckled fingers clutched and grabbed at the tablecloth, fighting an invisible enemy. The vase of hydrangeas toppled.

'Mama!' Milo ran into the room, knocking me forward. I dropped the pitcher. Glass and ice splintered across the hardwood. Water puddled at my feet. Milo shrieked and ran back to the playroom.

I froze while Trisha pressed her phone to her ear, repeating 'allergic reaction.'

Jill pushed Marian's chair away from the table and wrenched her skirt to the side, revealing pale skin thin as crepe paper and mapped with bluish-purple veins. The sight was too intimate. I looked away as Jill pressed the EpiPen's needle into the outside of Marian's thigh and Trisha pleaded into the phone, 'She can't breathe. Hurry! Please!'

Behind them, Poppy, startled by the sudden commotion, awoke and began wailing. My breasts leaked. In the morning rush, I'd forgotten to put pads in my bra.

'Mommy! Mommy! What happened?' Jasper appeared by my side, broken glass crunching beneath his sneakers, ketchup smeared across his white polo shirt.

'Keep the kids back!' Jill shouted.

Zoey steered Jasper and the others, eyes wide, toward the playroom.

'Mommy! Is Mimi OK?' Jasper called as we waited, hoping to hear the sound of sirens racing toward us.

TEN

Laurel

Crowding the tiny living room, police officers stood behind paramedics, their shirts white as flour against Marian's mottled face. Her head looked small, shrunken beneath the oxygen mask.

'Ma'am, were there nuts or shellfish in any of this?' an EMT asked. A sweaty sheen coated his forehead as he nodded toward the dining room where the aftermath of my failed lunch was on full display – food on the floor, hydrangeas on their sides, table-cloth crooked and crumpled. 'Ma'am?' he said again, removing a blood pressure cuff from Marian's arm where angry pink welts bloomed.

It was hard to think. The squawk of walkie-talkies competed with the high-pitched squeals of Jill's twins who wanted to ride in the ambulance.

'No.' I shook my head, rocking and swaying Poppy in an attempt to quiet her howls. 'My husband has a food allergy. I'm very careful.'

'Well, those are our biggest culprits.' He looked away to avoid staring at the wet spots on my blue shirt where my milk leaked.

Trisha inched forward. 'Was there crab in something? At first I thought it was chicken, but I don't know.'

I shook my head again. 'I–I don't think so.' Exhaustion made me doubt myself. I'd been so busy, I'd only taken a bite of quiche to make sure it was the right temperature.

'There was crab meat in something.' Jill nodded. Her certainty made my cheeks burn as if I'd been caught in a lie.

We watched them load Marian onto a stretcher. Her bony arms extended like a Halloween skeleton's before EMTs strapped her down and slid her into the ambulance.

'Is there anyone we should call?' Trisha bit her lower lip. 'You know, just in case?'

'She has a son.' Jill lowered her voice. 'But he's in Connecticut and they don't speak.'

My back ached. Poppy felt impossibly heavy. I wanted everyone to go home.

As if she could read my mind, Zoey said, 'I should get back to work, though I gotta say this was a lot more action-packed than I'd expected.' She disappeared through the kitchen to fetch Wyatt.

'I'll follow them to the hospital,' Jill finally offered. 'Laurel, is it OK if the boys stay with you until Pete can pick them up?'

What could I say?

The afternoon dragged. Poppy was inconsolable even after I nursed her. Trisha stayed for a bit – more to process what had happened than to help clean up or keep Flynn and Donovan under control. Jill texted updates from the hospital. *Marian improving! It was def the crab!*

I opened the cabinet below the sink to toss the leftovers. The stench of Poppy's diaper, which I'd hastily thrown in the kitchen garbage before music class, mixed with the pungent sweetness of strawberry stems. The bite of quiche swam into my throat.

'I feel sick.' I hadn't meant to say it aloud.

'You've had a long day.' Trisha placed a hand on my back then pulled it away with the slightest wrinkle of her nose. My shirt, damp with sweat, clung to my skin. The house seemed to grow hotter by the second.

It was six when Jill's husband finally collected Flynn and Donovan. Like his sons, he was big and boisterous.

'I'm Pete.' He extended his hand, thick and squishy as a ball of fresh mozzarella. 'I'm here for the boys, unless you want to keep 'em!' His shoulders shook as he laughed at his own joke.

I wouldn't have put him and Jill together. She was soft-spoken, petite. But then Rob and I were so different. He was outgoing, eager to charm everyone in a room while I pressed myself into corners, hoping to blend in.

'Heard you tried to kill the old lady,' he said, following the sound of his sons' squeals. 'She's one tough bird. You're gonna have to do more than that.'

My face flushed.

'I'm joking!' Pete's loud snort startled Poppy, who'd been dozing in my arms. She began to cry and I thought I might too.

'Daddy! Daddy!' The twins jumped at the sound of their father's voice.

'What's up, dudes?' He fist-bumped them and then turned to me. 'We gotta have you and the fam over soon, welcome you to town.'

'We'd love that.' I hoped he'd only said it to be polite.

'Hey, your oven's on.' He pointed to the red light as he strolled through the kitchen, his sons bolting out the front door without a 'goodbye' or a 'thank you.' 'No wonder it's a damn inferno in here.'

By the time Rob came home I felt as if I'd been awake for months. He found me upstairs, sitting in Poppy's room, nursing her in the glider. Jasper was across the hall sprawled on our bed watching Miss Cheryl's YouTube channel on the iPad.

'There you are!' Rob stood in the doorway unbuttoning his dress shirt.

I brought my finger to my lips. He walked over, kissed me, and brushed the pad of his thumb across Poppy's crinkled forehead, fretful even in her dreams.

'So, how'd it go?' Rob whispered.

Before I could answer, Jasper raced in. 'Daddy!'

Rob scooped him up. 'Hey, bud! How was your playdate?'

'Great! A ambulance was here! And police!'

I held Poppy closer, afraid the commotion would wake her.

'Why?' Rob's eyes flashed to me. 'What happened?'

Jasper nodded furiously. 'Mimi ate a bad thing.'

'She had an allergic reaction,' I clarified.

'That's awful.' Rob put Jasper down. 'Is she OK?'

Having delivered his news, Jasper scampered back to his videos.

'She's at the hospital. They expect her to be fine but they're keeping her overnight for observation.' I stood and carried Poppy the way I'd maneuvered a four-tier wedding cake – carefully, holding my breath. With her safely in the crib, I moved into the hall.

'What was it?' Rob followed me into our room.

'What was what?' I scooted Jasper over and collapsed on the bed beside him.

'The allergy? What did you make that triggered it?'

I didn't like what his question implied. 'They think it was

shellfish. People brought stuff; it could've been in anything. I have no idea.'

Rob rubbed his chin. 'I can't believe I didn't ask if she had any allergies when I invited her.'

A spark of anger flared in my chest. I'd forgotten he was the reason she was there.

'I mean, Christ, I know what that's like.' He sat on the bed and removed his socks.

I waited, knowing what would come next. Sometimes when his mother had too much wine, she'd recount the tale that Rob and his sister, Emily, referred to as her 'We almost lost him!' story. It was the week before Christmas. Rob was five and Emily two. The whole family had gone to Manhattan to see the tree in Rockefeller Center. Dennis had insisted on having dinner in Chinatown, which Susan said she adored but felt wasn't the best dining spot for two young children – even ones with sophisticated palates. Rob had an allergic reaction to the shrimp in the dumplings. It was the first time he'd ever had shellfish. The staff sprang into action and he was taken to the hospital.

'My little Robbie in the ER. I can't even bear to think about it.' Susan would shudder and reach for Rob's hand. 'We almost lost him!'

Rob had only vague memories of it, but he'd avoided all seafood since that night just to be safe.

'That must've been awful for Marian and the kids, too.' Rob tossed his dress shirt in the hamper and pulled on a tee.

'The police there . . . here . . . in our home . . .' The words made the hair on my neck and arms rise. I shivered though it was broiling upstairs. 'It was like I was twelve years old again, Rob. I've had this sick feeling in my stomach all afternoon.'

'Maybe you ate something bad, too.' Rob often ignored references to my childhood. And the truth was, that sick feeling in the pit of my stomach had been there for two decades. Nothing he could've said would've fixed it. 'Did you make the crusts from scratch?'

'No.' The sound of Miss Cheryl doing an acoustic, kid-friendly cover of 'Oops! . . . I Did It Again!' hurt my head. 'I didn't have time.'

'Well, there you go!' he said. 'Who knows what's in those?

Any thoughts on dinner for Jasper and me? I guess leftovers are out.'

'I don't know. I just need to rest for a bit.'

'When you're feeling better, let's talk about the will and guardianship.' He stood at the foot of the bed, voice low. 'I told the lawyer we'd get back to him soon.'

Watching Marian taken away in an ambulance made it seem more pressing than ever. And then there was the note. I wanted to show it to Rob. I thought I'd stuck it in the kitchen, but when I looked for it after Pete and the twins left, I couldn't find it. Trisha must've swept it into the trash.

'Emily and Colin are the obvious choice,' Rob said.

'For what?' I mumbled.

'The legal guardians,' Rob laughed. 'Wow, you really mustn't be feeling well.'

Had all the color drained from my face? I should've known he'd suggest his sister and her fiancé. Yet it surprised me. Emily and I couldn't have been more different, and I was still upset that she hadn't asked Jasper to be a ring bearer. I'd expected it to bother Rob too, but all he'd said was, 'You know how brides are. She probably doesn't want a cute kid stealing the show.' So I'd let it go. And Colin? We might as well have left the children unattended in the woods.

'Rob, I don't think they're the best—'

'I'm hungry!' Jasper squealed.

'We'll talk more about it later,' Rob said before turning to Jasper. 'How about pizza?'

'Yay!' Jasper bounced with glee.

I pressed my palms to my forehead as if it could make the pounding stop.

Rob reached down and touched my arm. 'What happened with Marian, Laur, that was a freak thing. You shouldn't feel bad or guilty about that.'

I nodded so he'd go downstairs and take Jasper and the screeching iPad with him. Then I closed my eyes. He was right. I didn't have any reason to feel bad or guilty.

At least not then.

When I awoke, moonlight streamed through the windows. I reached for Rob. He was beside me. What time was it? I'd left my phone downstairs. A headache was building at the base of my skull. My mouth was dry. I needed water. Advil.

Halfway down the stairs, a sound came from the back of the house. If Jasper got up during the night, he ran into our room; he didn't roam.

It came again. Faint music. One of his toys must've been left on, its battery dying.

The sound stopped.

I stopped at the bottom of the staircase.

Was someone in the house? I remembered the note and thought of Lyle, a chill rippling down my spine. I was about to turn, hurry up the steps to get Rob, when a beam of light from the playroom bounced off the kitchen wall.

A figure stepped out then jumped back. Something clattered to the floor. I screamed.

'Holy shit!' a woman gasped. 'You scared the hell out of me.'

In the dim glow of the microwave's nightlight, I saw Zoey, standing in my kitchen.

I struggled to catch my breath, my heart beating in my throat. 'What – what the hell are you—?'

Rob thundered down the steps, repeating my name. He flicked on the overhead light.

Upstairs, I heard Jasper's weepy 'Mommy?' muffled by Poppy's wailing.

Rob was suddenly behind me, squinting, hand on my shoulder. 'What's going on?'

'She – she was in the playroom,' I stammered.

'Wyatt left Waddles here.' Zoey waved the stuffed penguin. 'Can't sleep without him.' She raised her cell phone, its flashlight blinding me. 'Did you not get my text?'

'How did you get in?' I kept my hand pressed to my heaving chest.

'The door was unlocked.'

I spun around to glare at Rob.

'Relax. You're not in the big, scary city anymore.' Zoey stepped closer. We were inches apart. She was still wearing her dark eye makeup, her lips red as the strawberries I never served. 'This is a safe neighborhood . . . relatively . . .' She looked at Rob. 'Sorry if I scared you. I had no idea you went to bed before . . .' She checked her phone. 'Ten p.m. I'll see myself out.'

She glided past us as if this were the most normal thing in the world. I clutched the corner of the stove to steady myself.

'Rob . . .' I started, my breathing still ragged. 'The door . . .'

'I thought I'd locked it.'

ELEVEN

Corey

'What time will you be home tonight?' Ma stood in the doorway of my bedroom, which had been a guest room, not that anybody ever visited.

I swiped deodorant like I was spackling a hole. It wasn't even eight a.m. and already the Floriday sunshine snuck between the vertical blinds turned the cream-colored rug into a heating pad under my bare feet.

'Thought we might go to the diner. Two pretty gals out on a Saturday night.'

I slapped the cap back on my Speed Stick, its chemical-floral scent pissing me off, and slammed it on the dresser. 'Don't do that.'

'Do what?'

'Act like that. Like we're normal, like we're the same as everybody else.'

'I'm not, dear.' Morning light bounced off her glasses. I couldn't see her eyes. 'We still eat dinner, right? I just thought, well, it might be nice. Something different. But if you don't want to, that's fine. I'll defrost some salmon.'

'Yeah, why don't you do that?' I twisted my hair into a ponytail and shoved it through the opening in the back of the Hall's Garden Center baseball cap that matched the brown T-shirt before it faded. Half a uniform. At least we could wear jeans or shorts.

I remembered what Desiree said to me on her first day. 'If I wanted to wear shit brown, I'd have applied at UPS.'

To be fair, it wasn't all shit brown. There was a bit of green in the logo. The LLs in Hall's formed the trunk of a palm tree,

jade-colored leaves poking out up top. I was well past caring about
what I looked like. But Desiree wore a uniform to her Catholic high
school and said she spent all year blending in and was dead tired of it.

She didn't have to worry about that anymore. It had been a
week since Dave let her go. I'd tried not to think about it. But
her face kept popping into my head. The cash I'd taken that had
gotten her fired was still in the thermos. No point in giving it
back now.

I waited to hear Ma head down the hall toward the kitchen. The
crinkle and swish of her tracksuit made her sound like a toddler
cruising around in a diaper. But she didn't move. Just stood there,
awkward, shifting a little, like a baby deer getting used to its legs.
In the mirror, I could see her hands fidgeting, twisting her rings.
Her tell. She needed to say something, something she knew I didn't
want to hear.

'Aren't you burning up in that?' I waved a hand at her outfit.
She had a dozen of them in every color of the sherbet rainbow.
'You might as well be sealed in Saran wrap.'

'You know I'm always cold.' She chuckle-coughed, fingers
fiddling with a crumpled tissue.

'It's all those pills you take. Who knows what's in that crap?' I
sat on the edge of the bed, shoving my feet into thick socks that
saved me from getting blisters in my work boots.

'Listen, Corey, there's something I need to talk to you about.'
She moved out of the light. I could see her eyes, so much like
Frankie's, I had to look away. It wasn't just the greenish-blue. It
was the expression in them – like they were staring straight into
my soul, wanting, needing things I couldn't give, whispering,
'You've disappointed me.'

'I was going to wait until dinner but—'

'Just say it.' I stood. The mattress springs squeaked though I
hadn't been this light since high school.

She hesitated.

'Say it,' I repeated. 'You can't tell me anything that'll make my
life worse than it already is.'

'I'm not sure how much longer you can stay here.' She stared at
her white sneakers. 'The association has rules.'

'Screw the association.' I pushed past her and headed toward the
front door to grab my boots. 'You pay the mortgage.' I sank to the

couch, punched the cushion beside me. A cloud of dust rose from it. 'This is *your* place. I am *your* daughter.'

I pulled my boot laces tight and stood. The room tilted. I shut my eyes, waiting for the dizziness to pass. My stomach growled. When was the last time I'd eaten?

'Of course, I know that. I want you to stay.' She moved closer. S*wish swish swish*. 'But these places have rules.'

'Fuck the rules!'

'Language, Corey. Please. These walls are so thin,' she whispered. 'The bylaws state you can't have a guest for more than six months. That's just how some of these over-fifty-five communities are. At last night's bridge game, Alice Blackwell asked me again how much longer you were planning on staying. It puts me in a bad spot. If you need money, I can try to help—'

'Why does Alice Blackwell care where I live?' I hissed. 'And I don't need your money.' I hated what I had to say next. 'But I do need your car.'

'Take it. I've got nowhere to be.'

Picturing Ma in her La-Z-Boy talking to the TV all day was like imagining a flower shriveling in real time. I grabbed the keys off the ceramic reptile hanging by the door. Its tail formed a hook. On its body, someone had painted, 'See you later, alligator.' I wanted to smash it.

'I'll start looking for a place tomorrow.' My voice came out meaner than I intended.

'Honey, don't be . . .'

'Don't be what?' I stopped in the doorway. 'Disappointed that once again you put your needs above your daughter's? At least I know where I learned it.'

'Corey—'

The hollow snap of the door cut off the rest of her sentence.

In the driveway, I pressed the unlock button a half-dozen times, making the Corolla chirp like a child's toy, startling a power walker. If it had been Alice Blackwell, it would've taken everything not to gun the car in reverse, flatten her nosy ass, and try to pass it off as an accident.

But it was Irene Moffatt, a woman whose son had a hard-luck story about as bad as my own. Ma never missed an opportunity to remind me. 'Her son, Mike, the one who's a police officer. He lost his . . .' I cut her off every time, but it was like she had some primal need to finish her thought. 'Lost his daughter to a rare cancer. His marriage didn't survive it. Maybe you'd like to talk to him? There's kinship in hardship.'

I'd grit my teeth not to say the first thing that flew into my head, which was 'What fucking Pinterest board did you borrow that from?'

Mrs Moffatt waved. I threw up a hand and dropped into the driver's seat feeling like I'd already hauled ten tons of organic potting soil around the yard. I folded that stupid foil reflector Ma put in the windshield to keep the steering wheel from cracking in the heat, turned the key, punched the AC, and waited for it to cough up cooler air. I stared at the condo, its yellow stucco facade cheery as a daffodil. Another place I couldn't stay.

I could've moved out any time. I had money from the house sale. I didn't want to be by myself. If I was doing bad things while I was living with Ma – stealing shit because it reminded me of Frankie, drinking myself to sleep, struggling to make sense of how I ended up with nothing – how much worse would I be on my own?

If I were alone, I'd have to confront the question that slithered between the folds of my brain: Had I lost everything or had it been stolen from me?

TWELVE

Laurel

'Laur, Laur!'

I rolled over, disoriented. What day was it? Saturday?

Rob stood over me. 'Can't you hear Poppy?'

I always heard her. Cooing. Crying. Wanting. Needing. The air conditioner muted some of it, but her noises formed a soundtrack that looped inside my head.

'I fed her at five,' I groaned. 'I just fell back to sleep.'

'It's almost eight.' Rob turned. 'Jasper's been up for an hour. He misses you.'

I hadn't been myself since Thursday when the note arrived, Marian nearly died in our dining room, and Zoey scared the hell out of me in our kitchen. Rob let me sleep in the following morning.

Late that day, Jill texted to thank me for an 'unforgettable' after-noon. She added an upside-down face emoji. *Pete and I want to have you guys for a BBQ. Throw out some dates!*

I pictured Pete, face round and doughy as a potpie, his voice booming as he'd pointed to the oven and barked, 'No wonder it's a damn inferno in here!' I was in no rush to see him again. I didn't tell Rob about the invitation. He'd want me to respond right away. I wasn't ready for that.

Marian was home from the hospital. I thought about going over to tell her I hoped she was OK, that if she needed anything from the store I'd pick it up or drive her. I remembered my mother ferrying older neighbors to the market after knee replacements and cataract surgeries.

While I couldn't imagine becoming friends with Marian, I didn't want the bad feelings between us to grow and fester. She'd looked so vulnerable and alone on that stretcher. Jill said she and her son didn't speak. I couldn't imagine being estranged from my children. After she'd had a few days to rest, I'd check on her, maybe bring her flowers. Rob would like that.

He came back into our bedroom and placed Poppy in my arms. I expected him to return downstairs to Jasper. Instead he stood, watching us. I looked at Poppy's face, eyebrows like tiny brown feathers. Feeling Rob's gaze, I kissed Poppy's forehead before sliding the strap of my nightgown off my shoulder to feed her, her small mouth opening and closing like a newly hatched bird's.

Every time I shut my eyes, I saw them – two police officers in our home, shifting from foot to foot, not sure what to say or do as the paramedics hauled Marian away. It jolted me straight back to that December afternoon when I was twelve.

Basketball practice had ended. I sat on the curb, cold seeping through my sweatpants, waiting for my mother. She'd never been first in the pick-up line but she was never last.

Mr McCardle, the middle-school principal, came outside in a thin suit and rubbed his palms together before blowing into them. 'Not here yet? Let's give her a call.'

He was new. Mom said some parents thought he was too young for the job, but kids liked him. He'd take half-court shots when he cut through the gym. Sometimes he'd sit at the lunch table with a tray of French fries and get to know us. He didn't seem angry or disappointed the way other adults did.

I'd followed him to his office and glanced at the clock. Five-twenty-five. My stomach did a little flip, embarrassed that my parents had forgotten me, their only child.

'Maybe she's stuck at work?' he volunteered.

'The bank closes at five. She's a loan officer.' Nerves made me babble. 'She helps people borrow money so they can buy stuff like cars and houses.'

'She probably has even more paperwork than I do.' Mr McCardle laughed and fished out his phone from beneath a pile of folders. 'What's her number?'

He tried the bank. No answer. Even if she'd gotten stuck with a customer, she'd have picked up, apologized, and said she was on her way. Maybe she'd stopped at the grocery store. The forecast called for snow. At practice everyone had been buzzing about the possibility of a day off or at least a delayed opening. The market would be packed. My stomach growled. I wondered what she'd make for dinner, if she'd let me help. We'd been baking cookies together since I could reach the countertop. At the beginning of eighth grade she let me chop vegetables, boil water.

He tried our house. The machine came on and I heard my dad's recorded voice on the outgoing message. Mr McCardle looked at the clock, its tick extra loud in the empty building.

'You know what?' He looked out the window toward the lot. 'Why don't I just drive you?'

My parents wouldn't have liked me accepting a ride from a stranger. But your principal wasn't a stranger, I reasoned. I wondered what my classmates would think if they saw me getting into his hatchback, its doors freckled with rust spots. A Vanillaroma tree hung from the rearview mirror but the car still smelled like coffee.

To fill the awkward silence as we waited for the windshield to defrost, he said, 'So, the team's looking good this year. I wouldn't be surprised if you make it to states.'

'That'd be cool. Sorry about this,' I mumbled.

'No trouble at all.' He pulled out of the lot, switched on the stereo, and drummed his ringless fingers against the steering wheel in time with Coldplay's *A Rush of Blood to the Head*. I'd seen the disc's case on the floor and tried not to step on it.

'This band is gonna be big. Makes me wish I played piano.' He turned to me and smiled as we sat at a red light. When it turned green, the first flakes of the season hit the windshield, fat and white.

We yelled 'Snow!' at the same time then 'Jinx!' We laughed and I gave him directions. Right here, left at the next block. When we stopped at another light closer to my house, I offered to get out and walk.

'No way! This could turn into a blizzard any second.' He winked.

Christmas break began in four days. Things had started to feel kind of magical, and for a moment, I forgot we were in the car together because my mom hadn't shown up.

'Mine's the gray house on the . . .' The police car's red and blue lights flashed extra bright against the dark sky and the soft confetti of snowfall.

'Hmmm . . . what's this all about?' Mr McCardle scanned left then right as we coasted down the small slope toward the squad car parked at the curb just beyond my driveway.

'Um, our neighbor, Mr Casey, he falls a lot. Maybe . . .' My voice trailed off as I craned my neck, expecting to see an ambulance or a stretcher outside his house.

Mom's wagon wasn't in our driveway. Suddenly, the car seemed too hot. I needed air. I shoved the door open and grabbed my backpack.

'I have to go.' I heard the plastic CD case crunch under my foot as I stepped out. 'Sorry, um, thank you.' I wanted to run but the seatbelt yanked me backward.

Mr McCardle's hand on the sleeve of my puffy pink coat made me feel small and claustrophobic.

'Let me park and walk you to the door.'

When he didn't release his grip, I understood my life as I had known it was over.

Rob nudged my elbow. I jumped, eyes startling open. After I'd moved Poppy to my other breast, I started nodding off.

'Here, I'll burp her and put her back in the crib.' He hesitated as he reached for Poppy. 'You don't doze off regularly when you nurse her, right? Because I've read some real horror stories where—'

'No,' I interrupted him. 'I've barely slept. I'm exhausted.' I pulled my nightgown strap back to my shoulder.

His forehead wrinkled as he sat beside me, settling Poppy on his shoulder, patting her back. 'You'll still make it to Em's shower tomorrow, right? I know you're not feeling one hundred percent, but my mom will be upset if you're not there.'

My sister-in-law's bridal shower. How had I forgotten? Susan texted Thursday to ask how my first 'ladies' lunch' in our new home had gone and to ask if I could come early to help her set up for the shower. I knew she didn't need me; it was her way of being inclusive. I'd texted back, *Lunch was great, thanks! See you Sunday!* followed by a heart emoji. How could I tell her the truth? She'd never almost poisoned a guest, I was certain of that.

'I'll go.' Maybe a day out of the house, away from the children and the neighborhood, would make me feel better.

'I was thinking, while you're there, maybe you should ask Emily about the guardianship. It could be a really nice moment between you guys and then she can talk it over with Colin.' Rob smiled like he was presenting me with a gift.

I sat straighter and kept my voice neutral. 'I'm not sure that's a good idea.'

'What do you mean?' he frowned. 'Why not?'

'She and Colin aren't even married yet; they're just starting out. It took him years to propose. I doubt he'd jump at the chance to raise his niece and nephew.'

'Hopefully, it won't ever come to that,' Rob said, rationally, 'but we need to choose someone and Emily's family.'

'Let's think about it a bit more.' I reached to rub Poppy's foot but Rob shifted her to his other shoulder and scoffed as if I were being difficult.

My mind scrambled to find a name, other options. I had no siblings. My father and stepmother, Janice, were so wrapped up in themselves, they rarely visited. My best friend, Nina, was an artist who never stayed in one place for long. I had a cousin in California. We exchanged holiday cards and liked each other's social media posts, but we hadn't spoken since Jasper was born.

'There's not really much to think about.' Rob stood. 'If we don't ask Em, her feelings will be hurt.'

Emily hadn't cared about my feelings last winter when she announced that Rob would be escorting her friend Meredith down the aisle.

'You'll be in all the family photos, of course,' Susan had added quickly after I pieced together that I wasn't included in the wedding party.

'I don't want you to feel any pressure to fit into a bridesmaid's dress or chip in for the bachelorette party. You're having a baby and buying a house!' Emily reasoned as if my physical and financial comfort were her top priorities.

'Just give me a bit more time to wrap my head around it,' I said but Rob was already in the hallway, heading toward Poppy's room as if it had already been decided.

THIRTEEN

Corey

Ma's verbal eviction notice didn't inspire me to stick around for our usual morning chat about weather patterns, so I left for work early. Being late wouldn't have mattered. Dave, my boss, was in Maine for a family reunion. He'd been yammering about fireworks and lobster rolls since May.

'He's the type who'll get loaded and blow off his hand with an M-80, am I right?' Desiree had said. She'd gotten a laugh from Rex, the hot greenhouse manager whose hazel eyes gleamed almost gold in certain lights. I'd watched her float on that for the rest of the afternoon.

Dave would be gone ten days at least. I'd stayed off his street since the night he told me he let Desiree go. Her firing felt like the universe sending me a warning signal that for once I decided to heed. But how much longer could I hold out?

At the stop sign, I hesitated. I could drive by. Have a look. See

if the girl was outside her house like she'd been the day Ma and I
went to Publix. Dashboard clock read 8:12 a.m. Plenty of time.

I palmed the directional lever gently as if it were a stick of
dynamite. All I had to do was turn right, say no to temptation. I'd
reward myself with an iced latte, maybe an apple fritter, though it'd
been nearly a year since I had any appetite.

'Everybody's dealing with something, Cor, bluffing their way
through with an overpriced coffee in one hand and their phone in
the other, posting some bullshit about how awesome their life is,'
my ex, Kenny, had insisted. 'That's what normal people do. We
fake it.'

'Then I guess I'm not "normal people."' That was the last thing
I'd said before I left him staring into the creek as if he looked at it
long enough he could travel back in time and reverse its flow.

The intersection lay wide open. Not even a chipmunk or a gecko
skittered past.

That all-over itch was back, tiny sparks firing through my veins.
I craved the feel of something in my hand, something that belonged
to the girl. I'd seen her once by her driveway and then every day
since in my mind's eye – that tangle of brown curls so much like
Frankie's.

8:14 a.m.

Turn right! I told myself.

I tapped the gas and bolted left, leaving better judgement in my
rearview. In that moment, it seemed only like *a* bad decision, not
the bad decision, the choice that would set all sorts of shit in motion.
That's the thing about choices, you don't know which will be the
one that blows your world apart until you're trying to piece it back
together.

By the time I slow-rolled past Dave's house, I'd sweated through
my deodorant. My heart beat everywhere – in my ears, stomach,
hands. The neighborhood was dead quiet except for a few sprinklers
tsk-tsk-tsk-ing. My mouth had gone so dry I wanted to pull over
and sip from them like they were fountains of Mountain Dew.

I jerked to a stop when I saw her: the girl in a leotard, a tutu as
white as daisy petals around her waist. I lowered the windows.
Would she speak? What would her voice sound like?

'I told you not to put that thing on until we get there,' scolded
a woman – her mom, I guessed – following close behind, beach

bag on her shoulder, travel mug in one hand, gift in bright-colored birthday wrap in the other. 'I'm not stopping when you start whining that it's scratching your legs.'

A boy trailed them, bouncing a soccer ball on his knee. My eyes moved back to the girl's hands patting the tutu's netting. Her head was down, so focused I couldn't see her face. I willed her to turn my way. What if she looked like Frankie? What if she didn't?

She scrambled into the Pathfinder and I blew out the breath I'd been holding.

The woman swung the bag and present into the trunk's open mouth. A pair of pink goggles, the squishy kind that felt like jelly-fish, dropped in the driveway without a sound. As she closed the trunk, she glanced at me. I'd parked in front of their house, pulled as if by a magnet, watching like they were a family in a sitcom. Her gaze made me hotter than the sun beating through the wind-shield. I fumbled for my phone, pretending I'd stopped to answer a text.

When she looked at me, what did she see? A woman alone, not a kid or car seat in sight. Did she wish we could trade places? Did she think she recognized me? No. I was being paranoid. She prob-ably hadn't even noticed the things I'd snatched. She was moving through her days, dealing with the demands of raising young kids. To her, the items I'd taken were junk. To me, they were souvenirs from another life, precious as fossils.

She got in her car, too busy to care what I was doing there. I thought about waiting 'til they'd left then grabbing the goggles. But in daylight it seemed reckless. Across the street, a guy washing his pick-up watched me as he aimed the hose at a hubcap, the spray hissing.

I made a big show of tapping at my phone before putting it down. In the driveway, the Pathfinder idled. The woman was probably checking her messages – real messages – or making sure her kids were buckled.

I looked in the mirror, ready to pull away. The Hall's logo on my baseball cap stared back at me. *Shit.* Could anyone see it from outside? If they knew Dave, would they recognize it?

I pinched my thigh 'til it smarted then decided it didn't matter. I'd come to see *her* and there she was, sitting in her car seat with her small hand fluttering near the window like she was waving at me, her goggles on the ground so close I could almost touch them.

I got to Hall's with four minutes to spare, shame burning a bullet hole in my chest though I'd done nothing but look. I rushed toward the back office to clock in.

Rex sat at the round table tapping a mini-golf pencil inside a sudoku puzzle square. His hair was getting long, peeking out under his hat, curling around his ears and his tanned neck.

'Mornin'.' His cheeks colored. 'Cause of me or because it was Florida in July?

'Hey.' On my way past him, I bumped the table. His iced tea spilled. 'Shit! Sorry.'

'No biggie.' He lifted the dripping newspaper and balled it into a wet wad. 'I'm more of a crossword guy anyway.' He smiled as he tossed it into the trash. 'Rough night?'

'Nah, just too much coffee.' With acid churning at the bottom of my belly, it didn't feel like a lie. I pulled paper towels from a roll on top of the fridge to avoid his eyes.

As I started mopping up, he reached to help. When our fingers touched, the heat of memory made me light-headed. I pulled my hand back like I'd dipped it in a grease fryer. Rex made a 'huh' sound and nodded toward the cactus-shaped clock on the wall. One minute 'til nine.

'See ya out there.' He stuck the tiny pencil behind his ear and took the long way around the table so there'd be no chance of our bodies brushing against each other. He pushed the swinging door so hard it stayed open long enough for me to see the way light streaming through the front window outlined his broad shoulders and narrow waist.

Since the first day I saw him, I wanted to tell him to drop the bags of mulch, go to New York, find a modeling agent, sell sportswear, cologne, hell, even underpants. Save that beautiful body for something better than planting trees for people who didn't know how to care for them.

During my first month at Hall's, I'd gotten cornered by a customer ranting about a fungus. Seeing I was trapped, Rex told me I had a call in the office and he'd take it from there. He'd winked at me while the customer scrolled through more photos of his dying lawn.

Rex was young, maybe twenty-five. He knew I wasn't much for conversation. I kept my head down. Did the work. Being quiet made me mysterious, more interesting than I actually was.

We were clocking out around the same time the afternoon he saved me from that customer.

'If you ever want to talk more about funguses, maybe we could get a drink sometime?' His smile – that's what got me. How long had it been since anyone had shown me kindness that wasn't fueled by pity or twisted curiosity? Something stirred at the base of my body, a long-dead engine turning over, rumbling to life.

'How about now?' That stupid cactus clock ticked like a bomb as I stared at my boots and waited for his answer. What if he said, 'Now? Really? We smell like manure,' and I'd have to laugh it off or come back with some crack like, 'Oh sorry, I didn't realize you thought you were *The Bachelor.*'

What he'd said was, 'I've got the perfect spot.'

Did I know what I was doing? That one drink would spill into four? That I wasn't strong enough to resist the combination of his eyes and the water at sunset? That his calloused hand grazing mine to reach for the bar bill would be the same one that led me back to an apartment where we had hungry, urgent sex, once in the shower and then on the couch, its leather squeaking and sticking to our damp skin.

After, we laid there. His heart pumping so close to mine dragged me backward to Kenny, to the early days. I stared at the ceiling fan spinning to nowhere and felt the nothingness rush in, spreading through me like a disease.

'That was . . .' Rex let out a long whistle.

'A mistake,' I said at the same time he moaned, 'Fantastic.'

'Ouch.' He laughed. 'Is it 'cause I live with my parents? They're on a cruise and I'm getting my own place, I swear.'

I shook my head. Hell, I lived with my mother in a retirement village. I wasn't judging him. I couldn't let it happen again because to feel good, normal, only to remember what my life had become, was too much. When we'd been pressed together, our bodies bumping hard and fast as pinball flippers, it swallowed me. Everything fell away. When it was over, guilt slammed me with the force of a hurricane. That's when I vowed not to let anyone in again. To forget, even for a second, was a betrayal. I'd already failed Frankie enough.

*   *   *

For most of the day, I avoided Rex. My head throbbed, my mind spinning back to the goggles. Were they still in the driveway? Seeing the girl should've been enough. But even as I tried to distract myself, looking for shapes in the dark clouds, the thought of getting those goggles pressed down, relentless as a toothache.

It was afternoon when I saw her riding by on that crappy bike. Lots of cyclists didn't wear helmets. Desiree did. Her head would've looked like a Junior Mint if she hadn't covered her shiny black helmet with stickers – a skull and crossbones on one side, a red rose on the other.

Her circling made me twitchy. There was no way she could've known about the money – that *my* theft had gotten *her* fired. Still, I wasn't ready to talk to her.

'She looking for you or for me?' Rex snuck up behind me.

'Who?' I played dumb, glad I was wearing sunglasses.

'Desiree.' He nodded toward the street where she turned the corner. 'Shame about what happened. Seemed like a nice kid.'

Desiree's crush on Rex was subtle as a sledgehammer. I'd caught her staring at him one Saturday as he stretched to water hanging ferns. His T-shirt hitched up, revealing a pointy, black arrow, the bottom of a tattoo.

'Put your tongue back in your head,' I'd teased her.

When he'd gone to help a customer, Desiree sidled over to me. 'Rex,' she'd purred with a mock swoon. 'Even his name is se-x-y. See what I did there?' She laughed. 'Seriously, I'd give my fake AirPods to check out the rest of that tatt.'

I didn't tell her that I'd seen the whole thing. That I'd licked it. That he tasted like salt and earth and something that would make you a million dollars if you could bottle it.

'She *is* a nice kid,' I told Rex, shoving away that memory.

'Well, at least it got Dave to finally fix the camera,' he said, heading toward the bougainvillea.

'Right,' I called after him, acting like I'd known it, like my heart wasn't kicking against my ribs as I filed that information, another warning I'd be wise to heed.

The clouds burst. Wind sent cold rain sideways. I shivered as I started the car and leaned into hot air wheezing out of the AC vents.

That's when I saw it. A note stuck to the windshield. Loopy letters faced me. 'HMU.' Code for 'hit me up.' Desiree. Rain made the ink bleed. Her phone number was half gone. I could make out the top of an eight, the curve of a six. I wouldn't have called her anyway. I knew what she'd want. To meet. To ask me why Dave had shitcanned her. I couldn't sit inside the fro-yo place and try to convince her that she'd be just as happy working in a supermarket ringing up oranges and sunscreen.

The day she came for her interview, I'd been arranging birdhouses nearby.

'Why do you want to work here?' Dave had asked.

She'd flung her arms wide. 'I want to be surrounded by beauty, by things that are alive, growing!'

Most of Desiree's sentences hitched up at the end, making them sound like questions. Not that one. She knew what she wanted. And that honesty, that innocence, that enthusiasm, who talked like that? Only someone who hadn't been kicked in the teeth by life yet.

'I want to study landscape architecture,' she went on. 'It's a really competitive program so I was kind of hoping that if I do a good job maybe you'll write me a rec letter?'

Dave chuckled, beer belly bouncing like a mall Santa's. 'Well, now, let's not get ahead of ourselves. Come by Saturday, work the register, and we'll see how you do. Deal?'

She'd done great. Until I fucked it all up on her.

The afternoon I swiped the cash from the register she'd been in the greenhouse refilling Mack the white macaw's dish of seeds. Rumor had it Dave'd spent years trying to teach Mack to talk but he only ever sat on his perch, fluffing his feathers, silent as a monk. There was no way Desiree could've seen me. Guilt was making me paranoid. Still, I didn't want to find out for sure.

I flicked the wipers and watched her note get wetter, thinner, 'til it slid off the windshield in pieces. Then I threw the car into reverse and tried not to look at the white clumps of paper sinking into a puddle behind me.

The stink of fish smacked my face as I walked into the condo. Ma stood over a frying pan pushing scallops around like they were fat, white checkers.

'Hey,' I said.

'How was your day?' She turned and smiled like an amnesia victim, like the ugliness between us that morning had been wiped from her memory.

'Same as every other one.' I washed my hands and reached for the paper towels. A little shiver rocketed through me remembering Rex's fingers brushing mine.

'How about that thunderstorm?' Ma asked like it wasn't a daily occurrence in the summertime.

How long had we been talking to each other like strangers on a bus? Things got awkward around the time Dad passed and she moved to this sad, pastel-colored purgatory. They got worse after Frankie.

'It's stopped for now. Hoping to get a run in later.' All day my thoughts kept jumping back to the girl in the tutu, her goggles. I needed them. They'd be the last thing I'd take. I'd lay them in the closet beside the others. That would be enough.

We sat at the table, Ma still wearing oven mitts.

'Check you out, Iron Chef,' I said before I saw the plates. She'd made faces – scallops for the eyes and nose, a lemon wedge smile, wilted spinach for hair – like she'd done for Frankie. A lump clogged my throat.

'Oh, it was nothing.' Ma blushed. 'Plus, I thought we should celebrate.'

'Celebrate what?'

'You.' She opened a bottle of sparkling water. It hissed like a slashed tire. 'Your fresh start. If you're going to look for a new place tomorrow, who knows how many dinners we have left together?'

I mashed the food together. She hadn't forgotten.

'Irene Moffatt's—'

'Stop!' I threw down my fork and it clattered against the plate. 'I cannot hear about Irene Moffatt's son and her dead granddaughter one more time!'

Ma flinched then cleared her throat. 'I was going to say that her daughter is a real-estate agent. I'll give her a call.' She crinkled her napkin into a ball. 'When you find a place, we can go shopping for bedding and curtains. I've been saving coupons.'

She went on about different neighborhoods, which complexes had pools, tennis courts. Twice she offered me her blender.

I stood before I hurled my dish at the wall. 'I'm going for that run.'

'Is that a good idea so soon after eating?'

Ma's constant worrying wore me out, but I wondered: If I'd anticipated trouble lurking around every corner, maybe Frankie would still be here and I wouldn't be snapping at a woman who just wanted to keep me safe.

The rain cooled things down a degree or two. It was still drizzling, enough that people would stay indoors, hiding from humidity that made you want to climb out of your skin.

I passed a big-ass iguana hanging out between palm trees. I considered myself fearless, but they freaked me out, looking like beasts from prehistoric times with their whip-like tails and razor-sharp teeth. They weren't endangered – they were the danger. I admired it.

I ran, that shimmering, all-over excitement people talked about before a first kiss – the anticipation, bubbling inside me.

What would I do if the goggles weren't there? I ran faster, forcing my thoughts in a different direction. Maybe moving out wouldn't be terrible. What if staying with Ma was making me worse – turning me into a sullen teen again? If I found a place in the opposite direction, could I forget about the girl?

When I turned the corner onto her street, I slowed, wanting to savor the moment I spotted the goggles. Dave was still out of town. As I passed his place, the girl's house came into view. Beneath the streetlight and the sliver of moon, the lawn, freshly cut and slick with rain, glowed green. The smell made me electric with hope. I stood in the driveway. The Pathfinder was parked where it had been that morning, but the goggles were gone. I squatted, pretending to tie my sneakers, and checked under the car. Nothing.

I stood, dizzy, palms itching. I couldn't leave empty-handed. If not the goggles, then something else. Something of hers. I glanced around. No one in sight.

I moved toward the car and stared into the back seat. The tutu, its netting as white and fine as the baby's breath I wove into bouquets at Hall's, waited. My head swam. I needed it. To feel it. If I folded it just right, I could tuck it inside the waistband of my shorts. I imagined the roughness of it on my skin, pressed against the scar that Frankie made when she came into the world, spluttering, squawking, arms outstretched, already wanting everything.

The car had been unlocked when I took the purple thermos a couple weeks back. All I had to do was open the door. Slide out the tutu. My fingers twitched. I tried the handle. It lifted. I was in. I reached for it. A current shot through me. A connection. I pressed the tutu to my face. The smell – a mix of baby powder and pancake syrup – made my knees buckle.

'Hey! What the hell do you think you're doing there?'

I jumped and turned. A cell phone flashlight blinded me.

'I said, what the hell do you think you're doing there?'

I froze. Three feet from me stood a man with a dog. How had I not heard the jangle of its tags?

'I've seen you before,' the man said. 'This morning. Watching the house.'

I recognized him too – the neighbor who'd been washing his truck. I knew I should run. Running was the only thing I was ever good at, but my feet were glued to the ground.

'Your hat. You work with Dave?' He laughed. 'I've known people to steal cash, maybe even cars, but ballet shit?' He lifted his cell phone again. I clutched the tutu and heard a click. He took my picture.

Fuck me. Fuck this. Run. My legs didn't work. The dog bared his teeth and let out a low growl. *This was supposed to be the last time.*

The guy paced, prepared to block any escape I tried to make. He pressed the phone to his ear. 'Hey, Tommy, I'm right outside your house. Caught a prowler. Call nine-one-one.'

His stare burned straight through my skull. Behind me a door opened. A barefoot guy with a mop of curly brown hair shot out, gripping the neck of a baseball bat with his right hand.

'Jesus, what the hell is going on?' His eyes darted in all directions. 'Where's the prowler?'

'You're looking at her.'

'What?' He blinked and gave me the once-over. 'She's . . .' He shifted from foot to foot, loosening his grip on the bat. He wiggled his index finger. 'Why are you holding that?'

I couldn't speak. Just focused on the wet grass, wishing I'd run when I had the chance.

'I caught her in your car.'

'What's going on?' The woman I'd seen that morning came out of the house. She stood next to the guy with the bat and stared at my hands, confused. 'Is that Lyla's?'

I didn't answer. I was just hovering there, outside it all. Time speeding up and standing still. Tears bulged behind my eyes but I'd be damned if I'd let them fall.

'Why are you holding our daughter's tutu?' the guy with the bat asked again.

What could I say? That I'd seen his little girl and she'd reminded me of the one I'd lost? That I stole things she'd have loved and other shit, too, to remind myself that I wasn't completely dead on the inside?

I heard the *whoop* of a siren. Lights spun, turning everything blue and red, blue and red, making me dizzy. In the doorway of the house, a boy and girl stood together in pajamas.

'Mama, who's that?' The girl pointed at me. Even in the low porch light, I could tell she looked nothing like Frankie. Tears I'd been holding back slid down my cheeks, into my mouth.

Over my shoulder, I heard the guy who'd taken my picture babbling, all excited like he'd captured the leader of a drug cartel.

A police officer stood beside me. His fingers closed around my elbow. I barely felt it.

'Ma'am,' he said. 'I'm Officer Moffatt. I'm going to need you to come with me.' He kept his touch light as a sparrow's as he led me to the car and opened the back door. He wasn't nearly as rough as the rookie who almost broke my arm last fall when I'd had my final run-in with my psychotic neighbor.

I sank to the edge of the seat, cool leather giving me chills. He squatted so we were at eye level.

'Ma'am, what's your name?' In the interior light's creepy yellow glow, I got a better look at him. He couldn't have been much older than forty, but his short blond hair was already turning white at the temples.

'Ma'am? Your name?' he repeated. 'And can you tell me what you're doing here?' His blue eyes drifted to the tutu. I was petting it as if it were a wounded animal. I tried to stop crying but it was like somebody'd opened a tap and sadness kept spilling from it.

I took a gulp of air. 'Corey Sutton.' I'd gone back to my maiden name pretending that might help.

'Sorry, can you repeat that?' he asked. The radio's squawking had drowned me out.

I cleared my throat. 'Corinne Sutton.' Even in the shadowy dimness, I saw something, pieces of a puzzle clicking together in his head.

He took a step back. 'Mary Lou's daughter?'

I looked at him like he was a mentalist doing a parlor trick. Then it was my turn to connect the dots. He'd said his name minutes before. It floated up in my memory. 'Irene's son?' I mumbled.

'Yes, ma'am.' He searched my face. I was doing the same to his. He took a deep breath, chest inflating, working up courage. For what, I didn't know.

'Wait here,' he said. His lips, pink as bubble gum, puckered as he drummed his fingers on the car's roof, before he walked toward the others.

He took his partner aside and jerked his thumb in my direction. His mouth moved but I couldn't make out a single word over the buzzing in my head and the screeching of that damn radio. Moffatt kept talking while his sidekick swatted at mosquitos.

How much did Moffatt know thanks to *my* mother spilling her guts to *his* mother? Each time Ma had brought him up, I'd shut her down. I hadn't wanted to hear his sad story. But maybe he'd wanted to hear mine. After all, misery loved company. When Kenny lost his job, he couldn't wait to tell me about anyone we knew who was also out of work.

'Well that might make you feel better, but it doesn't pay the bills,' I reminded him.

Hearing that Moffatt had lost his daughter wasn't going to bring mine back. Messed up as I was, I didn't take comfort in another person's heartache. But after meeting Moffatt, I wished I'd known as much about him as he seemed to know about me.

On the street side of the squad car, neighbors gathered, inching closer. Nosy fuckers. I tucked my head and shielded my face with my hand the way celebrities and mobsters did.

Moffatt and his partner walked across the lawn, back to the girl's parents and that asshole with the phone. They took turns glaring at me – even the dog. The woman hugged herself. The man leaned the bat against a lamppost and nodded at the cops like a bobblehead doll.

My heart should've been knocking against my ribs, but I was numb, paralyzed by the full force of my stupidity. I'd been reckless. It wasn't the first time and, worse, I was pretty sure it wouldn't be the last.

After what felt like somewhere between a minute and forever, the partner offered the couple his card. The woman took it while Moffatt shook hands with the guy then motioned for the dude with the phone to move along. He hesitated, shoulders slumped, no doubt disappointed he wasn't going to witness a *Cops*-style throwdown, my face slammed against the hood, cuffed and stuffed. He crossed the street, dog squinting at the high beams.

Moffatt came over. I was the one who'd been bawling, but up close he looked every bit as sad as I felt.

'We're going to drive you home.' His gaze was steady, his tone the kind you'd use with a lost toddler. I dropped my eyes, afraid he'd see inside me and know there was nothing there. 'We'll need you to come by the station first thing Monday, all right?'

My head felt floaty, like a helium balloon after someone let go of the string. Was I getting special treatment because our mothers mourned their granddaughters together while playing bridge and sipping iced tea? Or, maybe swiping a tutu wasn't much of a crime? But I'd been inside that family's car. If that douchebag neighbor told them he'd seen me there that morning, they'd think I was staking out the house. Or maybe even planning to abduct one of those kids. It was all too much to think about, and at the same time none of it mattered.

'Before noon,' Moffatt added.

'OK.' What else could I say?

'OK,' he repeated and knocked on the roof. With his other hand, he started to close the car door.

I tried to swing my legs into the cruiser but they were rooted to the ground, heavy as tree trunks.

'Take your time,' he said in that same steady voice.

Before we pulled away, I turned back toward the house. The girl who'd been standing there looking nothing like Frankie was gone. Front door shut. Locked tight, I'd guess.

Moths circled the porch light beating their wings against a bare bulb. Did they know they were burning up? Probably. But they didn't care.

Some creatures can't help themselves.

On the ride back to the condo, my brain should've been cycling through scenarios, trying to figure out what would happen at the police station, but static filled my head. My body should've pulsed with shame, but I felt nothing as strip malls, churches, and shooting ranges slipped past under the black, starless sky.

They didn't ask where I lived. Of course Moffatt knew it was Whispering Palms, same as his mom.

I pictured Alice Blackwell, nose stuck to her window, that tacky flamingo windsock flapping in the breeze beside it. She lived right across from Ma. If she saw me get dropped off by the cops, she'd spread that news like a virus and force me out of the development even faster. Ma didn't need any more heartache than she already had.

When we were about a half-mile away, I leaned forward. 'Hey, can you drop me at the entrance?'

The partner shot a look at Moffatt, who dipped his head in a tiny nod. The car swung into the complex and rocked to a sudden stop. I jerked forward, throwing my hands up before my head smacked the divider.

I got out, legs weak and wobbly. The car didn't move. They were watching, waiting to see me head in the right direction. I took a step then turned back and knocked on Moffatt's window. Before he slid it down, I saw my reflection, eyes puffy like I'd been in a lame-ass bar fight.

As Moffatt lowered the window, I heard his partner sigh, no doubt pissed that they weren't rid of me yet.

My face felt hot and tight as I looked at Moffatt and forced myself to ask one of the most ridiculous questions of my adult life: 'Can you not tell your mom about this?'

FOURTEEN

Laurel

M y in-laws' house on Lennox Lane resembled a French chateau. Stately and elegant, it was the color of freshly churned butter, accented by black window frames and tendrils of ivy creeping up the stone chimney. The front lawn was an ocean of green bordered by rows of lavender. Their landscaper used photos of it in his promotional materials, something Susan loved to casually drop into conversation.

I was awe-struck the first time Rob brought me there. It was so different from the small, gray split-level in upstate New York where I'd spent my childhood, and nothing like the charmless condo in South Jersey my father and Janice moved to while I was in college, its walls so thin I could hear my stepmother cackling at late-night hosts' opening monologues.

There was plenty of room in the Wests' circular driveway. Still, I parked on the street to avoid getting blocked if I decided to leave early.

As I opened the trunk, a fresh wave of embarrassment washed over me. Beside the reusable grocery bags, Emily's present sat covered in Christmas wrapping paper. I'd ordered the stand mixer from her registry but had forgotten to buy a shower-themed gift bag or paper.

I'd wanted to run to the store but Rob convinced me it wasn't a big deal. Easy for him to say; he wasn't the one presenting it. As I hoisted the mixer out of the trunk, nose to nose with flying reindeer and 'Ho! Ho! Ho!'s in white bubble letters, I wished I hadn't listened when he'd said, 'No one will notice. You don't want to be late, right?'

It wouldn't have mattered. The shower wasn't a surprise. Emily insisted on having as much input as possible. Susan had hoped to host it outdoors on the stone terrace that overlooked the garden and pool, but the punishing heat and humidity spoiled her plans.

On each side of the double front doors a braided hibiscus tree bloomed, sending orange blossoms the size of satellite dishes toward the sky. I pictured the browning forsythia wreath that hung crookedly on my door as I balanced the mixer on my knee and rang the bell.

Susan appeared in a light pink sheath, strands of pearls looped around her neck. 'Laurel!' She air-kissed me and placed a cold hand on my arm to usher me inside. 'Oh dear!' She glanced at the enormous box in my hands, eyes lingering on the holiday wrap but reserving comment. 'That looks . . . heavy. Irma!' Her voice echoed in the soaring entryway as she summoned her housekeeper.

'Good morning, Mrs West.' Irma nodded at me. 'Nice to see you again.'

'You too, Irma.' I smiled. 'And, please, it's Laurel.'

'Put this with the others, Irma.' Susan waved her fingers, nails polished a shade deeper than her dress, toward the package then turned back to me. 'How are you?' Her hand closed around my arm, eyes laser-like.

Had Rob mentioned my failed lunch? Or was she referring to Lyle's release? I pictured the note. *I lost my family. Now yours is in danger.* I still hadn't mentioned it to Rob. I'd searched our house and hadn't found it – not even the envelope with the Florida postmark. The garbage had been picked up Friday morning. The note was probably long gone. If I told Rob, he'd demand to see it and then accuse me of being careless by misplacing it. Without being able to show him those two sentences in that menacing scrawl, it felt like I'd imagined it.

'I'm good, thanks. A little tired. Poppy's been up a lot.'

Her lower lip curled in an exaggerated pout. 'I wish Robbie and the kids had come!'

'I do too!' I said. Initially, Rob planned to bring the children and visit with his dad. But his father had a noon tee time with Colin, Emily's fiancé, and Colin's dad.

'Maybe Irma can mind the kids and I'll golf while you watch Em open kitchen appliances she doesn't know how to use,' my husband had suggested.

'Irma's going to have her hands full. Plus, Jasper barely knows her, and Poppy's a newborn.' I didn't bother adding that if the children's schedules were thrown off, the day would be miserable for everyone.

'We need to find a sitter,' Rob had said after deciding to stay home with the kids. 'Start asking around and I'll look online at those services that do the vetting for you.'

'I'm not leaving our children with a stranger you find on the internet!' I'd protested.

'My parents never missed an event or their standing Saturday night dinners at the club.' Rob scoffed. 'They'd leave Em and me with anyone with a pulse.'

'And look how you turned out!' I swatted his shoulder with one of the freshly washed burp cloths I'd been folding.

I'd kept our conversation upbeat. There was no reason to argue. Rob had to know I'd never leave our babies with a person I didn't know or trust completely. If anyone understood that regular people were capable of terrible things, I did.

Susan excused herself to check on the caterer.

On my way to the dining room, I passed an ornate gold mirror and admired the way the jade necklace and earrings popped against my plain black jumpsuit, making me look a thousand times more put-together. I had Addie to thank for that.

As I'd placed Emily's gift in the trunk of the car that morning in my driveway, I heard a voice behind me.

'Hey, pretty lady! Where are you headed this early?' Addie jogged up to me and removed her AirPods.

'My sister-in-law's bridal shower.' I hoped she hadn't seen my ridiculous wrapping paper.

She smiled, looking me up and down. 'Wait right here.'

Before I could say anything, she dashed into her home and returned a minute later with a strand of light green stones the color of mint chip ice cream.

She placed the beads over my head and took a step back. 'Perfection! I knew it.' She opened her palm, revealing matching earrings.

'They're gorgeous! Are you sure?'

'Of course!'

I turned to look at myself in the car window, the burst of color so stunning it changed everything. 'I love them!' I touched the necklace again. Since having Jasper, I hadn't bothered with accessories. They were just another thing he'd grab and break. 'Thank you,' I said. My hand flew to my mouth. 'I'm sorry, I still have your bowl from the pasta salad.'

'No worries.' Addie looked toward my house and waved. Rob and Jasper stood at the front door waving back. 'Bring it by one night and we'll have a drink or two.'

Each time I felt my energy flagging on the long drive to my in-laws', I thought of her invitation. It brought me back to life.

In the dining room, a wall of windows, flanked by silk drapes that cascaded like waterfalls, overlooked the sweeping front lawn. If Jasper were with me, his tiny handprints would be everywhere. I exhaled, relieved I didn't have to worry about him making a mess or breaking any family heirlooms.

In the center of the room, the table was set for a lavish brunch buffet. Pedestal cake plates of varying heights stood atop a navy linen tablecloth. Square vases overflowed with red tea roses, adding color and a light, summery fragrance.

'Laurel!' Emily squealed, throwing her arms around me.

I inhaled her perfume's rich notes of jasmine and bergamot and hoped my deodorant would last until the end of the day. She clasped my hands and pulled back, giving me a chance to admire the ivory wrap dress that highlighted her sun-kissed skin.

'You look fabulous!' I gushed.

She ignored the compliment and didn't offer one in return. 'I'm so happy you could make it.' She leaned in. 'Now be honest, does this room give off "Yankee Doodle meets Uncle Sam" vibes?' She cocked her head toward the table. 'All this red, white, and blue. I know it's almost July Fourth, but Jesus, am I right?'

'Everything looks stunning – as usual!'

The doorbell's chimes distracted her.

'Coming!' Emily sang, trotting off to greet her guests.

It was nice to see her happy. She and Colin had dated for six years. His long-awaited proposal was one of very few things that hadn't occurred within the West family's desired timeframe.

A server appeared carrying a tray of flutes. The first sip of the shower's signature drink – a blackberry and thyme champagne cocktail – fizzed against the back of my dry throat. My stomach rumbled and I turned back to the table where finger sandwiches, salads, and mini quiches made my mouth water.

One of the caterers entered through the pocket doors on the other side of the room. She placed slim white cards in front of each dish. *Had Susan done that before?* I took a step closer, squinting to read her perfect handwriting. Asterisks dotted the cards. *Contains Almonds! *Caution: Shellfish!

Blood rushed to my face. Rob *had* told Susan about Marian and my disastrous luncheon. How had I not known he would? The Wests shared everything. I used to admire it, the way their family formed a tight circle. But it had begun to feel suffocating – even as I remained on the outside.

Finishing my drink in one long swallow, I went to find another to settle my nerves, even if it meant pumping my breastmilk and pouring it down the upstairs guest bathroom sink.

I wanted to enjoy my afternoon out, but once the champagne burned off, a dull headache settled in, making it hard to connect with anyone.

Emily, on the other hand, was in her element. While I typically withered in the spotlight, my sister-in-law bloomed. She kept up a gracious stream of 'Aw, thank you!' and 'I love it!' Amid the pyramid of presents, mine, in its garish red and green wrapping, stood out, making me feel ridiculous. Before it was passed to Emily, I snuck away to pump upstairs and hide, certain no one would miss me.

After the gifts had been opened and dessert served, I carried empty plates and wine glasses into the kitchen where Irma and the hired help slid them soundlessly into Susan's twin dishwashers. Part of me missed working in a bustling kitchen, the camaraderie of it. But Irma shooed me away.

'You're a guest, Mrs West. Go sit!'

What I wanted was to leave. I'd never been away from Poppy for such a long stretch. My body ached to be near her again. As I turned to exit the kitchen, Susan and Emily formed a blond barrier.

'We know you're eager to get back,' Susan said, 'but if you have a moment, there's something we wanted to talk to you about.'

My face flushed for the dozenth time that afternoon. Had they noticed that I stayed upstairs for nearly an hour?

'Let's sit.' Susan took my elbow and steered me toward her 'sewing room,' though there were no sewing materials in sight. She deposited me in a floral wingback chair while she and Emily sat together on the long cream-colored sofa.

'So, exciting news!' Susan began.

'The invitations go out Monday!' Emily gave a silent little clap.

'And we wanted to explain—'

'Before you get yours—'

'There's a small note tucked inside.' Susan looked to her daughter. 'Emily?'

Had they rehearsed this?

Emily smiled. 'Well, it's just that Colin and I really want . . .' She paused, swiveling the sparkling diamond around her finger.

'They want this to be a really special day. Obviously!' Susan smiled and took a deep breath, her chest rising. 'An elegant affair where the entire focus is on them.'

Emily nodded and twirled a lock of her long blond hair.

'So the wedding weekend is going to be adults only.' Susan's voice was low but firm.

When I said nothing, Emily jumped in. 'You know I love Jasper and Poppy to the moon and back, but we want you and Robbie to be able to relax and enjoy the day – the entire event, really.' She settled into the downy back of the sofa and crossed her legs. 'We have so many amazing things planned. There'll be a scotch tasting bar with cocktail napkins that have fun facts about Colin and me printed on them.' She giggled, squeezing Susan's elbow. 'And Mom hired an artist who'll be there painting the entire scene.' Susan beamed at her daughter. 'Oh, and we've rented a photo booth! It's got this special lighting so your skin looks flawless.'

My hand shot to my face, a reflex. Were my cheeks as red as they felt? A hum filled my head. As their words filtered in and out, I caught only snippets.

'You'll join us Saturday morning to have your hair and makeup done. Our treat, of course.' Susan reached out and touched my arm, relieved the message had been delivered and I hadn't protested. I hadn't uttered a word.

'We wanted to give you plenty of time to make arrangements so you and the kids will be comfortable.' Emily tilted her head the way she'd done when she told me I wasn't a bridesmaid.

'Right, thanks,' was all I could muster. Working in the restaurant industry since I was seventeen had given me the ability to smile and nod in the face of anything – *This bread pudding isn't worth nine dollars! Your flourless chocolate cake is dense and dry* – but that didn't mean I wasn't furious.

Meredith, one of Emily's bridesmaids, appeared in the doorway. 'Em! Guests want to say goodbye.' She held out her hand to Emily. They left me alone with my mother-in-law, stupid grin plastered on my face.

'I know you're ready to get going.' Susan stood and brushed imaginary lint from her skirt. 'Let me just check with Irma, I asked her to pack sandwiches for Robbie and macarons for Jasper.'

On our way to the kitchen, Susan looped an arm through mine. 'Personally, I'd love to show off my gorgeous grandchildren,' she whispered, 'but it *is* Emily and Colin's special day.'

I drove home seething, gripping the steering wheel until my fingers cramped. Rob must've known the children weren't welcome. No wonder he'd started planting seeds about finding a sitter.

I pictured Susan and Emily calling him before I'd even reached the highway.

'Laurel took it well,' they'd say, because that's what I did, what I'd always done, because I wanted people to like me.

As I sat in traffic, breasts hard as rocks, their words, 'Bring a sitter maybe?' 'Not a kid-friendly venue,' and 'Better this way!' echoed in my ears.

Forty miles from home, the fuel light popped on. I cursed and took the next exit. My headache roared back as sunlight bounced off the car's trunk, blinding me while I filled the tank.

I was returning the nozzle to the pump when a car with a Florida license plate barreled toward me. Startled, I jumped and squeezed the trigger. Gasoline, cold and slick, trickled across my ankles and seeped into my sandals. The driver stepped out. His long, salt-and-pepper beard made me tremble. Was it the man I'd seen at the farmers' market? Was it Lyle? We were inches apart but I couldn't tell. He removed his sunglasses. One eyeball was milky white in the center where the dark pupil should've been.

'Did I startle you, darlin'?' His laugh turned into a wet cough. It couldn't be Lyle, not unless he'd picked up a Southern drawl in prison.

I got back in the car without answering. By the time I pulled into the driveway, I felt wrung out. My anger toward my in-laws and Lyle formed a tight, hard fist that lodged in my throat. As I stepped out of the car, I considered leaving the bag of sandwiches to rot in the heat.

I looked at Addie's house. Maybe I'd return her bowl after I tucked Jasper into bed. It would be a relief to see a friendly face. I could run the wedding situation past her, see if she thought I was overreacting, which was how Rob would undoubtedly spin it.

He must've heard my key in the lock. As I walked into the house he was there, finger to his lips indicating one or both children were asleep.

'Did you know?' The words were out of my mouth before I could stop them.

'Know what?' He shrugged. 'And "hello" to you too.' He kissed my forehead. 'How was the shower?'

'Where are Jasper and Poppy?' I walked into the kitchen and placed the bag of leftovers on the counter. After being at my in-laws', our home seemed exponentially smaller, our furnishings shabbier. I looked around, ready to pick a fight over dirty bottles, plates in the sink, and toys scattered across the floor. But the house was spotless. How had he managed it?

'They're in bed.' Rob followed me. 'I told Jasper you'd give him a kiss when you got in.'

I wheeled around. 'Did you know they're not welcome at the wedding?'

He exhaled. 'Oh, right. I wanted to talk to you about that.'

My chest tightened. 'It was one thing when Emily didn't ask Jasper to be a ring bearer, but, Rob, your family's acting like I've spawned a pair of feral animals.'

'Laur, it's not like that.' He shook his head and reached for my hand. 'Let's just calm down and talk about this rationally.'

'Do not tell me to calm down!' I stepped away from him. 'It's not just the wedding.' I held up my hand, ticking off events. 'There's the rehearsal dinner Friday night, the ceremony and reception Saturday, and then there's a Sunday brunch. Who's going to watch them? Is Mary Poppins going to descend from the sky?' My voice came out high and shaky, undermining me. I cleared my throat and clutched the countertop. 'Do you know what your mother said? "Why not bring a sitter with you?"'

'Well, it's an idea . . .' Rob ruffled his dark hair and massaged the back of his neck.

'And who's going to pay for that? Another hotel room and at least forty-eight hours of childcare?'

My husband rubbed his chin as if he were thinking about this for the first time. 'What about asking your dad and Janice to watch them here?'

I laughed. It came out like a snort. 'Oh yeah, right, because those two love kids! Were you not there when Janice called our daughter "Penny?"'

'Well, in Janice's defense, her full name is Penelope. We just chose a different nickname.'

'Seriously, Rob, will you ever stop taking everyone's side but mine?' I slumped into a kitchen chair and dropped my head into my hands.

'I'm not taking—'

'Mommy?' Jasper appeared in the kitchen doorway, hair damp from his bath. 'You're back!' He ran to me and flung his arms around my neck.

I scooped him onto my lap. 'I missed you!' I pressed his small body against mine and felt his heart beating fast as a bunny's. I tried to drink in the appley scent of his shampoo, hoping it would steady me. It had the opposite effect. I grew angrier at the thought of my in-laws excluding him. Squeezing him tighter, I nuzzled his neck.

'Stop, Mommy,' he giggled. 'You're crushing me!'

I relaxed my grip. 'How was your day? Tell me everything!'

He hopped down, pulled a piece of paper off the fridge, and raced back to me.

'I made this!' Beaming, he held a watercolor rainbow. 'With Mimi!'

I forced my eyes to stay on his painting. 'It's amazing!' I said before turning to my husband.

'I thought we should check on Marian,' he said. 'See how she's doing, ask if she needed anything.'

Rob was acting out of kindness. Why did it irritate me?

'That was nice!' I said in an exaggerated tone for our son's benefit. 'How long were you there?'

Jasper spread his arms wide, waving his painting like a flag. 'A long time!' He spun around. That's when I noticed them: small cuts on his neck, another behind his ear.

'Come here, sweetie.' I reached for him. 'What happened to your—?'

'Mimi cut my hair!'

My blood ran cold. It wasn't his first haircut, but who did that without asking?

'She said "don't move,"' Jasper continued. 'It only hurt a little.'

With his hair damp, I hadn't noticed. I ran my fingers through it and glared at Rob. 'What the—'

'She said she used to cut her son's hair all the time,' my husband said as if this were normal, acceptable. 'She offered to trim mine too, but I'd rather wait until right before the wedding.'

'That's insane, Rob,' I said, panic rising in my voice.

'She thought she was doing us a favor, Laur. It was getting kind of long and have you looked into a place that cuts kids' hair here?'

I shook my head. When did I have time?

'She invited Jasper to hang out for a bit while I put Poppy down for her nap.'

'You let him stay with a woman we barely know?' I was shouting now.

'Hey pal, can you go back upstairs?' Rob said. 'Mommy'll tuck you in soon.'

''K!' Jasper dashed back to hang the paper on the fridge and then turned to me. 'Soon, Mommy! Soon!'

I listened to the sound of his tiny bare feet slapping the steps as he returned to his room.

Rob walked to the fridge, took out a beer, and fumbled through a drawer for the opener.

I sat silent, stewing.

'Marian wanted me to tell you she's sorry about lunch.' He took a long pull from the bottle and started inspecting the leftover sandwiches. 'She feels really bad, like you went to a lot of trouble, and she ruined things.'

I ignored him, not sure that was even true. 'They're not goldfish, Rob,' I hissed. 'They're children; you cannot leave them with just anyone!'

'Laur, you're being . . .' Rob stopped, rubbed his eyes and started again. 'Did you have a chance to ask Em about the guardianship?'

'Are you kidding me? She doesn't even want the children at her wedding; I highly doubt she'd like to raise them!' I stood, and pressed a hand to my throbbing head. 'I can't do this right now.'

Rob stepped closer. 'Listen, we'll figure it all out. We still have, what? Six weeks to find a sitter? It's going to be fine. Better than fine. It'll be great.' He smiled. 'We could use a getaway – a couple of days just the two of us. We'll have some drinks, great food, dance a little.' He swayed his hips and pulled me into him. His fingertips, cold from the beer bottle, traced my arms, making me shiver. 'Am I crazy or do you smell like gasoline?'

Did I even want to go to Emily's wedding? If I had a hard time being away from the children for eight hours to attend a bridal shower, how could I leave for an entire weekend?

To some people I might have seemed pathetic, co-dependent, but my children had become my entire world, the family I'd craved since I lost my mom. I needed them just as much as they needed me.

Rob might not have understood how far I'd go to keep them safe. At that moment I didn't know either. But before six weeks passed, we'd both find out.

FIFTEEN

Corey

I woke up Monday morning in a puddle of drool, still wrecked from Saturday night. I hadn't cried like that since the afternoon I found Frankie, scarlet bruise blooming on her forehead, cheeks blue and rubbery.

For a few seconds, I lay there staring up at the popcorn ceiling, stiff from sleep. At first I didn't remember the shitstorm I'd kicked up Saturday night or the fact that I was due at the police station in a couple of hours. But then I rolled over. The closet was open just an inch but enough for the white netting to stick out.

They let me keep the tutu. I'd been clutching it to my chest in the back of the squad car as if it were as precious as oxygen. The mom told the cops she didn't want it back. Acted like I was diseased. Maybe she was right. I pictured her staring at me, face scrunched in a combo platter of horror and disgust. I got it. Would I have been freaked out if someone had been watching my house, my family?

The irony was, in my old life, someone *had* been watching, but I'd been too distracted to notice.

I thought of Laurel West. I wanted to warn her, but I had no proof of anything – just vague memories and a bunch of bad feelings. I had no reason to believe what happened to my family would happen to hers. Plus, I was in enough trouble.

Laurel West was on her own.

I showered, nerves making me nauseous, cool water offering no comfort. What did someone wear to meet a cop after stealing part of a child's ballet outfit? Which women's magazine had a listicle for that? I pulled a light-green sundress from the duffel bag in the corner. I'd lived with Ma for eight months and hadn't unpacked. I'd only meant to crash for a few weeks, but I had no one else, and no place would ever feel like home again. So I stayed.

I walked down the short hall and found Ma parked at the kitchen table, blowing on her coffee and refilling her pill organizer.

She smiled and held up a pale-pink tablet smaller than a Tic Tac. 'Doctor Goodwin prescribed something to help me sleep. She said she doesn't like to give these to seniors on account of them making you drowsy and increasing your fall risk.' She lowered her voice. 'But she knows our situation so she made an exception.'

'Our situation' meant she'd played the 'I lost my only grandchild' card. My jaw tensed.

'You're up early.' She snapped the organizer's final square shut.

'Got an errand to run.'

'What do you need?' She stood, chair legs squeaking against the white linoleum. 'I may already have it. Let me check. If not, add it to the list and I'll pick it up after my Bible study. And don't you look nice in that dress!'

'I'll have the car back before you need it,' I mumbled, ignoring her offer and her compliment.

'I do wish you'd join me.' She took off her glasses and cleaned them with a crumpled tissue.

Every week we did the same song and dance. She wanted me to go to St Cecilia's with her, and I wanted to know how she could still believe in anything.

'Faith is a balm, dear.' The pity in her voice made me want to smash the cereal bowl she'd set in the drying rack. Instead, I pressed my palm against the side of the coffee pot and held it there until the stinging heat cleared my head.

'So you keep saying.'

She sighed and I left without another word.

I pulled into the police station lot before nine and parked under a tree so I wouldn't have to deal with Ma's stupid tin foil sunshade.

I hoped Moffatt was already there. I needed to put this bullshit behind me and move on. Seeing that child, her face slim where Frankie's was round, her skin tan while my girl's was pale as cotton, hit me like a good, hard slap that snapped me awake.

My daughter was gone. Collecting crap she might've liked wouldn't change that. Plus, the feeling I got from taking those things, the buzz that kept me going back, wore off quicker each time. If someone asked me if it had been worth it, what would I have said? That depended on what Moffatt had planned for me.

Inside the station was cool and quiet. The air smelled like sharpened pencils mixed with a fake citrusy floor cleaner. A woman in a blue uniform that matched the walls sat behind a window playing Candy Crush on her phone.

I cleared my throat. 'I'm here to see Officer Moffatt.' That was as much as I'd rehearsed on the drive over.

She looked up and put down her cell, irritated like I'd interrupted the best game of her life.

'Have a seat.' She flicked her long nails toward the wooden bench behind me and picked up a landline.

I waited, half-reading posters about domestic abuse and the dangers of opioids. I tried to focus on the words and forget that this wasn't the first time I'd done something that landed me in a police station.

I'd gotten off before because everyone figured I'd gone mad with grief. What were the odds of that happening twice?

The woman mumbled 'here to see you' into the phone and she

looked at me again. Did she know I was the freak who stole a tutu? Or did she think I was a weirdo for sitting on my hands, staring into space? Most people would've been scrolling through their devices, killing time on social media, not wanting to spend a second trapped with their own thoughts.

I was the opposite – scared to be alone with my phone. Photos and videos of Frankie lurked there. Her first steps, the way she used to wave with her cupped hand backwards, kneeling at her dollhouse on her third birthday. If I jacked up the volume and pressed the phone to my ear, I could hear her raspy little voice whispering, 'Sleep, baby, sleep,' as she tucked a plastic infant into a crib the size of a rosebud.

I couldn't look without the whole world turning into a terrible dark forest where all I wanted to do was blur into the branches and bury myself below the earth. The ache was too deep, the pain so sharp it felt like someone had peeled off my skin and stuck me with a million needles.

When I saw Frankie animated, giggling, pointing to a butterfly, the creek lurking behind her like a predator, I needed to be with her again. But I couldn't do that. Not to Ma. Not after all she'd lost already. So I didn't look at any of them. So much beauty, I couldn't bear it.

Moffatt came around the corner. He looked shorter, broader in daylight. More compact. When he saw me, he slowed and walked over real hesitant, the way you'd approach a menacing dog.

'Morning, Corinne.' In the quiet of the station, his voice was deep, not over-the-top like a radio deejay, but strong. 'Do you prefer Corinne? Corey?'

'Doesn't matter.' I stood and braced for whatever came next.

'Well, you gotta have a preference, right?' He turned and led me down the hall.

'You'd be amazed at how little I care about anything,' I wanted to tell him but instead grumbled, 'Corey's fine.'

He showed me into a small room. A dusty ficus plant was dying in the corner.

'Have a seat.' Moffatt waved toward a chair. In his short-sleeve shirt, his arms looked thick like limbs of a bare tree in winter. No watch, no ring. Snippets Ma told me about him started swimming back. *His marriage didn't survive it.*

He walked around the table and stopped. 'Can I get you coffee? Water?'

My tongue was dry as a cat's but I didn't trust my hands not to shake. 'I'm good.'

'Then I guess I'll get right to it.' He sat across from me. 'So I talked to the Longs . . .' He paused, expecting me to speak, but 'Who the hell are the Longs?' was all I could think.

'The couple,' he continued. 'The homeowners?'

I nodded.

'I shared a little bit about your situation with them Saturday night as you could probably tell. They wanted some time to think about things.'

I sat a little straighter. 'And?' I needed to stay calm, not freak out or overreact, but my body was already betraying me. Sweat suction-cupped my armpits to my sides.

'I spoke with them just now. They've agreed not to press charges . . .' He stopped and looked at me.

'Thanks?' It came out like a question. Shit, I was turning into Desiree. But, really, what I'd done was pretty minor. What could they do to me?

'As long as you agree . . .' Moffatt's blue eyes drifted up as if the rest of his sentence might drop from the ceiling tiles.

I shifted in the chair, its wooden legs creaking. 'Agree to what?' I fought the urge to fold my arms across my chest, knowing it made me look hostile. I remembered how Kenny would see me in that pose, and say, 'Jesus Christ, Cor, what now?'

'. . . if you agree to not go by their house again,' Moffatt finished his sentence.

I shook my head up and down and side to side, confirming that yes, I agreed, and no, I wouldn't go back there. I stopped short of telling him that the Longs and their trinkets had lost their luster.

'And if you agree . . .' He was just inches from me, so close I could smell a mix of Irish Spring soap and the breath mint he must've popped before he came to get me.

Did he want me to reach over and pull the words out of him? 'If I agree to what?'

'If you agree to get some help.'

'Huh.' A bitter laugh rose up from deep in my belly. I bit my lip to stop from saying what I was thinking: *Give me a break. I stole a tutu. I didn't carjack anyone.* I stared into the parking lot through ugly metal blinds so I wouldn't roll my eyes, his gaze burning a hole into the side of my face.

How many times in the last year had some well-meaning jerk-off tried to give me the same advice? 'What about a grief counselor?' Kenny's mother suggested. His sister Lorraine told me I should find a psychic so I could 'talk to Frankie again.' Ma wanted me to visit the pastor at St Cecilia's. 'Yeah, right, 'cause he knows what it's like to lose a child?' It took everything not to punch a wall when people said stupid shit like that.

I turned back to Moffatt. His eyebrows were approaching his crew cut as he waited for my answer. I shook my head and laughed again. 'Help? What does that even mean?' It felt like someone had cut the AC. I wiped the sweat from my forehead. 'Couldn't I just pick trash off the side of a highway? I mean, I know what I did was wrong and it wasn't "normal."' I curled my fingers into air quotes to show that I wasn't that different from everyone else. 'But I don't need any help.' I stood, squeezing Ma's car key between my fingers until I thought it might snap in two. 'I won't go back there, and I won't go stealing anyone else's stuff either.'

He sighed and leaned forward on his elbows, hands folded. Maybe he was praying for patience.

'Look, there's this group, these meetings I go to. They help with the grief – and the anger.' He said the words real slow, making them seem more serious. 'I know you got into some trouble up north, so I think you'd better sit down.'

I dropped into the chair. Was he bluffing? What did he know? Had he seen my file or was he getting his intel from a pair of old ladies? How much had my mother confided in his?

My mind spun back to the early days after I'd just moved into the condo, to an afternoon late last fall. Ma and I had been sitting around watching Guy Fieri speeding toward his inevitable heart attack when she turned to me and, serious as a funeral director, asked if I'd checked on Kenny to see how he was holding up.

'Are you fucking crazy?' The words were out before I could reel them in. Ma flinched like I'd hurled a grenade at her, but I didn't stop. I couldn't. 'After everything, you think I give a shit about how he's doing?'

'I just thought—'

I'd shot up, stomped into the bathroom, and slammed the hollow door. An artificial floral arrangement sat on the toilet tank in between a tower of fancy soap and a tissue box wearing a little knitted sweater.

I grabbed the fake flowers and beat them against the vanity, sending dust particles swirling through the air, making me feel like I'd gotten trapped inside a snow globe. Silk petals and waxy leaves fell on the worn blue bath mat. I sat on the closed lid of the toilet, taking deep breaths, telling myself it had to get better. *I* had to get better.

But how? How was I going to move through each day without Frankie? What would I do with the rage, with the way my mind had become an angry hive of murderous thoughts buzzing round the clock? I took the green Styrofoam cube that had held the flowers together, squeezed it in my hands, picturing Kenny's face, and then tore it to pieces.

That's how I ended up at the garden center. I'd walked in looking for a Christmas cactus to replace the arrangement I'd destroyed and spotted a 'Help Wanted' sign on the door.

I had to do something with my days other than wait for the sun to sink below the horizon so I could start drinking myself into a state of temporary amnesia.

I'd asked about the opening and Dave had hired me on the spot.

If I didn't agree to what Moffatt had cooked up, would I lose that job? Did I even care?

'I'm sure your mom has told you about my daughter, same way mine told me about yours,' Moffatt was saying when I tuned back in.

Ma. I crossed and uncrossed my legs, itching to get out of there. I didn't know how much time had passed since I sped away from the condo. She'd be standing at the door, purse dangling from her wrist, Bible in hand. She hated to be late, especially for church.

'She said a bit. Not much.' She'd tried to give me every terrible detail, but I refused to let her. The weight of the sadness I already carried left me too weak to bear anyone else's.

'After everything happened . . .' He separated his hands and dropped his head into his open palms.

Don't you dare cry on me, dude, was all I could think as I willed him to pull himself together. I was better suited to scrubbing prison toilets than trying to comfort a grown-ass man.

He took a hard swallow. 'After everything happened with Ava, my daughter, I had this constant anger. I vibrated with it, you know.' He made a fist and cupped it with his other hand. 'I did some stupid things. Those bad decisions cost me even more.'

Somebody else might've wondered what he meant, what he'd done. Not me. I knew what he was up to, trying to act relatable, get me to care. *Good luck, pal.* I didn't want to hear any of it.

'People told me to get help. But did I listen?' He shook his head. 'Now, I'm not going to pretend to know what you're feeling, 'cause I don't really know you or your family, obviously, but I do know this isn't the first time you've gotten yourself into trouble. Getting help now could prevent you from doing some permanent damage and making things a whole lot worse . . .'

'So, what?' I sighed. 'What do you want me to do?'

'Join this group. Meets once a week. It's helped me. A lot.'

I wondered if that was why Ma was always bringing him up. She was probably dying to ship me off to this 'group' with him. 'How many times?'

'How many times . . .?' His mouth hung open waiting for me to complete the sentence.

'How many times do I have to go before . . .' I swirled my hands in a circle. 'This goes away?'

'Give it eight, maybe ten weeks. Who knows? You may be surprised and find that you want to keep going.'

Nothing was going to fix me, but what choice did I have?

'Fine,' I said. 'When is it and what's the address?'

He stood. I was eye level with his holster, staring at the grip of his gun, wondering what it would feel like in my hand, the cool weight of it. He moved toward the door.

'We meet Wednesday nights, seven thirty.' He stepped into the hall and motioned for me to follow. 'So I know you'll show, how about I pick you up?'

'Fine, whatever.' Just because I went to his group, that didn't mean I had to say anything or even pay attention. I'd gotten good at letting people talk, try to comfort me, my body there, my mind a world away.

He walked me out. Before I could ask, he added, 'I'll be at the front entrance where we dropped you Saturday night. Again, I think this'll be good, Corey. It's really helped me.' He stuck out his hand for me to shake.

I stared at his fingers, red and raw around the cuticles, nails bitten down to nothing, and wondered how many other lies he told himself.

SIXTEEN

Laurel

Mondays were always difficult. Getting back into the routine of juggling everything on my own after having Rob's help all weekend was a rough adjustment. The usual challenges were made worse by a stomach bug that kept Jasper up all night vomiting. The sour stench lingered in my nostrils and clung to my hair after he wiped his mouth on my shoulder as I carried him, limp as a stuffed animal, into our bed at four a.m.

I couldn't fall back to sleep with his knees digging into my spine so I got up around five thirty and made a pot of coffee. I was sipping from a chipped mug at the kitchen table when Rob came down after seven looking fresh in navy pants and a striped blue button-down.

'Oof, that was a tough night,' he said, though he'd only gotten up one of the four times Jasper had appeared whimpering beside our bed.

I grunted, still angry about the day before when he'd allowed a stranger to cut our son's hair, when he'd dismissed my irritation at the way his mother and sister ambushed me at the shower. If my husband noticed my irritation he didn't let on as he dropped ice into his travel mug and filled it with coffee.

'Got an early meeting. Shoot me a text and let me know how Jasper is when he wakes up.' He came over to kiss me goodbye.

'Don't get too close. I smell awful.'

'Too late.' He pecked the top of my head and wrinkled his nose. 'But, yeah, you may want to shower if you're heading out today.'

Where would I go with a sick child? I rolled my eyes behind his back.

'If you need me, I can come home early,' he offered on his way out the door.

He didn't come home early. In fact, he was later than usual, and by the time he walked in, I looked and smelled worse than when he left. I spent the entire day tending to Jasper, who couldn't keep down more than a few ounces of water, and pressing my lips to Poppy's forehead, checking her temperature, fearing she'd catch it next. Jasper had chills so I'd turned off the air conditioning. The house was stuffy, the air pungent, when Rob finally arrived.

'How's our patient?' he whispered.

I shushed him and made a so-so gesture. Jasper had finally fallen asleep on the couch under a blanket. I'd tried to keep him up in his bedroom, germs contained, but he hadn't wanted to be alone.

'What's for dinner?' Rob trailed me into the kitchen where Poppy fussed in her bouncy chair, ready for her next feeding.

Dinner. I hadn't given it a thought. 'I don't know. A can of soup?'

'It's July!' Rob laughed, bending to free Poppy from her seat. 'Not exactly soup weather. Thought I'd married a chef.'

He took one look at my face and said, 'Soup's fine. Or I can run into town and grab something?'

'No!' I protested. 'You just got home. I'm dying to shower. I'd like to go out for a bit actually.'

He frowned as he swayed, cradling Poppy, her cries shifting to coos. 'Really? Where?'

'Addie's.'

Around mid-morning, she'd sent a text. *Coffee? 10:30? Want to hear about the shower!*

Though I'd been at my in-laws less than twenty-four hours earlier, Emily's shower seemed like years ago. I'd forgotten that I'd borrowed Addie's earrings and necklace, and I still had her bowl from the luncheon.

Jasper's got a stomach bug, I wrote. *Stuck inside. Gonna be a loooong day.*

Hope he feels better!

I put the phone back in my pocket. It pinged again.

Wine tonight? You'll need it! Addie wrote.

I smiled. *Would love that. Thank you!*
See you @ 8!

As I'd washed Jasper's soiled pajamas and sheets, the thought of savoring a chilled glass of anything in a home that didn't reek of vomit kept me going.

'Addie's?' Rob stared at me. Was he thinking I was a bad mother for leaving my sick child, even if it was only to go next door?

'Jasper's fever broke about an hour ago,' I said, 'and Poppy should be ready to go down after I feed her. I have to return a few of Addie's things. I won't be long.'

Rob passed Poppy to me and went to the fridge to grab a beer. 'Sure. I'll hold down the fort.' He twisted off the cap. 'It's funny, you seem to really like her even though you two don't have much in common.'

My jaw tensed. Did he mean because Addie was beautiful with her toned runner's body? Or because she had a career and didn't have kids or vomit in her hair?

I didn't want to start another argument. 'She's nice and I know how eager you are for us to make friends here.' I kept the edge out of my voice, adding, 'Soup's in the pantry,' as I took Poppy upstairs to change and feed her.

Once she was settled, I stood beneath the shower's hot spray, a sour milk funk rising from my skin. When I returned downstairs, Jasper was still asleep, his breath a soft wheeze. Rob sat in a kitchen chair, scrolling through his phone and finishing his beer.

'There's my girl.' His eyes roamed my floral sundress. I crossed my arms in front of my stomach. 'Don't stay out too late.' He raised his eyebrows.

I knew what that meant. Sex. I'd had no interest lately. With so many demands on my body already, I was resentful of another.

In the glow of the late-day sun, Rob looked as handsome as ever. Still, something was off between us. It had been since we'd moved in. I'd chalked it up to my hormones and the adjustment of caring for a new baby and a new home. I imagined we'd get back to normal once life became more settled.

I walked over, kissed him lightly on the lips, and said, 'Text me if you need me.' I pulled a bottle of the Sancerre from the back of the fridge then gathered Addie's bowl, earrings, and necklace.

As I crossed our yard and entered hers, a lightness washed over me.

Addie opened the door before I rang the bell.

'Hey!' She smiled, looking summery and gorgeous in a turquoise halter top and white linen pants I could've worn for approximately two minutes before they ended up covered in stains. Silver hoop earrings brushed her golden shoulders. She hugged me and reached for her bowl. She smelled like fresh peaches.

'How are you?' Her eyes focused on mine, her concern genuine and unexpected.

'I'm good.' I'd learned long ago that most people didn't want to hear the real answer to that question. 'How are you?'

'I'm great,' she said. 'Come in!'

When I'd brought her a slice of strawberry pie weeks earlier, we'd chatted for a few minutes but I hadn't gone inside. Jasper had been waiting for me to read him a bedtime story.

Like my house, the front door opened into the living room. But that's where the similarity ended. While our homes may have had the same footprint when they were first built, hers had been renovated and expanded. Based on her perfect appearance, I'd imagined the interior would be stunning. It surpassed my expectations. Everything looked new, luxurious, expensive.

Where our fireplace was a faded, red brick eyesore, hers was slate gray accented by a rich mahogany mantel. Built-in floor-to-ceiling bookshelves flanked it. Between linen sofas the color of sea glass sat a round ottoman in a shade of ivory that made me think of buttercream frosting.

'Wow, your home is spectacular,' I gushed, eyes drawn to the far corner where a wide-leafed plant stretched toward the ceiling. 'I can barely keep a cactus alive.'

'Aw, thank you!' She laughed. 'It's getting there. Follow me.'

The wall that divided my kitchen and dining room had been removed so Addie had one flowing space. A white marble island stood across from a six-burner stove. I felt a pang of envy thinking about the pies and pastries, sauces and soufflés I could make with her high-end appliances.

'Have a seat!' Addie motioned toward a barstool. I sat and leaned into its tufted cushions. 'You must be exhausted!' She rubbed my arm on her way to the other side of the island where a bottle of wine waited in an ice bucket. Beside it, a cheese board held a wheel of brie surrounded by grapes, almonds, and wedges of crusty bread. I hadn't eaten dinner. My stomach growled just looking at the spread.

'Sounded like you had a rough day.' Addie uncorked the wine.

'Rough twenty-four hours.' I groaned and promptly spilled every-thing about the shower – focusing on the patronizing way Susan and Emily had tag-teamed me with the news that my children weren't welcome at the wedding.

'Ugh. Textbook Bridezilla.' Addie poured until each wineglass was beyond half-full.

'Cheers. To getting me out of my house.' We clinked glasses. 'Thank you!'

'Were you and your sister-in-law on good terms before this?' she asked. 'Did she grow up in your husband's shadow or something?'

'We were always friendly, not best friends, but close.' The wine tasted buttery and delicious. I took a longer sip as I mulled her second question. 'For the past six years, it's been all about Rob and me, I guess. First our wedding, then Jasper, then Poppy, and now the house. Maybe she feels like it's her turn in the spotlight?'

'If you were close before, I'm sure you will be again once the wedding stress dies down. But, yeah, so rude to not want your beautiful babies there.' Addie shook her head. 'And, listen, if you need a sitter, I'm here.'

'That's really generous of you, but it's not just a day – it's the entire weekend!' I grumbled. 'I mean, that's a big ask. I'm hoping maybe my friend Nina will watch them. She's supposed to visit in August anyway.'

I'd texted Nina earlier, feeling her out. *Still coming to NJ next month?*

She'd written right back. *YES! Boarding a flight to Brussels RN. Call me next weekend! XO*

Nina was a photographer who'd drop everything for a job, a guy, or the chance to explore an interesting spot.

'Well, if something happens, I'm always here.' Addie popped a grape into her mouth. 'How's Jasper feeling? Better?'

'His fever's down, thankfully. I don't know if I could make it through another day of that.' I twitched thinking about all the places Jasper had vomited.

Addie raised her glass. 'Seriously, I don't know how moms do it.'

Between her kindness and the wine, the knot between my shoulders dissolved. As my body loosened, my filter fell away. 'Speaking of Jasper, wait 'til you hear this! Yesterday, Rob took the kids to check on Marian. He left Jasper there and Marian cut his hair. Can you believe that?'

Addie clucked her tongue and stepped back. Had I gone too far? Was she going to say that Rob was a terrible father? That men didn't know the first thing about taking care of kids? Or would she say the opposite: Rob was a saint for minding the children while I spent the day alone at the shower?

Her eyes narrowed. I sat up straighter, embarrassed. 'Sorry! I've been talking non-stop.' I laughed, trying to play it off. 'I didn't mean to come over and treat you like a therapist.' I'd stopped seeing my actual therapist when we moved. 'I don't usually babble like this.' I covered my face with my hands. 'This is what happens when you don't talk to adults all day. Thanks for listening.'

'No, no. I'm just . . .' Addie swept a few loose strands of hair behind her ear. 'You don't think Marian would've given Jasper something?'

'Something?'

'I don't know . . .' Addie clicked her nails, red as ripe cherries, against the island. 'Something that upset his stomach – something that made him sick – you know, to retaliate for whatever happened to her at your house. I mean, he was fine when you left, he spent time at her house, then he's up all night vomiting. Coincidence?'

It was comfortable in Addie's kitchen, warm from the final rays of daylight streaming through the windows, yet a chill crept up my spine.

Addie held up her hands. 'I know it sounds crazy. But she's definitely creepy, right?'

I wasn't a fan of Marian's. She'd unnerved me from the start, but seeing her carried out on a stretcher and loaded into an ambulance had softened me temporarily. She'd looked so weak, so fearful, not nearly as intimidating as she'd originally seemed. But Addie wasn't wrong. I pictured Marian's cold, watery eyes and the small cuts on Jasper's neck and behind his ear. The wine on an empty stomach made it hard to think clearly. Would she give him something that made him sick?

'I . . . I don't know.' I thought of the scar on Jill's son's chin. He'd fallen while Marian was watching him. 'I mean, maybe? But that would be insane, right?'

'Forget it.' Addie waved her hand, dismissing the idea. 'I listen to too many true-crime podcasts. They make me suspicious of everyone. It's just she's always given me . . .' Addie shivered. 'I don't know, bad vibes, I guess.'

'No, it's definitely not you. I feel it, too,' I said, unable to shake the cold that had seeped into my bones.

'I'm sure I'm wrong. I shouldn't have said anything.' Addie downed the rest of her wine. 'But while we're on the subject of creepy neighbors, you don't think Zoey's trying to bump off Marian to get her hands on that house, do you? Everyone knows about her allergy, just like everybody knows Zoey wants out of the Barretts' "shed."'

I rubbed my hands up and down my arms where goosebumps sprouted and multiplied. 'And here I thought the city was dangerous.'

'Listen to me! You came over for a break and I'm filling your head with crazy conspiracy theories!' She motioned toward a screened-in area off the back of the kitchen. 'You look frozen. C'mon, let's sit out there.'

Addie carried the ice bucket while I brought the cheese plate. She switched on a lamp in the corner and lit a pair of citronella candles, their flames flickering beneath the lazy swirl of the ceiling fan.

I sat on the far end of a wicker sofa and spotted a basket of yarn in the corner. 'I've always wanted to learn to knit.' I pointed to the needles poking up from a Kelly green ball. 'Maybe you could teach me sometime?'

'I wish I knew!' Addie perched at the other end of the couch and refilled our glasses. 'That was my mom's favorite hobby.' She sat back, crossed her long legs, and looked out into the purple glow of evening.

My stomach cratered. I wished I hadn't mentioned it. 'Oh, I'm sorry, I didn't . . .'

'Oh no, don't be. This was – is – her house. I don't know how much you've heard from neighborhood chatter.' She tilted her head toward Marian's home, visible on the other side of my backyard. 'My mom's had some health issues. My dad passed away five years ago, and it took a toll on her. I hadn't realized how bad things had gotten – the loneliness, her decline. I'd call her on Sundays and sometimes she'd forget an actor's name, or she'd say, "I wanted to tell you something and now I can't remember what it was." It didn't seem concerning at first, but each time I came to visit, it got harder to leave. So I moved in.'

'I'm so sorry,' I said. 'That must've been really difficult for you, adjusting your whole life like that.'

'I'm lucky that I can work anywhere, and it's my mom, right? How could I not? We've always been super close. Growing up, she was more like a sister than a parent.' She sipped her wine. 'It started with small things – she left a door open and a squirrel got in. Do you have any idea how hard it is to catch one of those bushy-tailed bastards?' She laughed and tossed her head back. 'I had to use cheese and a snow shovel! Anyway, then the mortgage check bounced; the taxes hadn't been paid. Seeing it up close, watching her slip away before my eyes, was heartbreaking. When she left the oven on overnight, as much as she wanted to stay, I knew it wasn't safe for her here.'

'Or you,' I added, wishing I hadn't mentioned the basket of knitting.

'I found a nice place in Oakhurst. It's better this way.' Addie swirled the wine around the inside of her glass and took a drink. 'I visit every few days.'

'Well, if you ever want company, I'd be happy to go with you,' I volunteered. How could I not after she'd offered to watch Jasper and Poppy?

'Aw, that's really sweet of you.' She smiled, her perfect white teeth gleaming in the low light. 'I may take you up on it. Some weeks are worse than others.'

'Please do. I mean it.'

She looked around the room. 'When I moved in, everything was florals and pastels. There was this teddy bear by the front door – like a furry little bouncer – and she'd change his outfits with the holidays.' Addie rolled her eyes. 'I mean, I work for a toy company and even I was like, "You've got to be kidding me?" I've been updating the house slowly, but everything costs a fortune – unless you're handy, which I'm not.' She plucked a few almonds from the small dish. 'Is your family close by?'

I hated this part of making a friend – the getting-to-know-you phase. Where did I begin? How much was necessary?

'My dad and stepmom are about forty-five minutes away, but we don't see them very often.'

Addie divided what was left in the bottle between our glasses. 'Oh, that well-dressed blond woman who stops by, is that your mom?'

'No, that's my mother-in-law.'

'Ah, the infamous "no-kids-at-the-wedding" Susan.' Addie did a cranky old lady impression, pulled her lips down in a pout, then grinned.

She'd shared so much with me; how could I not be as open with her?

'My mom died when I was twelve.' Even after more than two decades, I still struggled to say it without my voice cracking.

'Oh Laurel, I'm sorry.' Addie stretched across and put her hand on my arm. Usually the attention that came with talking about my mother's death made me shy and uncomfortable, but from Addie it felt comforting.

If I left it at that, people assumed it was cancer, because, statistically, that was the most likely cause. But not telling Addie the rest seemed like a half-truth.

'She was shot and killed at work.' That never got easier either. Sometimes when I said the words aloud, it seemed like a terrible story I'd made up.

'Oh my God.' Addie set her glass on the low table in front of us. 'Laurel, that's . . . I'm . . .'

There were no words to convey how awful it was walking into my childhood home that December afternoon. The air hadn't smelled like dinner, only the industrial scent of radiators competing against the cold. As I'd turned to close the front door, I saw my principal, Mr McCardle, on the front lawn, his hatchback still running, exhaust melting the falling snow. He held up his hand in a gesture I couldn't decode. I had the sudden urge to run back to his car. Instead, I followed a trail of muddy boot prints into the kitchen where two police officers stood.

The only light came from the fixture hanging above our round table. Dad sat where he always did, surrounded by junk mail, a bowl of apples, and the cereal box I'd forgotten to put away that morning. He looked at me, his face white as the napkins in the cheery yellow ceramic holder I'd made at summer camp.

'Dad? What's going on? Where's Mom?' I asked, a buzz building between my ears. Little black circles floated in front of my eyes. My body felt weightless, like I was falling with no bottom in sight.

Addie squeezed my hand, pulling me back to the porch. 'Are you OK?' she asked.

I shivered. 'She worked at a bank in town and there was this customer. He'd lost his job; they were foreclosing on his home. He had a wife, a daughter, a son with medical issues. He bought a gun.'

I could still see the headlines: *Desperate Dad Shoots Up Savings & Loan*; *Overdrawn: Bank Customer Murders 5*; *Holiday Horror: Gunman Opens Fire Inside Bank*.

'He killed a father setting up his daughter's college fund, a teller just back from maternity leave, a teenager cashing his first paycheck, the bank manager, and my mom. It was a week before Christmas.'

Addie covered her mouth with one hand and placed the other over her heart.

Only a few miles from my school gym, my mother died while I practiced layups and foul shots. I could never remember if I'd heard sirens.

'The shooter, Lyle Hartsell, was released from prison right around the time we moved in.' I stared into the distance at the darkening sky and hugged my arms tight around my body. 'I know this sounds crazy, but sometimes I think I see him. It's like this dark energy hovering. It's . . .'

'Oh Laurel, I'm so, so sorry.' Addie looked up at the ceiling fan. 'Here I'm going on about trapping a squirrel and you've survived this terrible trauma. I don't know anything about the law, or sentencing, but how? How is he out?'

'Apparently the system's overcrowded, and Lyle was a model prisoner.'

We sat in silence, the only sounds coming from crickets and a barking dog.

'That note about my family being in danger, I think it could be from him.' My voice wavered. 'Lyle blamed my mom. He's had all these years to plot his revenge. I . . .' I rested my head in my hands, the wine muddling my thoughts.

'Shh.' Addie scooted over and rubbed my back. 'I'm sure that was just some asshole developer. Or Zoey. You haven't gotten another one, right?'

I shook my head. I hadn't, but each time I heard the mail slot open, my stomach plunged, fear flooding my veins as Jasper handed me the stack.

'Good.' Addie stared out at the creek, candlelight casting shadows across her face. 'There's so much evil in the world,' she sighed, 'sometimes you forget.'

When I got home, Rob was in bed. I sat on the edge of the mattress, careful not to wake him.

'Thought you said you wouldn't be long.' He'd been facing the wall but turned toward me as I pulled my sundress over my head, unhooked my bra, and slid between the sheets.

'We started talking and I lost track of time. How's Jasper?' I debated sharing Addie's theories about Marian and Zoey, but I was afraid it would make him defend them and dislike Addie.

'He's better, had some crackers and fell asleep watching the Yankees game. I carried him up around ten. Fever's pretty much gone.'

'Oh good.' I nuzzled into my pillow, exhausted. The wine made the room spin like the slow start of a merry-go-round. Rob massaged my shoulders and I moaned with gratitude. Working his way down my back, he slipped his other arm under my ribs and rolled me over into him.

My breasts were full, nipples hard as they grazed his chest. I should've grabbed a T-shirt. His free hand traveled up and down my body.

'Rob, I—'

'It's been a while,' he whispered, fingers skimming the thick waistband of my underpants.

'I know, but I'm so tired.' I yawned as if submitting proof. I wanted to shut my eyes and block out the kaleidoscope of my in-laws, Marian, Zoey, Lyle Hartsell, and Jasper vomiting all over his area rug. I tried to turn onto my other side but Rob's arm pinned me to him.

'Not too tired to hang out with a neighbor.' He kissed my neck and slid a finger inside me. My body tensed. He moved closer and I felt how hard he was, the wet tip poking my thigh. 'I missed you.'

I inched back. 'I'm still sore.' It was true. Recovering from my C-section took longer than it had with Jasper. My back, arms, and neck ached from holding and feeding Poppy. By the end of the day, I longed for my body to be mine alone. Rubbing my shoulders felt like a gift. I hadn't realized it was Rob's attempt at foreplay. The last thing I wanted was him on top of me, thrusting and grunting, my belly and thighs jiggling as he turned me this way and that, asking, 'How does this feel? Do you like it?' until he believed I was satisfied.

'I'm tired, too.' He pressed me onto my back. 'But it's like you've closed up shop down here.' He pushed a second finger in. It made me catch my breath. 'And you're so distracted lately. Even my mom said—'

I shot up, nearly headbutting him, and covered my leaking breasts with a pillow. 'You and your mother are talking about our sex life now? Or, sorry, our lack of sex life?' For once, I didn't care if I woke the children.

'Jesus, Laurel, no.' Rob propped himself up on his elbow and frowned. 'You're taking this all wrong. I talked to her this morning and she mentioned you didn't seem like yourself yesterday. I told her you were tired, and she said Poppy's almost two months old and things should be getting back to normal and—'

'If your mother's so wise and perfect, Rob, maybe you should try to fuck her?'

He recoiled. 'OK, you know what, I'm gonna chalk that up to too much wine or whatever you drank that's made you smell like you just finished a bar crawl, because this is not how you and I speak to each other. Whatever is going on with you, Laurel, fix it.'

I took my pillow and the throw blanket from the end of our bed and walked into Poppy's room. I settled stiffly into her glider and peered out the window. A light was on in Addie's kitchen.

When I was there with her, I felt listened to, comforted, understood. At home, I was there to serve the needs of others. Was it universal? Did all wives and mothers feel that way? Or was there something wrong with my marriage? Should I have gone back to our bedroom and tried to repair whatever was broken between us? Would I have been able to fix it?

That question haunts me still.

SEVENTEEN

Corey

I side-eyed Moffatt as he drove. In his cargo shorts and blue tee, he didn't look like a cop. He didn't really look like a dad either. With his light eyes and boy-next-door thing, plenty of people might've found him attractive – if they could get past the layer of sadness that clung to him like a bad spray tan.

He wasn't ripped like Rex, but strong. Solid. Kenny had let himself go after Frankie was born. He'd joke about his 'dad bod' while scooping second helpings of ice cream. A year before we lost Frankie, Kenny started running. I should've known something was up right then.

Squinting into the setting sun, Moffatt parked his beat-up minivan in the church parking lot.

I tugged at the handle to get out but the door was locked.

'Hey, before we head in, I wanted to tell you a couple things.' He shifted in his seat so his back rested against the door and he faced me. 'Usually you have to complete a questionnaire and do a short interview with Linda, the moderator, to make sure you're a good fit for the group, but I asked that they make an exception in this case.'

I almost laughed. He was acting like he'd gotten me into the hottest bar in South Beach. But since he looked so earnest, I whispered, 'Thanks.' If I played nice and seemed relatively normal, maybe I could wrap up this bullshit in four weeks, tops.

'Share, don't share. It's up to you,' he said. 'For a while, I kind of just sat there, taking it all in, but once I started talking, that's when I really got something out of it.'

It didn't seem like the right time to tell him I'd sooner gargle glass than speak about my child with a room full of strangers. Kenny had joined a grief group. He'd wanted me to go with him. That was back when I was numb and still pretending that I might eventually forgive him.

'Why?' I'd asked. 'So we can be somebody's sad story to tell over dinner? No way.'

'It's not like that, Cor,' Kenny had argued. 'It's anonymous, confidential, whatever you call it.'

Confidential, my ass. Kenny had gone twice before the whispers started. I was at the grocery store, drifting like a ghost through the aisles, trying to think of what I needed – other than a time machine – when I heard these women from our neighborhood talking. I was in my grieving-mother uniform – jeans, a hoodie, sunglasses. Last thing I wanted was to be recognized, pitied, or consoled by these vultures always scavenging for gossip.

'My mother-in-law says he's a mess,' one of the women said.

'Where'd she see him?'

'She's in a bereavement group, has been since my father-in-law passed. She said the guilt's eating him alive.'

'Have you seen him?' the other asked. 'He's lost a ton of weight. They both have.'

'My heart breaks for her. Him, too, of course.' The woman's voice got real low. 'But what was he thinking, leaving such a young child alone?'

'I heard there was a little more to it. Rumor has it the mom attacked a neighbor . . .'

I'd stood there, frozen, staring at the label on a can of sweet potatoes. I wanted to grab dozens and bash them against their skulls 'til they lost consciousness. That was the moment denial shifted to white-hot rage.

'Now Linda – she's a pretty straight shooter.' Moffatt was still talking. 'She's not warm and fuzzy, so don't expect a ton of sympathy. She tells it like it is, but a few of us were saying that's better than giving people false hope, right? I mean, it's not like we'll ever forget or move on completely. It's more, "How do you move forward without it ruining the rest of your life?" If that makes sense?'

I nodded. I'd have agreed to anything to get out of the van and into air conditioning.

Moffatt led me into a big room. What was left of daylight filtered through a couple of stained-glass windows, white doves trapped forever flightless in their centers. A piano sat silent under a tarp. The air reeked of mildew and coffee.

People gathered in small clusters. They ranged from early twenties to bald or blue-haired. One thing they shared was the stoop of their shoulders. Grief was a big, heavy coat you never got to take off. I wore it too.

Had I imagined that Moffatt would walk me around and make introductions like I was some kind of debutante? No. But I hadn't expected him to leave me to help a couple guys drag chairs into a circle in the middle of the room.

'Hey, Mike!' One clapped him on the back. 'Good to see you.' The other offered him a fist bump.

I picked up a bottle of water, hands so shaky I wasn't sure I'd even be able to twist off the cap. Without my nightly run, my skin crawled, legs twitched, my body staging its silent protest. I didn't want to have anything in common with these people who'd had their hearts run through a meat grinder and been forced to reassemble them and keep living.

A woman in a dark, sleeveless dress with curly white poodle hair walked toward me. She looked like my old neighbor.

Don't run. Don't freak out. Pretend you're normal.

'You must be Corey,' she said. 'I'm Linda. Welcome. We're glad you're here.'

I shook her bony hand. She didn't smile, simply gave a little bow before joining the group on my right.

I walked around, flipping through prayer books and bibles, pretending they were as interesting as steamy beach reads so no one else would try to talk to me. After a minute, Linda rang a small bell and people moved toward the chairs. Was I supposed to sit next to Moffatt? Could I hide in a closet and hope he'd forget about me? A seat was open beside him so I took it. The folding chair's cold metal stung the back of my thighs.

'We gather this evening carrying burdens no one should bear, our hearts heavy, bodies tired, spirits and minds weary.' Linda's 'grounding meditation' felt more like a half-assed attempt at a prayer. 'Let us find comfort here in this space among others who travel down these same dark roads, recognizing that we are each on our own journey, going at our own pace.' She closed her eyes while I rolled mine and tried to steal a glance at Moffatt. His face was buried in his hands. 'Take what serves you and leave the rest behind. There is no perfect path forward. Let us try to be the best we can for one another and ourselves in our time together,' Linda continued. 'As always, we respect the trust we've established within this circle.'

'Amen,' a few people mumbled.

Linda held her upturned hand toward me. 'Corey has joined us.' It was met with a chorus of 'Hi' and 'Welcome.'

My insides jangled from the weight of their stares. I could hear their thoughts. *Who'd she lose? When was it? Does she pretend every ladybug or cardinal is her lost loved one too?* I gave a small wave then focused on Moffatt's frayed running shoes, stretched out in front of him, crossed at the ankle.

It was quiet except for the *whoosh* of the air conditioner and a few squeaks as people tried to get comfortable in their chairs. Eyes bounced around the circle. Who'd go first?

After a few seconds, a young woman with limp, carrot-colored hair raised her hand. 'I'm having a rough week,' she said. 'Sunday was my birthday. *Our* birthday. First one without him.'

'Firsts are hard,' Linda said.

Heads bobbed in agreement.

The girl wiped her eyes with the back of her hand. 'Sorry.' She took a breath, shoulders floating up. 'When we were little there were always two cakes. This year, there was one.' Her neck got splotchier with each sentence 'til it nearly matched the pattern of her tie-dyed tank top.

The woman to her left handed her a tissue. 'Thanks,' she mumbled. 'Curtis wanted us to go out to dinner. I said I didn't really feel like celebrating. He got pissed. Bottom line, he doesn't think he can do this – be with me – anymore. He said some really awful things – about Scotty, mostly. Yeah, he had problems, and he hadn't been himself in a long while, but that doesn't mean I can't miss him.'

'Did you share your feelings with Curtis?' Linda asked, casual as if they were chatting about the weather.

'I try. He doesn't get it. He says I should be over it by now. But Scotty was more than my brother; he was my twin. I knew him before we were born. How crazy is that?' She mopped a little river of eyeliner with the tissue.

I squirmed in my seat, itching to leave. The whole thing seemed too intimate. I felt like a peeping Tom, peeking into someone's soul during their darkest hour.

'I swear I can feel him. He's still with me.' Sara knocked on her chest. 'The restlessness. He never could sit still. Part of it was the drugs, but it was there before that. Maybe that's why he started using in the first place.' She looked around the circle like she hoped someone would confirm her theory. 'Anyway, I feel bad saying it, but he was ruining my life while he was alive, making me worry all the time. If I lose Curtis, it's like Scotty's ruining it from the grave.'

'Death is the end of a life, but not the end of a relationship,' Linda said. 'You're reliving not only the trauma of Scotty's death but also of his life – a life that no one would want for their sibling. You're entitled to your feelings, Sara, and if that makes Curtis uncomfortable, then Curtis will decide what's best for him, and you should decide what is best for you.'

'What's best would be for someone to kick Curtis in the dick,' was what I wanted to tell Sara.

Moffatt shifted and turned toward me, eyes wide. If he thought I was going to share, he was crazy. He cleared his throat. I stared at the scuffed tiles, afraid he was getting ready to speak. I didn't want to know how bad off he was and then have to suffer through an awkward ride home with him.

He held up a hand, same as he'd done when he'd pulled up to the Whispering Palms entrance.

'Yes, Mike?' Linda said.

'So, I'd been doing OK – not great but, you know, all right. I took Ryan fishing on Sunday. That's kind of become our thing. He caught a small bass. We threw it back. It was a good time. We didn't talk about Ava. Ry wanted hot dogs for dinner so we hit Publix on the way to my place. So we're in the frozen food section getting these waffle fries he likes and I see this little girl trying to push the cart, but she can't reach the handle, not even on tiptoes. Her mom's like, "When you're older. When you're bigger." But this kid, she's feisty.' He stopped and laughed for a second like he was picturing her in his mind's eye. I wondered where he was going with his story and if Linda ever thought about setting a time limit on how long people could 'share.'

'She's jumping up and down, getting closer,' Moffatt said, 'and the mom's tossing frozen peas into the cart, not really paying attention, just repeating, "Someday. When you're bigger."'

He shifted again. The tension in his body crept into mine.

'And it hit me – boom!' He raised his arms. 'How many times had I said that to Ava? "Someday." "When you're bigger." I thought we'd always have more time.' He tipped his head back and pinched the area between his eyes. 'It messed me up for the rest of the night. But because I had Ryan, I had to shove it aside, and then I'm betraying her again – her memory. The whole time we're watching the Marlins game and eating ice cream, it's there. I could be having a regular day and sadness, guilt, anger – they're waiting to ambush me – and I'm thrown back to where I was the day we lowered her into the ground.'

'Grief's a fucking hijacker, man,' a skinny guy across the circle said.

'You know it, baby,' an older woman agreed.

A few others *mm-hmm*'d.

'Thanks for sharing, Mike,' Linda said. 'As we know, mourning doesn't follow a linear path. There's no timetable, no expiration date.'

A lady pulled a cocktail napkin out of a purse the size of a bulldog and wiped her eyes.

'There will be times when those feelings surface out of nowhere and that's perfectly natural,' Linda added.

More nodding. I looked around again, thinking, *That's it? This guy pours his heart out and that's the best you've got?*

I glanced at Moffatt, quietly nibbling his thumbnail down to a nub, and wondered how anyone found this helpful.

When the meeting ended, a few ladies hugged Sara, the girl who'd lost her twin. The woman who'd passed her the tissue came up to me.

'I hope you join us again, hon,' she said. 'I'd like to say it gets easier but I'd be lying.' She gave me a tired smile and then reached out to rub Moffatt's arm. I hadn't realized he was beside me. 'Take care now, Mike, you hear. See you next week.'

'Thanks, Shirl,' he said. 'You do the same.'

We walked to the car in silence. It was still hot, but at least there was a hint of a breeze.

'Powerful stuff, right?' Moffatt asked.

More like terrible, I wanted to say. The rawness, the way these people could be vulnerable . . . grieving wasn't a competitive sport, but they were so far ahead of me. I couldn't even talk about her. About any of it.

'Yeah, powerful,' I repeated, thinking about Linda saying, 'Firsts are hard.'

Frankie would've turned four just days after we buried her. Her birthday had barely registered. The shock and pain were so deep and numbing, nothing seemed real. Weeks earlier, I'd sent invitations to kids in the neighborhood. She'd wanted a mermaid theme. Kenny suggested we rent an inflatable waterslide. I told him we didn't have the money.

'C'mon, live a little, Cor,' he'd said.

I'd caved and booked one. We'd forgotten about it until we heard the guys hammering the plastic spikes into the ground in our back-yard hours before the party was supposed to begin. With the flick of the generator's switch, the slide rose off the ground, coming to life like a monster in a horror movie. Kenny went flying outside screaming, 'Shut it off! Shut it the fuck off!'

Nearly a year had passed. Her fifth birthday was weeks away. Firsts are hard, Linda said. Were seconds any easier?

'Hey.' Moffatt broke the silence as he turned left out of the church parking lot. 'I usually get a donut and a cup of coffee on my way home. Any interest?'

I looked at the clock on the dashboard.

'Coffee? It's after nine.'

'Gotta keep that cops-and-donuts stereotype alive.' He chuckled. 'Plus, I don't really sleep anymore. Do you?'

'Not without a shit ton of alcohol.' I stared into the darkness, not wanting to go with him but not ready to go back to the condo either.

'So, how 'bout it? There's a little—'

'I told Ma I was meeting with a real-estate agent to look at places. I should probably get back.'

He slowed for a red light and smirked. 'Yeah, I heard Alice Blackwell wants you gone.'

I shook my head. 'Wow, shout out to the Whispering Palms' breaking-news alert system.'

'Hey, I was just grateful to hear my mom talk about something other than inflation and how worried she is about Ryan.'

'Well, then, I'm glad Alice and I could oblige.' I laughed.

'The same woman who started a petition to protect the rights of those creepy-ass iguanas won't rest until I'm homeless. Gotta love it.'

The light changed and he tapped the gas pedal. 'Next time then.'

'Next time what?'

'We'll grab coffee next time.' He gave a firm nod like it was a done deal.

'Yeah, maybe.' I tipped my head back, took in the blackness of the night sky.

How lonely must he have been to want to spend time with a loser like me?

I didn't need to ask.

I knew.

EIGHTEEN

Laurel

For days Rob and I tiptoed around each other, speaking only on an as-needed basis about things like which child was due for a bath or who'd skipped a nap. Nothing beyond that until Friday night.

I sat on the floor beside Jasper's toddler bed reading *Go, Dog. Go!* for the third time when Rob peeked in.

''Night, pal,' Rob whispered.

He was waiting in the hall as I blew Jasper a kiss and closed his bedroom door.

'I don't want to spend the weekend like this – us not talking,' Rob said, hands buried in his shorts pockets. 'Look, about the other night, I'm sorry. I knew you'd had a rough day with Jasper and I shouldn't have . . . It's just . . . you haven't seemed like yourself lately and I'm worried that . . .'

'I know.' I cut him off. I didn't want him to go down that road again, to remind me of my failings as a wife, a mother. 'I'm trying, Rob, I really am.' I looked down at my feet. Pregnancy made them expand to the width of flatbread while the heat caused my ankles to swell, thick and pink as canned hams. 'It's a lot here. But I'm OK, really.' I swallowed the lump in my throat. I couldn't cry. It would be another symptom he'd add to the list I was certain he was tallying: tired, no interest in sex, weepy.

'I want things to be good between us again, Laur.' He didn't move or touch me, and the perverse thing was that after days of living like roommates, I missed him, the feel of his hands, the sandalwood scent of his shaving cream.

'I want that, too,' I said. 'When I was at Addie's, I told her about my mom and about Lyle getting out, and . . .' I tried to keep my tone even, unsure if I should tell him I thought I was seeing my mother's killer everywhere. 'And we never talk about any of it. I wait for you to bring it up and—'

'I don't bring it up because I know it upsets you.' An edge crept into his voice. He ran a hand through his hair. 'I feel like I can't win here.'

'It's not about winning, Rob,' I snapped. 'It's about acknowledging that I've lived through a nightmare, and the man responsible for it gets to walk away and move on with his life. It's over for him, but not for me. I'm never going to stop missing my mother – my mother who isn't here to see her grandchildren.' *Or to teach me how to be a mother*, I thought but didn't say. 'I'm sorry I can't magically move on too.'

Jasper opened his bedroom door. 'You're being loud. You're gonna wake the baby!' he whispered, repeating what we often told him.

'You're right, bud, sorry,' Rob said.

'Can somebody tuck me in?'

'C'mon.' I placed my hands on Jasper's shoulders and steered him toward his bed. As I fluffed his quilt and kissed his forehead, I wished I could stay there beside him where things were simple and soft.

I stepped out of Jasper's room. Rob sat on our bed. I hadn't put up curtains and the space was gray and dim with evening. I felt lost, trapped by a sadness that my husband believed was well past its expiration date. I closed the door and sank to the edge of the bed unsure where we'd go from there.

He turned to face me, our knees touching. 'We have everything, Laur – a beautiful family, a nice house. I have a good job. You're

able to be here with the kids and yet you're still not happy.' His
eyes drifted toward the floor. 'And it's so frustrating for me because
I don't know what else I can do.'

From his perspective, I sounded so ungrateful. From mine, he
was taking and twisting my trauma, making it about how my
sadness affected *him*, how my mother's death impacted *his* life. I
debated pointing that out but knew he'd tell me I had it all wrong
again.

'I want to fill this place with love, laughter, silliness.' His lips
parted in a slow smile. 'And I get that that sounds like some cheesy
saying you'd read on a throw pillow, but I mean it. I want our kids
to have everything I had growing up.'

'I know. I do too.' In that moment, my anger lessened. Part of
what drew me to Rob was his love of family. I knew he'd be the
kind of all-in father I didn't have. And his belief that, in spite of
everything, I'd be OK made me believe it, too.

When we were dating, I'd told him about the therapist I'd been
seeing who'd said, 'Maybe you need to accept that this is how you'll
always feel.'

'Or maybe you need to find a new therapist?' he'd countered.

The room grew darker. I rested my heavy head on his shoulder.
I was too tired to argue, to try to make him understand that happiness wasn't something I could slip on like a pair of shoes.

I thought of Janice, my father's wife, how she'd say, 'You're as
happy as you make up your mind to be, Laurel. It's as simple as
that.'

Janice had worked at the bank with my mother. She'd left early
for a dentist appointment the day Lyle Hartsell came in with his
gun. How many times had I wished she'd been there instead of my
mother?

Rob wrapped his arm around me. We couldn't go on the way we
had been. Even Jasper had picked up on it. 'Talk, Mommy! Talk,'
he'd begged Wednesday night as I sat silent during dinner, pushing
green beans around my plate. I couldn't allow him to feel even a
hint of the sadness that filled my childhood home after my mother's
death.

Rob laced his fingers through mine and touched my chin with
his other hand, turning my face toward his. 'I've missed you – us.'
His eyes were filled with tenderness, not need or want.

Something inside me shifted. If I leaned toward his kindness and away from my fears, could we get back to where we once were? What if it were as simple as that? I wanted him to believe in me again.

His hand left my face and traveled to my bare thigh, his finger tracing small circles above my knee. 'Is this OK?' he asked.

'Yes.' I nodded and unbuttoned his shorts, slipping my hand inside his boxers. I kissed him deeply, hungry to get to a better place.

I woke Saturday morning to the smell of bacon. Sunlight streamed through the windows. I looked at the clock: 9:04 a.m. Rob had let me sleep in. He was standing at the stove flipping pancakes when I walked into the kitchen.

'Mommy!' Jasper shrieked from the table where he waited, a fork in one hand, butter knife in the other, legs dangling inches above the floor.

'Good morning!' I felt better than I had in weeks. 'Now *this* is the perfect way to start the weekend. Thank you.' I kissed Rob, the closeness of the night before lingering between us.

'You're welcome.' He smiled and sprinkled a handful of chocolate chips into the bubbling batter. 'Sit with the kids. I'll fix your coffee.'

I pecked the top of Jasper's head, then turned to Poppy, parked in her bouncy chair beside the fridge, hands and feet flailing like a tiny kick-boxer.

'Hey, baby girl!' I scooped her up and sat beside Jasper. Rob, busy, happy, poured from the French press we only used on week-ends. The day felt fresh, full of promise. Rob and I were finding our way back to each other. It seemed like as good a time as any to bring up my idea.

'So . . . I've been thinking about asking Nina if she'd stay with Jasper and Poppy while we're at the wedding.' I rubbed Poppy's toes, tiny and pink as bits of raw ground beef. 'What do you think?'

'No-Show Nina?' Rob laughed as he delivered Jasper's pancakes and my coffee. 'Like that would ever happen.'

'Who's Nina-no-shoes?' Jasper asked, flooding his short stack with syrup.

Rob removed the bottle from his hands. 'She's your mom's flaky friend.'

'Flaky like a croissant?' Jasper asked.

'Spoken like the son of a pastry chef. Bet he's the only three-year-old in town who knows what a croissant is.' Rob smiled.

I grinned back. 'I'm serious. She said she's coming in August, so why not ask her?' I leaned over to Jasper. 'She's the one who sent you that froggy towel you love.'

'Ribbit!' Jasper stuck out his tongue pretending to catch a fly the way I did when I swaddled him after a bubble bath.

'I thought you only wanted to leave them with someone they knew?' Rob leaned against the counter and sipped his coffee.

'Maybe she can get here a day or two early and spend time with all of us?'

He lowered the mug, mouth tight, lips pressed in a thin line.

'What?' I stole a piece of Jasper's bacon.

'Nothing . . . just . . . maybe we should have a backup on standby.' He shrugged and returned to the stove where smoke rose from the griddle.

His lack of faith in my friend made me defensive, protective. 'She's busy with her career. I'm happy for her. I admire her – everything she's accomplished.'

'I know,' he said, 'it's just I've seen how many times she's disappointed you, and this isn't dinner reservations or concert tickets, Laur. It's my sister's wedding. There's a lot riding on her showing up – if she even agreed to do it in the first place.'

Our conversation was interrupted by the clap of the mail slot. Each time I heard that sound, my heart stopped. We hadn't received any other notes, but I hadn't told Rob about the one I'd misplaced. If it was nothing but a scam like Addie had said, there was no need to worry him.

Jasper jumped down from the chair. Seconds later he was back, handing me a pile. I picked through it carefully, afraid of what I might find. It was mainly bills and a postcard from a local real-estate agent, Rachel Barnes. The words 'Thinking of selling?' seemed to confirm Addie's theory about the current housing shortage.

I pushed the mail aside and looked at Rob. 'Don't forget, No-Show Nina is the reason we're together.'

'Fair,' Rob conceded, opening the window above the sink before the smoke detector emitted its piercing shriek.

I brushed my lips against the top of Poppy's head, my mind

traveling back to seven years earlier. Rob and I were strangers, pacing the overheated corridors of New York's Penn Station, each of us waiting for someone, checking our phones for updates. It was the Monday before Thanksgiving and an early snowstorm had caused delays up and down the East Coast.

I'd noticed him. It would've been impossible not to. With his dark hair and hazel eyes, Rob was handsome, but it was more than his looks that caught my eye. A man had been asking people for change. Most ignored him. Rob bought him pizza, pressed some cash into his palm, and wished him a good night.

'Hey!' I blurted when Rob passed me. 'That was nice.'

He stopped. 'Probably would've preferred booze.' He held up his hands. 'No judgement. I could go for a drink myself.'

'Same.' I laughed. 'Who are you waiting for?' I wasn't usually that bold, but it had been hours since I'd spoken to anyone and I didn't want him to walk away.

'My sister, coming up from D.C., trying to beat the holiday rush. You?'

'No one. I just like to hang around dirty train stations on my night off.' I watched his confusion morph into a smirk then a genuine smile that made the emptiness inside me shrink. Nina had that effect on me too. I'd been so excited to see her, I'd raced up there in the freezing cold so she wouldn't have to walk or take an Uber alone to my apartment.

'My college roommate,' I said. 'She lives in Boston. We're hanging out before she visits family on Long Island.' I wasn't in the habit of chatting up strangers, but Rob's eyes were kind, encouraging.

In my rush, I hadn't put on any makeup or even a bra, just hurried out in the bulky down jacket I wore pretty much from October through April. I wished I'd made an effort, especially when a petite blond in a navy velvet coat tapped Rob on the shoulder.

'Rob-bie!' she sang.

'Em!' He hugged her, lifting her off the ground, while a broad-shouldered guy looked on.

'Rob, this is Colin.' She introduced the linebacker behind her with a dramatic flourish. 'We met on the train.'

Emily was giddy, glowing. I'd have killed for a fraction of her radiance. As she explained she and Colin were headed to a bar, my phone buzzed in my pocket. A text from Nina. *Met THE hottest guy. Getting off in New Haven to check out a band. Don't hate. Be there by lunch tomorrow. XOX*

I groaned. It pinged again.

Sorry! Thought I sent that an hour ago. Train Wifi sucks! XOX

'Fucking typical.' I hadn't meant to say it aloud. I zipped the phone back into my pocket feeling the emptiness inside me growing, spiraling. When I looked up, Rob was still there.

'Let me guess, your night got derailed, too?' He grinned. 'Get it, derailed? We're in a train station.'

'Ha.' I didn't laugh. I'd looked forward to Nina's visit for weeks. I shared a tiny apartment with a distant cousin of Janice's. Whenever she came into the common areas, she was clutching a ferret neither of us acknowledged. I was staring down Thanksgiving with my father and Janice at their cramped condo. I could already hear Janice asking me if I'd considered Match.com and assuring me that if I wore makeup and put in a little effort, someone would find me attractive. Nina's visit was the lone bright spot on my otherwise bleak horizon.

'So, I'm still in the mood for that drink. How about you?' Rob asked. 'My family has this tradition – the first snowfall of the season, you stop what you're doing and have an Irish coffee. Random, I know. But fun, right?' He smiled, then frowned. 'I mean, when we were young, Emily and I had cocoa,' he babbled nervously, which made him that much more adorable. 'I don't want you to think my parents get little kids drunk or anything.'

The memory made me smile as Poppy squirmed in my lap.

'Without Nina, you wouldn't be here,' I told Jasper, stroking his soft cheek, bulging with pancakes.

'So give her a call. Ask her,' Rob said. 'And while you're on the phone, I'll start thinking of a backup plan.'

The air was warm but not oppressive for a summer afternoon in mid-July. In the shade of an elm, I swung in the striped hammock I'd gotten Rob for Father's Day. Jasper and Poppy were napping while Rob caught up on work email.

I slipped my phone from my pocket and called Nina, wondering which time zone I'd find her in or if I'd get her voicemail.

'Laurel!'

My heart somersaulted the way it always did when I first heard her voice. 'Neen!' I said. 'Where are you?'

'Bruges. Belgium,' she added. 'I wish you were here, Laur, you'd die. The coffee, the waffles, the chocolate – I may never leave.'

There was so much to catch up on but our calls often ended abruptly with her rushing off to somewhere more interesting.

'Well, as delicious as it sounds, you *must* leave because I can't wait to see you next month! You're still planning to visit, right?' I looked at the leaves fluttering above me and braced for disappointment. Rob's nickname, No-Show Nina, wasn't inaccurate.

'Of course!' she said. 'Third week of August. I haven't seen my parents since Christmas. They're about to write me out of their will.' Her laugh was rich, throaty. I pictured her out until dawn, voice raised to be heard above the music in a piano bar or more likely a nightclub with bottle service and lighting that came with a seizure warning. 'I want to see you and meet—'

'Poppy!' I jumped in to avoid any awkwardness in case she'd forgotten.

'And I'm dying to see your new house!'

I looked at our home through Nina's eyes. Small, roof faded, a few shingles missing, the whole place in need of a power washing – nothing like the villas of France or the modern lofts of Soho where her glamorous gigs took her.

'How's life in the 'burbs?' she asked. 'As blissful as people on Instagram want me to believe?' I heard the smirk in her voice followed by the flick of a lighter. I'd have to ask her not to smoke in the house or in front of the children.

'Hmmm, not quite.' Out of the corner of my eye I spotted Marian in her yard refilling a bird feeder. I lowered my voice. 'Honestly, Neen, it's weird.' In the background, spoons clattered, a man spoke French. I needed to ask before she had to go. 'So, I have a small favor.' I bit my lip. 'Actually, it's a big favor. Rob's sister is getting married next month—'

'Wait, not to that meathead who got completely hammered at your wedding?'

'Yes!' I laughed, imagining Susan and Emily hearing the impression Colin had made. 'It's the sixteenth through the eighteenth, and I'm hoping maybe you could watch Jasper and Poppy?' Silence. I cringed but continued, 'I don't really know anyone here yet, and it's just that my dad and Janice—'

'Say no more. Of course, I'll do it. I'd love to! And, no offense, but I wouldn't leave a stray cat with your dad and Janice.'

Relief rushed through me. 'Oh my God, Neen, thank you.'

'Happy to help!' She blew a long, slow exhale. I'd only ever smoked when I was with her. I hadn't realized how much I missed it.

'Honestly, I'd rather stay here with you.' I looked up as if Rob might suddenly appear and overhear. 'I'm dealing with a textbook Bridezilla. It's this big, long—'

'Listen, Laur, I have to go, but I'm in. Just don't get carried away and forget to come home. My maternal juices dry up after seventy-two hours max. Text me the deets. Love you!'

I rested my phone on my stomach and pushed my foot against the grass, making the hammock sway. For the first time, I started to look forward to the wedding. I'd miss Jasper and Poppy, of course, but they'd love Nina and she'd adore them. It would be good – the motivation I needed to take better care of myself. I'd start exercising, eat more fruit and less of Jasper's mac and cheese. Then I'd look for dresses for the rehearsal dinner and wedding, maybe something casual but cute for the Sunday brunch. Without the stress of juggling the kids, Rob and I could reconnect.

I closed my eyes and savored the sounds of birdsong and the creek burbling behind me. While I was thrilled Nina had agreed to stay, her joke about her parents' will reminded me that Rob and I still needed to draft one and appoint a guardian. Because we'd barely spoken all week, we hadn't discussed it since the night of Emily's shower. The wedding would be the first time we'd traveled together without the children. We had to complete the paperwork before we left. But other than Emily and Colin, who could we ask? I stood to go inside, prepared to start what would likely be a challenging discussion.

Maybe it was getting up too quickly, the heat, or the hammock's movement, but I felt lightheaded as I walked slowly toward the house.

'Yoo-hoo! Laurel?'

I turned and saw Marian standing where our yards met.

'Oh, hi,' I said without moving closer. I hadn't spoken to her since the luncheon. She looked pale in a mint-green dress, her cotton ball of hair less puffy than usual.

'Where's Jasper?' Her tone bordered on accusatory.

I looked around as if I'd misplaced him. 'Napping.' I took a step toward my house.

'I made another batch of blueberry muffins. He liked them so much when he was here on Sunday. He said they were the best he'd ever tasted.' She paused to let that land. 'In fact, he had three. I said, "Doesn't your mother feed you?"' She snickered and rocked a little on her heels, color rising in her cheeks.

Though I was standing in a patch of sunlight, a chill settled over me as my thoughts slipped back to earlier that week in Addie's kitchen.

'You don't think Marian would've given Jasper something?' Addie had asked. 'Something that upset his stomach – something that made him sick?'

The dizziness that hit me when I first stood returned. I forced myself to stay calm. 'Well, then I'll have to get your recipe.'

'A baker never gives away her secrets.' Marian shook her head as if I were the most foolish woman in the world. 'I'd expect a pastry chef to understand that.'

How did she know my occupation? Rob must've told her.

'Anyway,' she continued. 'When Jasper wakes up, bring him by.'

I pictured the nicks on the back of my son's neck from the haircut she'd given him without my consent. I considered telling her she was crazy if she thought I'd 'bring him by' after that, but I could imagine the ways she'd justify her outrageous behavior and I didn't want to hear it.

Instead, I smiled. 'If he'd like a muffin, I'll send him over with Rob.'

She grinned back but her cold eyes narrowed like she could read my thoughts and knew I had no intention of mentioning it to either of them.

NINETEEN

Corey

The back room at the garden center smelled like a bag of armpits as I waited to clock out. The air buzzed, charged with the promise of Saturday night. It didn't make any difference to me which day it was. I was headed home to Ma for another night of nothing.

As I grabbed my wallet and keys from my locker, Dave popped his head in. 'Corey, stick around a minute?'

Was that a question or an order? A prickly feeling crept up the back of my neck. 'Sure, what's up?' I followed him to a supply closet he considered his office.

'Have a seat.'

I perched on the rung of a stepladder while he leaned against a shelf full of empty vases. Was he going to tell me I should smile at the customers or have more patience when the dumb ones asked, 'Do I need to water this?'

'So I've been out of town for a while.'

I caught myself before a 'duh' slipped out. 'Yeah. Maine, lobsters, family reunion, I remember.'

'Bumped into my neighbor last night. Guy across the street? Spends half his life washing his truck.'

My heart started knocking fast and hard. Where was he going with this?

'Anyway, I'm rolling out my recycling when he tells me this crazy story about you stealing a—' He stopped and cleared his throat. 'A tutu from another neighbor's car.' He laughed, rattling the vases behind him.

All the blood in my body shot to my cheeks, betraying me. There was no point in lying.

'Yeah, and?'

'Yeah?' He stopped laughing and stared like he was seeing me for the first time. 'So he's not making it—'

'Nope.'

'Ah, Jesus.' Dave took off his baseball cap, rubbed the top of his head like he was part ape, and tugged the hat back into place. When I said nothing, he sighed, his coffee breath nearly knocking me off the ladder. 'None of my business . . .' He looked right and left like he was crossing traffic and dropped his voice. 'But you're not having an affair with Tommy Long, are you? Or, shit, who knows nowadays – his wife, Teresa?'

'No. It was a weird, one-time mistake.'

Dave's eyes got all squinty like a TV detective's. 'Really? 'Cause I remember seeing you on my block at least twice.' His lips puckered. 'The money – the cash that went missing from the register up front – that you?'

I couldn't admit to that too. Moffatt went to bat for me once. I doubted he'd do it again.

'Wasn't me.' My hands cupped my knees, dirty fingernails digging into the skin, leaving little ruts behind like a bird had pecked there.

'You sure now?' His eyebrows arched toward the brim of his cap.

I nodded.

'Well, either way, I'm afraid I'm gonna have to let you go. Not 'cause of any of this.' He waved his hands like he was clearing away a fart. 'Slow season. Gotta make some cuts.'

I didn't need his shitty job and, still, it clobbered me. I'd never been fired. That was Kenny's department. I was a hard worker, got things done, kept to myself.

'Sure, whatever.' I stood. I wanted to stare him down, make him feel as bad as I did, but I couldn't force my eyes to meet his.

'Keep the hat and shirt!' he hollered, but I was already rushing out the back, giving Mack the macaw a lame salute and wondering when I'd stop letting my bad choices put me in a cage of my own.

I hurried to the car, focused on the ground in case Josh and the others were still hanging around trying to outdo each other with their fake plans for the night.

I was almost at the Corolla when I saw them – knockoff Doc Martens and a bicycle tire. All facing me. *Fuck this*. I wasn't in the mood.

'What are you doing here?' I asked, arms limp at my sides.

'You didn't think I was going to let this beautiful friendship end, did you?'

I squinted at Desiree, blinded by the late-day sun bouncing off her helmet. Her knuckles turned white as she gripped the handlebars of that sad-ass Schwinn. 'Don't you have any friends your own age?'

'None as interesting as you, Corinne Stevens.' She smirked. Stevens – my married name. She'd googled me like she'd threatened. 'When you didn't text me after I left you that note with my number, I decided to find yours. Man, what a crazy rabbit hole that was.' She shook her head, still safely encased in her helmet.

'If you've come to blackmail me, you're too fucking late. Dave fired me.'

The bike tilted to the side as her hand flew to her mouth. 'No way. That sucks.'

'Whatever. Screw him. I don't need the money.'

'Must be nice.'

I moved toward the car. She rolled forward to block me. I pressed my hand to my head. A dull ache spread from the part of my brain that was smarting from my time with Dave. I wanted to get the hell out of the parking lot before I had to see him again.

'What is it, Desiree?' I groaned. 'What do you want?'

'I don't know.' She gave a sad smile, her tough exterior melting amid the heat rising off the asphalt. 'I thought maybe we could get fro-yo like the old days?'

'Old days? That was like, what, three weeks ago?' I snorted. 'I would, but I have to—'

'Get the car back to your mom?' She finished my sentence and frowned. 'Do you even have a mother? I read some stuff about you, and now I'm like, who are you? Really?'

That stung but I wouldn't let it show. 'First off, everyone has a mother. Second, I'm just a loser who can't hold down a part-time gig at a garden center.'

'Welcome to the club.'

For a second, I'd forgotten I was the reason she'd been fired.

Chewing her bottom lip, kicking gravel around a pothole, she looked so young.

'All right, fine, let's get some yogurt.'

I stood outside Yo Momma wondering what the hell I was doing there while Desiree locked up her rusty bike like it was a top-of-the-line Cannondale.

Inside, the air conditioning was a relief but it was brighter, more colorful than I'd remembered. The forced cheeriness of it made my head throb.

'What flavor you gonna get?' Desiree bounced on her steel-enforced tiptoes.

'Does it matter? They all taste like paint with a hint of vanilla.'

'There's that cynical charm I've missed.' She fake-punched my arm.

At the register, I pulled out a twenty while she patted her pockets.

'I got this,' I said.

'You sure?'

'Yeah. Consider this our Hall's Garden Center retirement party.'

When we sat, she whipped out hand sanitizer, grabbed my wrists and squeezed a quarter-sized drop into my palm. 'Your nails,' she shuddered and took off her helmet. Her pixie cut had grown into yellowy-orange chunks shooting out of dark roots.

'I see you staring. Way to be subtle.' She shoved a lock behind her ear but it sprang forward again.

'What the . . .?'

'I know. It's bad, right?' She scrunched up her face.

'You look like a Duracell battery.'

'I've been babysitting a ton. Unlike you, I need the money. I swim every day and the chlorine turned it this funky color. My mom's gonna make me dye it back to my regular shit brown before school starts anyway.'

'Well, at least that's a decent shirt.' I nodded at the navy halter top with its lime green embroidery. It was one of those pieces that weighed less than an ounce but probably cost seventy-eight dollars.

'Thanks. It's a hand-me-down from one of the families my mom cleans for. At first I was like, "No way am I wearing somebody else's rejects." Then I saw the label. Anthropologie, baby. So I was like, why cut off my nose to spike my face, right?'

'Spite.'

'What?'

'It's "spite" your face.'

She rolled her eyes in an 'if you say so' way and reached for my phone.

'Hey!' I snatched it back. Even with my head pounding, my first thought was to guard the videos and photos of Frankie. 'Don't touch that!'

'Geez.' She looked offended but recovered fast. 'I was going to give you my contact info. Chill.'

I put my finger on the home button and handed it to her. She said her number and spelled her name as she added everything.

'Now enough about me.' She placed the phone face down. 'I want to talk about you!' She licked her lips and pointed her finger guns at me.

The flavor I'd picked, sea salt caramel truffle, left a thick, furry coating on my tongue. 'I'm really not that interesting.'

'Au contraire.' She smiled. 'Am I saying that right or did you want to correct me there too?'

'Nah, you're good.' I tried to think of a way to sidetrack or stonewall her. I didn't talk about my past with anyone – not with Ma or Moffatt with his pleading 'confide in me' eyes, and definitely not with that grief group.

'You were an event planner?' she asked.

'Yeah. Why? You weighing your career options?'

'Sort of. That landscape architecture program I want takes five years and money's tight.'

'My job sounds more exciting than it was. I just brought a lot of moving parts together. Stayed on top of vendors. I can be a ballbuster when I have to be.'

'Really? I hadn't noticed.' She smiled and looked around. The shop was empty except for us and the girl behind the counter who was scrolling through her phone. 'So, is it true?' Desiree whispered. 'Did you really break into those houses?'

My day just kept getting better. 'Yup. I did.'

Her jaw dropped and her eyes bugged out. She'd been expecting me to deny it.

'Badass,' she purred into her empty cup.

I thought of Frankie, how she'd take two hours to eat a carrot but would scarf down an ice-cream cone in thirty seconds then wait until I gave her mine.

'Want the rest?' I tilted my nearly full yogurt toward her.

'Gross, but yes. Please.' She tapped her blue nails against the tabletop. 'You still think one of your neighbors is responsible for what happened to your little girl?'

'I don't know what I believe anymore.' Images flooded my mind. Small hands poking out of the ground. Brownish-green water. The foul, sulphur stench of it came back so strong I might as well have been standing beside the creek, mud squishing between my toes.

I twisted my ponytail, pulling hard until the memories faded. It had been nearly a year. Each day that passed, I got a little more certain it wasn't 'a freak accident.' Someone had wanted to hurt us.

'How come you didn't get in more trouble? With the police and everything?'

'Nobody pressed charges. Everybody assumed I'd gone crazy – from grief.'

She pushed away her fro-yo. 'I'm sorry about your daughter. I had no idea. That must've been really, really awful.'

Beneath the table, I pinched the back of my knee where the skin was thinnest. The stinging stopped the tears that burned my eyes whenever anyone told me how sorry they were.

'Do you ever think about . . .' Desiree hesitated, turning to look at the girl behind the register before locking her eyes on mine.

'Think about what?'

'Going back?' she whispered. 'Figuring out what happened?'

'Nah.' I ran my tongue over the rough edge of the plastic spoon. 'I have to move on. No other choice, right?' I shrugged like that was it. Case closed.

I didn't tell her that I thought about it every minute of every hour and that it was only a matter of time before those thoughts became actions.

TWENTY

Laurel

I took Jasper and Poppy for an early walk, determined to start the day and the week off right.

Mondays were a bit like New Year's but on a small scale, offering a chance to *be* and *do* better than the week before. If I walked for an hour each day, I could look and feel more like myself in time for Emily's wedding.

By the time we arrived home, the fresh air had knocked Poppy out. She napped in her crib while Jasper watched his beloved music videos in the playroom. Other than the faint sounds of G-rated versions of Maroon 5 and Flo Rida songs, the house was deliciously quiet. I opened the windows. A light breeze carried in the scent of fresh-cut grass. I showered and took my time getting dressed. Instead of my usual maternity skirts and oversized T-shirts, I found loose shorts and a white sleeveless top. I pictured Addie, always so put together, and reached for the pair of amethyst earrings that had belonged to my mother.

As I applied moisturizer, I thought about how we'd spend the day. Jill had recommended a playground her twins adored. Maybe I'd pack a picnic lunch. Jasper would love that.

In his room, I gathered his dirty clothes, then peeked in on Poppy. I crept down the steps carrying the laundry basket, hoping the old oak floors wouldn't wake her. Still, I heard a creak. Out of the corner of my eye, something moved. The front door groaned open several inches. Could the breeze have done it? I was certain it was shut – locked – before I'd gone upstairs.

Was it Zoey again? Rob had seen her on his walk to the train the morning after we found her in our kitchen. She'd apologized again, he said. She'd been close with the former owners, she told him, adding they had 'an open-door policy with the neighbors.'

'Well, we have a closed-door policy – no, a locked-door policy,' I'd said, 'at least until we know them better!'

'Fair enough,' Rob had agreed.

I set the laundry basket on a chair, locked the front door, and hurried to the kitchen.

'Jasper?' I called. 'Jasper!' I expected him to run to me, bare feet pitter-pattering against the hardwood. He didn't. He probably couldn't hear me over the music. In the playroom, kids in neon colors danced across the TV screen. My son was nowhere in sight.

'Jasper?' My chest tightened on my way to the half-bathroom. He loved to unspool dental floss, stringing it from the sink faucet to the toilet paper holder, creating make-believe spiderwebs.

He wasn't there. I tried not to panic. My mind bolted to the front door. Would he have opened it? Could someone have come in? Taken him?

No. This was a safe neighborhood. But that's what people said about the town where I grew up, the place where my mother was killed. Her murder drove me to imagine the worst, even when there was nothing to fear.

Jasper had to be in the house. But I'd been in his room, he wasn't there. The basement was unfinished. Rob had put a latch at the top of the door because the steps were steep.

'Jasper! Jasper!' I shouted, ducking under the dining-room table. Sometimes he pulled the tablecloth to one side and pretended he'd built a fort. 'Jasper!' I yelled louder, smacking my head against the table's underside as I crawled out.

Poppy's cries traveled down from the second floor. I didn't have time to get her. I needed to find him. My thoughts turned to Lyle.

Where was he?

Where was my son?

Through the kitchen window my eyes landed on the creek. I told Jasper we'd play catch. Would he have gone outside without me? Through the front or the back? I spun in circles, pulse pounding, not knowing which was more dangerous: the street or the water.

I raced out the mudroom door. 'Jasper! Jasper!' I could barely catch my breath as I ran to the shed where we kept his tricycle, though I knew he couldn't be in there; the lock on the outside was still latched. My eyes darted across to the neighboring yards and beyond. Nothing. Not a child. Not a swing set. Only a pair of squirrels sprinting through Addie's hydrangeas.

A scream rose up from deep in my belly. 'Jasper!'

My phone buzzed in my pocket.

'Rob? Rob, I—'

'Laurel, what's wrong? You sound—'

'I can't, I can't find Jasper. I—'

'What? Slow down. Where are you?'

'I was taking a shower and when I came downstairs, he was gone. I'm outside. Rob—'

'Why are you outside? Go back in the house and look—'

I struggled to form the words. 'Rob, the front door was open.'

'What do you mean? Wasn't it locked? You were the one who made such a big deal about Zoey—'

'Rob, please, I—'

'How long was he alone? Why weren't you with him?' His tone, so harsh, so thick with blame, brought back a flood of terrible memories, ones I spent two years trying to forget. 'I'm coming home. I'm leaving now but I won't be there for at least an hour.' I pictured him running his hand through his hair, palming the back of his neck the way he did when he was stressed. 'Call the police, then call me back!'

'Rob, I'm—'

He ended the call.

I shoved the phone into my pocket and shouted. 'Jasper! Jasper!'

'Laurel?' Addie appeared beside me, popping out her AirPods. 'I was on a conference call on my sunporch. I thought I heard you.'

Tears pooled in my eyes. The backyard swam out of focus. 'Addie.' My chest heaved up and down as I tried to catch my breath. 'I can't find Jasper. I was in the shower and, and . . .' Weakness flooded my joints like a sudden case of the flu.

Addie's head swung toward the creek as she touched my arm. I followed her gaze. Flies swarmed above the water. It hadn't rained in days. A sulphur smell hung in the air. I thought I might vomit. 'The front door was open and . . . and . . .' I felt dizzy, strange, like I was watching my life fall apart from above. I doubled over, then shot back up. 'Jasper!' I screamed again.

'Mommy?'

I spun around. He was there, hazel eyes wide, lips blue, standing in Marian's yard like a garden gnome amid her pots of red geraniums. I nearly collapsed on the grass.

'Jasper!' I gasped, hot tears spilling over. I rushed forward and scooped him into my arms.

He giggled as I buried my face in his neck. 'Mommy, your nose is wet. Like a doggie!'

Marian stepped outside, wiping her hands on a tea towel. 'What's all this commotion?'

The hint of laughter in her voice made me murderous.

I cradled Jasper's head against my shoulder, my body and voice shaking. 'Did you come into my home and take him?' The phone buzzed in my pocket. *Rob.* I needed to tell him Jasper was safe. But first I had to deal with Marian. 'Do you have a key to my house?' I demanded, sticking my neck out like an animal on the verge of attack.

'No yelling!' Jasper shrieked in my ear. 'You'll wake up Poppy!'

Poppy. I'd left her crying in her crib. I had to go to her, but I couldn't let Marian off that easily. She had to know what she'd done was unacceptable. What Zoey had done was bad enough; this was worse.

'What the hell were you thinking?' Sweat streamed down my back and stomach.

'Laurel, dear, take a breath, my goodness!' Marian said. 'I rang your doorbell and invited Jasper to come for a muffin. I told you how much he liked them, but you didn't send him over.' She tilted her head like she was talking to a child. 'Jasper said you were in the shower, which, frankly, surprised me, given that—' she held up her arm to study her slim silver wristwatch. 'It's nearly eleven a.m.'

'I had no idea where he was!' Anger surged through my veins like a narcotic.

'I'm sorry that you've gotten yourself so worked up. I left a whatchamacallit – a Post-it note – for you. I stuck it to your banister so you'd see it when you came downstairs and you'd know he was with me.'

I pictured the staircase. I'd been carrying the laundry basket, but I couldn't remember seeing anything. 'There was no note and even then—'

'Isn't that your baby crying?' Marian jutted her chin toward my house where Poppy's screams traveled through the open window. 'Sounds like she needs you. Jasper, I hope to see you again soon.' The smile she flashed my son vanished when she looked at me.

I stared in disbelief as she turned toward her house and disappeared inside.

'Thanks for the muffins, Mimi!' Jasper called, waving one hand, a muffin in the other.

'Holy shit,' Addie mouthed. She placed a hand on my shoulder as we walked toward my house, each step a mile on my trembling legs.

I hugged Jasper tighter. He wiped his blueberry-stained lips on the shoulder of my white shirt.

'Are you OK? Because that was pretty fu— messed up.'

'Who does that?' A coppery taste filled my mouth like I'd been sucking pennies.

'Can we play catch now?' Jasper asked.

I ignored him.

'Do you want me to come in for a bit?' Addie volunteered. 'I have another call,' she held up her phone, 'but I can reschedule it.'

'No, but thank you. We'll be OK.' I put Jasper down. A throbbing ache was forming behind my eyes. 'The front door was open. I completely lost it. Who comes into someone else's home and takes their child? Who does that?'

'Fucking Marian, that's who,' Addie whispered as she gave me a quick hug. 'Text me later.'

Before we went inside, I took the muffin out of Jasper's hand and hurled it toward the creek. I didn't care if Marian was watching from her window.

'Mommy! No!' Jasper tried to sprint after it but I caught him, reflexes sharp from leftover adrenaline. 'I want it,' he cried. 'It's mine! Mommy, get it!'

'In!' I ordered, making sure to lock the mudroom door behind me. I marched him toward the bathroom. 'Wash your hands and face.' In the mirror above the sink, I saw that my lip was bleeding. I must've bitten it. I closed the toilet lid and sat, taking deep breaths. 'Jasper, we don't open the door just because the bell rings. It could be a stranger.'

'Mimi's not a stranger. She's my friend. She gives me muffins.' He shook his head. 'And I didn't open the door. I'm thirsty!' He dried his hands on his shirt and darted toward the kitchen. I trailed behind.

'Did she have a key? Jasper? How did Mari— How did Mimi get in?'

'Poppy's crying!' He tugged at the fridge door, grabbed an organic juice pouch from the lowest shelf, and ran into the playroom. I wanted to interrogate him, but how reliable was a three year old?

Poppy's howls grew louder as I neared the staircase, but I didn't go to her. I needed to look for the note Marian claimed she'd left. My phone buzzed again. *Rob.* I swiped to answer, still panting. 'Hey, Jasper's—'

'I'm in an Uber. I'm on my way.'

'Rob, he's here. Jasper's here. I've got him.' A drumbeat of relief thumped inside my stomach.

I heard him exhale. 'Where was he?'

'He was with Marian.' Rage replaced relief as I pictured her walking back into her home as if she'd done nothing wrong. 'She came over while I was in the shower and took him to her house for muffins. Who does that, Rob?' While I spoke, I searched for her note, upending couch cushions. Nothing. 'She's not normal.' Words poured out of me. 'First the haircut, now this! Something's not right, Rob, *she's* not right.'

I took a breath and waited for Rob to agree, to say that Marian had gone well beyond any reasonable boundary. I wanted him to promise he'd go over and talk to her, tell her to stay away from our family.

I looked up and down the staircase again and behind the fake plants Susan had brought, knowing I wouldn't be able to keep real ones alive. No Post-it.

When he said nothing, I thought our call had dropped or he'd entered a tunnel and lost service. Then I heard him sigh.

'I get that you were scared, but why didn't you check with Mimi?' he asked. 'You know Jasper's crazy about her. When Em and I were kids, we roamed the neighborhood from sun up 'til sundown.'

'Do not twist this around on me, Rob!' I sounded hysterical as I sifted through junk mail on the entryway table in search of Marian's note. 'She took our son out of our home without asking me!'

'To give him a muffin, Laurel. Honestly, do you hear yourself? She's trying to be helpful. She knows you're overwhelmed.'

I gripped the table. 'Why does she think that? I barely see her. Did she say something to you? Did you say something to her?'

I heard how I sounded: paranoid, manic.

'Where is Poppy? Why is she crying like that?'

'She just woke up. I'm going to get her now.'

How long had she been crying? Ten? Fifteen minutes? When I opened her door, she was a sweaty, writhing mess, tiny hands balled into fists, diaper full. The smell made me gag.

'I left work because I thought our son was missing!' Rob's voice was low but sharp. 'You have to pull it together, Laur.' I imagined his lips curling inward as he spoke. 'We have two children now,' he said, as if I didn't know, as if I hadn't carried each of them inside my body for three-quarters of a year. 'I need you to put your paranoia aside and focus on them. At all times. You need to be strong. For them.'

His words shamed me as I lifted Poppy out of the crib and placed her onto the changing table.

'Just because she's an older woman that doesn't mean she isn't dangerous, Rob. She's still a stranger. Would you have let him hang out with that lady from our apartment building? The one who roamed the hallway all night humming the *Jeopardy!* theme? A change of zip code doesn't make everyone good or kind—'

'You're spiraling,' Rob interrupted. 'I'm halfway home. We'll talk more when I get there.'

I didn't want to talk more. I wanted him to say, 'Yes, Laurel, what just happened was insane. I'll set Marian straight.' I knew what he'd want to discuss. I looked at Poppy, fist in her mouth. Her crying had stopped while my tears dropped onto her bare stomach.

Rob would go back to that December day two years ago. The anniversary of my mom's death was always an awful day but that one had been particularly brutal. The sky was dark with the threat of snow, just like the afternoon she died. From the moment I forced myself out of bed that morning, I'd felt the deep kind of sadness that seeped into my bones and settled in every cell. The air had teeth, its biting cold cut through my coat. I'd bundled Jasper into his stroller, determined to stay busy, keep moving. I took him to the Natural History Museum, to the Central Park Zoo to see the polar bears, places my mom and I had visited together. I remembered the ham and Swiss sandwiches we ate while riding the train from Albany. Just the two of us. 'An adventure,' she'd called it.

I felt closer to her as Jasper and I stood below the blue whale at the museum and smelled roasting chestnuts as we crossed the park.

I'd walked miles behind the stroller, cell phone in hand, waiting for my father to call. We didn't have a ritual – no meeting at the cemetery, no lunch or dinner to share stories, recounting the way my mom started a joke but forgot the punchline and we'd end up laughing anyway. As years passed, I longed to add to my small catalog of memories. When I pressed my father for more about her – how they'd met, interests she'd had before I was born – he'd only say, 'She was a good woman, Laurel. Now stop, please, you know this makes Janice uncomfortable.'

It had been eighteen years. Why did I think that day would be different? Still, Jasper was almost a year old. Each time I saw how Susan doted on him, I ached for my mother. The loss of her was more acute since I'd become a mom. I wanted her support, her guidance, to hear her tell me that motherhood was hard but that I was doing a good job and everything would be fine.

With a blanket over his pale-blue snowsuit, Jasper napped on and off as I trekked dozens of blocks to see the tree in Rockefeller Center. The area teemed with tourists, happy families taking selfies. It was too much. The emptiness stretched and grew inside me, wide and soaring as the mighty evergreen in front of us. As I wheeled Jasper home, snowflakes caught in my eyelashes and I began to cry. When I reached our building, my phone chimed. A text from Rob. *First snowfall!! Get out the Jameson, it's Irish coffee time! Can an eleven-month-old have cocoa?*

A headache spread from temple to temple. Maybe it was the pressure in the atmosphere, Rob's enthusiastic exclamation points, the day, or all of it at once.

I tucked the stroller into the back storage area and carried Jasper up the four flights to our apartment. I stripped off his snowsuit. We'd been gone for hours. His cheeks were chapped. His diaper sagged. I'd give him a bath, make dinner. The day was nearly over. I counted down the hours until I could sleep again on a single hand. The anniversary of a terrible thing – there was no word for it. Maybe a drink with Rob would numb the pain, ease my head.

I lowered Jasper into the tub, placing him in the bath seat Susan had given us. The warm water felt so soothing against my hand, red and cracked from the cold. I left Jasper for a moment to grab a washcloth and the soft froggy towel from Nina. Rob had done the laundry the night before. The basket sat on the floor in front of the bed. I heard the water cascading into the tub, Jasper squealing and clucking. I looked at the white down comforter, soft as a cloud. I'd only rest for a minute. Just a second. Close my eyes. It had been such a long day. Such long years without her. A piece of me gone. The pillow was like a cool, gentle hand beneath my cheek. I began to cry. Tears flowed as water continued spilling into the bathtub. I don't know when I drifted off or how I did so suddenly. Maybe it was the headache, all that walking, bearing the weight of the grief that I carried.

I awoke to Rob screaming my name, grabbing my arm.

'Jesus Christ, Laurel!' He shook me by the shoulders. Jasper lay beside me on the bed, lips blue. 'What the hell are you doing?'

The room was dim, only a half-halo of light traveled in from the bathroom, yet I could see his eyes were wild as a spooked horse's. He pulled me off the bed with such force it was as if our building were on fire. I looked past him, disoriented. Towels covered the hall floor.

Jasper, blubbering, held up his small, chubby hands to me. I touched his fingers, wrinkled as raisins. I could feel the chill coming off him like a draft. We must've run out of hot water. I reached to pick him up, his skin slick as a seal's.

'No!' Rob snapped. 'You do not get to touch him! You do not go near him!'

'I'm sorry,' I said, the first in a string of a million apologies.

'I told you I'd stay home today.' Rob covered his face with his hands, unable to look at me. 'You said no. You said you'd be OK. This is not OK, Laurel! This is not even close to OK!'

His voice took on the slow distorted quality of a talking toy with a draining battery as I stood there, processing how close I'd come to another tragedy.

'My five thirty meeting got canceled. What if I'd stayed, Laurel?' He paced in front of the bed running his hand through his hair. 'The water was up to his neck. *His neck!*' he shouted.

Jasper began to cry. I bent toward him. Rob blocked me and scooped him up. 'You need help, Laurel.'

'I don't,' I sobbed. 'I was just . . . it's the day.'

'You do! For Christ's sake, if I hadn't come home when I did, he could've drowned. Our child could have drowned!'

The words toppled me. I sank to the bed. 'I hadn't meant to fall asleep. Please, you have to believe me.' My insides churned. I thought I'd be sick.

Still, Jasper reached for me. The sweetness of it, the guilt I felt when I looked at him cracked me open. Rob pivoted and swept Jasper's hand into his chest as if I were as dangerous as a hot stove.

'It doesn't matter what you meant to happen, Laurel, what you intended. That's not the point!'

I knew he was right.

I'd promised to find a new therapist, get help, whatever it took to regain his trust, earn his forgiveness. I begged him not to tell anyone – especially his mother.

Was I a negligent, terrible parent? At that moment, yes. But always? No.

Would I forever pay the price in Rob's eyes? Maybe.

As I waited for him to come home, I searched the house for Marian's note. If he found it before I did, if it was somewhere obvious and this had all been for nothing, he'd be even more upset with me.

I turned the place upside down while rocking and shushing Poppy, but I couldn't locate it, which I believed proved my point: Marian was a liar, someone who couldn't be trusted – especially not with our son.

*　　*　　*

It was only in September, when we were packing to move out, that I found Marian's note stuck behind the living-room radiator. The breeze must've blown it there. Dust clung to the adhesive on the back. I studied her handwriting, loopy and large, slanting to the right. *Bringing Jasper to my house for a . . .* She'd drawn a little muffin where the word should've been. *Will return him shortly!*

If I'd seen the note that morning or even that afternoon, would it have been enough to change my mind about Marian? Would I have seen her the way Rob and Jasper did? No, probably not.

My dislike for her was as permanent as the blueberry stains on my shirt.

TWENTY-ONE

Corey

The air stood still, damp and close as a mouth-breather perched on your shoulder. That didn't stop Whispering Palms' power-walkers from taking their nightly laps around the development's retention ponds. Pairs of them circled, eyeing me suspiciously from under their visors thanks to Alice Blackwell's campaign to get me evicted.

Moffatt was ten minutes late. I'd decided to give him another five before I bailed when he rolled up.

'Hey!' he said as I yanked at the handle. The door was locked. 'Whoops, sorry 'bout that.'

Whether he'd had a great day or a shitty one, I couldn't tell. Moffatt had an evenness that made me want to punch the dashboard.

'Hey.' I cringed at the feel of the seat, moist as a wet sponge against the back of my legs. It had been raining on and off all week, but lightly, the universe spitting at me.

He pulled onto the main road. 'Thinking about sharing tonight?' he asked, voice raised to be heard over the screech of his windshield wipers.

Like a slow-motion hangover, a headache was building.

'Sharing what?'

'About yourself, your feelings?' He shook his head. 'What'd you think I meant? Gum?'

He grinned as I chomped the wad of Big League Chew I'd picked up at the liquor store that afternoon.

I turned to look at Moffatt. 'Uh-oh.'

'What?' he asked, serious.

'I'm afraid my sarcasm is rubbing off on you.'

'Wouldn't be the worst thing.' He drummed his thumbs on the steering wheel. 'I've gotten a little soft over the past couple years.'

Funny, I'd gotten hard as diamonds – minus the beauty and the brilliance.

We drove in silence. Without the garden center gig, my days were worthless. When I wasn't up by seven thirty Monday morning, Ma opened the guest room door all flustered and concerned. 'Corey, dear, are you sick? Did you call out?'

'I quit,' I lied.

She'd gasped the way she did when her favorite *Wheel of Fortune* contestants blew the final puzzle.

'When?'

'Saturday.'

'Didn't you give them two weeks' notice?' She pulled a wrinkled napkin from the pocket of her tracksuit and went to town cleaning her glasses. 'That's the professional thing to do, Corey. They've been good to you there.'

What the hell was she talking about? 'Good to me? How?'

'Well, they paid you on time—'

''Cause I worked my ass off.'

'Don't you need to state your place of business on your apartment rental applications?'

I pulled the comforter, its cheap filling bunched into uneven mounds, over my head and groaned like an asshole teenager.

That's probably when my headache officially began.

Moffatt parked and we got out. He aimed his key fob at the van and waited for the chirp.

'Really?' I asked. 'You're worried about *that car* in a church parking lot?'

'You'd be surprised when and where thefts occur.'

I spotted a faint smile and wondered if he wanted to say something like, 'Who'd expect a middle-aged woman to steal a tutu on a Saturday night, am I right?'

We walked into the meeting, same drill as the week before but because we were late the circle was already set up.

After Linda's 'moment of mindfulness,' a woman raised her hand. I'd tried hard not to stare at people during the last meeting so I couldn't remember if I'd seen her.

'Yes, Louise, go ahead.' Linda nodded.

'So I'm just having a day, y'all.' She fiddled with a gold charm bracelet. 'It's Wednesday and that was our day – the day Mama and I'd go to Costco. She loved those free samples. I was cleaning out her sweater pockets this afternoon, getting her clothes ready for donation. I wanted to keep 'em, but Earl says somebody out there could use 'em and that's what Mama would want.'

I shifted in my seat, stuffing down the urge to scream, 'Get on with it!'

She took a breath so big she could've sucked all the air out of the room. 'I found a whole bunch of those white sample wrappers tucked in her pocket. A little stack all smushed together but kinda fanned out too. It looked like a carnation. That was her favorite flower. Y'all, I think she sent it to me, like a sign. I just started bawling.' Her bracelet jangled as she dug through her purse to show us this 'sign.' She held it up to a chorus of 'oohs' and 'ahhs.' 'After Costco, we'd go to her place and split things up: paper towels, that jumbo tub of chocolate-covered raisins, the two pack of Sweet Baby Ray's barbecue sauce.'

Jesus, the level of detail. I hadn't meant to, but I groaned. Moffatt shot me a look. He was probably the only one who hadn't mistaken the sound for commiseration.

'Yes, Corey?' Linda asked. 'Is there something you'd like to share?'

More 'sharing' – as if we were a passel of kindergartners at show-and-tell not grown-ass adults baring our misery.

The fire that burned in the bottom of my belly kicked in like a furnace. Heat spread all over my body. I needed to contain it. 'Nope.' I pressed my lips tight.

'Go on, sugar, you can say anything here,' Louise encouraged. 'I was done anyways.'

That was all it took. 'I get that you miss her and your afternoons buying in bulk or whatever, but . . .' I knew I should stop but I couldn't. 'How old was your mother?'

'She was seventy-nine – would've been eighty in September. I was going to have a party, get one of those Costco sheet cakes. You can feed an army and they're not too—'

'You had your mother for decades!' I exploded, voice bouncing off the cinderblock walls, my hands clenched around the sides of the folding chair. 'A child *should* outlive a parent. That's the natural order of things. Not the other way around. I had my daughter for four years. Not even. Three years, three hundred and fifty-seven days!' Tears slid down my face.

Across the circle, Sara, the girl with the dead twin, looked down at her Crocs. The Costco lady whimpered. Moffatt put his hand on my arm. I shook it off.

'You seem angry, Corey.' Linda spoke with a calm that made me want to rush over and choke her.

'You think?' Snot dripped into my mouth. 'I don't know how not to be. Isn't everyone here fucking furious?'

An older woman tutted.

'Language, please,' Linda reminded. 'Would you like to talk about the anger you're feeling right now?'

'How about the anger I feel all the time? What do I do with it – aside from imagine all the ways I want to punish the people responsible? You got a remedy for that? Or maybe a meditation?' My voice swelled with hatred.

I had to give Linda credit. She didn't react. Just started spouting wisdom she probably picked up from dozens of self-help books and 'Dr Phil' reruns. I closed my eyes and tuned her out. I'd never planned to utter more than 'hello' and 'goodbye' here, but that burning in the pit of my stomach kept getting harder to smother.

When the meeting ended, Moffatt folded the empty chairs. A woman touched his arm and leaned close to whisper something I guessed was, 'How'd you end up friends with the crazy lady?'

I sat, waiting for people to leave, face in my hands. I didn't want to talk to anyone about my outburst, didn't want to see their pitying smiles or listen to that bullshit about the stages of grief – like it wasn't possible to feel them all at once or get stuck in one forever.

Outside the sky was black. The rain had stopped and the air was cooler. August lurked right around the corner. Back in Jersey, fall decorations were probably out cluttering storefronts. Pumpkin spice, Halloween costumes, candy corn every five feet. At least in Florida, it just felt like one long season with varying degrees of humidity.

Moffatt unlocked the van and I got in.

'How about that for sharing?' I tried to make a joke. Neither of us laughed.

He let out a low whistle I couldn't decode. For once, Moffatt seemed to have nothing to say. Had I embarrassed him by taking out my mess and flinging it everywhere?

As we pulled onto the main road, I stared out the window. I couldn't imagine going back to the condo, to Ma and her questions about new jobs and apartments.

'I'll get that drink with you, if you want,' I offered. 'But it sure as shit better be something stronger than coffee.'

Moffatt drove to a bar. The inside was all dark wood, red leather booths and barstools. An old-school jukebox blinked like a carnival ride. A pool table took up most of the back area. The place was packed with couples on dates or groups in business casual clothes, their post-work happy hour spilling from appetizers into burgers and third pitchers of beer. People living their lives without a care in the world. That's what got me: how much the average person took 'normal' for granted.

We ended up at a table for four in the middle of the place. Moffatt sat next to me so we could hear each other over the crowd and the music.

I pressed the heels of my hands to my eyes, burning and itchy from crying. What a wreck I'd become. It had been too hot to run during the day. Without the release, I was jumpy as a dog tied to a chain-link fence.

When the waitress appeared, I took my hands away from my face and cracked my knuckles under the table. We ordered – bourbon for me, a craft beer for Moffatt.

'IPA, eh? I figured you for a Bud Light man,' I said, hoping we could stick to alcohol as our main topic.

'I'm full of surprises.' His smile faded fast and I knew he was waiting for me to say something about the meeting.

'So about what happened back there . . .' I wished the waitress would hurry the fuck up.

Moffatt kept his fingers steepled, his eyes on mine. 'Kind of a breakthrough?'

'More like a breakdown,' I said. 'I – I don't think it's for me – the group thing, you know.'

The waitress brought our drinks. 'Here's a couple menus.' She gave Moffatt a long, appreciative look like he was dessert.

'Thanks,' he said and turned back to me. I'd already started drinking since we weren't exactly about to make a toast. It took everything not to finish in one gulp.

'It's hard at first – getting comfortable talking about it with strangers.' He poured his beer into the frosted pint glass. 'What you said? That constant anger? I felt it, too, but mine was aimed mostly at myself.' He took a baby sip. 'Ava, my daughter, she'd had the tumor for a while before . . .' He waved off the end of that sentence. 'Heather, my wife, my ex-wife, she'd noticed things. Ava'd had headaches and her vision wasn't great. We got her glasses. Thought that would fix it. She had a lot of stomach bugs. But what school-aged kid doesn't? I told my ex, "Stop looking for trouble." I couldn't see any reason to put Ava through a bunch of tests only to be told there was nothing wrong. No one expects them to actually find something, right?' He stopped, took a longer swallow.

For the first time, I was grateful for Jimmy Buffett squawking about cheeseburgers in paradise, filling what would've been brutal silence.

'Bottom line, we lost a lot of time. Because of me. Would six months, a year, have made a difference? I don't know, but I live with that question every day. I took this job to protect people. I couldn't even save my own child.' He looked at his beer, its foamy head gone.

I was the worst at offering sympathy, maybe because I knew that even the kindest, loveliest words didn't help. I wasn't touchy-feely either. I'd never be the type to hold his hand or pat his back. I focused on the menu. A blob of barbecue sauce the size of a quarter blocked the description of the bar's famous nachos. I thought of Louise from the group and her Sweet Baby Ray's twin pack. What an asshole I'd been to her.

'I'm sorry,' was all I could think to say. 'I didn't know what happened . . . with your daughter. Ma would bring it up and I . . .'

He nodded, absolving me. 'Tell you one thing, I appreciate every second I have with my son. You try to find the silver lining, right?'

Sadness sat like a third wheel at our four-top. A whoop erupted from the crowd at the pool table. I was glad for the distraction.

'How's your drink?' He glanced at my almost-empty glass.

That was like asking a kid if they liked chocolate milk. 'It's bourbon. It's fucking great.' I tipped the rest into my mouth, savoring the sweet rush of it, warm and familiar as an old pair of jeans fresh out of the dryer. 'And now it's gone.'

He flagged the waitress and ordered another round. It seemed like a goodwill gesture designed to keep me talking.

'So, earlier you said "people responsible."' He tapped his fingers against the side of his glass, hesitating, as if we weren't already in the middle of some deep, dark shit. 'I'd heard you blamed your ex. Want to tell me about the other person?'

How much could I say without coming off like a nut? How much did he already know?

'There was this woman – a neighbor. She took a shine to Kenny right away, acted like she loved Frankie, our daughter, too. She had no use for me. And that was back when I was somewhat likable.'

Moffatt smiled. Maybe it was the liquor, but my cheeks flushed.

'Anyway, I don't want to get into it because it makes me sound crazy – crazier than you probably already think I am – but I was pretty sure this woman did something that led to Frankie . . .' I bit down hard on the inside of my lip. 'But I couldn't prove it. Still can't. Shit, you probably know all this from "my file" anyway.'

The waitress dropped off our drinks. 'Can I get you anything to nibble on?' She did this weird little rabbity thing with her teeth and hands, blond ponytail swishing from side to side.

Moffatt raised his eyebrows at me.

'Nah, I'm good.' I was starving but I liked the way the bourbon punched harder on an empty stomach, the way it made my head swim.

'We're fine, thanks.'

'I'll check back soon.' The waitress winked. Was it that obvious that Moffatt and I weren't together?

He kept staring at me so I went on. 'Local cops looked into it. Ruled her death an accident. No foul play. They thought I was hallucinating, desperate, looking for someone to blame – other than myself for working too much and missing what was right in front of me.'

Thinking about it stoked that blaze in my gut. I wanted to open the fire door, let it burn and scorch everything in its path. Didn't I owe it to Frankie's memory to do something? And what about the woman who bought my house? Laurel West. Was her family in danger or was my messed-up mind playing tricks on me?

We were quiet for a second. The first licks of a Lynyrd Skynyrd song blared from the jukebox.

Moffatt leaned closer. Compared to mine, his drinks were about as powerful as Capri Suns, but the way his shoulders loosened told me he was a lightweight. 'Want to hear something crazy?' he asked.

'Always.' My voice came out flirtier than I intended.

'It's about Alice Blackwell.' He bugged his eyes.

I smirked. 'I'm all ears.'

'My mom and Alice are in a book club and also a restaurant group where they try new places. After every meeting, Alice leaves nasty reviews online.'

'Only surprise there is that she's tech savvy.'

'Here's the weirdest part . . .' He laughed into cupped hands, making him look boyish despite the skinny lines creasing the corner of his eyes. 'She uses an alias.'

'Nice.' I slapped the table and snorted. 'So what is it? Bitterest Bitch in Boca?'

'Teri J – name of the lady she bought her condo from.' Moffatt shook his head.

'Wow, top-notch investigating.'

'Wish I could take the credit. My mom figured it out. She leaves positive reviews, praising the waitstaff, complimenting an author. She noticed this Teri J was trashing the places she'd just eaten, the books she'd just read. Alice – excuse me, Teri – states her complaints same as she does at meetings. "The chicken was rubbery!" "The music's too loud!"' Moffatt's cranky-old-lady voice was spot-on. 'She hates unlikeable narrators . . .' His blue eyes bounced between my face and my glass. 'And female characters who drink too much.'

I laughed. 'Shocker!'

'When Teri wrote, "You want to read a real novel? Try *A Tree Grows in Brooklyn*," that sealed it for Mom. I swear she'll make detective before I do.' He shook his head. 'Now that I've said this all out loud, man, I need to get a life. Guess it's my turn to say, "Can you not tell your mom about this?"' He drained the rest of his pint glass.

My cheeks hurt from grinning; my body had forgotten how to use those muscles. I needed to pee but I didn't want to break whatever spell it was that had me feeling not terrible for the first time in forever.

His eyes didn't leave mine as he set down his glass.

'What?' I asked.

'Nothing.'

I kicked his foot under the table. 'What?'

'It's nice to see you smile.'

'Don't get used to it.' I pulled my lips into a side pucker.

'C'mon now, you don't want to end up like Bitterest Bitch in Boca, do you?'

'Already well on my way.' I polished off the last sips of bourbon. I wanted another, knowing it was best to leave before I ruined things.

'On the weekends I have my son, I take him over to visit my mom. You want any Whispering Palms gossip, I'm your guy.' He poked his chest with his thumb.

'Noted.' I fought to keep the corners of my mouth from turning up. Music vibrated in my chest, but my headache was gone.

Moffatt raised his hand for the check. 'Afraid I'm gonna have to call it. Got an early start tomorrow.'

A weird wave rippled through me, a feeling I couldn't place. Disappointment?

He threw down his credit card. I pulled two twenties from my wallet. He pushed them back at me. Did he know I'd lost my job?

'Seriously, c'mon,' I said. 'This isn't a—'

'You get it next time.'

As we walked out, a guy behind the bar shouted, 'See ya, Mike!'

Moffatt waved. I wondered if he was a regular and what his life was like on the weekends he wasn't with his son or the evenings he didn't work or have the group.

Outside, the night was clear, the sky wide and navy.

'Better than coffee, right?'

'Ask me again in the morning.' He laughed. 'I live a few blocks from here so I'm gonna walk. You're welcome to stay over.' His eyes searched my face.

The bourbon and his invitation swirled together, stirring something at the base of my body. I stalled for time. 'What about your precious minivan?'

'I can leave it in the lot. Phil, the bar owner, and I play on a softball team together. So . . . how about it?' When I didn't answer, he added, 'I'll sleep in Ryan's room.'

'Ma's up before roosters. She'll have a million questions if I'm not there. But thanks . . . for the offer.' I pulled out my phone and opened the Uber app.

He took a step back. Was he hurt? How much was him being a good guy; how much was more?

'You sure?' he asked. 'You've had a lot to drink.'

He had no clue how much I could handle. 'Car's on its way. I'm good.' I hated that I was sort of curious about his place, that I wondered what would happen if I went. The driver, Melinda, was three minutes away. 'See you next week.'

'I don't like the idea of you going by yourself. I can—'

'Nothing worse can happen to me.' I shrugged. 'You try to find the silver lining, right?'

He frowned. 'I don't know how much help I can be, you know, looking into what happened to your daughter? But I'd like to try.' He swayed a bit.

I pulled him toward me before he bumped into the couple passing behind him. 'Maybe I should see that *you* get home safely, officer.'

He put his hand on my shoulder to steady himself and left it there. His fingers felt cool, strong. In the glow of the bar sign, the kindness in his eyes seemed as infinite as the night sky. He leaned closer. Was he going to kiss me? Would I pull away?

My phone pulsed in my hand. The Uber I ordered lurched to a stop behind us, bass thumping.

'I should go because this is taking on Hallmark movie vibes.' I inched backward toward the car. 'Thanks for the drinks.'

He didn't move, just held up his palm, and smiled.

I slid into the back seat.

The driver turned down the music. Her eyes met mine in the rearview mirror. 'That's right, darlin', leave him wanting more.' She made a jerky K-turn. 'That's what keeps 'em interested!'

I looked down, silent, not caring if she gave me a one-star rating. I was thinking about Moffatt's offer and wondering if maybe he was exactly what I needed.

TWENTY-TWO

Laurel

The doorbell rang. It was Saturday morning. We weren't expecting anyone.

'I'll get it,' I said, glad for an excuse to leave the kitchen where Rob sat paying bills.

Things had been tense between us all week. He'd called from work multiple times each day. With the forced friendliness of a telemarketer, he said, 'Just checking in.'

More like 'checking up.' I'd lived under Rob's microscope before. How long would it continue this time? After I'd fallen asleep and left Jasper in the tub that awful December day, our relationship had been strained for months. He swore he hadn't told his mother about that night but Susan began showing up at our apartment once a week. I hoped Emily's final wedding prep would keep her too busy for that.

In addition to his calls, Rob texted me the names of therapists who accepted our insurance. The idea of starting from scratch – telling someone not just about my past but my present: Rob, the children, Lyle Hartsell, Marian – overwhelmed me. By the time I shared it all, Jasper and Poppy would be adults. I lied and told Rob I'd left messages for several. It was easier than arguing, as much as I wanted to point out that this time I wasn't the problem. Marian was to blame. How would Rob have reacted if she'd taken Jasper while *he* was in the shower?

I'd avoided Marian all week yet there she was, standing on the other side of my front door, holding a blue fluted pie plate, finger poised to ring the bell again.

'Hell-o.' She issued her two-syllable greeting and tilted her head as if addressing a simpleton.

'Hell-o,' I parroted, body rigid, insides simmering. I wanted to say something cutting and sarcastic, like *Did you lose your key*? or *Oh, so you do know how a doorbell works?* But I was frozen.

'It seems like we've gotten off on the wrong foot.' She thrust the dish toward me.

Was whatever lay beneath plastic wrap a peace offering? I kept one hand on the knob, the door pulled close to my back as if we had a pet I didn't want to escape.

'I . . .' How would I finish that sentence? *I want you to stay away from my family.* I didn't get the chance. Rob walked up behind me and swung the door open wide.

'Mimi!' he said in the voice he reserved for his beloved aunts. 'This is a nice surprise. What do we have here?'

Marian's eyes brightened. 'Just a little something I whipped up.' She held the plate aloft as if presenting him with bars of gold. 'I hope you'll enjoy it.'

'Mimi!' Jasper squealed, worming between Rob and me.

'My goodness! What a lovely greeting!' Marian beamed.

'I think I hear Poppy.' I backed away as Rob took the plate. I wondered if it was still hot, hoping he might drop it.

'It's a mixed berry crumble,' Marian said. 'You can top it with ice cream!'

'Ice cream!' Jasper jumped up and down.

Upstairs, I slipped into the bathroom. Sitting on the edge of the tub, I pulled out my phone and texted Addie: *Wine tonight?* It was a long shot – short notice *and* a Saturday. I waited a minute in case she wrote back then stepped into the hall.

Marian's voice, girlish and giddy, floated up the stairwell. 'I won't keep you!'

'Don't be silly,' Rob said. 'Look how happy Jasper is that you're here.'

It was true. My son was practically levitating, so thrilled to see her, as if I'd kept him in solitary confinement.

I crept into Poppy's room and sank into the glider. The air was filled with that warm baby-napping scent that reminded me of baking bread. Through the crib bars, I watched the almost imperceptible rise and fall of my daughter's chest.

Forget about Marian. Focus on Poppy, I told myself. It had been difficult to convince Rob to try for a second child. When Jasper turned two, nearly a year after I'd left him in the bathtub, I found the courage to bring up getting pregnant again. Rob told me he wasn't ready. I knew what he really meant: he wasn't ready to take on more worry. He might have forgiven me for my negligence, but it was clear he'd never forget.

That Christmas, Susan and Dennis gave Jasper a doll that came with a bottle and blanket. Jasper carried him everywhere, tucking him in on the sofa, offering him crackers and brie.

'Wouldn't he just adore a sibling!' Susan's eyes flitted from Rob to me and back to Jasper. 'He'll make such a wonderful big brother!'

'Just like Robbie!' Emily pinched Rob's cheek on the way to refresh her martini.

Though Susan unknowingly helped my cause, sprinkling seeds that took root in Rob's mind, the insensitivity of her comments struck me. What if we'd been trying without success? When it came to the Wests, there were no boundaries they wouldn't push and, ultimately, cross with perfect smiles and the offer of 'another cocktail?'

About a month later, Rob came into the kitchen as I was about to take my birth control pill. He put his hand on mine. 'Maybe don't.'

It happened right away. We'd been lucky. But as I watched him read the word 'pregnant' on the test stick, his happiness didn't feel as pure as it had with Jasper. Even in the operating room, when the nurse placed Poppy on my chest, fear clouded his face. I knew that expression. He was thinking, 'I hope this wasn't a terrible idea.'

But Poppy was here and she was perfect. I listened to her gentle breathing and the tick of the giraffe clock on her dresser. It wasn't even eleven a.m. I couldn't let Marian ruin another day. The front door closed. I strained my ears, hoping she'd gone back to her house rather than settling in for a visit.

I stood and rubbed the bottom of Poppy's socked foot. She didn't move. I pinched her toes. 'Sorry, sweet girl,' I whispered.

She startled and let out a whimper that turned into wailing. I hated to wake her, but if I went downstairs without her, Rob would accuse me of hiding from Marian.

After I changed Poppy's diaper and nursed her, I found Rob in the kitchen, leaning against the counter, staring at his phone.

'Hey, good news!' he said. 'Emily and Colin are stopping by for dinner.'

'What? When?' I asked.

'Tonight.' His thumbs bounced across the keypad. 'Em just texted. They're driving back from visiting Colin's parents. Should be here around six. She's dying to see Jasper and Poppy. It's been a while, right?'

I remembered Emily's voice on the day of her shower. *You know I love Jasper and Poppy to the moon and back, but . . .* The fake sweetness turned my stomach.

'The fridge is empty. I haven't started the grocery list.' I usually shopped on Saturdays. I looked forward to the time alone.

'No problem.' Rob slid his phone into his back pocket. 'I'll pick up steaks, maybe some chicken. We'll grill. And now, thanks to Mimi, you don't have to worry about dessert!'

Her dish rested on the stovetop. Would she be an ongoing presence in our lives? Always lurking? Stopping in whenever she felt like it? How would I deal with that on top of everything else?

'Hey Jasper,' Rob called into the playroom, 'want to go to the store? We can pick out ice cream to go with Mimi's crumble.'

'Yay!' Jasper leapt from his beanbag chair.

'Grab your shoes!' Rob turned back to me. 'Perfect timing. We can ask them about the guardian stuff in person.'

If something happened to us, I couldn't imagine his sister raising our children. Emily's warmth turned on and off like a space heater, and despite how long they'd been together, what did we really know about Colin? 'Rob, I still don't think—'

'Don't think what, Laurel?' His voice was low, his tone impatient. 'If it came down to it, and hopefully it never will, we want them with family.'

How could I argue with that logic? He stopped just short of pointing out that I had little family, few friends. The will and guardianship had been my idea. We were out of options.

I rubbed my temples.

'Listen, Laur.' Rob took my hands in his. 'This is just a precaution. Nothing's going to happen to us.'

I wish he'd been right.

While Rob and Jasper were out, Addie responded to my *Wine tonight?* text.

Sounds great! Your place or mine?

I groaned. *Last-minute change. Bridezilla and fiancé coming for dinner.* I thought about Rob springing Emily and Colin's visit on me. *Join us? Six-ish?*

You sure? Not a fifth wheel?

No way! Would love to have you!

See you soon!

As the steak marinated and the wine chilled, I set five places at the dining-room table. Rob peeked in.

'Little late for Jasper to eat, no?'

'I'll feed him around five, same as always. Addie's joining us.' He opened his mouth, but before he could speak, I added, 'What was it you told me your mother would say? "In for a penny, in for a pound?"' I smiled and placed a steak knife to the right of each plate.

Emily and Colin arrived while I was upstairs getting ready. My daily walks were paying off. I felt stronger, less swollen. A pair of black pants fit again. I paired them with a sleeveless lilac top. I hunted around for the amethyst earrings that had belonged to my mother but couldn't find them.

'Jaspy!' I heard Emily squeal. 'You're getting so big! And, Pops, oh my goodness, your hair! And those cheeks!' Poppy began to cry. I could go to her or maybe if I let her sob long enough, Emily and Colin would turn down the guardian request.

I settled for pearl earrings, jabbing them in place as I walked down the stairs.

Emily spun around. 'Oh, Laurel!' She floated over to air-kiss me. 'You look so much better than the last time I saw you!'

The doorbell rang. Emily froze. 'You didn't invite Mom and Dad, did you, Robbie? I need a night off from them. Did you hear Mom deleted the tracking info for our favors and now two hundred and fifty monogrammed pouches of fair-trade coffee beans are God-knows-where? I should've hired a wedding planner.'

'It's a friend of mine, actually,' I said, opening the door.

'A neighbor,' Rob added.

In a flowy emerald dress, Addie looked like a goddess with her dark hair spilling in long waves around her tanned shoulders.

I introduced everyone and enjoyed watching Emily adjust her

posture, trying to make herself taller as she raked her eyes over Addie. Did she, like her brother, wonder what we could possibly have in common?

Gold bangle bracelets jingled like sleigh bells as Addie handed a bottle of sauvignon blanc to me and a gift bag to Jasper.

'Aw, thank you, you didn't have—'

'Yay!' Jasper flung the tissue paper to the ground and removed a small wooden dachshund on wheels. Its eyes moved side to side as Jasper pulled its red string.

'How retro!' Emily said, her elegant version of a put-down.

As Rob and Colin stood beside the grill, smoke rising, beer bottles in hand, I filled wine glasses for Emily and Addie and poured an inch for myself.

Jasper ran outside and returned with a football. 'Aunt Em, play catch with me?'

'Aw!' Emily winced. 'I would, but I don't want to ruin my manicure.' She wiggled her fingers, her diamond throwing prisms across the ceiling.

Jasper's face fell.

'I'd love to play with you!' Addie placed her glass on the table and swept her hair into a bun as she followed him out the mudroom door.

Through the kitchen window, I saw Colin watching Addie, his gaze lingering as she cheered for Jasper when he snagged the ball out of the air. Her earrings, hammered gold circles that nearly skimmed her neck, shimmered in the late-day light.

Emily kept her back to the window. 'Plus, the mosquitos in New Jersey?' She rubbed her hands up and down her arms and shuddered. 'Gross. I could never live here – no offense.'

Throughout dinner, Emily steered the conversation from one wedding 'nightmare' to another. Her florist's vision wasn't unique; the wedding singer needed back surgery and might not recover in time.

'She has the most magnificent voice, like Bettye LaVette, right, Col?'

'Right.' Colin laughed and refilled his glass. 'Whoever that is.'

'OK, you're cut off,' Emily said. 'I'm driving.'

'Well, if you're driving . . . don't mind if I do.' Colin splashed another two inches of white wine into his glass.

We were on our third bottle. At the rate he was going, we'd soon be on our fourth. I'd begun to relax. There was no way Rob would ask them about the guardianship in front of Addie, and especially not if Colin was drunk.

'Who's ready for dessert?' Rob asked.

'Me!' Jasper marched in from the playroom, something silver raised above his head.

Emily gasped. Rob jumped to his feet. Between the wine and Colin rambling about adding golf clubs to their wedding registry, it took me a few seconds to process what my son held. A knife, its serrated teeth shining beneath the chandelier.

'Jasper!' Rob seized the blade by the handle. 'Where did you get this?'

I came around the table, lightheaded from getting up so quickly.

'In my kitchen. Under the sink,' Jasper said.

'Your play kitchen?' Rob stared at me then Jasper whose head bobbed 'yes.'

I knelt beside my son, turning his hands over, checking for cuts.

'Laurel.' Rob's voice was sharp as the knife's edge. 'How could you leave this in there?' He placed it on the table. Its red pearlized handle gleamed like a Twizzler.

'I – I didn't,' I stammered. 'It's not ours.'

'What do you mean?' Rob demanded. I didn't need to look to know our guests were all staring at me. 'How else would it get there?'

The wine and so many sleepless nights dulled my brain. 'Ours all have black handles with silver circles.'

'That's right,' Emily chirped. 'I remember you'd registered for a cheaper set but Mom insisted on getting you the Wüsthofs.'

'Think Susan would buy me a Scotty Cameron putter?' Colin asked.

Emily shushed him.

Rob ignored them, his jaw square. 'You must've taken it from one of the places you worked.'

'I wore an apron home once, Rob. I never stole a knife.'

'Jasper.' Addie stood as a tense silence fell over the table. 'Why don't we get dessert started?'

'Then where did it come from?' Rob pointed at the knife.

He was waiting for an answer, but I was thinking of something else. The note: *I lost my family. Now yours is in danger.* I hadn't gotten another. Was this a second warning with a more disturbing delivery method? I still hadn't said anything about it to Rob. With everyone there, it wasn't the right time.

I pictured Zoey standing in our kitchen the night she'd been in the playroom, but that was weeks ago.

The hours before Emily and Colin arrived were a blur. We'd been in and out for most of the afternoon. Rob and Jasper went to the grocery store; I walked Poppy to the wine shop. Could someone have come in and hidden it? How long had it been there? Rob still hadn't changed the locks. I'd call someone first thing Monday.

As Addie brought in the mixed berry crumble, I pictured Marian standing on our doorstep that morning.

Had Rob let her inside while I was in Poppy's room?

'The main thing is Jasper didn't cut himself.' Rob rubbed the back of his neck. 'Let's hit the reset button. Laurel, you and I will talk about this later.'

I went back to my seat, confused, powerless, shamed.

As Rob served Marian's crumble, Emily said, 'Just the smallest bit. I have a gown to fit into in a few weeks! You booked the hotel room, Robbie, right? The block's almost sold out.'

'Done!' Rob went to pass me a piece. I waved it off and he gave it to Colin. 'Coming up fast!'

'Who's watching the kids?' Emily asked.

Did she really care or was that her way of reminding me the children weren't welcome?

'My friend Nina,' I said.

Emily's head spun toward Rob. Did she know Nina's nickname?

'She's the one with that unfortunate tattoo?' Emily cringed as if the Roadrunner on Nina's ankle, the result of a drunken dare, were a terminal illness.

When I didn't answer she took a bite and moaned. 'This is outstanding, Laur. One of your best.'

'I didn't make it, actually.' I held Jasper on my lap. I'd given him a scoop of vanilla ice cream but I wouldn't let him have any of Marian's dessert, not knowing what was in it. I squeezed him tight, unable to get the image of the knife in his hand out of my head.

'Laurel would've whipped up something delicious, I'm sure,' Rob added in his salesman voice, 'but our neighbor brought it over.'

Colin smiled at Addie. 'You can throw a perfect spiral *and* bake? Damn!'

Addie shook her head and dabbed her lips.

'Other neighbor.' Rob tilted his head toward Marian's house and shot me a look. What did it mean: *See? She's a good person! I told you!*

I narrowed my eyes, sending a message: *Let's not do this now.*

'What?' Emily wagged her finger from Rob to me, grinning. 'I saw that. What's going on?'

'Hey, Jasper, can you stick the ice cream back in the freezer?' Rob asked.

Jasper raced to the other end of the table. When he was out of earshot, Rob glanced around to make sure the windows were closed. 'Our neighbor, the one who made this, is a lovely older lady.' He smiled and kept his voice low. 'Jasper's crazy about her. But Laurel doesn't trust her.' He served himself a second helping of crumble, one eyebrow arched like he was about to tell a joke.

'Do you think she's like a wicked witch from a fairytale?' Colin asked with his mouth full. 'Like that wolf who dressed up as a grandmother?' Berry juice dribbled down his white shirt, collecting in the pocket, spreading like a bloodstain. 'Was that *Red Riding Hood* or *Hansel and Gretel*?'

'She took Jasper to her house while I was in the shower.' I did my best to keep my voice even. 'When I came downstairs, I had no idea where he was.'

Emily dropped her fork. 'Holy sh—'

'To give him muffins,' Rob jumped in, a smirk on his berry-stained lips.

'Aw, that's kind of precious, actually.' Emily smiled and patted my hand. 'That's what small town living's all about, right? Befriending your neighbors.'

'This was—'

'Aw, Laur, your hormones are turning you into a Mama Bear!' She growled, her hands curled as if they were paws.

Colin let out a laugh and he topped off his wine.

Addie, who'd been quiet through most of dinner, cleared her throat. 'There was nothing funny about it.'

Colin attempted to cover his frat boy chuckle with a cough. Rob hid his grin by taking a sip of water.

'I'm not raising a child and I'm guessing you're not either, Emily, but I think we can both imagine the terror Laurel felt in those moments when she didn't know where her son was.' Addie paused.

I wanted to high-five her as I watched Emily's cheeks flame.

'Even if we weren't talking about a child, no one likes it when a person comes along and takes something that doesn't belong to them – especially without asking.'

'No, right, of course.' Emily deflated.

Because Addie was beautiful, stylish, and well-spoken, I knew her words would carry weight with my sister-in-law, but would Rob hear them?

'Well, it seems like everything's fine now, right?' Emily attempted to cut through the awkwardness. 'Jasper doesn't appear to be trau-matized. Or maybe he does?' Her voice turned playful as she pointed over my shoulder at Jasper who'd left my lap to do a headstand on the sofa.

'Somebody's ready for bed,' Rob said.

'I'll take him up,' I offered, grateful for the perfect excuse to step away and end the conversation.

Jasper said goodnight before heading upstairs. I helped him brush his teeth.

I wished I could've stayed in his room for the rest of the night. It was so peaceful beneath his glow-in-the-dark stars, but I felt guilty leaving Addie down there, a captive audience for Emily's wedding rants.

Jasper's eyes were shut before I finished the second story. I closed his door and peeked in on Poppy, listening for her gentle snuffling. Tiptoeing down the steps, I overheard Emily and Rob discussing Dennis's cholesterol.

'That cheese-of-the-month club probably wasn't a great Father's Day gift, Robbie.'

'Laurel thought it . . .'

So I was to blame for that too. I craved more wine, knowing I needed water. As I turned the corner into the kitchen, I heard faint sucking sounds. Had Rob loaded and started the dishwasher? I looked up and stopped abruptly, eyes adjusting to the light. Colin had Addie pressed against the sink. His mouth covered hers. His hand cradled the back of her neck. On the other side of the wall, Emily laughed at something Rob said. I felt dizzy. Was I imagining it? Would I blink and find myself on Jasper's area rug having dozed off while reading *Julius, the Baby of the World*?

No. It was as real as Colin's thick fingers squeezing Addie's breast inside her dress. He let out a low moan and I gripped the corner of the stove, knocking the kettle into a roasting pan. Addie pushed him and he stumbled back, wiping his mouth on his forearm. He and I stood frozen while Addie smoothed her hair and her dress, her cheeks crimson.

I could barely speak. 'What . . .?'

'I – I should go.' Addie's eyes refused to meet mine. She looked different, messy. I'd never seen her not perfectly composed.

Before I could say another word, she slipped out the side door into the darkness.

Colin pointed after her, spluttering, 'She started it. I swear.'

'Laur?' Rob called. 'Everything OK in there? Did you break something?'

I glared at Colin. I was exhausted, disoriented, but also suddenly sober.

'Please,' Colin pleaded. 'You have to believe me.'

A lump lodged in my throat. I swallowed it and walked shakily toward the doorway that connected the dining room and kitchen. 'Just bumped the kettle. Anyone want tea?'

Colin cut through the living room and appeared at the other end of the table. 'Thanks, but I think we should head back.'

'Party pooper!' Emily stood and tossed her napkin on her plate. 'Let me help clean up first.'

'I've got it. Go,' I said, head spinning.

'If you insist!' Emily smiled. 'Where's Addie?'

Colin started coughing.

'Her mom's care facility called. Some emergency,' I lied. 'She said to tell you goodbye.'

'Yikes.' Emily turned to Rob. 'I am not looking forward to those days with Susan and Dennis!'

Near the front door, Emily leaned in for an air kiss. 'Thanks for having us. Everything was delicious.' She squeezed my arm and smiled. 'And thank you for asking us to be the children's guardians! We're truly honored, aren't we, Col?'

My eyes flashed to Rob. Could Emily see the horror in my face?

'I asked them while you were putting Jasper to bed. I figured Colin had had enough wine, he'd agree to anything.' Rob punched him in the arm. 'Papers are all signed and everything.'

'Just don't go dying.' Colin punched Rob back. 'Em, let's hit the road.' He nudged her toward the door.

Didn't Rob or Em notice how jittery he seemed, how he couldn't even look at me?

'Now, Laurel, watch out for dangerous neighbor ladies!' Emily teased, winking at Rob, the two of them relishing a joke at my expense.

How badly did I want to tell her that her fiancé had his tongue in the mouth of one of my 'neighbor ladies,' his sausage fingers buried in her bra?

The wine had loosened my tongue, too. 'What can I say, Em?' I swung the door open wide. 'If only I were as trusting as you are.'

TWENTY-THREE

Corey

When I got back from my run, Ma was in the kitchen, phone pressed ear to shoulder, sun-spotted hands slicing celery for the tuna salad she made every Sunday after church.

'I'm really pleased to hear that, Irene. Truly,' she said. 'With all he's been through, he deserves to find happiness.'

I usually didn't pay attention to Ma's calls, but my ears pricked at the name 'Irene.' I grabbed a water bottle from the fridge and peanut butter from the pantry. Spooning a wad into my mouth, I stood there eavesdropping on a seventy-five year old.

'Well, that *is* a good sign. Such a nice young man. I'll keep my fingers crossed and my toes, too.' Ma chuckled. 'OK, talk to you soon. Right-o. Bye-bye.' She placed the phone beside the sink, and let out a *tsk*.

'Why are you doing that?' she asked.

'What?'

'Eating straight from the jar.' She swept the celery, cut like little commas, into the bowl.

'Do you eat peanut butter now?' I licked the last bit off the spoon.

'That's not the point.' She exhaled and I heard the familiar rattle in her chest.

'Do you eat it?' I repeated, my bitch switch permanently stuck in the 'on' position.

'You know I don't.'

'Then don't worry about it.' I plunged my spoon into the jar again.

'We have bread.' She sliced an onion, nose twitching. 'It's not difficult to make a sandwich. I'll do it for you if you'd like. I'm happy to see you eat something. But don't spoil your appetite. I opened two cans of tuna today.'

As if I couldn't smell it. The whole place reeked like seagulls had landed in the kitchen. I gulped the water and nodded toward the phone. 'What was that about?'

'Irene Moffatt.' She knocked a jar of onion powder against the counter. The humidity made it clump. 'She thinks her son, Mike, the one who's a police officer, the one—'

'I know, Ma. Jesus. I don't have dementia.' I squeezed the plastic water bottle. Its angry crinkle made her jump and then go stiff with annoyance. We were losing patience with each other. I needed to dial it down or she'd start up about apartments and jobs again.

She took a breath. 'Irene thinks maybe he's found someone.'

'Like a missing person?'

'No, Corinne. A girlfriend.'

My turn to tense up. 'What makes her think that?' I never asked questions. Would she get suspicious or would she simply be thankful I was making conversation?

'Well, she noticed he sounded a little more chipper the past couple of days.' She reached for the mayo. 'Irene invited him for supper tonight. Sundays are hard on him once his son goes back to his mom and all. Anyway, Mike said he's planning to ask a gal to dinner.'

The peanut butter glued my tongue to the roof of my mouth.

Ma wiped her hands on a dishtowel. 'She sounded relieved. I think she's been more worried about him than she lets on.'

'Huh.' I hated how much I wanted details, all the details.

'It's nice to have someone to share things with.' She looked at me over the top of her glasses but knew better than to say another word. The last time she tried the whole, 'You're only thirty-six, there's still time for you to start over,' I'd pelted her with an angry 'Stop!' through gritted teeth.

'I'm gonna take a shower.' I stuck the peanut butter in the pantry, pinching my fingers in the crack of the door, to get my mind off Moffatt. The sting wasn't enough to make me forget *his* fingers on my shoulder, his eyes shining beneath the streetlight outside the bar on Wednesday night.

I'd just stumbled out of the Uber and into the condo when he texted *Home safe?* He was so earnest, if I ignored it, I could see him calling his own ride to come over and make sure I was all right. So I wrote back: *Yup.*

The bourbon had made my head light, my body liquid. It also made me dreamy, curious. *Would he write back?* I'd stared at the phone as I kicked off my shoes.

If he did, what would he say? I'd wondered as I sat on the toilet in the dark and peed for two straight minutes.

This wasn't part of the plan, jackass. I'd stuffed my phone in the bottom of my duffle bag in the corner of the guest room. I'd gotten in the habit of shutting it off for days at a clip. Each time it randomly served up photos of Frankie – *Here's a memory from two years ago!* – my heart imploded.

I wouldn't miss anything except maybe a text or two from Desiree. Earlier in the week she'd sent a video of a cat eating frozen yogurt. I gave it a thumbs-up. *Hang out soon?* she wrote. I hadn't replied.

The phone was still off, buried beneath clothes that now hung off me.

I turned on the shower and stepped under the trickle. Old dogs could piss with more force.

Who was Moffatt inviting to dinner and why the hell did I care?

I dropped the soap and stared down at my stomach, my legs, lean and hard. After I had Frankie, I'd been soft for so long. That body was gone. Both of ours. I was a different person.

On some level Ma was right. I could start over, but I wouldn't until I set things right, until I dealt with Frankie's death on my own terms. Moffatt had offered to help me with that, but our views on closure were drastically different.

I had to focus on that – not on the way he looked at me without pity or judgement – or how he'd seen the darkness in me and hadn't flinched.

But if he was interested in some 'gal,' where did that leave me?

Even after the shower, my skin itched like fire ants were scrambling through my veins. I couldn't stay in the condo. I got dressed fast, ran a brush through my wet hair, fished my phone out of the duffle bag, and grabbed my wallet.

Ma sat at the kitchen table eating her sandwich. An identical one waited for me on a paper plate.

I swiped her keys from the alligator holder. 'I'm going to the bank.'

'It's Sunday. Bank's closed.'

I'd been out of work one week; did she think I'd forgotten which day it was?

'The ATM,' I said. I'd started going every few weeks, then every couple days, withdrawing a chunk at a time, money from the house sale. I kept it in a shoebox in the back of the closet.

'I have cash,' Ma offered. Gritty crumbs from the bottom of her English muffin rained down as she rubbed her fingers together.

'Thanks, but I want to get out for a bit.'

'You were just out, Corinne.' A blob of tuna salad plopped onto her plate. She licked her thumb and stared at me. 'Where do you go?'

'Huh?'

'You're gone such long stretches. Even now, I'm sure you won't be back for hours, right?' She waved a napkin toward the door. 'What do you do out there?'

Why was she asking? Had Moffatt said something to his mother and she put it in Ma's head? I hadn't gone back to the neighborhood where I stole the tutu and he hadn't asked. Had he enlisted Irene to do it for him? The imaginary ants under my skin marched faster.

'Just around, you know. Checking out different areas for apartments,' I lied.

'Well, if you'd like company, I'd be happy to go with you sometime.'

'Thanks,' I mumbled. She still had the power to make me feel small, guilty. Or maybe I did that all by myself.

I sat in the Corolla, wallet and phone on the passenger seat. In the rearview, I saw Alice Blackwell watching me while she watered her pots of zinnias. I wanted to give her the finger. Instead, I gripped the steering wheel until it seared my palms, then gunned it in reverse, and got a messed-up thrill watching her scoot back onto her walkway afraid I'd mow her down.

At a red light, I glanced at my phone. Still off. I needed to know if Moffatt texted back Wednesday night or since. I didn't want to care either way. I looked at the clock on the dashboard: 12:52 p.m. At one o'clock, I'd turn it on, go from there.

At the ATM, I withdrew the maximum, counted the bills, and stuffed them in my pocket.12:59 p.m. The phone might as well have been a bomb, that's how gently I moved it into my lap, black case scorching my thigh. I pressed the button, placed it back on the seat and waited for it to glow to life. The pinging pulled my eyes off the road and toward the bright green of a new message, followed by another and another and another. It was either Ma, Desiree, or Moffatt. I'd blocked Kenny months ago.

I picked up the phone and swiped, steering with one hand.

My place?

Tonight?

Want to have dinner?

Had fun last night.

My head buzzed. Moffatt. I checked the time. He'd sent three around noon today and one on Thursday morning. I looked up. I'd driven past the turn I should've made, my eyes dipping down to read the messages in order.

Had fun last night.

Want to have dinner?

Tonight?

My place?

I heard it before I saw it. A horn. A car speeding toward me. I'd crossed the double yellow line. I dropped the phone. Tugged the wheel hard to the right. Another horn blared, this time behind me as I swerved back into my lane without looking. I braced for impact, a cold sweat sweeping over me. When I glanced in the rearview mirror, the car was nearly in my back seat, but we hadn't collided. I pulled to the shoulder.

'Learn to drive, bitch!' the passenger shouted as they passed. My arms were too weak to even flip him off. Plus, it was my fault.

I rested my forehead on the hot steering wheel and took a dozen deep breaths. Then I read the texts again.

Want to have dinner?

Tonight?

I was the 'gal', the reason Moffatt seemed – what had Ma said? 'A little more chipper?'

My fingers typed 'yes' before I could stop them.

In the late afternoon, Ma went to the clubhouse to watch *Singin' in the Rain*. She invited me to join her but I told her I was meeting up with people from the garden center.

Moffatt texted his address. I pulled an unopened bottle of Maker's Mark from my closet stash. The whole way over, my heart stopping and starting again, I told myself I was going there for one reason.

He opened the door before I knocked.

'Hey.' He smiled.

I heard noises inside, high-pitched musical notes. 'You got a bird in there?'

He stepped outside and pulled the door shut behind him. 'My son, Ryan, is here. Heather – his mom – was supposed to pick him up, but she's running late. I told him you were coming by, that you're my friend from the group.'

I handed him the bottle of whiskey. 'Well, I'm sure as shit not your personal trainer.'

The skin around his eyes creased as he grinned, but he didn't move to open the door. My heart did a little stutter-step.

'Look, if this is weird, I can go. I mean, if that's easier.' I tried to read his face. 'I will need to take that bottle back with me though,' I joked, hoping to hide the waves of disappointment rippling through my belly.

'No, no, I'd like you to stay. I didn't want to cancel, I just didn't want you to walk in and . . . I don't know . . .' He frowned.

'See a child and freak out?' It clicked. 'I can be around kids. How old is he?'

'Nine.'

I nodded. I didn't want things to get dark or serious. 'I won't steal any of his shit if that's what you're worried about . . . unless he's got a tutu.'

'Well, in that case, come on in.' He stepped back and I walked past him, my bare arm brushing his.

It was pretty generic inside, like he'd gone to a furniture store and bought an entire display, right down to the big circular wall clock and a bowl of twine balls that I couldn't imagine served much purpose.

'Nice place.'

'Thanks. My mom kind of took over the decorating. Did a good job except she put out these little dishes of potpourri. Ry and I each took a mouthful thinking they were fancy chips. Remember that, Ry?' he asked the boy sitting in the middle of a beige sectional playing a video game on the large flat screen. The kid ignored him as his fingers jabbed at the controller.

'Ryan,' Moffatt tried again, 'this is my friend, Corey.'

'Hey.' I waved.

The boy came out of his gaming trance, dropped the controller, walked over and shook my hand. His dark hair was a little longer than a crew cut. His eyes were blue but not as light as his dad's.

'I was going to make my famous shrimp fra diavolo, but Ry wanted pizza. Hope that's OK,' Moffatt said.

'Who doesn't like pizza?' Jesus, I hated how peppy and fake I sounded.

'I'm just gonna grab cash for the tip.' Moffatt disappeared down the hall.

'You can sit,' the boy said, 'if you want to.'

'OK.' I left an empty cushion between us.

'Ever play Minecraft?'

'Nope.'

'Wanna learn?'

'Not really.'

Moffatt returned empty-handed. 'Must've left my wallet in the van.'

'I have cash.' I pulled a wad of twenties from my pocket. I'd have given him a hundred bucks not to be left alone with a nine-year-old stranger.

'Be right back.' The door closed before I could say, 'I'll go with you.'

Rain started falling in the video game, but the kid wasn't playing. He was staring at me.

'You have it too?' he asked.

'Huh?'

'A hole.'

'Excuse me?'

'A hole! In your heart.' He pressed his hand to his chest, Pledge of Allegiance style. 'A hole . . . where the person used to be. My dad said . . .' He looked down, cheeks reddening the way Ma's did when I said the F word. 'My dad said you've got one too.'

'Right.' I knocked my fist against the middle of my rib cage. 'Yeah, I guess I do.'

'Dad said it shrinks a little bit at a time and then one day, it may just close up and I won't feel it. Or not as much.' He shrugged, tossed his controller in the air and caught it.

That sounded like some Linda-based bullshit. I hated to act like her, but I couldn't stop myself. 'And how do you feel about that?'

'I don't want it to.' He shook his head real fast. 'What if that means I forget her? If she's in the hole and it closes, she's gone, like forever.' He frowned and scratched behind his ear.

Where the hell was Moffatt?

'I know what you mean,' I said. 'The hole makes you feel awful, but it reminds you how much you loved that person, right? Sucks either way. Shit, sorry, that's not helpful, is it?'

He smiled.

'What?'

'My dad said you ought to come with a foul-language warning.' I smirked. 'He sure as hell isn't wrong.'

Ryan giggled, then looked at the door. 'Want to see where my dad keeps his gun?'

My eyes went as wide as his. 'You bet I do.'

'Look what I got!' Moffatt walked in carrying two large pizzas and a white bag with a growing grease stain. 'Perfect timing. Found my wallet under the cupholder when the delivery guy drove up.'

'It's in a box in a drawer next to his bed,' Ryan whispered.

'How does he open it?' I whispered back.

He held up his hand and wiggled his index finger.

'Come and get it while it's hot,' Moffatt said.

'It's summer, Dad, it can't not be hot!'

The three of us ate on the couch.

'Mom never lets me do this.' Ryan bounced on a cushion, oil dribbling down his chin. 'You think she'll be more chill when she and Gary get married?'

On a scale of one to ten, Moffatt's wince was a five. If I hadn't been sitting there, would it have been at least a twelve?

'Guess we'll have to wait and see,' he said.

We talked about baseball. Ryan asked my favorite team (the Yankees), where I liked to sit when I went to a game (the bleachers, 'cause the fans were more interesting), and did I think it was weird that his dad didn't like hot dogs (yes).

I didn't mind the questions. I'd been in my own world so long I'd forgotten how to talk to people – especially sober. But seeing them together was a reminder. As much as Moffatt tried to act like it, he and I weren't the same. He had this great kid to live for. I had nothing.

The doorbell rang. Ryan muttered, 'Mom,' like she was the ultimate buzzkill, but he might have done that for his dad's benefit.

As I watched Ryan sling his Spider-Man knapsack onto his shoulder, I thought of Ma saying, 'Sundays are hard on him once his son goes back.'

'Good to meet you.' I stood and jerked my thumb toward the hall. 'Gonna use the bathroom.'

I wanted to see Moffatt's ex, but it was better to avoid the situation. I wondered how long Moffatt would be distracted. Did I have time to sneak into his room, open that drawer?

After a minute, I shut off the water and pressed my ear to the bathroom door, straining to listen.

The knock made me jump.

'They're gone. You can come out now,' Moffatt said.

I took a second to look in the mirror – not great, not awful – and opened the door, expecting to see him standing there, but he was in the kitchen holding the bottle I brought.

'How about a drink?' he asked.

'Sounds good.' Without the boy there, I suddenly felt awkward.

'It's cooled down a bit.' He handed me a glass. 'Want to sit outside? Enjoy the view?'

I followed him onto his balcony overlooking a dumpster and slid into a white Adirondack chair.

'Handsome kid,' I said. 'Looks nothing like you.'

'You were right the other night – this is definitely taking on Hallmark movie vibes.' He smiled, touched his glass to mine and took a sip. 'Ryan liked you. I could tell.'

'I'm good with kids and dogs – not so great with adults, even worse with old people.'

'Alice Blackwell, case in point.' He swished the ice around, the liquid making it crack and pop.

The breeze picked up and blew a folded-over newspaper off a low table. We reached for it at the same time, nearly bonking heads. Our faces were inches apart, his eyes, warm and hopeful, met mine. My insides flipped, pushing the air out of my lungs. I looked away, turning the paper over. He'd almost finished the *Sunday Times* crossword puzzle.

'You really are full of surprises,' I said.

He reached for my hand. 'I like you, Corey.'

'That's probably a bad idea.'

'Let me help. Give me the names of the people – person – you think could be responsible. I'll do some digging.'

I nodded. He leaned closer and touched my chin. Goosebumps spread up and down my arms. I didn't want to feel them. I needed to not care. This wasn't a movie – one of those stupid 'love grows out of sadness' tearjerkers with a ridiculous happy ending. Fuck. That. I was here for something else.

But I could smell the bourbon on his breath. I liked the way it mixed with his wholesome clean scent. I closed my eyes and didn't pull away.

TWENTY-FOUR

Laurel

Finding Addie and Colin kissing haunted me. Even if they'd had too much wine, that was no excuse. Despite Colin's immature 'She started it,' he'd been the one pressing her against the sink, his hands everywhere. Yet, until I bumped the kettle, Addie hadn't shoved him away.

I'd wanted to tell Rob as soon as Emily and Colin left, but I was furious with him for asking them to be our children's guardians – especially when I wasn't in the room. If I told my husband what I'd seen, I imagined him twisting the situation, making it my fault for inviting Addie. He'd want me to end our friendship. I couldn't. Addie had been there for me so much more than he had the past few months. She had my back with Marian. She listened when I spoke about Lyle. She talked me down when I opened that threatening note. Her friendship felt like a rare and unexpected gift. I wasn't ready to give that up.

Seeing Colin all over her with his fiancé in the next room confirmed he could never be part of Jasper and Poppy's future. The guardianship paperwork sat on the kitchen table inside a salmon-colored folder awaiting my signature. I ignored it. There was something more disturbing I needed to address. The knife. The image of it in my son's small hands left me shaken, unable to focus on anything else. My mother had been murdered – nothing could happen to my children.

Sunday morning, while Rob played with Jasper in the backyard, I left messages for locksmiths. I considered buying cameras, placing them by the front and side doors, in the playroom and children's bedrooms, but I knew Rob would object to the expense and insist the knife was mine.

Monday couldn't come fast enough. With Jasper and Poppy down for their afternoon naps and Rob at work, I sat at our dining-room table waiting to see Marian back out of her driveway. Her garden club met every Monday at three p.m.

At two forty-five, she left her house, straw bag over her shoulder. I forced myself to stay still until I saw her Subaru rolling toward the corner, then I slipped out the mudroom door and hurried across our backyard into hers, determined to find the rest of the knife set. When I did, I'd show it to Rob and he'd finally see Marian for who she was.

Her back door was unlocked. I snickered. People didn't realize how unsafe the world truly was. *I knew.*

For a moment before I stepped inside her avocado-colored kitchen, I wondered if I could be wrong. What if the knife wasn't Marian's? What if Lyle Hartsell was lurking, waiting to hurt my family? It was possible. But the woman next door, who seemed to despise me from the moment we met, who'd been to our home the day the knife appeared, was the more likely suspect.

I left Marian's back door open a crack and tiptoed in like a burglar. A cookie jar shaped like a pig wearing a chef's hat and an electric can opener sat on one countertop. A wooden breadbox rested on the other. I opened the drawer beside her stovetop and found pens, paperclips, coupons for Metamucil. I moved to the drawers on the other side of the sink. They weren't on rollers and made an awful screech as I shimmied them loose to look inside. Utensils were stacked in a gray plastic organizer. The other drawer contained spatulas, a whisk, and a meat thermometer. No knives matched the one Jasper had held, but I wasn't finished looking.

As I headed into the dining room, the sound of crushed gravel in the driveway traveled through an open living-room window. I ducked behind the far side of the china cabinet, pulse quickening. What would I say if she caught me?

The front door opened and closed.

'Eleanor? It's Marian. I forgot the minutes from last week's meeting. Start without me. I'll be there as soon as I can.'

The steps creaked as she headed upstairs. I chewed my bottom lip and focused on the framed prints of irises hanging on each side of her dining-room window. The chandelier twitched. She was directly above me.

I kept my back pressed against the wall as the staircase groaned again. The front door opened. It was almost over.

'Now how'd that happen?' she mused.

Was she still on the phone? No. She was moving toward the kitchen, her footsteps growing closer. She was on the other side of the wall. The back door had blown open. She was going to close it. A light breeze whispered around my bare ankles, making me shiver. Lacing my fingers together, I tried not to breathe. She was inches from me. Out of the corner of my eye, I saw her cotton ball of hair and thought I might faint.

I was trespassing. I had no proof Marian was guilty of anything other than being overbearing and rude. But my gut told me she'd put the knife there.

The back door clicked shut. Were the kitchen drawers the way I'd found them? Sweat slid down my spine. I closed my eyes. Waited. I could no longer hear her footsteps over the pounding of my heart in my ears.

Finally, the front door closed. When the sound of gravel turning over came again, I exhaled and all but collapsed on her dining-room floor. I wanted to keep searching, but I was shaking from that close call. What would I have done if she'd found me? What would she have told Rob?

Legs weak, I stumbled back to my house, storm clouds gathering overhead, flies swarming above the creek, more desperate than I'd felt in years.

*   *   *

Months later, when Marian's son held an estate sale to clear out her house, I found the set. Two slots in the block were empty. I bought it anyway. I keep the knives in my new kitchen. Their blades are dull but they're a sharp reminder that you can never be too careful about who you let into your home.

TWENTY-FIVE

Laurel

Colin's messages started arriving Monday afternoon. He must've found my number in Emily's phone. Each one was cryptic, coded. For someone so boorish and sloppy, he could also be quite cunning.

His first voicemail came shortly after I'd returned from Marian's:

Hey Laurel, it's Colin. Thanks for dinner Saturday night. I may have been over-served. Just calling to apologize for any questionable behavior.

Texts followed an hour later:

No need to say anything and get people worked up over nothing, right?

You know how much this family means to me.

He sent others the next day:

What did she tell you?

Things aren't always what they look like. Remember that.

You should get some new friends.

And the day after:

I know you're busy in Mommyland, but I'd appreciate a response!!

I wasn't going to engage with him until I knew what I wanted to do. I went over and over it as I sliced apples for Jasper's snack, as I nursed Poppy, as I stared at the ceiling wide awake at three a.m. Each time I closed my eyes I saw Colin and Addie together, their bodies strange and distorted in the reflection of the kettle's shiny silver surface.

The wedding was just weeks away. If I told Rob, and if he told Emily, would they believe me? Even if they did, I wasn't sure it would be called off. So much time, effort, and money had been poured into the whole event, it was like the runaway train from the book I read Jasper. It was too far down the track to be stopped.

* * *

Each time my phone pinged I hoped it was Addie writing to explain what had happened, but it was always Colin, continuing his text assault. As days passed and I ignored his messages, they became more aggressive.

It's my word against yours.

Along with the wedding, Colin's livelihood was at stake. Dennis had called in a favor to secure him a job after the line of craft beer he'd started with a fraternity brother failed spectacularly. Susan and Dennis were generous – as long as you were doing right by their children. One phone call from Dennis had the power to upend Colin's life, and he knew it.

We all think you're fragile. Maybe even unstable. Susan and Dennis worry about your mental health, did you know that? You left a knife in your kid's playroom. WTF?

When I read it, my hands shook so badly I dropped the phone and slid to the floor.

You should've seen how she was flirting with Rob.

Open your eyes!

I was being harassed by the man who could end up with my children if anything happened to Rob and me. The anger left me lightheaded. I picked up my phone, a spiderweb of cracks splintered the screen, and wrote:

Text me again and I'll tell everyone I've ever met.

It had been a day since he'd last written. Still nothing from Addie.

At the sink, I rinsed and peeled carrots while facing Addie's home, wondering if our friendship could get back to where it had been. Jasper was at my feet, pulling the wooden dog she'd given him.

'Mommy? Is this money?' He handed me a gold disc.

Addie's earring. I pictured Colin's fingers against her neck. I'd taken her silence to mean she was embarrassed, complicit, not ready to talk about it, but after Colin's messages, I was certain she was a victim, not a participant. I owed her an apology.

I stared at her house, broken earring in my soapy hand. Poppy was asleep. I grabbed my phone and texted her. *Want to have coffee? Here?*

It took a minute, maybe two before dots appeared and then vanished just as quickly. Finally, she wrote: *Sure. When?*

Now?

She responded with a thumbs-up.

I waited for her on the living-room sofa. The sky was gray, the air cooler. An August breeze carried the first hints of autumn. Leaves rustled as a light rain fell.

'Hey,' she said as I opened the door.

'Hi.' I smiled, admiring the light-blue cardigan she wore over a white tank top. 'Want to sit in the kitchen? There's coffee and Jasper and I made apple cinnamon squares this morning.'

She followed me and took a seat at the kitchen table, tucking a leg beneath her. 'I'm so sorry—' she began.

'No,' I interrupted. '*I'm* sorry. I should've reached out sooner. I just—'

'When he came up behind me, I should've pushed him off right away.' Addie swept her long hair over to one side and shook her head. 'It's just . . . I spend so much time working or focusing on my mom.' She stirred cream into her coffee. 'It's been a while – not that that's an excuse. It sounds dumb or selfish, but it felt nice to be wanted. Even though . . .' She wrinkled her nose the way Jasper did when Poppy had an explosion. 'Colin's . . .'

'Gross? A loser? A lecherous jerk?' I kept my voice low. Jasper was nearby pretending to do magic tricks for his stuffies.

'All of the above.' Addie picked at an apple square and sighed.

I must've been frowning.

'What?' she asked.

'I didn't date much, and I'm sorry if this comes off as prying, but . . .' With only a swipe of mascara and a hint of lipstick, she was still one of the most attractive women I'd ever seen in real life. 'I can't imagine you'd have a hard time finding someone.'

'You have no idea.' She laughed and covered her face with her hands. 'The thing is, I tend to make bad choices.' She flicked crumbs from her fingertips. 'I trust someone and then they disappoint me. When my engagement ended, I was pretty messed up, like, really lost, for a while.' She blew on her coffee. 'So I took a break for a bit.'

I waited, hoping she'd say more.

'I was seeing a guy – this was a little over a year ago – and, well, it's a long story. Promise not to think less of me?'

I nodded.

'He was married.' She paused, gauging my reaction. I kept my face neutral. I didn't want her to stop talking.

'He swore he was leaving his wife – said he loved me and we'd be together. This went on for months.' She laughed. 'What a cliché, right? He had a child and he couldn't bring himself to break up the family. It got complicated and it ended badly. Believe me, I'd never do that again.' She shuddered like she wanted to shake off the memory. 'After that, I dated a guy who worked in town, but that didn't last long. So it's been a while. Colin caught me off-guard and I got swept up in the moment. I'm sorry.' She put her hand on my arm. 'I know I've put you in an awful spot.'

'No, I'm the one who should apologize,' I said. 'I've never been a fan of Colin's but I didn't think he—'

'Have you told anyone? Rob?'

'No.' I looked toward the playroom. Jasper was busy at his train table. 'We've hit a rough patch the past few weeks and I didn't want to make things worse.'

'Want to talk about it?' Addie sipped her coffee.

I glanced at the documents at the other end of the table. The paperwork for our will was complete, tucked neatly inside the orangey-pink folder. Rob had filled in Emily and Colin's names. All I needed to do was send everything back to our attorney.

'I thought we should draw up a will. Rob wants Emily and Colin to be the children's guardians.'

Addie set down her mug. 'I heard. I hope I'm not overstepping, but I couldn't believe he asked them without you there.'

My chest tightened. 'We'd talked about it, but, yeah, it was really . . .'

'Disrespectful.' Addie tore an apple square in half. 'I mean, these are your babies.'

'Totally,' I agreed. 'But at the same time, it's like, who else could we ask? I'm an only child. My closest friend is halfway across the world most of the time. Emily is family, even if . . .'

'She's a b-i-t-c-h.' She spelled it, knowing Jasper was probably listening. 'I mean, Bridezilla is the tip of the iceberg.'

I laughed ruefully while Addie clicked her nails against her mug.

'Hey!' she said, blue eyes wide and twinkling. 'What about me? I mean, of course, I hope you'd never, ever need me, but what about putting my name down as guardian? I adore your children. I have a job, a house.' She swept her open palm toward her lovely, well-kept home.

Her idea made me sit up straighter. It seemed crazy. I'd known her less than two months. But at the same time, she'd tossed the football with Jasper while Emily worried about her nail polish. And then there was Colin, groping her with his fiancé ten feet away. Still, putting Addie's name in place of theirs seemed reckless, insane, and yet I thought about Rob's words: 'Hopefully, it won't ever come to that.'

It was tempting, but I hesitated. 'I'd love that, but Rob already—' I pulled the folder close and opened it. Emily and Colin's names stared up at me.

'I'll take the papers back to my office. I have a scanner and a printer. I'll make some changes, then you send them back.' She smiled. 'Rob will never know. I'm sure you'll live to be a sweet little old lady making these fabulous apple squares for your grand-kids. It'll be our secret.' She lowered her voice. 'Your own little F-U to Emily and Colin.'

I sat with it for a moment, waging an internal debate. Rob would kill me if he found out, but maybe he never would.

'When I handled everything for my mom, it was like a crash course in wills, estates, and trusts,' Addie continued. 'Exhausting, but I learned a lot. Sometimes I had to get a little creative.' She winked.

Was she going to replace their names with her own? I almost asked but didn't want to know. Switching the guardian behind my husband's back seemed mad, a major breach of trust, but it was also kind of perfect. I was so angry – at him, Emily, and especially Colin. His text – *Susan and Dennis worry about your mental health* – screamed like a siren inside my head.

I thought about Addie's compassion when I told her about my mother's murder and Lyle Hartsell's release. If anything happened to us, I'd want Jasper and Poppy to be raised by someone loving, someone who listened.

But there was a question I needed to ask, and I had to do it delicately. Because of losing my mom and not having any siblings, all I'd ever wanted was a family of my own. Not every woman felt that way, and I understood – even more so since becoming a parent. I needed to know Addie was all in.

'Sorry if I'm prying again, but . . . raising kids? Is it something you'd really want?'

'After seeing you with yours,' she squeezed my arm, 'I think, yes, I'd love it.'

I ruffled the papers. 'How – how would you do it?'

'Don't worry, everything will look completely authentic,' she said. 'My mom's documents were filed without a second glance.'

It would be so nice to take back some of the control I'd lost, to have a say in this enormous decision. Addie's warmth, wisdom, and willingness to take charge were exactly the qualities a parent should possess. Still, could I do something so impulsive?

'Thank you.' I placed my hand on hers. 'I'm so grateful you'd even consider it. Let me think it over a little longer.'

A flash of disappointment clouded her face. Understanding quickly replaced it.

'Of course! Take your time,' she said. 'Before I found the right home for my mom, I was a wreck. I know this is different, but at the end of the day you want to know that the people you love most are in good, safe hands.' .

'Totally.' I slid the papers back into the folder.

Addie stood. 'I should probably head back to work.'

I walked her to the front door.

She stopped and picked at the brown wreath I still hadn't changed.

'There's something I wanted to . . . I hope I'm not . . . When I was coming back from my run this morning, I saw Zoey and Rob talking. It looked like they were exchanging numbers.'

An anxious fluttering filled my stomach.

She touched my arm again. 'I thought you should know.'

TWENTY-SIX

Corey

Ma switched off the television, bringing another afternoon of riveting court TV to a close.

'It's time, Corey.'

Jesus, what now? Sometimes she wanted to talk about her 'end of life plans,' like things weren't depressing enough.

'Time for what?' I tried not to jump down her throat. Maybe it

was something simple like, 'Time to defrost the chicken for
tomorrow night's dinner.'

'Time to find you a new place.' She took off her glasses, probably so she couldn't see my face, and rubbed her eyes. 'I made an
appointment for Saturday.'

'If this is about Alice Blackwell again, I swear I'll slash her tires.'

Ma sighed. 'You shouldn't talk like that, Corinne. You're a grown
woman. Wouldn't you like a place of your own?'

'I'm working out a plan.'

'You said that before and then you quit your job.'

Her voice held so much disappointment it was as if I'd resigned
from my post as Secretary of State, not part-time plant-waterer. She
put her glasses on and slid them up the bridge of her nose.

'Now I know you're – what do they call it, between jobs? But
you have all that money in the bank. That should count for something, right? And I'd be happy to co-sign your lease agreement if
it helps.'

I put my feet on the coffee table, knowing she hated that, and
folded my arms across my chest. 'Wow. You're that desperate to
get rid of me?' Sweat pooled in my armpits.

'Please don't do that.'

'Do what?'

'Twist this around.' She fiddled with the zipper on her lime
tracksuit. 'It's just that this isn't good – you sitting around all day
like this. It's not healthy. You go for those runs and I don't know
how smart that is in this heat. You barely eat. I want more for you.
I want *you* to want more for yourself.'

'So what you're saying is if I'm going to waste my life, you'd
prefer not to watch?' My face burned. 'I forgot that you're busy
curing cancer in that back bedroom.'

Ma hung her head. Her sagging shoulders rose as she took a deep
breath that led to a coughing fit. 'That's not . . . I want you to make
a life for yourself. Yes, you've suffered a terrible loss, but you can't
hide from the world forever.'

'Oh, you mean like you did after Dad died?' I snorted. 'You
couldn't run away fast enough.'

'We've been over this, Corey. I couldn't be in that house anymore.'
She pulled a tissue from her pocket and dabbed the corners of her
mouth. 'There was nothing left for me there.'

'*I* was there!' My voice hovered between a whimper and a growl. 'Not in that house, but nearby. You knew Kenny and I were trying to have a baby. Sorry I couldn't make it happen fast enough for your timetable.'

'You were busy with your own life. You and Kenny and your new home. You didn't need me—'

'I did need you! I'd just lost my father. My marriage was turning to shit even then with Kenny changing jobs and the cost of IVF nearly bankrupting us.'

'Well, I wish you'd said something.'

'I didn't think I had to!'

Her head drooped like a wilted flower. I wanted to get up but she looked so small, like if I left her there alone she'd disappear. We sat like that – a couple feet between us that might as well have been a canyon – until a horn outside cut the silence.

'So I made the appointment for Saturday, one o'clock.' She held out her hands, knuckles big as acorns. 'Maybe after we can go for mani-pedis?'

I stared at my feet. The nails on a bunch of toes were purplish-black from running.

How could you live with someone and not really know them at all?

It wasn't the first time I'd asked myself that question.

Ma drove. I looked out the window, hissy as a cat on its way to the vet. What did I expect? That I could stay with her forever? No, but I'd wanted to take my time, wait until things were clearer in my mind. She'd given me a deadline – out before Labor Day – serving up some nonsense about how September was the 'perfect time' for a fresh start. 'Just like the beginning of a new school year!' Ma had taught second grade. It explained a lot.

I couldn't blame her for wanting me gone. I dried dishes, took out the trash and recycling, but I was no joy to live with. I thought about telling her not to worry, I'd be gone soon enough, but I didn't feel like answering a dozen questions.

She switched off the radio, sparing us from an update about another mass shooting.

'I have three complexes in mind. I found this one myself that time I got lost on my way back from CVS.'

It was a little after noon when she pulled into the parking lot of a two-story converted motel. Beyond a patch of weeds, a pool not much bigger than a pothole stood empty.

Ma opened the car door. 'C'mon,' she said.

A sign announcing '1 and 2 bedroom apts. available now!!' was attached to a chain-link fence, rust peeking through its turquoise spraypaint. Available was spelled wrong and the exclamation points reeked of desperation.

'I think *Dexter* was filmed here,' I said.

'Is that good?' Ma stuck out a leg and reached for her giant white handbag.

'No. Get back in. I'm not living in a fictional serial killer's building.'

Ma dropped into the driver's seat. 'I don't know what that means, but OK, let's try the next one.'

As we looped through back streets, the morning haze burned off and the sun began heating up the car quicker than a microwave.

'We're a little early,' Ma said as she angled the Corolla into a spot beside an old green Jaguar with the vanity plate: ISLL UBY. 'But it looks like she's here.'

'Who?'

'Irene Moffatt's daughter, Michelle. Remember I told you she's a real-estate agent?'

Shit. I'd been trying not to think about Moffatt. When he kissed me on his balcony on Sunday, I didn't resist though I'd stopped things there. He picked me up as usual for the group session Wednesday night, but he was quiet on the way. When the others were 'sharing,' he didn't do his typical nodding and commiserating.

On the drive back, he turned into a high-school parking lot, rolled down all the windows, and cut the engine.

I shifted to face him. 'Just so you know, I draw the line at having sex in a minivan, even one as classy as this.'

He stared out the windshield, chewing what was left of his thumb nail.

''Cause I did way too much of that in high school,' I tried again, wanting some reaction, expecting he'd grin and go back to normal.

Nothing.

I leaned forward to see what had caught his eye. I hoped he wasn't going to do some weird astronomy shit like pointing out the

Big Dipper, thinking it was romantic. The sky was blank, a big dark void. 'Hey, you OK? If this is about the other night, I—'

He looked at me. 'Heather – Ryan's mom – she's marrying this guy, Gary.'

I nodded.

'She called me last night, which is rare 'cause she usually texts – and then it's like five words tops. So I figured something must be up.'

'And?'

'Gary's been offered a new job. He's supposedly a tech wizard.'

I waited.

'It's in Texas. She wants to take Ry. Soon. Enroll him in school there. He'd start in a couple weeks.' He rubbed his forehead.

'You can fight her, right? Take her to court?'

He shook his head. 'I could, but she'd win.' Even in the dark, I saw the lines between his eyes deepen. 'Remember that day at the police station when I told you I'd made some bad decisions?'

'Yeah.'

'After we lost Ava, I was drinking. A lot. One night, it all got to be too much. I drove out to this abandoned warehouse where my buddies and I used to hang out back in high school. We'd pass around bottles we swiped from our parents' liquor cabinets and talk about how great our lives were going to turn out.' A sad laugh bubbled up. 'Anyway, I fired six shots into the ceiling. A developer had built a gated community not too far away. Someone called it in. I'd been up for a promotion. Got suspended instead.' He dropped his head. 'I know how that would play out in court.'

Nothing I could say would help, so I put my hand on his arm. We sat there listening to the traffic and the buzz of the overhead parking lot lights until he finally said, 'I already lost my daughter. I can't lose my son, too.'

The knock on the car window pulled me back to the apartment complex. I lowered the tinted glass, dreading everything that would come next.

'Welcome to Magnolia Grove!' Like an excited puppy, Michelle Moffatt stuck her face so close to mine I thought she was going to lick me. 'Your possible new home! I'm Michelle, but you probably already guessed that! I can't wait to give you the grand tour.'

Her enthusiasm made me want to crawl into the trunk. But Ma and I climbed out so Michelle could walk us through a vacant two-bedroom where everything was white: floors, walls, countertops, cabinets.

'Talk about a "fresh" start?' Michelle giggled as she pulled back shutter-style doors to reveal a white washer and dryer.

'Isn't this nice?' Ma asked. 'There's something so familiar about it.'

'It looks like your dentist's office,' I mumbled while Michelle ran ahead to open the blinds in the primary bedroom.

The sameness of it all depressed the shit out of me. Not that the house Kenny and I had shared was any architectural wonder, but we'd made it our own. Kenny was good with his hands. That's how we'd met. I'd been working for a wedding planner. He'd been hired to construct a pergola with a dome on the bride's parents' property. My boss sent me to check on his progress.

'Wow. I had zero hope for this, but it actually isn't awful,' I'd said as he knelt beside one of the footings.

'That's a hell of a testimonial. Mind if I include that in my marketing materials?' His sarcasm won me over even before he turned around and knocked me flat with his big brown eyes.

He pushed a lock of wavy black hair away from his face and pulled off a work glove.

'Kenny Stevens.' When he shook my hand, more than an electric shock ran through me. It was like I'd been Tasered.

The home we bought was cheap. The owners had lost their son years earlier in a hiking accident and let the place fall into disrepair. But nothing we couldn't tackle.

'Small, but good bones. Nice neighborhood,' Kenny had said, arm around me as we stood on the sidewalk after the open house. 'Let's do it.'

While he updated the bathrooms and restored the floors, I painted each room a warm, vibrant color. When we finished a project we'd sit back, split a six pack, and admire our progress.

Over time, I planted fig trees and hydrangeas, forsythia and lilacs. When I was pregnant with Frankie, Kenny built a window seat in the bedroom that would be hers.

'This way my ladies can sit and read while overlooking the grounds.' He did the funny rich-guy voice he used when he imitated his clients.

The fall Frankie was three, she squatted in her pink Crocs helping me plant tulip bulbs on each side of the walkway. I dug the holes, and she'd dropped them in, repeating 'Points up! Points up!' patting the dirt with her pudgy hands.

When I'd seen the listing online last fall, any trace of us had been erased. Every wall was white like the interior of the apartment Michelle was saying could be mine by September first.

'What do you think?' she asked.

'Not for me.' I folded my arms across my chest.

Michelle frowned, but quickly recovered. 'No problem! Plenty more to show you.'

Ma and I followed her to the next place. I stared at the back of her car and wondered what would possess someone to get vanity plates when Ma asked, 'Do you think she looks like Irene? Same blue eyes but different mouth.'

I'd been trying to figure out if she looked like her brother when I realized we were turning into his complex. Part of me wanted to see him, but would we pretend not to know each other? I couldn't exactly tell Ma he'd bailed me out after I got caught stealing a tutu.

We parked beside Michelle's car, afternoon sun sparkling off her hood ornament like it was the star atop a Christmas tree.

'So believe it or not, my brother lives just over there!' Michelle pointed a manicured nail, red like her dress, toward a building on the other side of the lot. 'He loves it here.'

She was so convincing, if I didn't know better I might've believed her.

'Your mom thinks he met someone special.' Ma raised her eyebrows.

'Oh geez, I hope not.' Michelle lowered her voice and spoke out of the side of her mouth. 'Just between us, he has the worst taste in women. He's a great guy. He should be able to find somebody decent, but he's got this thing for troubled souls – like the more issues, the better.' She rolled her eyes. I wanted to gouge them out. I didn't care that she was implying I was a loser, but I was pissed for Moffatt. Who shared shit like that with strangers?

Ma just shook her head. 'I'll keep him in my prayers.'

'Now I think you're really going to like this one!' Michelle led us to an elevator.

We got off on the third floor. On the way to the apartment, we passed a child's riding toy – a white plastic horse on wheels with a purple mane. Frankie had the same one in pink. The yogurt I'd eaten for breakfast swam up into my mouth. I swallowed it down.

Michelle opened the door. The place was similar to Moffatt's, only bigger.

'Oh, Corey, look how nice!' Ma said.

'Maybe *you* should rent it,' I muttered.

The sliding glass doors in the living room led to a balcony that overlooked a pond. Water was the last thing I wanted to see. Sometimes I woke up just before dawn, heart hammering, sheets stuck to my skin, flashes of the creek so real I could almost smell the damp, dank earth.

'I bet you'd spy all sorts of birds!' Ma exclaimed, ticking off species: herons, egrets, cranes, like she was an ornithologist.

'Would you look at this closet space?' Michelle gushed as we trailed her into the bedroom.

In my camo cargo shorts and white tank top, did I look like someone with a fancy wardrobe? I was living out of a duffle bag.

'You'll come to treasure the amount of morning light you have here,' Michelle continued as if I were Claude fucking Monet. 'Do you have any questions?'

Yeah – how fast could I get back to the car? I shook my head as Michelle turned on a ceiling fan and said, 'Voila!'

'I'm going to stand on that balcony again,' Ma said. 'Maybe I'll spot a pelican.'

Once she left the bedroom, Michelle did her weird talking out of the side of her mouth thing again. 'Hope I'm not crossing a line here, but your mom mentioned that you've had . . .'

I waited, a *tic tic tic* thrumming behind my eye, jaw tensing. I wouldn't fill in the blank. Whatever she wanted to say, I refused to make it easy.

'. . . some hardships.' She rubbed my arm and pulled her lips down in an exaggerated pout. 'Wouldn't this be a wonderful place to begin again?'

'Absolutely!' I nodded and smiled, showing all my teeth. 'Did I see a sign for a fitness center on the lower level?'

'You did!' She clapped her hands.

'I'd love to check it out. Do you mind staying here with my mom in case she has any questions?'

'I'd be happy to! We'll meet you down there in a few!'

I hurried out the door before Ma could call me over to look at a robin. I took the steps two at a time. I was so light, it was almost like flying. Seconds later, I stood in front of Michelle's vintage Jaguar, glancing over each shoulder. No one else in sight.

I wrapped my hands around the hood ornament, burning beneath the blazing sun, and yanked and tugged and wrestled, the veins in my forearms rising to the surface, until it loosened and broke free.

What had I planned to do with it? Toss it in the bushes? As I stared at the silver cat, its mouth open mid-roar, body lean and ready to pounce, I knew I had to keep it. Stuffing it in the pocket of my shorts, I darted toward the fitness center.

In the distance, I heard the ding of the elevator, the tinkle of Ma's laugh. I stepped inside the small gym area, the blast of air conditioning a welcome relief, and exited just as they rounded the corner.

'Oh my goodness!' Michelle said. 'Look at you! Breathless and sweaty already!'

'She's quite a runner!' Ma bragged. 'Didn't get that from me, even though I dress the part!' She ran her hand over her fuchsia tracksuit.

Michelle fake-laughed and led us back toward the parking lot. 'And there are tennis courts just over there.' She flicked a finger to the left. 'Such a nice, safe community where you can . . .' She stopped mid-sales pitch. 'Goddammit!'

Ma reeled back. 'What is it, dear?'

'My Leaper!' She stomped her foot.

Ma looked confused. I gasped as Michelle pointed to the hole.

'My hood ornament!' she whined. 'I've already replaced it twice.'

'Maybe this isn't such a safe community after all?' I moved closer to Ma as if protecting her.

'This really bums me out,' Michelle said. 'Do you mind if we call it a day?'

'Don't mind at all.'

As Ma drove back to the condo, she listed every feature she liked about the last apartment while my mind traveled back to Wednesday night, to the high school parking lot. Moffatt had been just about to start the car when he turned to me.

'You were going to say something but I interrupted you.'

I shook my head. 'I don't remember.'

'You said, "If this is about the other night," and I cut you off. What were you going to say?'

I squeezed my eyes shut. When I opened them, I saw one tiny star, or hell, who knows, maybe it was an airplane.

'Well, now this is going to make me sound like an egomaniac, but I thought maybe you were acting different because I left after one drink Sunday night.' I planted my feet on the dashboard and forced myself to face him. 'I was going to say, "If this is about the other night, I like you, too. But it probably won't end well for either of us."'

His lips formed a slow, sad smile. 'Another Hallmark movie moment.'

Ma pulled into the condo driveway and slapped the steering wheel.

'What?' I asked.

'I forgot all about our mani-pedis.'

'Next time,' I said. My fingers were already occupied, stroking the silver Jaguar's head buried deep inside my pocket.

TWENTY-SEVEN

Laurel

As much as I appreciated Addie's offer, I couldn't go through with it. And, by the time I looked for the will and guardianship documents the next afternoon, they were gone. Rob must've taken them to mail from his office. Jasper had scribbled wild dark spirals across the front of the folder. I'd expected Rob to blame me for leaving an uncapped pen nearby but he hadn't mentioned it.

Still, I wanted to thank Addie. Just believing that I'd had another option had made me feel better, not as powerless.

'Can I take you to dinner Friday?' I asked as she stood in my kitchen and I told her it was too late to change the paperwork.

The light left her eyes. 'I'm supposed to visit my mom. Her case manager wants to talk about some of her new "behaviors."'

'I'll go with you!' I volunteered. 'It's the least I can do.'

'Thanks, but you really don't want to do that. It's pretty miserable.'

'Seriously, I insist,' I said. 'Rob's company has summer Fridays. He'll be home by four. We'll get dinner after. You shouldn't always have to go alone. Let me be there for you the way you've been there for me.'

She hesitated.

'Or I can go alone. Give you a day off.'

'That's very sweet, but I really can't let you do that.'

'Then Friday it is,' I said.

Eventually, she relented.

We zipped along backroads on the way to Oakhurst. Addie had put her convertible's top down. I settled into the comfortable seat and admired the leaves, crisping at the edges, some already starting to fall. Even though we were headed to the memory care unit of an assisted-living facility, I was happy to be out with a friend.

'Busy for a Friday afternoon,' Addie mused as she swung her Audi TT into a parking spot.

It was close to five p.m. We'd have time for a short visit before her mom ate dinner.

'I should tell you a few things before we go in.' Addie put the top up but kept the car running so we didn't melt in the August heat. 'Sometimes she doesn't know who I am. Other times she does, and she accuses me of terrible things – like sticking her here.'

I looked up at the building. With its colorful landscaping and wide porch adorned with white rocking chairs, it was far nicer than the nursing home where my grandfather had spent his not-so-golden years in Schenectady.

Addie clutched her keys. 'It can be a lot. Don't say I didn't warn you.'

The smell hit me as soon as we walked through the double doors.

Addie wrinkled her nose. 'Friday is fried fish and broccoli night.'

A woman behind the front desk smiled as we signed in.

'Hello Miss Conroy!' An aid greeted us in the hallway. 'Got to let you know, your mom's real agitated today – has been since we told her you were coming.'

'Lovely.' Addie squared her shoulders.

'But Joyce is glad you're here. She wants to talk with you.'

'Well, she knows where to find me.' Addie managed a smile, and whispered, 'Case manager,' to clue me in.

The faint scent of urine followed us down the hall.

'Knock, knock!' Addie said cheerfully.

A white-haired woman sat in a wingback chair facing the window. At first I thought she didn't hear us, but as we got closer, she turned. Her eyes were blue like Addie's but with none of their sparkle.

'Nice of you to finally show up,' she said angrily, spit bubbles forming in the corners of her mouth, 'though I wish you hadn't.'

'Mom, this is my friend, Laurel.' Addie bent to kiss her mother's cheek but the woman shrunk back and fixed us with a harsh glare.

'Hi.' I waved, suddenly understanding why Addie had protested when I insisted on accompanying her.

'She stuck me here and stole my house!' she hissed, gripping the arms of her chair.

Addie straightened and gave me a withering look before turning back to her mother. 'You're safe here, Mom. You've made new friends . . .'

'It's a lovely room.' I gestured toward the floral wallpaper border and the windows, which overlooked a garden and walking path.

'Want to trade places?' she snarled at me. When I didn't answer, she let out a nasty cackle. 'Didn't think so!'

'Addison?' A woman in a crisp white blouse and navy pants stood in the doorway. 'Nice to see you again. Can I speak with you in the hall for a moment?' She grinned at Addie's mom. 'Don't worry, Helen, I'll have her back to you in a flash.'

'You can keep her,' Helen grumbled.

Addie squeezed my elbow and mouthed, 'I'm sorry,' before following Joyce into the hall.

Helen jutted her head toward her bed for me to sit. 'How long have you known her?'

I settled on the edge. 'A couple of months. We moved in right next door.'

She made a *harrumph* sound. 'Ah, yes, the house that nobody wanted.'

'I'm sorry?'

She turned back to the window, wringing her hands. 'Well, just don't say "no" to her. She doesn't like that. That's how I ended up here. I didn't want her to come back. I didn't want us to live together.' She shook her head violently. 'Guess what? Now we don't!' She paused, eyes widening. 'And that poor boy. Look what happened to him!'

I peered through the window. Was she talking about a child outside? The garden and walking path were empty.

'What day is it? How long have I been here?'

I glanced toward the hall, hoping Addie would return soon. 'Addie's been great, really welcoming. It's made such a difference.'

Helen's eyes followed mine, her long fingers pointed at the slim slice of her daughter's arm that overlapped the doorframe.

'I blame myself. I was almost forty when I had her. My only child. I couldn't say no to her. Created a monster. We never got along. Never.'

She was talking more to herself than to me. I didn't know how to respond. Her head swung toward the hall. 'It's a shame. She's a beautiful girl.' She leaned forward, straining to take my hand in hers. Her yellowed fingernails dug into my wrist. My instinct was to pull back, but her voice was a whisper. 'That's how she fools people. They think, "How could someone so attractive on the outside be so rotten on the inside?" Did she tell you about the toy company?' She threw her head back in an open-mouthed guffaw and pulled her hand away to slap her thigh.

Addie returned looking worried, but she rearranged her features into a smile. 'It's nice to hear you laugh again, Mom.' She put a hand on her mother's shoulder. Helen shrugged it off.

'You want to hear me laugh?' She emitted a sharp cackle that sounded almost crow-like.

Addie stepped back, face contorting.

'Not funny enough for you?' Helen demanded. 'Then get out of here! I mean it, fuck off!'

I'd read that people living with dementia sometimes used profanity. Hearing it aimed at my friend by her own mother was too much.

'Should we leave?' I stood. Addie nodded, head lowered, hair shrouding her face.

We were almost out of the room when her mother's voice came again. 'And we both know that wasn't a squirrel! That was my dog!'

In the car, Addie pressed her fingertips to her forehead. 'Joyce, the case manager, said the doctor wants to try new meds, but my mom will have to undergo some tests first, and that rarely goes well.'

'I'm so sorry,' I said, struggling to find the right words.

'*I'm* sorry. I hope she didn't scare you. Sometimes she's sweet and kind – the way she used to be – but lately, I never know what she might come out with.' She exhaled and looked in the rearview mirror, wiping beneath her eyes. 'Do you mind if we get dinner another time? I feel a migraine starting.' She twitched. 'And I can't wait to shower.'

'No, of course,' I said.

Before meeting Addie's mother, I'd never considered that in losing my mom so suddenly, maybe I'd been spared having her disappear in a different but equally devastating way.

When I got home, Rob and Jasper were watching a baseball game. Seeing them together filled me with gratitude for our simple life – even as the pizza box rested on the stovetop and their plates sat beside the sink. After we tucked Jasper in, Rob and I watched a movie, my head on his shoulder. Before bed, I texted Addie to see if she was OK. She responded with a simple: *No. But I will be. XO*

After Poppy's two a.m. feeding, I had trouble falling back to sleep. Helen's voice, her words, *Ah, yes, the house that nobody wanted*, played on repeat in my mind, an earworm, worse than one of Jasper's Musical Munchkins songs. I almost woke Rob to ask him if he had any clue what she meant. But he was snoring and I already knew what he'd tell me: *She's confused, Laur. That's why she's there. Don't look for trouble where there isn't any.*

Still, something about it gnawed at me – there was a connection my brain tried but failed to make. I sensed it swimming to the surface just as I fell asleep.

TWENTY-EIGHT

Laurel

Saturday morning I stood at the stove waiting for the kettle to whistle when my phone pinged. A message from Jill brightened the screen: *BBQ tonight? Come around 5 if you're free!*

I was relieved it wasn't Colin resuming his text assault.

'Cool! Let's go!' Rob said, peering over my shoulder.

I didn't share his enthusiasm. I'd barely slept and wasn't really up for seeing Jill's rowdy twins or her husband, Pete.

When I didn't start typing back immediately, Rob frowned. 'You like her, right? Maybe other kids Jasper's age will be there, too. Class lists come out next week. It'd be nice to meet more people.'

I couldn't think of an excuse to decline so I wrote back: *Sounds fun! Will bring dessert! (Nut-free!)*

'This is great!' Rob kissed my cheek.

'I'll head to the store once Poppy's in for her nap.'

'Can I go, too?' Jasper asked.

'Not today, pumpkin.' I liked going alone, taking my time, not having to say 'no' to his countless requests for candy and toys.

'But I went with Daddy,' Jasper whined. 'He let me pick the ice cream.'

'Tell me what flavor you want and I'll get it!' I hadn't had coffee yet and my patience was nearing an all-time low.

'No! I want to go!' He dissolved in a heap of tears on the kitchen floor.

'You can take him, Laur,' Rob said. 'You'll be a big helper, right, pal?'

Jasper's sobs ceased as he ran to fetch his shoes.

'Ah, peace restored.' Rob smiled as I curled my fingers around my empty coffee mug to stop from smashing it.

* * *

It had taken a few weeks, but I'd come around to the suburban supermarket. I appreciated the wider aisles and larger selection, but still I backtracked quite a bit as I learned the layout.

I tried to coax Jasper into the cart but he'd have none of it.

'I wanna walk!' he repeated, arms folded defiantly, and stomped his foot.

'Fine,' I said, 'but you need to stay by me the entire time. Deal?' He nodded.

We filled the cart with baby items and ingredients for the desserts I planned to make for Jill's barbecue. We were picking apples when I saw the man – late-fifties, dark hair riddled with gray, full beard. He'd been watching us but darted away once our eyes met. His were deep-set. Just like Lyle's.

I was so tired of being afraid, of my heart stopping each time the mail arrived, of laying awake listening to every rattle and creak in our new home. I dropped the bag of Granny Smiths and raced after the man. In the cereal aisle, I caught up to him and grabbed his arm. He turned, surprised. Was it Lyle? I couldn't be sure.

Like trying to scream in a nightmare, I could barely force out the words. 'What do you want?'

His mouth hung open. I waited for him to speak. I'd know Lyle's voice.

'You were staring at me, at . . . at my child,' I stammered.

'Aye, your son reminded me of my boy at that age.' His tone was soft with the hint of an Irish brogue. 'I seem to have misplaced the wife.'

It wasn't Lyle. I had a sweeping sense of vertigo. I clutched a shelf. Boxes toppled to the floor.

'Are you all right, miss?' The man cocked an eyebrow.

'Fergal! There you are!' A woman came toward us, basket dangling from her arm.

'I – I'm sorry.' My face burned with shame. Who was I becoming, chasing a stranger through a store? I spun around. Jasper wasn't beside me. I'd left him by the apples. I lurched away, stumbling in sandals. As I rounded the corner, I didn't see him. My stomach dropped. I hurried through the produce section, pushing carts out of my way, shoppers watching warily. *Who let the madwoman into the market?*

'Jasper! Jasper!' I called.

'Mommy?'

At the deli case, I saw him and, to his right, Marian holding his hand. She smiled as she gave him a slice of cheese. I stopped, panting. I'd found Jasper but I had a new worry. Marian. She stepped in front of my son, protective, judgement radiating from her thin frame.

'Where were you?' she demanded. 'Anyone could've come along and taken him!'

Like you did while I was in the shower, I thought, anger building. 'Are you following me?'

'I'm here every Saturday. But this isn't about me, Laurel,' she hissed. 'How could you leave him like that?'

I'd never seen her there and I shopped every Saturday too.

'Come on, Jasper.' I took his free hand. If Marian didn't let go of the other, we'd be in a tug of war. After a beat, she slid her palm out of his.

'I know you mothers today think you have so much going on and you're so busy, but you really must be more careful.' She scowled. 'Tragedy can strike in the blink of an eye.'

I fought the urge to flip her off and took Jasper to find our abandoned cart. Someone had dumped a half-dozen loaves of French bread in it. I paid for everything and left.

Rob was sitting on the couch, scrolling through his phone when we got home.

'How'd it go, pal?' he asked.

'Great! Mommy ran away and Mimi gave me cheese.'

In the car, I'd debated telling Jasper that seeing Marian at the market was our secret, but what kind of mother did that?

'Mommy ran away?' Rob's eyes scanned my face.

I was spiraling, unraveling. I hadn't wanted to tell him but maybe if I did, he'd understand and help me. I set down the grocery bags and sank into the sofa.

'I thought I saw Lyle.'

Rob frowned.

'Lyle. Lyle Hartsell. There was a man who looked like him and he was staring so—'

'So what? You ran after him?'

'I followed him, but I was wrong. It wasn't Lyle. Jasper was only alone for a sec—'

'Laurel, that's—'

His cell phone rang on the couch cushion between us. *Mimi* flashed across the screen. I didn't know he had her contact information.

'Figures,' I scoffed. 'She's dying to tell you what a horrible mother I am.'

Rob stared at the phone. 'I'm sure she's just concerned . . .' He reached for it.

'Do not answer it!' I pleaded. 'I'm trying to tell you—'

'Tell me what, Laurel?' he asked, teeth clenched.

Upstairs, Poppy began to cry. I had to pee and my breasts were leaking. I wanted to tell him that I kept thinking I saw Lyle, that I felt this dark presence looming, but we'd gone off track.

'Marian's own son doesn't speak to her. Did you know that? What does that tell you?'

Rob's face contorted. 'Her relationship with her son has nothing to do with *you* not watching *our* son!' He took a breath, searching for patience. 'Laurel, please. I know you're tired and stressed, but you have to pull it together. I'm counting on you to take care of our family when I'm not here. You have to be stronger than this.'

He stood to tend to Poppy. As I rested my head in my hands, his phone beeped – a voicemail notification.

I waited until I heard the creak of the changing table overhead then I picked up his phone, deleted Marian's message, and blocked her number.

That evening, we walked the half-mile to Jill and Pete's. I carried the desserts while Rob pushed the double stroller. A chilled bottle of wine in an insulated bag rested in the storage basket beneath the seats. My mouth watered for a glass after a long day of uncomfortable silence. Maybe the twins' wildness and Pete's booming voice would be a welcome change after all.

'You made it!' Jill said as we entered their backyard guided by smoke rising from a grill and the sound of little boy laughter. Jasper ran to the swing set where Flynn and Donovan were attempting to push one another off the top of the slide.

I introduced Rob to Pete and Jill. Regardless of what was going on between us, I knew he'd be friendly, charming. I was the one who struggled to fake it, making too big a fuss over the paper lanterns and fairy lights strung from the red umbrella and around the deck railings.

'So it's just us!' Jill said. 'Trisha's down the shore.'

Earlier I'd wondered who else would be there, if I could fade into the background. Though I was out of the house and away from Marian's prying eyes, I couldn't put the morning's episode behind me. Normally, I'd have been curious to see the inside of Jill's home, but I was too preoccupied.

As I took Poppy out of the stroller and placed her in the baby sling, Rob watched me. He pushed Jasper on the swing while talking with Pete, who flipped burgers and barked out orders for Jill to bring him another beer, a serving platter, cheese. Each time Pete was distracted, Rob's head swiveled toward me.

'Later Pete'll expect me to thank him for all his "hard work!"' Jill joked as she made her dozenth trip from the kitchen to the grill.

'Right.' I laughed, only half-listening.

Rob asked Pete about youth sports leagues and his eyes followed me. I was under his microscope again. How long would I remain pinned beneath it this time?

When the burgers were ready, Jasper and the twins sat at a kid-sized picnic table on the grass while the rest of us stayed on the deck.

After dinner, Rob looked around the property. 'I'll have to get the name of your fence guy. We've been meaning to put one up,' he said.

'You haven't yet?' Pete's eyebrows arched. 'Man, I'm surprised. That would've been my first—'

'Pete!' Jill interrupted. 'Flynn's eating a dandelion behind you. Can you stop him?'

'What? Your legs don't work?'

'Let me check.' She kicked him under the table.

'I'm just saying, with young kids and everything.' Pete lumbered toward the lawn to clap Flynn on the back until he coughed up yellow petals. 'You get a storm and that creek swells like a mother—'

'It's been on our list,' I said in our defense. It was the first time I'd spoken in a while. Did my voice sound as strange to them as it did to me?

Jill stood and changed the subject. 'Wait 'til you see the desserts Laurel made!' She collected our dinner dishes. I got up to help.

'Don't,' she said. 'Please. How many times a night are you up? Once? Twice? I remember those days. Sit. Pete'll help me.'

'I will?' he asked.

Through the sliding glass doors, I watched them. Despite Pete's gruffness, they worked together in a choreographed dance, covering leftovers, placing them in the fridge, fetching clean plates for dessert, chatting animatedly. They were a team. I looked at Rob. He was focused on Poppy, asleep on my chest, and didn't meet my eyes. We'd become opponents.

Pete carried out the cookies Jasper and I made, calling for the boys to 'come and get 'em.' Jill followed with the fruit tart.

'This should be on the cover of a magazine, seriously,' Jill said. 'How long does it take to become a pastry chef? I'm in awe.'

'You're a pastry chef?' Pete sat and opened another beer. 'I thought you were a lawyer.'

Rob laughed as Jill passed him a slice.

'What made you think that?' I asked.

'I don't know. Jill said you were pretty interested when she told you that Flynn took a header down the deck stairs on Marian's watch. I figured maybe you were sniffing around trying to drum up a lawsuit – negligence, that type of thing.'

Though it was dusk, I saw Rob's eyes settle on me. My stomach pitched. Had I seemed overly curious when Jill told me about Flynn needing stitches? Why did she tell Pete about it? Did she also think Marian was troubled?

I'd had a glass and a half of wine – enough to make me bold. In a tone I hoped sounded more casual than nosy, I asked, 'Any idea why she and her son don't speak? I can't imagine—'

'Laurel,' Rob chided, 'that's none of our business.'

'For the record, I side with the son on that one,' Pete snorted.

Jill held up a finger indicating she'd weigh in once she'd swallowed her bite of tart. 'It was an accident!' She took a sip of wine. 'Could Marian have handled it better? Of course.'

'Well, now you *must* tell us!' I set down my dessert fork and smiled encouragingly even as Rob stiffened.

'Patrick – Marian's son – and his husband went on a cruise and Marian was supposed to watch their dog.'

'Now you gotta understand,' Pete interjected, 'these guys loved that dog more than most people love their kids.'

'Fiona was her name,' Jill said. 'Cute little thing. A puggle, I think. Marian let her out to do her business, expecting her to come right back—'

'And bam!' Pete clapped his fleshy hands. 'Hit by a car right in front of your house. Killed instantly.'

'That's awful,' I gasped as a small spark of vindication flickered inside me.

'Patrick texted to check in, and Marian told him in a message.'

'Guy was devastated.' Pete shook his head.

'Marian said she was sorry but it wouldn't have happened if he'd done a better job training her.'

'Ouch!' Pete said.

'Needless to say, that didn't help,' Jill continued. 'Then she made things worse by telling him, "It's only a dog. Just get another one." He picked up Fiona's remains and hasn't spoken to Marian since.'

It was horrible, yet I felt a smug satisfaction. Marian was far from perfect. Rob would have no choice but to finally acknowledge it.

On our walk home, we weren't halfway down the block when Rob said, 'We're new here. Do you really want to be known as the type of person who gossips about her neighbor? Who thinks the old lady next door is some sort of villain?' He paused. 'Did you actually call any of the therapists I forwarded to you? Or do I have to take that on too?'

I started to defend myself but stopped. Zoey was walking Harriet on the other side of the street. Rob waved.

Once we were out of earshot, I asked, 'Did you give Zoey your phone number?'

'What?' Rob scoffed.

'Did you?'

'I gave her my email so she could send me her resume,' he said irritably. 'Are you spying on me now?'

I didn't answer. I was thinking about Marian and about my mother, how she'd known something was off with Lyle. The week before the shooting, I'd overheard her tell my father about him, how he'd hurled a mug of pens at the wall, knocked over the flag, and shoved a customer as he barreled out the door.

'I'm sure he's just making noise, hoping to scare people into giving him what he wants. Don't let him intimidate you, Kathleen!' Dad had said.

'It's more than intimidation, Bill. You had to see him. He was possessed.'

'Listen, I'm sure he'll come up with the money, and this'll all blow over.'

'If he could come up with the money, he'd have paid his mortgage months ago,' Mom had argued. 'I tried to get him another extension. His family is going to be evicted days before Christmas. I have a really bad feeling.'

If my mother had trusted her instincts, had run when she saw Lyle enter the building that gray afternoon, would she still be alive?

People didn't believe women, and that made us doubt ourselves. I wouldn't make the same mistake – even as Rob tried to convince me I was wrong about Marian.

As we approached our home, I avoided looking at the street where that dog had been killed. Instead, I stared at the swaying treetops. A storm was coming. Branches extended over our roof like menacing hands.

Rob stopped the stroller and turned toward me. I refused to meet his eyes. 'When we get back from the wedding, you need to get help,' he said. 'I cannot keep doing this.'

'I can't either,' I agreed, knowing we were talking about two different things.

The house seemed stuffier than usual. I chalked it up to the August humidity and the anger simmering inside me. Rob took Jasper up for a bath while I nursed Poppy. We went to bed with our backs to one another.

Hours later, a beeping woke me. I opened my eyes to see Rob pulling on a T-shirt, rushing around the room.

'Laurel, get up!' Rob shook my arm. 'It's the carbon monoxide detector. I called nine-one-one. We have to get out of the house. Now!' He opened the windows, tossed me my robe, and went to wake Jasper, who was asking for pancakes when I met them in the hall a minute later.

Rob turned on the overhead light. The brightness burned my eyes. I grabbed Poppy and hurried downstairs where the beeping blared.

'I don't understand . . .' I began, too disoriented to finish my sentence.

Rob ushered us outside as the police arrived.

'Anyone dizzy, nauseous, tired?' an officer asked.

It was two a.m. I was all those things but no more than usual. I shook my head 'no' and Rob did the same.

Red lights flashed, bouncing off the windows of our neighbors' homes.

'A fire truck!' Jasper jumped and pointed.

Firefighters filed past as we stood confused, helpless, the grass cold and wet beneath our bare feet.

'Found the source,' a firefighter's voice boomed. 'Oven was left on. Turned up to five hundred. You didn't smell it?'

'Jesus Christ, Laurel!' Rob spat. 'You didn't shut it off?'

I stared into the dark night, trying to recall pushing the 'off' button after removing the cookies. 'I'm sure I . . .'

Rob shook his head, disgusted.

A light flickered in Marian's upstairs window. We'd been out for hours. She easily could've snuck in. We'd also passed Zoey walking Harriet. She'd let herself into our home before.

I looked at the police officer. Could I tell him about the note, the knife, the way Zoey appeared in our playroom, or how Marian had followed me to the store? No, not without Rob thinking I'd become completely paranoid, hysterical.

Someone was literally turning up the heat while I stood there and watched. That needed to change.

TWENTY-NINE

Corey

When I walked into the kitchen Monday morning, Ma was at the table with her laptop open. She shut it as I passed behind her on my way to the fridge.

'Geez, what are you looking at? Porn again?' I was in a rare decent mood. Moffatt had texted. Wednesday night's grief group meeting was canceled. The church needed the room for a tricky tray fundraiser. He invited me to his place for dinner.

'I wish you wouldn't talk like that.' Ma reached for her pill organizer. I noticed a little tremor in her hand. She hadn't looked at me or asked how I slept. I opened the fridge and grabbed a yogurt.

'Seriously, what were you doing on there? If you forgot a password, it's no biggie, I can help you reset it.'

Kenny and I bought her a new computer when we came down to visit for Mother's Day when Frankie was two. I'd shown her how to pay her bills online. Kenny got her on Facebook and joked that he was setting up an eHarmony profile for her.

'Flash me your sexiest smile, Nana!' he'd joked, aiming his iPhone at her.

'Stop! Stop!' She'd blushed and waved her arms in protest, laughing.

That was back when things were OK, before Kenny had lost his job and I'd started working twice as hard to compensate. Plus, Frankie was there, making us all better versions of ourselves.

The kitchen was quiet except for the whirring of the fridge's ice maker. I pulled a spoon from the drawer and waited. Ma didn't answer me.

'You know I can just open the laptop myself.' I smirked, feeling like Desiree when she'd said, 'You know I can just google you.'

Ma sighed and raised the screen. Against the yellow of her robe, she looked washed out. I came around behind her and braced for a nasty email from Alice Blackwell asking when I was moving out, or a notice that the price of one of Ma's meds had gone up again. What I saw was worse.

'You're still friends with him?' I stepped back, dizzy. Sick. 'Are you kidding me?' I threw my spoon across the room. Vanilla yogurt streaked and splattered like a bird shitting everywhere.

'Corey, please.' Ma looked at me. 'This is not how I expect you to behave.'

'This is not how I expect *you* to behave!' I growled. She shrunk in her chair. 'You are *my* mother! Frankie's grandmother! Where is your loyalty? To her? To me?' My throat hurt from straining to not yell louder. 'How? Why are you still in touch with him?' I glared at Kenny's photo, his face tan, his arm slung around a dark-haired woman I'd never seen before. I wished I could reach inside the screen and strangle him. It was night in the shot, but the foreground was lit up. They were standing on sand, ocean behind them, tip of a whitecap brightening the corner of the picture. How could he ever be near water again?

'I want to talk about her with someone, someone who knew and loved her,' Ma said softly. 'You won't do that with me and I have respected that.'

'Someone who knew and loved her?' I couldn't process it. Every sentence that left her mouth struck me like a hammer to the head. 'You're talking about someone who failed her, who left her alone!'

'He's already suffered so much. You don't know because you shut him out. He's trying to start over. He's met someone.'

'No shit!' I pointed at his idiotic grin, his overpriced shirt with its blue whale. He looked happy, like a man who'd never known loss. I wanted him to look haunted – as haunted as I was. 'I wonder how she'll feel when . . .' I couldn't finish my sentence.

Ma took a breath. I listened to the wheeze and whistle in her chest. 'He tried to call you, but he said you blocked his number.'

I waited. She took off her glasses and rubbed her eyes. 'The headstone is in.' She paused. My heart hit the floor. 'He wanted to know if you planned to go home – to see it.'

'I don't have a home,' I snarled.

'She's close to your dad, Corey. Their names will be right near one another. Francis and Frances.' I heard the catch in her voice but she swallowed it. 'There's gonna be a – what did he call it . . .?' She put her glasses on and scrolled. 'An installation of the stone. Kenny said a priest is coming to bless it.'

'Let me know if he can raise her from the dead and then I'll be there.'

I threw the rest of the yogurt in the garbage and ran to the bathroom, dry heaving 'til I was wrung out. Then I rested my head on the toilet rim, cold porcelain offering no comfort.

Ma knocked on the door. 'Let me in, Corey. Let me help you,' she pleaded. 'I can go with you – back to New Jersey – if you want. You don't have to do this alone.'

But I did. I couldn't bring anyone else down with me.

THIRTY

Laurel

Rob called from work around noon on Tuesday.
'Any word from Nina?'
With the wedding days away, he'd dropped the 'No-Show' nickname.

'Not yet.'

I'd tried her all weekend. But my texts – *When do you get in? . . . Happy to pick you up at the airport! . . . Send me your ETA & I'll be there! . . . Can't wait to see you!* – had gone unanswered.

I'd called but her voicemail was full. I planned to give it another day before phoning her mom.

'I'll try again now,' I told Rob, wanting to add that I'd happily stay home with the children. I had no desire to see Colin again.

'Keep me posted.' Rob sighed. I knew he had to be biting his tongue not to say, 'I told you so.'

Since we'd gotten home from Jill and Pete's Saturday night, we'd kept our exchanges short, direct.

I scrolled to Nina's number and typed: *Hey! Hope you're still coming! Would love to know when you'll arrive. Jasper can't wait to meet you!* Coated in a thick layer of embarrassment, I hit send. All the exclamation points – it felt like groveling.

As I stared down at my pathetic messages, a bubble appeared. She was there – who knew where – but there, typing. I watched, holding my breath. The bubble disappeared. I exhaled. *Shit! Shit! Shit!* On top of everything else that was wrong between us, telling Rob that No-Show Nina was definitely not showing would be unbearable. I groaned just as the phone rang in my hand.

'Neen!' I shouted, startling Jasper, who dropped his just-opened juice pouch and watched in delight as the liquid trickled across the kitchen floor. I was so relieved she'd called, I didn't care.

'Laur,' she whispered. 'Can you hear me?'

'Yes! How are you? Are you on your way?'

'Yeah, I'm wheels up, but listen, have you heard of this band Ladyfinger?'

'Like the sponge cake?' I laughed. 'If Kidz Bop does a cover, yeah, I probably know them.' I leaned against the wall, thrilled she was in flight.

'They're from Manchester. I was hired to shoot their album cover and the lead singer, Simon Burton, and I have kind of become a thing.'

Jasper giggled as he danced in the growing puddle of grape juice.

'We're headed to this music festival right now.'

'Cool. Where is it?' In my excitement at hearing her voice, I'd lost track of which day it was. 'Wait, when is it?'

Stupid Laurel. Did I not understand, or did some part of me know but still need to hear her say it?

'So that's the thing.' She made an *errrr* sound. 'It's this weekend. In Edinburgh.'

I slid down the kitchen wall to the floor. The house must've settled unevenly. Jasper's juice flowed slowly toward me. Dragging my hand through my greasy hair, I said, 'But I thought you—'

'Laur, I'm so sorry. If it were any other weekend, you know I'd be there, but Simon and I – we've gotten really tight. No one knows this, so please keep it on the down-low, he's got this, like, paralyzing stage fright. He says my being there's been a huge help – like a total one-eighty.'

I said nothing as Jasper opened the fridge and tossed more juice pouches to the floor, hoping they'd burst.

'I can come in October! Maybe around Halloween? I'll take a shot of your kids in a pile of leaves. You can use it as your holiday card. It'll be fab.'

I heard a voice. 'Miss, we've repeatedly asked you to turn off your phone!'

'Laur, please don't be—'

I ended the call, set down the phone, and crawled to where Jasper lay on his belly, licking the floor.

'Like a cat, Mommy.' He giggled.

I rolled onto my back and stared at the ceiling. Rob's voice saying, 'I've seen how many times she's disappointed you,' drifted back to me.

I wanted to be furious with Nina, but it was my fault for believing this time would be different. I was down to my last option.

Pulling a dishtowel from the oven handle to mop the sticky floor, I sat up.

'I have to make a call,' I told Jasper. 'I'll fix you a sandwich in a few minutes, OK?'

'Sandwich!' he shouted and ran to get the bread.

I dragged myself back to my phone, found my father's number, and said a silent prayer that he answered, not Janice.

'Laurel! What a surprise!' he said. 'What's new? How are the kids?'

'They're good, Dad, thanks. They're actually the reason I'm calling—'

'Hold on, hold on.' His voice traveled away then returned. 'Laurel, Janice wants to talk to you.'

'No! Dad! I need to ask you—'

'Need to ask him what, Laurel?' Janice interrupted. 'Not for money, I hope. We just bought an inflatable hot tub. It's done wonders for my sciatica.'

I bit my lip. I'd never asked them for anything.

'Actually, while I have you, I wanted to ask *you* something.' Janice's nasally whine brought back a flood of bad memories. My head throbbed. 'You'll make the desserts for this year's picnic, right?'

The annual picnic, held in September because December was too cold, had been Janice's idea. I'd hated it from the very first one. Families who'd lost loved ones in the bank shooting and workers who'd been there that day stood around Lincoln Park – all of us bound by tragedy, eating sandwiches like it was a normal Saturday.

As the years passed, the misery expanded. The parents of the boy who was cashing his first paycheck divorced. The mom blamed the dad for telling the teen to do it that afternoon rather than loaning him twenty dollars and leaving the errand until the weekend. The girl whose father had been setting up her college fund was in and out of rehab. The bank manager's son showed up drunk once and insisted 'they had it coming' for being part of 'our greed-fueled capitalist system.'

On the tenth anniversary, the bank set up a scholarship fund that went to a high school senior who planned to major in finance. Janice was instrumental in that too, according to my father.

'Isn't that nice?' he'd asked. 'Going to make a real difference in some kid's life.'

'Too bad the bank wasn't as generous a decade ago. They could've helped Lyle Hartsell refinance and then maybe he wouldn't have killed my mother – your wife. Now *that* would've made a difference in *my* life.'

'You shouldn't let her talk to us like that, Bill!' Janice fumed.

Later that night I heard her through the thin walls of the condo: 'Either she goes or I do.'

The following month they moved me into the apartment with Janice's odd cousin.

'Laurel! Did you hear me?' Janice squawked in my ear. 'I know you're busy with the kids, but you can still make the desserts for the picnic, right?'

'We're not going this year,' I said.

'What? Bill, Laurel says they're not going this year!'

I heard a clicking sound, probably her fake nails as she handed the phone to my father. In the background she muttered, 'You know how hard I work on that all year – and to honor *her* mother.'

'What's this now?' Dad asked.

'It's too long a ride, too long a day for a baby – not to mention it's incredibly sad,' I said.

'But, Laurel, it's tradition,' Dad insisted.

'Tradition!' Janice parroted.

'Listen, Dad, I called to ask you a favor.' My stomach twisted. If there were any other way, I wouldn't make the request. 'Rob's sister, Emily, is getting married this weekend, and I was hoping you and Janice could stay with the kids?'

'This weekend? Jan, what are we doing this weekend?' Faint sounds of rustling and mumbling filled my ear as I waited. 'We have tickets to see a comedian in Atlantic City.'

I almost laughed at the irony. Janice was the most humorless person I knew.

She took the phone. 'Laurel, your father can't get up in the middle of the night with young children anyway. And what is this – a shotgun wedding? Why did you wait 'til the last minute to find a sitter?'

'I thought I had one lined up, but—'

'I remember Rob's sister from your wedding. Don't worry, she'll have a second marriage. You'll go to that one.'

'Poppy's crying. I need to get her,' I lied.

'Reconsider the picnic, Laurel. Your mother would want you there.'

Barefoot, I kicked the wall wishing it were Janice's face. Pain shot up my shin as I ended the call.

Hours later Rob texted: *Any luck?*

No, I wrote back. *You called it.* It hurt a fraction less if I said it. *No-Show Nina's headed to Edinburgh.*

It was for a different guy and a different band, yet so similar to how she'd left me standing in Penn Station the night I met Rob.

At least she's consistent, he wrote back.

I tried my dad. He can't do it.

It was the most Rob and I had said to each other in days.

Don't worry, we'll figure it out! he responded and I wondered for the millionth time what it must be like to go through life believing everything would be fine.

At the stove, I stirred a vegetable curry and attempted to answer Jasper's questions about sloths when I heard Rob's key in the lock.

I wiped my hands on a dishtowel and met him in the living room.

'It smells fantastic in here,' he said, inhaling the fragrant spices – ginger, cinnamon and cardamom – wafting through the house. He handed me a bouquet of white roses. A truce?

'For you.' He pecked me on the lips. 'Listen, I'm sorry about Nina. I know you were excited to see her.'

'Thank you.' A swell of warmth spread through me, touched by his words, the gesture, the absence of an 'I told you this would happen.'

'And I know dealing with your dad and Janice is never easy, so I appreciate you reaching out,' he added.

'I tried.' I buried my face in the flowers but they had no scent. 'I'd typed up Poppy's nap and feeding schedule, Jasper's favorite foods, the bedtime routine. My outfits for the rehearsal dinner, wedding, and brunch are in the garment bag in the closet.' I turned down the corners of my mouth. 'I'm really sorry I'm going to miss it – especially seeing you in your tux.'

He smiled, eyes gleaming. 'You're not going to miss it.' He took my hand. 'I found someone to stay with the kids. Someone who knows them. Someone Jasper's crazy about.'

I frowned. Everyone on his side of the family would be at the wedding. 'Who?' I asked.

'Mimi.'

I squeezed the bouquet. Thorns pierced my fingers.

'I stopped by just now. She said she'd be "delighted" to watch them.'

'No. Rob. You're joking?' The shock of it made me laugh out loud.

'I'm not joking, Laurel.' He shifted from foot to foot and tossed his keys onto the entryway table. 'We're lucky she's willing to do us this favor. You can't skip my sister's wedding. Em, my parents – they'd be heartbroken.'

'No, Rob . . .' My voice faltered as I searched his face. How could he be serious after he knew how I felt about her? Tongue thick and slow, I forced out the words. 'I am not letting that woman in *my* house to stay with *my* children.'

He put his hands on my shoulders. I shrugged them off. 'We've been over this, Laurel.' His voice was stern. 'She's a nice woman – with no hidden agenda.'

'No!' I shook my head. 'She's not a nice woman!'

'What exactly has she done to you – aside from give our son a muffin and express a little concern about his safety at the grocery store? And before you say anything about Jill and Pete's son getting hurt while she was watching him, we both saw that kid. He's a maniac.'

I stood frozen, arms slack, bouquet wilting at my side. Too stunned to argue.

'She'll be here Friday. At noon.'

'Who'll be here?' Jasper ran in and wrapped himself around Rob's leg.

'Mimi!' Rob's eyes never left my face.

'Yay!' Jasper jumped. 'Will she bring me muffins?'

'See?' Rob pointed to Jasper. 'Look how excited he is?'

'C'mon, Daddy, play trains with me!' Jasper tugged Rob's arm.

'One minute, pal, I'll meet you in there.' Jasper darted off while Rob kept his focus on me. 'I think you'll see once we get there that you need a break, that maybe all this – new house, new baby, lack of sleep – it's gotten to you.' He looked me up and down.

I touched the top of my head. Oily, limp, strands spilled out of my ponytail. I hadn't had a chance to shower after our morning walk. Had I showered the day before? Or the one before that?

'By the time we get back Sunday afternoon, you'll see I was right. You'll thank me.' As he moved toward the playroom, he leaned close to my ear. 'And for the record, this is also *my* house and these are *my* children, too.'

While they were in the playroom, I texted Addie. *Drinks tonight? Emergency!!*

The bar is open. Come anytime! she wrote back.

I put the roses in a vase and stuck them on the dining-room table. I nursed Poppy and served dinner but barely touched my food. After I put the baby down and tucked Jasper in, I told Rob I was going to Addie's.

'Sounds good,' he said. 'Got some work to catch up on before we head out of town.'

Addie answered before the doorbell finished chiming.

'Hey!' She rubbed my arm. 'Not that I ever mind having a cocktail on a Tuesday night, but what's wrong?'

'My friend who was supposed to watch Jasper and Poppy bailed, and Rob, thinking he's being helpful, or, I don't know, not thinking at all, asked Marian to stay with them!'

'Holy shit!' Addie's mouth hung open.

'And she said yes! She's coming at noon on Friday.'

'OK, this is so much bigger than Pinot Grigio. We're going straight to scotch.' Addie took my hand and led me to the bar cart in the corner of the dining room. She filled two rocks glasses halfway. 'Let me grab ice,' she said but I'd quickly guzzled mine.

We sat in her living room on opposite ends of the couch.

I rubbed my temples. 'I don't know what to do anymore. Am I overreacting? Is Marian the sweet old lady Rob thinks she is and *I'm* the monster?'

'You could never be a monster. Trust me.' Addie played with the fringes on a throw pillow. 'Marian on the other hand?' She rolled her eyes.

'You sense it. It's not me, right?'

Addie shifted, resting an arm on the top of a couch cushion. She looked out the window and back at me, lips parted.

'What?' I asked.

'It's . . . nothing. I mean, I'm sure you already know part of it.'

I shook my head, confused.

'About your house?'

'No,' I said. 'What?'

'Hold on, we're going to need more scotch for this.' Addie went to the dining room and returned with the bottle. My head was already swimming as she refilled our glasses.

'What's my house got to do with anything?'

'You seriously don't know?' She stared wide-eyed, voice low.

'Stop, you're scaring me,' I said.

She took a long sip so I did the same.

'The couple who lived there before you . . .' She reached over and put her hand on mine. 'Their little girl drowned in the creek.' Her expression remained neutral. She was trying not to upset me further.

'Oh my God, that's . . .' My voice trailed off. Beyond the windows of her airy kitchen, I imagined moonlight bouncing off the water, high from recent rains. The conversation between Rob and Pete about the fence came rushing back to me. Pete's insistence – *You get a storm and that creek swells like a mother* – blurred with Addie's mother's voice – *Ah, yes, the house that nobody wanted.*

I buried my face in my hands, the room spinning from more than the drinks. 'I – I can't . . . I had no idea. That's—'

'It was heartbreaking.' Addie's soft voice was infused with sadness. 'Maybe I shouldn't have said anything. I assumed you knew. I mean, that's why the house was a steal.'

I dropped my hands. 'We benefited from someone's tragedy.' I felt sick. I wanted details. How did it happen? I couldn't bring myself to ask, knowing it would break me.

'The only reason I brought it up is because the girl's mother always thought a neighbor had something to do with it.'

'What?' It got more awful by the moment.

'It was all rumors.' Addie looked down at her glass. 'Everybody wanted to keep it hush-hush because there was no evidence and people assumed the poor mom had gone mad with grief.' Addie shuddered.

'How could she not?' I knew what it was like to lose a parent; I couldn't fathom losing a child. 'Were you close with the mom? The family?'

'I liked the dad more, actually. But I always thought if a neighbor *had* been involved,' Addie's eyes narrowed, 'it was most likely Marian.'

'Our house was vacant for months, wasn't it?' The listing photos spun through my head like a slideshow. That was the connection my brain had been struggling to make. Rob saw the house in April, but it was autumn in the pictures. The elms' leaves were full and golden rather than newly green or barely there.

'They had a tough time selling it.' Addie nodded.

'Rob knows.' My stomach dropped. 'Rob knows and he's never said a word. How could he not tell me something so . . .' I was spiraling. Colin's text – *We all think you're fragile* – flashed through my mind.

'It's such an upsetting thing. I'm sure Rob thought he was sparing you. And there's no way he'd have heard anything about Marian's possible involvement.'

'If I try to tell him, he'll never believe me. He thinks I'm para-noid, losing it . . .' Embarrassment stopped me from saying more. 'I can't let her be alone with Jasper and Poppy. I can't.' My brain was short-circuiting. 'What am I going to do?'

The gleam in Addie's eye reappeared. 'What if you served her some shellfish and sent her back to the ER?'

I waited for her to laugh. She didn't.

'Addie, that's crazy.'

'Is it?' She raised an eyebrow and tilted her glass back.

I watched her swallow and waited for her to say she was joking. She said nothing.

'Yes! It is crazy!' I said. 'Plus, everyone knows I'm well aware of her allergy. She left my home in an ambulance! I'd be convicted in a heartbeat.'

She poured more scotch.

'Well . . .' She clicked her nails against her glass. 'What if it was something else then? Something no one knows about? Hold on.' She hopped up, dashed toward the kitchen, and returned with her laptop. 'I just read this article about people eating poisonous mushrooms. Apparently, they grow all over New Jersey and they're easily mistaken for edible ones.' Her fingers flew across the keyboard. 'What was the headline? Something about "mushroom roulette?" They have a cool name. Here it is!' She pointed as an image filled half the screen. 'The death cap.' She gave a little shiver. 'It says, "Taking the 'fun' out of fungi, these death cap mushrooms look fairly harmless and quite similar to their safe-to-consume counter-parts, but they're deadly poisonous."' She glanced at me as I stared at the laptop, then continued reading. '"Cooking does not make it safe to eat a death cap mushroom."' She paused to interject a 'Duh,' and went on. '"Even as little as half of this pale yellowish-green mushroom cap can kill an adult, while a tinier portion could be fatal to a dog."' Addie cocked her head. 'I'm not a big dog person, are you?'

'This whole conversation is insane.' My head ballooned from the scotch. 'I couldn't possibly . . .'

'Anyway, I'm not saying kill Marian, just, you know, sideline her for a few days. Then you can stay home. Or, if you want to go to the wedding, *I'll* watch Jasper and Poppy – anyone but Marian.'

'That's crazy,' I slurred. Pulling her laptop toward me, I studied the article and clicked on a sidebar piece: *Where the Death Caps Dwell in NJ*. Photos of a nearby hiking spot flooded the screen.

I spun the laptop back to Addie.

'No way,' I said. 'If I did something like this, then I really would be a monster.'

'*Or* would you be a mom protecting her family *from* a monster?' she asked. 'Because, let's face it, you're never going to be rid of her. Women like that live to be one hundred and twelve. They thrive on drama and bad vibes.'

'And blueberry muffins.'

We laughed. Addie poured another round. 'Anyway, just some-thing to think about.'

The more we drank, the less desire I had to go home, to see Rob – Rob who'd played dumb when I repeatedly asked how and why our bid on the house had been accepted.

I could wake him, tell him everything Addie had shared, but it wouldn't make a difference. He'd talk in circles, twist things, convince me that he was only trying to protect me. He'd argue that he'd been looking out for the family, making a good investment, thinking of the children's future. He'd promise to call a fence guy first thing in the morning.

Addie opened Spotify and a woman's voice, high and sweet, echoed through the room, singing about problems with her drug dealer.

'Hey, have you ever heard of a band called Ladyfinger?' My mind drifted to Nina, then my father, Janice, Rob. Anger churned at the pit of my stomach. How many people had disappointed me and I'd simply absorbed it?

'No, and with a name like that, I'm glad I haven't,' she snorted. 'I can look them up?'

'No.' I finished my drink. 'I should probably go.'

Addie and I stood at the same time, each of us swaying slightly.

'C'mere.' She wrapped her arms around me. 'Whatever you decide to do, I've got your back,' she whispered.

Her peach scent mixed with the scotch's woody notes, comfort and danger colliding.

'Thank you,' I whispered back.

Our bedroom was dark except for the faint trace of moonlight. I stumbled over the bag Rob had begun packing for the wedding weekend. His snores competed with the droning of the window unit air conditioner. I crept into bed, still in my clothes, expecting to fall right to sleep, but my fury burned through the haze of alcohol. I lay wide awake thinking about mushrooms, Marian, my marriage, and the little girl who drowned less than fifty feet from where we lay.

I looked at Rob, sleeping with his hand tucked beneath his pillow, and wondered how many other secrets he was keeping.

THIRTY-ONE

Corey

Ma was getting ready to leave for a three-day tour of historic churches in St Augustine with the senior group from her parish. Irene Moffatt was driving her to St Cecilia's to meet the bus. Even though she was an atheist, Alice Blackwell had signed up, probably so she could write nasty reviews of restaurants and tour guides when she got back.

As Ma shuffled around the kitchen, I watched, memorizing her movements: the way she leaned a bit to the left because she kept putting off a knee replacement, the tilt of her head, how she looked at me like I was still worth something. I stored it all in my brain for later.

Had our time together taken a toll on her? Did her mouth turn down like that before I showed up last fall? Was she always so thin?

She hummed softly as she placed her pill organizer inside a large plastic bag alongside a banana and a small box of raisins for the road. I'd already helped myself to what I needed from her pharmaceutical collection. The pills were wadded in a tissue stuffed deep in my pocket.

When Ma got in the shower, I slipped a note inside her suitcase on wheels, buried it under the blue-and-white seersucker dress she saved for special occasions. It took me two hours to come up with a few lame sentences:

Thanks for trying to piece me back together.
Sorry I'm still broken.
I love you but I'm bad at showing it. Sorry about that too.

I enclosed a twenty-dollar bill and wrote:

P.S. Bring me back a keychain with the pope on it.

If I didn't write something dumb or jokey, she'd worry. It took so little to make her anxious.

When Irene drove up, I reached for Ma's suitcase on wheels to walk her out.

'You should probably stay inside,' she said.

'Why?'

Ma's shoulders drooped. 'Alice Blackwell thinks you attacked her cat.'

'What?' I almost laughed but Ma's eyes narrowed as they studied mine. Could she believe I'd become the kind of person who'd harm a pet? 'I didn't even know she had a cat!'

'She just spent six hundred dollars at the vet. The cat came home bloody and limping. She said you always fly out of the driveway. She thinks you hit Pepper-Pot on purpose to retaliate for her, well, trying to get you evicted.'

'It probably got in a fight with one of those fucking iguanas Alice loves!'

'Your language, Corey! Please.' Ma let out a small sigh. 'I'll be home in time for dinner Saturday. Oh, and if you could put out the recycling—'

'Friday morning. Yeah, I got it.' I nodded, apologizing in my head, knowing I'd fail her on even that small task. I pulled her into a weird, fast hug, accidentally stepping on her white sneakers, leaving a dirty smudge across the top. I let go just as fast. She looked confused, like she'd been mugged rather than embraced by her daughter. She straightened her glasses.

'Have fun,' I said, 'or as much as you can have looking at statues and crucifixes in the suffocating heat.'

After she left, I started getting antsy. If it was possible to look forward to something and dread it at the same time, that's how I felt, stomach spinning with butterflies and bad intentions. I wasn't due at Moffatt's until six but I wanted to get there early. Catch him as soon as he got off work. I had a few other things I needed to do before then. The first was text Desiree:

Meet me at Yo Momma at 4:30? I wrote.

She gave it a thumbs-up emoji.

Bring a backpack. I have something for you.

?? she replied, adding a big-eyed emoji.

I didn't answer, just put the phone in my pocket and opened the guest room closet.

* * *

I turned left out of the complex. I hadn't been back to that neighborhood since the night I took the tutu, the night I met Moffatt.

The whole way there I prayed no one would be around. Not
Dave, not the family with the little girl who looked nothing like
Frankie, and definitely not that jackass who called the cops on me.
My heart punched so hard it forced the air out of my lungs. By the
time I turned onto the street, I was breathless, sweating like I was
driving a getaway car not an old lady's Corolla.

Dave's driveway was empty. I pulled in and grabbed the envelope
on the front seat. I'd stuck the two hundred and forty-three dollars
I stole from the register inside along with a note:

Sorry I took this.

Also sorry I lied about it.

P.S. You should rehire Desiree.

I tossed it through his mail slot and ran back to the car.

Slow-rolling down the block, the family's Pathfinder wasn't there.
The house looked smaller than I remembered. A green jump rope
snaked across the sidewalk. I felt nothing as I knelt and placed the
thermos, barrette, and chunk of chalk beside it.

I kept the tutu, not because of the girl, but to remind me of
Moffatt.

When I got to Yo Momma, Desiree was already there, sitting in a
raspberry booth, laughing at something on her phone.

I slid across from her and put the box on the table.

'Hey!' She looked up, a big smile I'd done nothing to deserve
splashed across her face. 'I was surprised to hear from you. Happy
but surprised.'

'Almost didn't recognize you.' I flicked my eyes toward her hair,
dyed back to its original dark brown.

She groaned. 'My mom made me do it. School starts next week.'
She stuck out her tongue before turning her attention toward the
box.

I had no clue where Ma kept her gift wrap, so I'd covered it in
foil and taped a few of Alice Blackwell's zinnias on top. Beneath
the bright lights of the fro-yo shop, it looked like a bad science fair
project.

'What's with the mystery package?' Desiree whispered, moving
her thick eyebrows up and down.

'Let's eat first.' I stood and put the box under my arm.

'Keeping me in suspense? That's cool.' She crossed the shop in a few long strides and handed me a cup. 'Must be pretty valuable if you're carrying it with you.' She pointed with nails the bright yellow of off-brand mustard.

'You have no idea what it cost me.'

I paid and we sat again. I was too jittery to focus, checking the time on the neon wall clock hanging beside a sign for Yo Momma's rewards program. I took a lick of my vanilla-chocolate swirl. The cold made my teeth ache. Desiree downed hers like she hadn't eaten in days. In between bites, she told me about the kids she babysat, a cute boy who watched her Instagram stories but still hadn't 'liked' one. Every few minutes she gave the silver package a side glance like it was a bomb about to detonate.

Finally, I slid it toward her. 'Here,' I said. 'Don't open it in front of anybody.'

Her eyes popped. 'Why? Is it a dildo?' She held her hands a foot apart. 'My friend Vanessa's mom has this—'

'Jesus Christ! It's not a dildo!'

'OK, OK, chill, it's just . . . you seem like an independent woman who probably has, I don't know, experience . . . or . . . wisdom to share in that . . . area . . .' She pointed toward her lap.

I snorted. 'It's for school.'

She tapped her nails against the lid, foil crinkling, before shaking it. Of course, it wasn't breakable, but still, it made me nervous. My legs bounced beneath the table. I was burning up even as we sat under a blower pumping out cold air like we were in a polar bear exhibit.

'There's a note inside explaining what to do, how to use it, to keep unwanted eyes off you.'

She leaned closer. 'Is it the answers to the AP calc and physics tests?' She grabbed my wrist. Her fingers, soft and fleshy, cracked something open inside me. 'Because that would, like, totally make my senior year so much easier.'

'Sorry, no, it's not that.' I took a big breath. 'But it is for your future, so put it somewhere safe.'

Desiree frowned, probably thinking it was a thesaurus, not fifty-two thousand dollars in cash – money from the sale of the house where I lost everything that mattered.

She bit the pink plastic spoon. 'I don't mean to sound ungrateful, but why are you doing this?'

'Doing what?'

'Being nice. Taking an interest in me. Giving me a present.'

This kid and the questions. I wanted to leave her with something encouraging like, 'I'm doing this because I think you're smart and you deserve a really great life,' but I didn't want to freak her out. Instead, I said, 'Think of it as a birthday gift.'

'Again, totally appreciate the gesture.' She held up her palms. 'But my birthday was in May. Don't you remember? I wore a tiara to work?'

'Must've blocked that out.'

'Well, thanks.' She shrugged. 'I don't know what to say. I know that's hard to believe 'cause I'm usually babbling, but I'm not really good at being gracious. Don't have tons of practice.' She smiled. 'You know what my mom got me for my birthday?'

'What?'

'Socks and underpants.'

'Could've been worse.' I smirked. 'Could've been maxi pads and acne cream.'

She wriggled like her gummy worms had come to life then looked at me. 'I don't know, I sorta feel bad.'

'Why?'

'I didn't get you anything.'

'Next time.' My nose tingled, a lump wedging in my throat. With her brown hair and loose curls framing her face, all I could think of was Frankie, what she might've looked like if she'd had the chance to grow up. Under the table, I twisted the skin on the back of my thigh and glanced at the clock. Four fifteen. I swiveled and stuck a leg outside the booth. 'Gotta hit the road.'

She walked me to the car, package in one hand, bike helmet in the other, and peeked in the back seat.

'Um, what is that?' She jutted her chin toward the head of Alice Blackwell's flamingo windsock. Its hacked-up pink threads spilled across the seat. I planned to mail it to her with a note that read: *Hey Teri J, you're a zero-star person* from somewhere that would confuse her, like maybe Delaware.

'It's—'

'Forget it.' She put the box on the roof of the car, sun glaring off the foil. 'I don't want to know.' She snapped on her helmet, zipped the box into her empty backpack, and slid her arms through the straps.

'Yeah, you probably don't.'

As I opened the car door, she threw her arms around me, whacking the side of my head with her helmet.

'Sorry! Sorry!' She stepped back. 'I'm just getting this weird vibe like this is goodbye or something.'

'Well, yeah, it's goodbye. I'm getting in my car and you're getting on your bike – going different places. That's how goodbyes work.'

She screwed her lips into a side pucker. 'Fine. See you around.'

I watched her pedal away. At the stop sign at the edge of the parking lot, she turned back and dipped her head toward her knapsack. 'Thanks – for whatever this is!'

From the driver's seat, I waved with one hand, the other in my pocket, making sure the pills were still there.

I was waiting on Moffatt's welcome mat when he turned the corner.

'Hey.' A smile spread across his face. 'You're early.'

My pulse picked up. Was I happy to see him or was it adrenaline?

'I was running errands and it didn't seem worth driving back to Whispering Palms. Sorry, I can always go wait in my mom's hot car.' I jerked my thumb toward the parking lot and grinned.

'No, I'm glad you're here.' He opened the door and let me in first. 'I'm gonna change real quick. Make yourself at home.'

'I'll fix us a drink.' I held up the wine I brought with me.

'Sounds good.'

As I opened his cabinets hunting for wine glasses, I listened for sounds from Moffatt's bedroom. Had his kid told me the truth? What if Ryan made it all up? Everything was riding on intel I'd gotten from a nine year old. What the fuck was I thinking?

I put the glasses on the counter, hurried down the hall, and knocked on Moffatt's bedroom door, nudging it open at the same time. He sat on his bed, back to me, top drawer of his nightstand open. There it was – resting inside a black and silver case. He closed the lid and turned, his shirt half-unbuttoned. I stood there frozen, mouth open.

'Don't tell me you saw a gecko in the kitchen? Ry spotted one last week and I called—'

'No, no, sorry,' I stammered. Seeing the gun – a reminder of why I was there, what I needed to do next – made my head buzz. I'd started something. Could I finish it?

I shook myself out of my trance. 'Where's your corkscrew?' Sweat beaded on my forehead. What if he didn't have one? He was a single dad who told me he used to drink too much. I should've gotten a twist-off or stuck with bourbon. I held my breath, waiting for him to blow my plans to shit.

'Drawer to the right of the dishwasher.'

'Gotcha.' I pulled the door closed and raced back to the kitchen. Would he be out in five minutes or thirty seconds? Inside the drawer, my fingers grazed the knives, savoring the sharpness of their edges, before grabbing the corkscrew.

At the liquor store, I'd picked something I didn't like – merlot – so I wouldn't be tempted. With a heavy hand, I poured two glasses and took out the tissue that had held the pills I'd crushed into a fine powder while waiting in Moffatt's parking lot. I stirred the mixture with my finger, fought the urge to lick it, and rinsed my hands.

From the time he finished his drink, he'd be awake for thirty minutes tops. I knew because I'd tried it. Took Ma's sleeping pills, ground them up the same way, added them to a few inches of wine and started a stopwatch. I sat in bed, waiting for sleep to drag me under. When I couldn't keep my eyes open another second, I hit stop. Twenty-three minutes and eleven seconds. Moffatt was bigger than I was, but his tolerance was likely lower. I had to time it just right.

He walked into the kitchen in a blue polo shirt, khaki shorts, and sneakers. I hoped he wasn't going to suggest we take a walk. I handed him a glass, barely able to meet his eyes. Would he think it was nerves? In his mind, was this a date? Or two messed-up people killing time?

'Cheers.' I raised my glass and touched it to his. 'To a Wednesday night without Linda.'

'Would you care to share why you're feeling that way?' He did a spot-on imitation of our grief group leader.

I smirked and took a sip, hoping he'd copy me keep period. It worked.

He sniffed the glass. 'Maybe it's my dishwasher pods, but this tastes kind of chalky. Gritty, right?'

My heart beat so hard I half expected my shirt to vibrate. 'Swirl it like a wine snob.' I swished the liquid, the color of dried blood, around my glass. I swallowed a bit to cover my mouth where a twitch was kicking up along my jawline. 'You get used to it. Lady at the store said it's a top seller.'

Moffatt set the glass down. If he poured it out, it was over. I had no back-up plan. I held my breath as he moved away from the sink and opened a cabinet. I exhaled and took a baby sip as he dumped a bag of chips into a large bowl and a jar of salsa into a smaller one.

He carried them to the coffee table in front of the couch and I followed with our glasses, making sure I knew which was mine.

'Mind if we sit for a bit before I start dinner? Didn't have time for lunch and I'm embarrassed to say I think I can already feel the wine hitting me.'

'Lightweight.' I smiled.

'Out of practice,' he said.

We sat, dipping chips and crunching. I studied his hands, his fingers. When I'd asked Ryan how his dad opened the case, he'd held up the index finger on his right hand. Kids weren't known for getting the details down. Was that the right finger? The right hand? I could not fuck this up.

I knew I should ask Moffatt about his son – if the move to Texas was still on, how he was doing with all that. Would the stress of talking about it make him drink faster? It seemed like an asshole move, even for me. Still, it was ruder not to bring it up after how distracted and down he'd been last week.

'Any chance your ex broke off her engagement? Decided the whole "everything's bigger in Texas" lifestyle isn't for her?'

Moffatt took a long swallow. 'Move's still on. Ry doesn't know yet. We're gonna tell him together Sunday when Heather comes to pick him up. She says it's better if he doesn't have too long to think about it. I don't agree – with any of it – but my opinion doesn't carry much weight with her anymore.'

He took another sip. Half of what I'd poured was gone. My body started tingling. I looked at his big wall clock. Ten minutes had passed. He rubbed his forehead. 'Long day.'

'Anything out of the ordinary?' I scraped a tomato off the edge of the bowl with a chip. I had no appetite but who knew when I'd eat again.

'This older lady came in. Phone scam victim. They got her for a couple grand. Bad, obviously, but what struck me was how much she didn't want to go home. She was so lonely. Confused. Fearful.' He drank more wine and shook his head. 'It made me think about my mom. If I end up following Ry to Texas, who's going to look out for her? My sister's here, but she's caught up in her own stuff.'

Like finding a new hood ornament, I almost said, nerves making me manic.

'With your work, you ever find it hard not to lose faith in humanity?' Why did I ask? To gauge how much he'd hate me after?

'Sometimes.' He tipped the last half-inch of merlot into his mouth. 'Growing up, it was all I ever wanted to be. Closest thing to a superhero, right? Thought I'd be able to protect people, save them. Some days you make a difference. Others, you don't.' He picked up a chip and dropped it in the bowl. 'Sorry,' he said, his speech slow. 'I'm really beat.' He slumped against the couch.

My heart was a woodpecker knocking hard against my chest.

'You had a long day. This heat . . . Want to rest for a bit?' I put my glass on the table and folded my hands between my knees to stop them from shaking.

'Yeah, that'd be . . .' He started to tilt toward the far end of his couch.

'In your bed?' Was it too much? I waited, bending my fingers backward 'til my knuckles cracked.

'Wow.' He grinned, even as his eyelids drooped. 'Didn't see that coming.'

'Let's go.' I held out my hand slick with sweat and hoped he'd assume it was from the punishing August heat.

He led the way and dropped onto the bed. I curled under his arm, gently nudging him closer to the nightstand.

'Hey, sorry, I'm . . . I promised you dinner.'

'I didn't come here to eat,' I whispered.

He half-moaned, half-laughed as I rested my head on his shoulder. His hand slid down my back. I tried to soak it all in – the feel of his skin on mine, his scent, the sound of his breathing.

For a few seconds, I thought about changing my plans – maybe staying there in Moffatt's bed, helping him work through whatever was coming his way with his son. It could all be different. He wasn't Kenny, who'd cut corners at work, at home, who'd lost job after job because he thought he was smarter than everybody else. I could start another life. But Frankie wouldn't be part of it. If I moved on, her memory would fade. Like Ryan said, the hole would close. Moffatt would fill it. I couldn't do that. Frankie deserved more.

'I was gonna wait 'til after dinner.' He pulled printouts of newspaper articles from his pocket and handed them to me. 'Did a little digging, made some calls. Don't know if this helps.' His eyelids fluttered then shut. 'You'd been searching names, should've been looking at the house. Your house.' His voice trailed off.

I skimmed the pages, then read each again, slowly, a picture forming in my mind. A blinding clarity making my scalp tingle.

Moffatt's breathing deepened, shifting from light to heavy snoring. Gently, I rolled him onto his side and crept off the bed. Opening the drawer, I took his arm. It was heavy as a log as I pulled it closer. He groaned. I stopped. My stomach spun, mind turning back to the kitchen drawer, to the knives. No. Severing his fingertip was too much. I couldn't hurt him more than I'd originally planned.

I held my breath as I maneuvered his hand toward the case. It just reached. I swept his index finger down the front and held it there 'til I heard the soft click. It barely registered over my pulse echoing in my ears. I placed Moffatt's arm back on the bed.

The gun felt light, magical in my palm. I aimed it at the floor and brushed Moffatt's lips with mine.

'Thanks, Mike,' I whispered. 'But not everyone can be saved.'

THIRTY-TWO

Laurel

I kept my back to the kitchen window, unable to bear the sight of morning sunlight glinting off the water. How could we continue living in this house?

Rob poured coffee into his travel mug and walked to the table. It had been more than a day since Addie told me a child drowned in the creek, and still I'd said nothing about it to my husband. I didn't want to hear him attempt to justify how or why he'd failed to tell me something so terrible yet significant.

I didn't look up as he pulled out a chair and sat across from me. Instead, I focused on Poppy, nursing in my arms.

'How do we fix this, Laurel?'

'I don't know, Rob.'

'We leave tomorrow for three days . . . for a celebration . . . not to mention the first time you and I will be alone without the kids in who knows how long. I want us to have a good time.'

'I know you do.' I shifted Poppy onto my shoulder to burp her. 'Do you remember that therapist I saw in the city?'

His eyes widened, probably hoping that I was going to say I'd scheduled an appointment with her.

'She told me that I shouldn't ignore my feelings. She said I should explore them, express them.' Rob nodded. 'I've told you I don't trust Marian and you've dismissed me every time.'

In the past, my eyes would've stung as I blinked back tears. Instead, my body simmered with anger.

'Well, I'm not a therapist, obviously.' Rob leaned forward as I arched back. 'But do you think maybe you're projecting all your fears onto this one woman?' He kept his tone even, soft. 'You have trust issues because of what happened to your mom, and I get that. But you're wrong about Mimi.'

My eyes locked on a baby carrot beneath the table. What more could I say?

'I love you.' He stretched out his hand. I kept mine on Poppy's back. He sighed. 'I want us to have fun together again.' He stood, pushed in the chair and grabbed his travel mug. 'It's going to be great, you'll see.' He placed a finger under my chin and tilted my face up to meet his, swaying his hips side to side, trying to lighten the mood. 'We'll dance. The food's supposed to be outrageous – you'll love that. And the kids will be just fine. Trust me, Laur, everything's going to work out.'

He kissed me lightly on the lips and squeezed Poppy's hand before walking toward the door.

'I'd like to believe you, but as you just said, I have trust issues.'

He turned, unsure if I was being sarcastic, but said nothing. The kitchen was quiet except for the rhythmic patting of my hand on Poppy's back.

'Have a nice day,' I added, eager to be rid of him.

'I'll try to come home early,' he said.

I'd heard that before.

I deposited Poppy in her crib while I dressed Jasper in pants and a long-sleeved shirt.

'It's too hot, Mommy,' he whined.

'We're going on an adventure!' I bent down and cupped his chin. 'There'll be ants and spiders and all sorts of creepy-crawly things!' I tickled him lightly from his belly to the top of his head. He giggled.

'What about snakes?' he demanded.

'Maybe!' I stood and took his hand. 'Let's go find out!'

I parked beneath a tree, hoping the shade would keep our snacks cool while we were gone. I put on a baseball cap and sunglasses before scooping Poppy out of her car seat and wiggling her into the carrier. Jasper continued the *We're Going on a Bear Hunt* chant he'd started in the driveway.

He tried to pull away but I held his hand as much for safety as to steady my nerves until we were deep in the woods. Poppy pressed to my chest slowed my racing heart; still my eyes darted left to right and back again, waiting to spot what I needed.

An older couple, outfitted like Patagonia spokesmodels, passed. Were they taking note of what we were wearing? What we looked like?

'Morning,' they chirped.

I waved and pretended to trip over a rock, stepping in front of Jasper to obscure his face. Though it was cooler in the forest, sweat pooled beneath my breasts and dripped down my stomach. After ten minutes, my shoulders and back began to ache from Poppy's weight, but I was stronger than I had been in months – and I was determined. I'd spent Tuesday night and all of Wednesday considering my options. After Susan called Wednesday afternoon to say she was pleased to hear 'Robbie found a solution,' and to tell me how lucky I was to have such a caring neighbor, the decision crystallized in my mind.

When I was sure we were alone, I put my sunglasses on top of my cap and studied the underbrush. We hiked forty, fifty more yards, pockets of crisp air driving me forward. The musty scent of pine and damp earth flooded our nostrils, birds screeching overhead providing an eerie soundtrack. At the base of a tree, beneath ferns, I saw them – a trio of mushrooms that matched the ones I'd seen on Addie's laptop.

I stepped closer. How would I know for sure they were the ones? How could I be certain she'd eat what I brought her? Was she as distrusting of me as I was of her? I removed the plastic sandwich bag from my pocket. How many did I need?

'Keep going, Mommy!' Jasper swatted my arm as I crouched low to study the caps, Poppy's drool soaking the neck of my T-shirt. 'What are you doing?'

'Just thinking of a new recipe.' I turned, reached up and tugged the bill of his baseball cap lower so he couldn't see. As I put the bag over my hand and plucked the mushrooms, they separated from the earth easily, like they wanted to be mine.

'Hey! I can't see!' Jasper shouted. 'Mommy!'

I tucked the baggie in my pocket and straightened Jasper's cap. 'I spy a chipmunk!' I pointed up the trail. 'Let's go say hi!'

He ran ahead. I followed, my hand returning to my pocket, pressing my thumb into the caps' tender flesh. I watched Jasper's small legs pumping, arms flung wide. My heart swelled. I looked down at Poppy, her hair soft as goose feathers, fingers shoved in her tiny pink mouth. There was nothing I wouldn't do for them, to keep them safe.

The words Lyle Hartsell spoke at his sentencing echoed in my head: 'I was trying to protect my family. When I felt like I couldn't, something dark inside me took over.'

I knew what he meant.

Jasper sat at the kitchen table while I rolled out the pie crust on the flour-covered countertop.

'I wanna help!' he whimpered, exhausted from the hike.

'You can help with dinner, OK?'

I pressed the dough into Marian's blue fluted pie dish, the one she'd used for her berry crumble. I'd forgotten to give it back. When I discovered it in the cabinet, it felt like a sign – the perfect excuse to go over there with something homemade. A thank you.

'No!' Jasper bellowed. 'I want to help now!'

'OK.' I gave in. 'Press your fingers here,' I directed, watching him push the crust up the sides of the plate. 'There. All done.'

I topped the dough with foil and pie weights to pre-bake and placed it in the oven.

'That's it, mister. Nap time!' I didn't want him to do any more, to be complicit. I doubted he'd ever distinguish one walk in the woods from another, one quiche his mother made from all the rest. But still.

Together, we tiptoed up the steps to avoid waking Poppy. I lay beside him reading *Are You My Mother?* and patted my pocket until his breath became a whisper and I could slip away.

Downstairs, I assembled the ingredients I'd collected at a farmers' market on the way home from the hike: tomatoes and onions, eggs and cream, a wedge of gruyère. I'd picked an array of mushrooms – shiitake, portobello, oyster – there too. I placed those in the fridge and pulled the baggie from my pocket. Beads of condensation clung to the plastic. The greenish caps felt slimy as they dropped into my palm. I didn't rinse them, afraid water might reduce their potency, if they were even the right ones.

In my panic that the mushrooms might not work, I'd stopped at a seafood market. My hands trembled as I plucked the shrimp from their shells. *What was I doing? How had it come to this?* I minced the silvery-white fish into minute slivers. I needed only a tiny amount – enough to cause a reaction but not so much that she'd smell or taste it. I swept the rest inside one of Poppy's dirty diapers. No one would look there.

Tears stung my eyes while I chopped, whisked, and poured the filling into the cooled crust. Sliding the quiche into the oven, its heat made me dizzy. *Who was I? What had I become? Breathe*, I commanded. *You're doing this for your family.*

I moved around the kitchen in a daze, wiping countertops, washing bowls and utensils. I started a load of laundry while the quiche baked. Through the basement window, I saw Marian's legs, ghostly white against her floral sundress, as she puttered in her yard, watering can swinging low by her side. Guilt rose up in my throat. Then I thought about the knife in the playroom, the oven set to the highest temperature, and I swallowed it. If I didn't stop her, what would happen next?

When the timer sounded, I eased the quiche from the oven. It was beautiful, golden, puffed up like it was proud of itself. The edges weren't perfect because I'd let Jasper help, but I'd explain that to Marian and she'd eat it up.

Through my dining-room window, I looked for her car. It wasn't in her driveway. Moving quickly, I swept the egg shells, the empty cream container, onion skins, and gruyère wrapper into a small plastic bag and hurried out the mudroom door.

As I crossed the backyard to sneak everything into Marian's garbage can, Addie called to me.

I jumped like I'd stuck a wet finger in an electrical outlet. 'Hey!'

'Whatcha got there?' She pointed to the bag.

'Tried a new recipe thanks to your suggestion.' I bounced on my toes, manic with adrenaline. 'Just taking out the trash.'

'I hope it does the trick.' Addie winked.

'Me too.' Talking about it made me more anxious, so I changed the subject. 'What are you up to today?'

'Headed out for a run in a bit.'

'Enjoy!' I called, moving toward Marian's, the plastic garbage bag leaking, leaving a trail behind me.

Back inside, I showered while the quiche cooled. I slipped into a nice skirt, a ruffled blouse, a pair of sandals – the image of a home-maker. I looked for my mother's amethyst earrings but still couldn't find them.

As I crept down the steps, my head buzzed. It was three p.m. Jasper and Poppy would be awake soon. I peeked out the window again. Marian's car was parked in her driveway. My pulse sped up. I needed to make the delivery.

Walking across my lawn to hers, my heart thundered in my ears. I glanced over each shoulder, toward the street, then the creek, and thought of the girl. Her family. Where were they? I heard Addie's voice in my head – *I always thought if a neighbor had been involved, it was most likely Marian* – and continued toward her front door.

'Laurel,' Marian said. 'I wasn't expecting you.'

Was it wrong that it gave me a little thrill to see her thrown off? She looked as if I'd awakened her from a nap, her puff of white hair flattened on one side.

'Hi!' I smiled, tilting my head like she often did. 'Rob and I can't thank you enough for agreeing to watch Jasper and Poppy,' I said exactly as I'd rehearsed in our bathroom mirror. 'You're sure it's not too much trouble?'

'Of course not! I'm delighted.' Her eyes softened and, for a moment, I thought about turning back.

'Well, you're going to need to keep up your strength, believe me!' I held her pie plate aloft, the way she'd done on my doorstep. 'I'm sorry I'm returning this so late. I'm sure Rob told you your crumble was a huge hit.'

A rosy pink bloomed on her pale cheeks.

'I hope you like quiche. I got the vegetables from the farmers' market!' I sounded so fake. Could she tell? 'Oh, and Jasper insisted on helping, so you'll see his fingerprints all over the crust. But his hands were clean, I promise!' I laughed, laying it on thick as my insides turned to cottage cheese.

'It looks very tempting.' She reached for the dish. It was in her hands. I shoved mine deep into my skirt pockets. I thought I might faint.

'Nice and light for a summer evening,' I added.

'And I'm famished,' she said.

'With all your gardening, you must work up quite an appetite!'

'I'll have it tonight,' she declared with an exaggerated nod.

'I hope you do!' My stomach cartwheeled. 'I started writing up the children's routine. I can bring that over to you later.'

'Rob said he'll give me a key to your house in case I want to take them to the park.'

My God, she was good at this. I wouldn't let her get away with it. 'But you already have a key.' I smiled.

'I don't,' she insisted, shaking her head.

'Then I'll be sure to bring one along with my notes on Jasper and Poppy's schedules.'

'There's really no need for that, dear.' She cocked her head. 'I know what children like. Speaking of little ones, where are yours now?' She craned her neck in the direction of my home.

'Napping,' I said. 'The house is locked. They'll be up shortly. I wanted to bring you this while it was still warm.'

'I know you're only a few feet away, but you shouldn't leave them like that, Laurel.'

My name coming out of her mouth made my skin prickle. 'You're right. I should go.' I nodded toward the quiche. 'I hope you enjoy it!'

Walking back across the cool grass, I forced myself not to run, to stay calm and breathe. The hardest part was over.

But what would Rob say when Marian landed in the ER? Would he know that I caused it? That it was intentional? If he found out, I would apologize, of course, and say I'd gotten the mushrooms from a farmers' market.

'There must've been a terrible mix-up,' I'd gasp and toss out the ones waiting in our fridge. Maybe I'd even search for the articles Addie had shown me and tell him it wasn't uncommon.

Marian was hardy. I'd seen her carrying full bags of mulch and potting soil. She'd recover quickly.

Rob would go to the wedding alone and, amid the majesty of Emily's scotch tasting bar, he'd forget about everything else.

At my first restaurant job, I'd worked under a chef who constantly reminded us, 'Taste your cream. Use only the freshest eggs. Consider the temperature of your butter. One bad ingredient ruins everything.'

In my mind, Marian had become the spoiled cream, the rotten egg, the cold butter. If I didn't stop her, she'd ruin everything.

THIRTY-THREE

Corey

Powered by Red Bull and rage, I flew up I-95, passing eighteen-wheelers, hillsides littered with cows, and endless miles of nothing. I drove as dusk drifted into darkness and dawn slipped into day, stopping only to pee, get gas, and choke down fast food to chase the caffeine jitters.

I didn't have a deadline other than to get there before Moffatt woke up and realized his gun was gone. How fast would he figure out where I was? How quick could I put a hole in her heart the way she'd done to mine?

Each time I touched the gun under my seat, Moffatt's face floated into my mind. I shoved it out. He was a means to an end – never *the* end, I reminded myself, changing lanes, pressing the pedal to the floor.

It was nearly a year to the day since I lost Frankie. It felt like a minute ago but also a lifetime. Parts of that evening were blurry. Others arrived in high-definition, their colors sharp, scenes spooling out behind my eyes like a movie beamed into my brain from a satellite. I replayed them, anger keeping me alert, fueling me like gasoline.

I'd left work a little early that afternoon because it was Friday and I'd already put in sixty hours that week if you counted the emails I answered after Frankie was in bed. The guilt that came from tapping out a text while she told me about her day had been eating me up. She needed more attention. I knew Kenny wasn't giving her enough. He parked her in front of the TV or the iPad so he could scroll through Facebook or nap. I'd joked that I was going to get a nanny cam to spy on my husband. If only I'd done it.

I wanted to keep Frankie up later, 'til nine or ten, so I could spend more time with her, but Kenny had said no, that she'd be crabby the next day.

'You could put her to sleep at midnight, she'll still be up before seven and she'll be a demon by noon,' he'd argue.

When I'd pulled into our driveway that afternoon, Kenny's truck was there. It was quiet inside the house. I figured he'd taken Frankie to the park or the pool. They could walk to both. Kenny said he was teaching her to swim. But the bag with her goggles and sunscreen sat beside the door. I kicked off my heels and charged my laptop, knowing I'd need to get back to clients, put out a few Friday-night fires after Frankie was asleep. In the kitchen, I pulled an open bottle of white wine from the fridge and poured a glass.

On weekends, I tried to make a nice dinner: pasta with shrimp and pesto for Kenny and me, butter and a snowstorm of cheese for Frankie. I planned to take her to the zoo the next day. Just the two of us. She loved the monkeys, the otters, the prairie dogs playing peek-a-boo. Other than that, we had nothing scheduled. Kenny was more distracted than usual. Not focused on Frankie, me, the house, or his job search. I planned to get on his case about finding work. Frankie was starting full-day preschool in September.

I pulled a bag of frozen shrimp and the garlic breadsticks Frankie loved from the freezer and stared out the back window. The creek was high. A hurricane down south had brought days of wind and rain our way, sending Frankie scrambling into our bed, scared by tree branches slapping the windows.

I glanced outside again. It was the first clear, dry day we'd had in a while. Maybe we could have dinner in the backyard. Beyond the picnic table, something orangey-pink caught my eye. It looked like Frankie's floral dress. She would've worn it every day if we let her. It must've blown off the clothesline and landed in the creek. I'd have to fish it out, wash it again. If it had gotten ripped on a rock, she'd be crushed. I grabbed a box of penne from the pantry. Clock on the microwave said it was nearly six. They'd be home soon, probably starving. Kenny usually forgot to pack snacks. I'd told him to stop wasting money at that overpriced ice-cream truck.

The mudroom door squeaked open. I pressed the oven's preheat button and spun around. 'Where's my girl?'

'Hey.' Kenny looked surprised. 'You're home early.'

I crossed the tiny kitchen, expecting my daughter to be a few steps behind him. She wasn't. Kenny's eyes moved toward the playroom.

'Where – where's Frankie? Upstairs?' His flushed face paled a little as he shoved a dark curl from his sweaty forehead.

'What do you mean?' I asked. 'Isn't she with you?'

'Frankie!' he shouted and pushed past me.

The house was so small, there's no way she wouldn't have heard him – us. I'd been there long enough to start dinner and drink half a glass of wine. She'd have come running down to see me if she were upstairs. Maybe she was in my closet, trying on my heels again.

Kenny raced up the steps. I followed, confused more than concerned – unaware I was still on the other side, living in the sweet before, the glorious unknowing.

'Where were you?' I demanded as Kenny flung back the shower curtain. 'Why wasn't Frankie with you?'

'I went next door for a minute. I told her to go back in the house, to wait for me here.'

I trailed him from room to room, searching under beds, in closets, calling her name, eyes scanning my jewelry, makeup. All untouched.

'Why couldn't she just go with you?' My tongue felt thick, slow. He couldn't look at me. In an instant, I knew everything. I smelled it. Where he'd been. What he'd been doing. The little flag of fabric – the orange and pink flowers. The creek. I turned, shaking, and nearly fell down the steps, tripping over the flip-flops Kenny stacked up on the sides, promising he'd put them away, never doing it.

My heart thumped like an animal caught in a trap. I ran out the side door, legs shaking, late-day light leaving a gauzy haze over everything. I saw it all in slow motion. The dress, its colors darkened by the water. Her hair fanned across the rock where she'd smacked her head. Her face covered by the brown-green water. The skunky, foul smell. My brain couldn't take it in.

I screamed. A wail that started at the base of my body and reached the top of the tallest elm. Staggering into the creek, I pulled my baby into my arms. Her lips were violet. Blood from the red gash on her forehead trickled into the dirty water.

'Frankie, Frankie!' I pleaded in her ear, stroking her rubbery cheek. 'Frankie! Please!' I waited for her to open her sea-green eyes.

On nights I worked late, we played a game: I'd kiss the top of her head, thinking she was asleep, and her eyelids would fly open. 'Gotcha!' she'd squeal, wrapping her arms around my neck until I tickled her and tucked her in again.

But her eyes stayed closed, her mouth silent. I carried her, mud squishing between my toes, to the mossy bank.

Kenny dropped to his knees, repeating, 'No,' his hands tearing at his hair.

How many compressions? How many breaths? People tell you in an emergency it all comes back. It didn't. Not for me. How long did I try before Kenny took over? I watched his hands and wondered what he'd done with his wedding ring. Irrational thoughts dove in and out of my head.

The EMTs tried too. Who'd called them? Legs encircled us along with murmurs and the words 'no pulse.' I sank into the cold, wet ground to lay beside my daughter as they strapped her to the stretcher.

In the ambulance, an older lady, a volunteer, held my hand. 'Never give up hope. Never give up hope,' she whispered so fervently I knew it was over. My life was over.

We left the hospital with only Frankie's dress, still damp, smelling like the creek that claimed her.

Days later, I sat on the playroom floor, delirious, wrecked, going over and over it – the endless hows and whys. A picture formed in my mind: plastic hands sticking up from the other side of the creek. A doll? Is that what Frankie saw? Is that what tempted her to try to cross it? Another image surfaced: a lock of blond hair poking out from beneath leaves and vines.

I stood and raced outside in only underpants and a tank top. I waded into the icy cold water that had stolen my only child and tore through the soil and stones, the worms and muck, until my hands were filthy but still empty. Had I imagined it?

Who would bury a doll on the far side of a creek, knowing a child who couldn't swim would try to reach it?

Someone who wanted to destroy my family.

Across the street from the house, I rested my head on the steering wheel. I'd driven close to twenty hours, body cramped and aching. I'd vowed never to return to this place. But I'd come to do one thing. I shrugged on the cardigan Ma kept in the back seat. It covered the bulk of the gun tucked inside my shorts. I started to open the car door when a woman walked out of my house – my old house – carrying a blue dish.

She looked over her shoulder in my direction, then back the other way toward the creek. I slunk down in the seat as she talked with Marian for a couple minutes, handed over the plate, and hurried back to her house.

My stomach churned, coffee mixing with greasy hash browns and a breakfast sandwich that had tasted like plastic. No flowers bloomed along my walkway. No potted plants waited on the stoop. Frankie and I would've been buying mums, picking pumpkins, decorating the front steps. Sadness hit me quick and hard, sudden as a car crash. I closed my eyes for a few minutes waiting for it to pass. When I opened them, Laurel West was leaving my home, sticking a baby and a boy in a double stroller and rushing toward the other end of the block. I watched until she turned the corner.

It's time. I touched the tutu for luck and stepped onto Cold Creek Lane.

*　*　*

The door to her side porch was unlocked. I snuck in like a thief. I wanted to surprise her. How would she react? I hoped she'd shit her pants with fear. But knowing Addie, she'd play it cool, like she'd been expecting me.

I inched inside her fancy kitchen real slow in case she'd spotted me through her front windows and decided to hide. Her flashy convertible was parked in the driveway, but that didn't mean she was home.

I scanned for clues she was there – an afternoon cup of coffee, a pre-dinner glass of wine – focusing on anything other than the fireworks exploding in my stomach. The house made the usual noises: the humming of the fridge, the sighing of the central air she'd installed. I looked around the kitchen, living room, and dining area at all the changes she'd made after railroading her mother, Helen, into that facility – Helen who remembered the ages and birthdays of every kid on the block.

Her decor was what other people might call 'chic' or 'stylish,' but to me it looked staged, fake, just like Addie. No large pieces, no china cabinets, nowhere for her to hide what I came to see.

At the bottom of the staircase, I listened. Quiet up there too.

I'd start in her cellar. The smell hit me as I opened the door. Years of the creek spilling over, seeping into the concrete floor, made my breath catch. I flicked the switch at the top of the stairs, flooding the small dank space with yellowy fluorescence. I kept my hand on the gun, my back pressed to the wall, steps groaning beneath me.

My eyes struggled to adjust. I'd expected to see containers, boxes, tubs. Helen's life condensed. Addie must've tossed it all. There wasn't much down there – Christmas decorations and an old roll-top desk. I slid the lid up. A key peeked out of a cubby. I ran my fingers over the familiar grooves and the monogrammed keychain Kenny told me he'd lost. In another sat a pair of purple stone earrings. An engagement ring. I plucked a piece of paper from the back, unfolded it, and saw my own handwriting – the note I'd sent Laurel West.

I lost my family. Now yours is in danger.

How had Addie gotten in? I was grinding my teeth, my pulse pounding in my temples. Tucked in a larger section was a stack of photos. The top shot was of a boy with dark hair and freckles standing beside hydrangeas. Hydrangeas I'd planted. In others, he held a football, so close to the creek, it made my knees buckle. It was the same kid who'd just climbed into the stroller. The boy I'd seen in the farmers' market photo. Jasper West. Other pictures – of a baby, a couple asleep – had been taken through a window. A shiver shot up my spine. I set down the photos and opened a pink folder. I held the top sheet to the light for a better look. Last Will and Testament of Robert and Laurel West.

How was Addie plotting to rip their lives apart? I leafed through the pages, dread settling in the pit of my stomach. I stuck the folder in the back of my shorts, Ma's cardigan concealing it. A termination letter from the 'It's Your Turn!' toy company, dated a year ago, stared up at me.

I almost missed the knife, but its red handle caught my eye. What role did it play in Addie's twisted plans? My hand traveled back to the gun.

I started to open a drawer when I heard the creak of floorboards above me. A door closed. I waited, mouth so dry I could barely swallow.

Water rushed through the pipes overhead, a toilet flushing, I took the steps two at a time.

I was there, outside the bathroom door, when she opened it.

'Jesus Christ!' She jumped back. Her face, already flushed from her run, burned a darker pink. 'I had a feeling you'd be back,' she said, like I was a nuisance, a Girl Scout returning to collect cookie money, not the mother of a small child whose death I was certain she'd had a hand in.

Addie had been dismissing me since the second she came to town, saving all her attention for my then-husband.

She stepped into the hall. I followed her eyes as they darted to the block of knives on the kitchen island. My head buzzed. I couldn't believe I was looking at her, smelling her – sweat mixed with that peach scent I'd picked up on Kenny but had been too distracted to place. Rage crackled inside me, an electric current. I needed to harness it, focus.

'Where is it?' I demanded.

'Where's what?'

'You know what. The doll.'

She let out a sad laugh. 'This again?'

'I know you put it there and I bet you still have it.'

Why did I need to see it? To prove that it was more than an accident, more than just Kenny's negligence? To remind myself that I wasn't crazy?

'We've been over this.' She put her hands on her hips, manicured thumbs on her bare waist where her running tank didn't meet her matching shorts. Her voice held its usual assuredness but I heard a slight waver. 'There is no doll. You imagined it. You were out of your mind with grief. Do you not remember your husband – your ex-husband – saying that as you were taken away in handcuffs after you ransacked our homes?'

Of course, I remembered it. I remembered all of it.

'I can still hear Kenny apologizing for you.' She shook her head like I was pathetic.

I pulled the gun from my shorts and pointed it at her. 'Give me the doll or I will put a bullet between your eyes.'

She let out a small gasp, but I had to hand it to her, the bitch barely flinched, just held up her palms. 'I dropped the charges against you,' she purred, a patronizing hush, 'because I felt sorry for you. Because you're sick. I get it. First, your husband betrays you, then your daughter dies in a freak accident. I can only imagine how that would make you lose your mind.'

'Fuck you.' I aimed the gun at her face and steered her toward the staircase.

She walked up the steps backward. 'Have you tried therapy?' she asked. 'I think it could help you.'

How could she be so confident? Because she was the crazy one, not me.

I started to hum, like Ma did, to block the sound of Addie's voice. My legs trembled from lack of sleep and close to a full day in a compact car, but adrenaline took over. I backed her into a small bedroom on the right.

Peeling floral wallpaper and a black-and-white wedding photo on the dresser told me it had to be the room where Addie had stuck her mother before convincing doctors and then the state that Helen was sick.

'Open the closet. Then the drawers. Take everything out.' If she found something she could use as a weapon, I was ready, my finger curled around the trigger.

'Dump the boxes.' I pointed toward the top of the closet. Bank statements, receipts, manuals fluttered to the floor.

It was ten degrees hotter upstairs. I'd dreamt of this moment, but, in it, I was nauseous, clammy.

'Next room,' I ordered.

The bigger bedroom must've been Addie's. With a blue velvet chair tucked in the corner, it looked like a posh hotel. A vase filled with white peonies sat perched on her dresser opposite a king-sized bed smothered with pillows.

I thought of Moffatt. Was he awake? Was his head pounding the way mine had after I'd mixed the pills with wine?

'There's nothing here for you, Corey,' Addie whispered as if I were a child on the verge of a tantrum. 'You need to accept that and go. Leave. Start your life over. Don't make it worse than it already is.' She tilted her head. A strange smile danced across her lips. A dare. 'I bet that gun's not even loaded. You don't have it in you. Just like you didn't have the guts to confront Kenny about us. You had to know.'

'Open that fucking closet,' I roared.

There was a hitch in her step as she moved toward the white barn doors that hung from a black wrought-iron track. Kenny had probably put them up for her. I turned for a second and looked out the window, straight into the bedroom he and I had shared. How had I started there and ended up here?

Kenny was to blame, of course. Unfaithful. Careless. But Addie was worse. Malicious. Calculating.

She slid the door back a foot.

'All the way,' I growled.

She nudged it a few inches. I stepped closer. 'More.'

The door shuddered. Her eyes flicked up. A tell. Small plastic feet poked out from the top shelf in the back corner above rows of high heels and handbags.

A sound came out of me. Half-laugh, half-cry. I almost fell to the floor.

'Give it to me,' I said finally.

She took the doll down. It was clean, like new, blond hair shining, blue eyes open.

I kept the gun on Addie as I cradled it for a second, the way Frankie would have, and then tucked it under my arm. Tears stung my eyes. I blinked them back.

'How? How was it not in any of the police photos?'

She rubbed her throat, scratching the hives rising on her skin.

The gun felt so heavy. I wanted to put it down, to be done.

'How?' I repeated through clenched teeth, my jaw tense and aching.

'I slept with the lead detective. I found a way to get rid of them.' She pointed at the doll. 'I'd put that thing there weeks before she died, actually.' She laughed. Was it nerves or pure evil? 'You have no idea how many times Kenny left her alone while he was with me, and knowing she couldn't swim . . .' She shook her head and tsk-tsked. 'He was only staying with you because of her. I was sure once she was gone he'd leave.'

'You could've had him,' I sneered. 'And the guy who lived there before? Your fiancé? His family told police he'd been trying to end your engagement. Then one afternoon you two went for a hike and he never came back.'

'That was a terrible accident.' She pressed her hand to her heart. 'I was broken after that.'

'I'd say you've been broken this whole time.' I waved my arm toward my old house. 'I found the Wests' will in your basement.' The folder's sharp corners poked into my back. 'You're their children's guardian? How'd you manage that?'

'Got a little creative.' Addie's smile returned. 'Just like with your daughter, I'm afraid you're too late to stop things there. Laurel wasn't really fit to be a mother anyway.'

What was she talking about? I looked at my old house as if that would help me make sense of her vile words.

While my head was turned, she lunged for the gun. I jumped back, out of her reach.

The doll dropped to the floor as I brought my hands together to steady the weapon and aim it at her heart.

She whimpered. I saw it, finally – fear in her eyes as I forced mine wide open. I pulled my finger back hard. The kick of it rocketed through my body. A thrill ride.

It was over in a second. She crumpled, blood spreading like a dark rose blooming as it seeped into her sheepskin rug.

I stood there, arms limp, swaying. Satisfied. For how long? I couldn't say.

Police officers moved all around me. Did they shatter a window, break down the front door or simply walk right in as I had? I didn't know.

All I heard was the sound of the shot echoing, a delicious ringing in my ears, making an *eeeeeee* that stayed with me for days. A souvenir.

An ending. A beginning.

THIRTY-FOUR

Laurel

After delivering the quiche to Marian, nervous energy zinged through my body. Upstairs, I changed into shorts and a T-shirt and woke Jasper and Poppy. Cutting a nap short usually led to meltdowns and tears, but I couldn't sit still. I needed to get out of the house.

Despite my enthusiastic cry of, 'Let's go to the park!' Jasper was slow to leave his toddler bed. Poppy was cranky, too. Once we were out in the fresh air, we'd feel better, I told myself.

After wrestling them into the stroller, I stuck my cell phone and house keys in the basket beneath the seats along with an apple and a baggie of crackers for Jasper. I wanted to stay away from Cold Creek Lane as long as possible.

Passing Marian's home, I gave it a side glance. Would she really have the quiche for dinner or did she say it to be polite?

As soon as I turned the corner, I felt a bit calmer, like I could breathe again. Walking uphill, I looked down through the little plastic window in the stroller's canopy and reminded myself I'd done it for my family, to send a message, to keep them safe.

'Mommy! What's that smell?'

I pretended I couldn't hear him. Poppy's dirty diaper filled with the shrimp I didn't use was in the stroller's back pouch. I'd wrapped it in plastic but it still stunk. I tossed it in the dog waste garbage at the park's entrance.

It was close to four p.m. and the playground was practically deserted. Jill told me that by mid-August the town emptied out as families took last-minute vacations before school began. Normally, I'd have welcomed the quiet. The lack of a crowd made it easier to keep track of my busy three year old. But I craved distractions – another mom to chat with, even if it was just to complain about the heat.

I placed Poppy in the carrier and pushed Jasper on the swing.

'Higher! Higher!' he shouted, my nerves fraying a bit more with each shrill command.

I tried to focus on other things, but my mind kept spinning back to Marian. What would happen next? Had I really just done this outrageous thing? What would Rob say if she became seriously ill? Would Susan or Emily even care if I missed the entire wedding weekend? Or would they make an exception and allow the children to attend some or all of the festivities?

Questions looped through my head as I watched Jasper climb to the top of the slide again and again. When he got bored, he made small piles of wood chips and knocked them down with sticks. He sang the 'Hello' song from Musical Munchkins, begging, 'Sing, Mommy! Sing!'

I tried to be present, but my thoughts were chaotic. *What had I set in motion? Was there time to stop it?*

In the distance, a siren screamed. My heart lurched. The sound grew closer.

'Police car! Police car!' Jasper jumped up and down, hoping it might pass the park.

Which direction was it heading? Horns blared. I envisioned drivers yielding to make way. I waited, listening for the wail of an ambulance as a slow-simmering panic made me pace around the jungle gym faster, bouncing Poppy anxiously.

As I passed the stroller, I heard my phone buzzing. My stomach twisted. What if it was Rob? What if it was Marian calling to tell me she was ill and needed help? I didn't want to look but I forced myself to fish it out.

'Dad?'

'Hi Laurel, listen, have you given any more thought to the picnic? Janice is going to be really upset if you don't bring the desserts.'

'Dad, this isn't a good time—'

'It's only a few weeks away and she needs an answer.'

'I . . .' I stopped, hypnotized by flashing lights blazing past the park in the direction of our home.

'A ambulance!' Jasper shouted. 'Two ambulances!'

'Think about your mom, Laur—'

'I do think about her. Constantly. It would be nice if you did more than once a year because Janice tells you to!' I ended the call and shoved the phone in my pocket.

'Mommy!' Jasper pointed toward the street. 'I wanna see the ambulance!'

My phone vibrated. I assumed it would be my father calling back. I pulled it from my pocket. Jill texted: *Hope you are OK!*

My legs wobbled like I'd sprinted a dozen miles. I sat on the nearest bench.

Yes! I wrote, guilt making my tongue taste metallic.

'I wanna snack!' Jasper whined.

'One sec, buddy,' I said.

Why do you ask? I added and hit send, palms clammy.

Just heard police cars are on your street??

My stomach cramped. 'Act surprised, concerned. She doesn't know anything,' I told myself.

Yikes! I responded. *I took J & P to the park. We've been here for ages. Heading home soon. Will text you if I see/hear anything!!*

Be safe! she wrote back.

'Mommy! Snack! Now!' Jasper bellowed.

I handed him the baggie of crackers, my pulse thrumming throughout my body. I went to put the phone back in the stroller basket and fumbled it into the wood chips. When I picked it up, I saw I'd missed a call from Rob an hour earlier. He hadn't left a voicemail. Even if he had, I wasn't sure I would've listened to it. Our conversation that morning confirmed he no longer heard me. He'd been dismissing my concerns for months. I had no choice but to take matters into my own hands.

I checked the time. It was close to five thirty. Rob said he'd try to get home early, but that was a promise he rarely kept. I scrolled back to Jill's text: . . . *police cars are on your street??*

The longer we stayed away, the better, but Jasper was getting irritable.

'Want to go on the swings again?' I asked.

'I wanna go home!' He threw the baggie to the ground and stomped on it.

'In a little bit,' I said. 'It's so nice here. You've got the whole playground to yourself!'

The few nannies who'd been there had rounded up their charges to head home for dinner.

'I want chicken nuggets!' Jasper shrieked.

Poppy started fussing in my arms. I didn't want to start back. I wasn't ready. I hadn't thought the next part through. What would I say when Marian told the police I brought her the quiche? I'd feign shock and maintain that it was a terrible but honest mistake. I'd say I'd planned to prepare the same mushrooms for my family that evening. I was a young mom. I didn't seem like the type who'd knowingly poison an older woman. I had nothing to gain in their eyes. If anything, I just lost my weekend babysitter. I talked myself down, taking deep breaths.

'Mommy!' Jasper blubbered. 'I'm hungry!'

'Fine,' I said, losing patience. 'Get in the stroller. We'll go home.'

Nerves jangling, I took the long way, gripping the stroller tighter, Poppy strapped to my chest, the only thing tethering me to the ground.

As we turned the far corner, Jasper wriggled in the seat, straining against the straps, punching the stroller's canopy. 'Police cars!'

I squinted in the late-afternoon sun. The cruisers looked closer than Marian's house. I walked faster. My mind traveled back to that December afternoon with Mr McCardle, the police car in front of my childhood home, officers waiting inside to tell me my mother was gone.

They weren't at Marian's. They were at Addie's, moving across her lawn, setting up yellow tape, cordoning off her front steps.

A policewoman came up to me as we got closer.

'Ma'am, we need you to cross the street.'

'Go! Mommy!' Jasper yelled, bucking back and forth.

'What happened?' I asked the officer.

'It's an active investigation, ma'am. I'm not at liberty to share any details. Now if you'll please cross to the other side,' she repeated.

Neighbors stood on the sidewalk, gaping. I hurried past Zoey and Wyatt, too jumpy to do more than wave. Cars slowed, drivers gawking as they slipped down our street beneath the canopy of elms. I crossed and then crossed back again, parking the stroller beside our front steps, my head swiveling from Addie's house to Marian's.

I unbuckled Jasper, grabbed my phone and house keys. The front door was unlocked.

'Go wash your hands,' I said, distracted. 'Rob?' He must've gotten home early. He didn't answer. Maybe he was in our bedroom, finishing packing for the wedding weekend.

With Poppy asleep, pressed against me in her carrier, I climbed the steps. She'd be up until midnight, but I was thankful one child was quiet. 'Rob?' I whispered.

He wasn't in any of the bedrooms. Maybe he'd gone to see what happened next door. He had a way of charming people. He'd get more information out of the cops than I had.

'Mommy!' Jasper yelled. 'I'm hungry!'

As I turned to go downstairs, I glanced out the window. Police officers moved in and out of Addie's house. I pulled my cell from my pocket and texted her: *Are you OK? Been at the park for hours with the kids. Please let me know you're all right.*

Downstairs, I walked into the dining room. The white roses Rob gave me days earlier hadn't opened. Instead, their shriveled heads drooped, petals brown at the edges. Beyond them, I looked at Marian's house. My eyes shifted to her backyard, her birdbath. She was nowhere in sight. I opened the windows. A lawnmower droned in the distance.

I remembered Rob called but hadn't left a message. Maybe he'd tried our home phone.

'I want chicken nuggets!' Jasper came out of the bathroom whimpering and wiping his wet hands on his shirt.

'Give me two minutes.' I turned on the television in the playroom and went to the kitchen to preheat the oven.

I reached for our landline. We had two new messages. My father's was first: 'Laurel, I think we got disconnected, so I'm trying you at home . . .' I deleted it.

Then I heard Rob. 'Hey! Good news! I'm on the three twenty-three express train. Should be home by four.' I glanced at the microwave: 6:01 p.m. His words were muffled as a robotic voice announced the next station stop in the background. '. . . go over to Marian's, drop off a house key, and thank her again for watching the kids. We really need this weekend away, Laur. It's going to be great.' He yawned. 'Man, I'm starving. I'll try you on your cell.'

Go over to Marian's . . . I'm starving.

I dropped the phone. It clattered to the floor, smashing, batteries flying out, rolling under the fridge. Poppy started fussing. Jasper ran in, broken plastic crunching under his small sneaker.

'No! No!' I whispered, panic building. 'Please! No! No!' I moved slowly to the dining-room windows and stared at Marian's house again. No movement, no signs of life. 'No!'

'Mommy, why do you keep saying that?' Jasper tugged on my shorts, frowning.

I grabbed my cell and dialed Rob's number. I'd tell him there was an emergency; I needed him home right away. I heard his ringtone. Maybe he was in the backyard? I darted to the kitchen window. He wasn't there. I raced upstairs, Jasper on my heels, following the ring. Rob's phone shimmied against his nightstand.

'Jasper, Jasper!' I barely got the words out. My head felt empty, so light it might've lifted off my shoulders and floated away. 'I need you to be a big helper and watch your sister. I have to go over to Mimi's for one minute.'

'I want to go with you!'

'No, no, not this time. I'm going to put Poppy in her crib and you're going to sit in the glider. You can look at the police cars from her window, OK?'

On Addie's lawn, officers swarmed, purposefully moving in and out. I stopped for a second. Something a policewoman carried caught my eye. A pink folder, dark scribbles coiled like springs across it, poked out of a box.

I pressed my face to the glass. Our will and guardianship documents had been in that folder. Why did Addie have it? A wave of nausea gripped me and I clutched the window frame to steady myself.

Who was this woman I'd thought was my friend and what was she capable of? Why was her property crawling with police? What had she done and what would she do next?

I staggered back from the window. The fear in my eyes must've frightened Jasper because he nodded, suddenly agreeable to staying with Poppy.

Downstairs, I rushed outside and ran across the lawn to Marian's, my heartbeat pounding in my ears. I rang her bell, then banged on her door. I told myself I was overreacting, jumping to the worst-case scenario because of what happened to my mother. If Rob were with

Marian, they were probably having cheese and crackers, talking about lawn care or the kids. I stabbed the doorbell and heard its flat *ding-dong!* again and again. No one answered.

I hurried around the back, tried that door. This time it was locked. I pressed my face to the window but I didn't see Marian or Rob. I couldn't hear their voices. I ran to the front, pounded on the door again.

'Ma'am, is everything all right?' A young police officer appeared behind me on Marian's flagstone walkway. My face must've gone as gray as the slate.

I took a deep breath and forced a smile. 'I hope so. I'm trying to get in touch with my neighbor. It's very unlike her not to answer the door. Her car is here.' I motioned toward the driveway. 'My husband said he was going to stop by to see her but I haven't heard from him either.'

The officer's eyebrows arched.

'No, no, it's nothing like that. She – Marian's – older, a bit frail. I'm afraid she may have fallen. She doesn't have much family nearby, and . . .' I babbled. 'With whatever's going on over there,' I gestured toward Addie's and tried to calm my shaky voice, 'I'm worried. She's supposed to watch my children tomorrow.'

The officer looked toward the squad cars. 'We've got our hands full. Let me see what we can do.'

I stood there, helpless, horrified, unable to tell him every second mattered.

When I didn't move, he asked, 'Where are your children now, ma'am?'

'I live right there.' I pointed, fingers trembling. Did he notice? 'They're inside.'

'Go home. We'll take it from here. Let you know what we find.'

I bit my lip not to scream, 'Break down this fucking door right now!' How could I say, 'I may have poisoned my husband!'

I lurched back to the house where Poppy was howling upstairs in her crib. The oven beeped, reaching its preheat setting.

'Mommy?' Jasper came down the steps. 'Where's Daddy?'

'I don't know, sweetheart.' Tears swam into my eyes. The floor beneath me felt as if it were moving – a ride I couldn't get off. A ride I'd started.

'Is my chicken ready? Can you make Poppy stop crying?'

On autopilot, I turned off the oven, microwaved the nuggets, and let him eat in the playroom. I got Poppy from her crib and nursed her, rocking softly as I sat on the dining-room floor beneath the open windows, listening as police broke the lock on Marian's front door.

The voices of the young officer and the policewoman who'd told me to cross the street drifted in.

'I was on duty the day that dog got hit right over there. Remind me never to buy a house on Cold Creek Lane. Jesus,' the young cop said.

'Like you could ever afford one?' The policewoman laughed, then coughed. 'You working the day that girl drowned in the creek?'

'No, but I heard about it.'

'Girl's mom's the one who shot and killed Conroy. Didn't even try to deny it. Just stood there smiling at the body. I've seen a lot, but that shit gave me chills.'

Shot and killed Conroy. I scrambled to my knees to peek out the window, cradling Poppy's head, my heart in my throat.

'That's messed up,' the young cop said, shaking his head, his back to me. 'Is it true Detective Phillips dated her – the victim?'

'Yeah, but not for long. Said she was batshit crazy.'

Addie? Shot and killed? My brain couldn't grasp it. *Batshit crazy?* I pictured her hours earlier, winking at me as I took the trash over to Marian's. 'I hope it does the trick,' she'd said.

She'd been manipulating me from the beginning. I remembered Colin's messages. Was there a shred of truth to them? *You should've seen how she was flirting with Rob.*

Rob. Where was he? Inside Marian's? I couldn't look, just sank to the floor, pressing Poppy to my chest, whispering, 'No, no, no, please, no.'

I rocked back and forth, waiting. I thought of Lyle Hartsell. While he was on trial, his wife filed for divorce. At his sentencing, he'd said, 'In trying to protect my family, I destroyed it. If I could go back, I'd do it all differently.'

Even as sirens punctured the evening quiet and ambulances pulled up next door, I prayed I was wrong, that I wasn't the same as the man who'd murdered my mother.

I was still slumped against the dining-room wall when the doorbell rang. Struggling to my feet, I wiped my eyes, bracing for police to once again stand inside my home and deliver the worst possible news.

The two officers I'd watched go into Marian's home waited on my steps.

'Mrs West?' the taller one asked. 'May we come in?'

I opened the door and tried to stand straighter, my insides quaking.

'You should sit down, Mrs West,' the shorter one said.

I dropped to the couch, Poppy's diaper leaking onto my shorts. When was the last time I'd changed her?

Jasper danced into the living room, ketchup on his cheek. 'More police officers!' He pointed.

I looked at my son standing in front of me, my daughter in my arms. Whatever the police were going to tell me, I needed to handle it the right way. Be brave for my children, strong in a way Rob never believed I could be.

'Jasper, if you're done with dinner, you can get a fruit pop from the freezer.' I sent him away as the men loomed over me. 'What is it? What's happened?' I glanced from one to the other.

'Ma'am, we found your husband and your neighbor unconscious.'

I focused on pieces of broken pretzels crushed into the fibers of the area rug, afraid the men would look in my eyes and know what I'd done.

'It appears they ate something . . .' one said.

'Toxic,' the other added.

'My – my husband has a seafood allergy.' My voice cracked. 'Is that it? He carries an EpiPen.' It seemed like the logical thing to say. 'Where is he? Is he all right now?'

'I'm sorry, Mrs West. Your husband was unresponsive. Mrs Murdoch, too.'

'They're gone, Mrs West.' The shorter one lowered his head, his words spooling out in slow motion. 'We're very sorry.'

I felt as if I were watching myself from above, Poppy slipping from my arms toward the coffee table's edge. I clutched her back to me.

'I'm sure this is a terrible shock.' The other officer's voice sounded far away.

'I – I don't understand. That can't be right. Rob . . . no . . . no. I don't—'

'There was a pie – a quiche – tomato, mushroom. We'll have it tested. It may take a bit of time for the results to come back, but let me assure you, we'll—'

'Mommy makes quiche!' Jasper was back in the room, juice from the mango fruit pop dripping down his chin.

A roar filled my head, a swell of emotion – anguish, horror, guilt, followed by instinct – survival, opportunity. An image surfaced in my mind: my hands as I gave Marian back her dish. My fingerprints were all over it.

'Mrs West?' The tall officer leaned forward, his arm extended like he might rub my shoulder. Instead, he watched as I brushed my cheek against Poppy's fine hair, self-soothing.

Rob's voice clawed its way to the front of my muddled mind: 'You need to be strong. For them.'

'Marian loved to bake,' I said finally, tears sliding down my cheeks. 'I worked as a pastry chef so she liked to share her latest creations. Just this afternoon she asked me to look at that quiche. She even had me lift the dish. She was so proud of how light it was. And it was – really perfect,' I said, certain they thought my ramblings were caused by delirium, grief. 'She wanted me to have a piece, but I said no thank you – the baby weight. Rob's sister is getting married on Saturday. Oh my God, Rob. His family . . .' I closed my eyes. 'I can't . . . It doesn't seem real.' A howl, a keening, rose from deep inside me as I cried for my husband, for what I'd done.

Did he know, as his throat closed, as he gasped for his last breath, that I was the cause?

I wiped my eyes. I could mourn later. I had to get the next part right. I needed to finish it.

'Marian mentioned that she'd used some vegetables our neighbor Addie brought her.' I watched the officers lock eyes. 'Marian was so excited. She kept saying "fresh is best, fresh is best." Did Addie eat them, too?'

Jasper placed his fruit pop stick on the coffee table and rubbed his eyes. 'Where's Daddy?' he asked.

The policemen bowed their heads, this question beyond the scope of their duties.

I looked at the front door. Rob wouldn't be returning. I was in charge now.

'Come here, sweetheart.' I patted the sofa cushion. My son curled up next to me and I kissed the top of his head. 'Mommy's here. You're safe.'

EPILOGUE

Laurel

We moved in late September. Even with Cold Creek Lane's terrible history, the house sold quickly. Some people aren't put off by living alongside tragedy. Rob certainly wasn't.

With Addie gone, would the new owners have a different, better outcome? Who can say? Not all fresh starts lead to happy endings.

I left a lot behind: our shabby furnishings, most of the small appliances and china we'd received as wedding gifts, Jasper's football. I need to be open to new things. Rob always said that, so I'm sure he'd be pleased. He wanted the best for us. After Poppy was born, he'd increased his life insurance. I hadn't known about that.

Jasper asks when he'll see his dad again, if Rob will be able to find us at our new address. I purchased a charming home on a large piece of land. The best part is the distance between us and the neighbors. Poppy is too young to understand, to truly miss him. Of course, I know what it's like to lose a parent. I'd never wish it on anyone, but I'll fill their heads with good memories, do for them what my father never has for me. I'll tell them that their dad made friends easily.

I'm the opposite. That's what made me so susceptible to Addie's charms. I'd been lonely – in my marriage and for most of my life, really. She sensed it; she seized on it. Her kindness and friendship cast a spell, a deadly one. She'd convinced me Marian was evil when all along she, Addie, was the dark presence I'd felt looming.

Did Addie see something I had and decide she wanted it? Or had I awakened that darkness in her by rejecting her offer to serve as the children's guardian? How often have I thought of her mother, Helen, cautioning, 'Just don't say "no" to her?'

Was she hoping I'd kill Marian so she could come forward and tell Rob and the police I'd gone mad? Given her history, would she have wooed Rob and tried to replace me? And if he hadn't been interested, would he, too, have suffered an 'accident?' With her forged documents, Addie might've gotten custody of my children. Did she even care about them or was it a game to her? I'll never know.

Addie's death was shocking. But also a gift. Without her, I had the luxury of rewriting that tragic afternoon on Cold Creek Lane. Her laptop's search history confirmed my story. When her mother came forward, she provided a motive. She told police that Marian had offered to pay for private evaluations to prove she didn't belong in that facility. Marian had spoken with a lawyer about elder abuse and fraud perpetrated by Addie. They pulled Marian's phone records; it checked out. If Addie had known, she would have wanted Marian gone. Maybe that's what I was to her. A pawn. Someone who'd get rid of Marian for her. I remembered when she stood in my living room and told me, 'People resort to crazy things when real estate and money are involved.'

Rob was an unfortunate casualty.

I try not to think about my husband. I've spent so much of my life looking back. Where has it gotten me? It's time to look forward.

Jill wanted to set up a GoFundMe and establish a trust for the children. It reminded me too much of Janice and her scholarship. I said no thank you.

Emily's wedding was postponed. I've tried not to point out that if Jasper and Poppy had been welcome, Rob never would have been at Marian's house, but I may have let it slip once or twice. If a new wedding date is set, I'll have to decide if I want to share Colin's texts with Emily. For now, the Wests have endured enough.

And how am I feeling? In a word: stronger. I ended two lives, but in doing so, I created a new one for myself. Without my husband or neighbors watching my every move, I'm free, more alive. Unafraid.

I covered my tracks, stuck to my story. The only thing I hadn't considered about that afternoon was the woman in the small car with the Florida license plate.

Corey

Moffatt moved to Texas to be near his son. Ma said he found a job as a security guard. Dull, but it paid well. She got me his address. I wrote him once.

I know you probably think I used you, but I did care about you. I just cared about revenge more.

Hardly poetry, but words were never my thing. I got a note from Desiree with a photo of her standing beside a new bike. She was wearing a Hall's Garden Center T-shirt, her brown curls spilling out from under the matching cap.

Look what I bought with the 'birthday money' you gave me. New wheels!

Without you here, I may finally have a shot with Rex.

Write me back. I always wanted a pen pal. A letter from a women's prison would totally up my street cred at Holy Trinity High.

Plus, I'm ready to hear about that decapitated flamingo now.

XO

D

I scribbled a dozen letters. Was I writing to her? To Frankie? To exorcise my demons?

Didn't matter. I never mailed any of them.

Ma visited once. She came up to see the headstone, to talk to Dad and Frankie as if they were both there, waiting beneath the earth, listening. I like to think they're together wherever they are.

Ma's tracksuit looked bigger on her, her glasses too. She asked if she could've done anything differently that might have led to a better outcome. I told her this: Mothers need to stop blaming themselves.

I told her I'd rather feel at peace in here, than like a caged animal out there.

I had another visitor. I didn't know her, but I'd seen her before.

Once online, once from a short distance. She had dirty-blond hair, shoulder-length, nicely dressed. We looked nothing alike, but in her eyes I recognized something familiar – she'd known loss, the deep dark wideness of it.

'I lived in your house,' she said.

I stared at her. We had more than that in common.

'I'm very sorry about your daughter. I know that doesn't help.' She sat straighter in her chair. 'What I came here to say is thank you. You saved my family. You saved me.' She lowered her voice. 'I saw you in your car that day and you saw me, what I was carrying. I must've blocked it out. A week later, I was peeling an orange for my son and pictured your license plate, you, there on Cold Creek Lane.'

I wasn't sorry to hear about Marian. A few days after Frankie died, she came by with a basket of baked goods and told me she wished she'd spoken up one of those times she'd seen Frankie alone at the edge of the creek.

'I didn't want to interfere,' she'd said, lips twisted in a sad smile. 'Now I think perhaps I should have.'

'Take your muffins and get the fuck out of here,' I'd told her.

I looked at the woman who'd moved into my house and back out again. We were mothers, murderers, both of us driven to the edge, neither of us particularly remorseful.

I smiled at her. 'I didn't see a thing.'

Acknowledgements

Thank you to everyone who picked up this novel, read and shared it. Time is precious and I appreciate yours.

I began drafting this story at The Writers Circle and am grateful for the support of instructor Michelle Cameron and fellow writer-turned-dear-friend Liz Schlossberg, who stuck with me to "The End" and beyond.

To my editor Vic Britton, thank you for giving Laurel and Corey a home and for being such a joy to work with each step of the way. My deepest appreciation extends to the entire team at Severn House who helped bring this book into the world.

Thank you to friends old and new and all the generous librarians and readers who've welcomed me into their book clubs and homes. (I'm sorry if I ate all your cheese.)

To my pen pal William Beck (and his cat, Becky) who kept their fingers (and paws) crossed for me as I wrote and revised. Your encouragement means the world.

Thank you to my mom who read an early draft and said, 'It's making me anxious.'

To my husband, Rich, and sons Sam, Ben, and Charlie, thank you for indulging my constant requests for character names and stronger verbs.

Though she probably won't read this, I'm forever grateful for my cat, Bubbles, who keeps me company while I type.

For more, visit lizalterman.com

Book Club Discussion Questions for The House on Cold Creek Lane

1. Have you ever had a neighbor you found suspicious? How did you handle it?
2. Laurel talks about her struggle to make friends. Discuss the challenges of forming new friendships as an adult.
3. Rob keeps the house's history a secret from Laurel. Given her past, do you agree with his decision?
4. Overall, did you feel that Rob was protective of Laurel or overbearing?
5. After Laurel meets Addie, she says, 'If a tribe could consist of a single person, I'd found mine.' What drew Laurel to Addie, and would you, too, have been taken in?
6. Addie states, 'People resort to crazy things when real estate and money are involved.' Discuss this as it pertains to the novel. Do you agree?
7. Mother-child relationships throughout the novel are complicated. Consider the feelings Laurel, Rob, Addie, Corey, and Desiree had toward their mothers and the breakdown of Marian's relationship with her son.
8. Corey and Desiree form an unlikely friendship. How do they impact one another?
9. Corey's relationship with Mike Moffatt takes several turns. Did she care for him, was she using him, or both?
10. After attending the grief group, Corey reflects on her daughter's birthday and states, 'Firsts are hard, Linda said. Were seconds any easier?' Discuss loss as a central theme.
11. Rob and Laurel's extended family plays a role in creating tension between them. What do you think of Emily's choice not to include children at her wedding?
12. Laurel and Corey change over the course of the novel. Is their behavior understandable?

13. At the end of the novel, Corey tells her mom, 'Mothers need to stop blaming themselves.' Discuss how the guilt Corey carries shapes her decisions.
14. Did the ending surprise you? What do you think happens next for these characters?

Would you like to arrange a virtual book club visit
with the author?
Visit LizAlterman.com to schedule it.